The Last Resort

Also published by Hodder

This Bed Thy Centre
An Impossible Marriage
The Unspeakable Skipton
The Holiday Friend

PAMELA HANSFORD JOHNSON

The Last Resort

HODDER

First published in Great Britain by Chapman and Hall in 1956

This paperback edition published in 2018 by Hodder & Stoughton
An Hachette UK company

1

A CIP catalogue record for this title is available from the British Library

Paperback ISBN 978 1 473 67994 8
eBook ISBN 978 1 473 67995 5

Typeset in Plantin Light by Hewer Text UK Ltd, Edinburgh
Printed and bound CPI Group (UK) Ltd, Croydon, CR0 4YY

Hodder & Stoughton policy is to use papers that are natural, renewable
and recyclable products and made from wood grown in sustainable
forests. The logging and manufacturing processes are expected to
conform to the environmental regulations of the country of origin.

Hodder & Stoughton Ltd
Carmelite House
50 Victoria Embankment
London EC4Y 0DZ

www.hodder.co.uk

I

After dinner it rained so heavily that nobody went out. The public rooms at the Moray were crowded: fires had been lit. It was abnormally cold for June.

I had nothing left to read and all the magazines had been taken by other people. I thought I would try to 'think', which was something Gerard could do *in vacuo*, sitting motionless for an hour at a time absorbed in the cinematic projections from his own head, but which I always found it hard to do for more than five minutes unless I were doing something else as well. Although I was then in my late thirties, I was well below the average age of the other visitors. I felt oppressed by elderliness and by the rain, resentful as a young girl who feels her life racing by when there are no entertainments and she has to sit still. I began listening to conversations; which was not easy, for voices at the Moray had the comfortable wash and muffle of the sea and were very seldom raised. But it is possible to throw the hearing as a ventriloquist throws the voice, and I was able to adjust my ear to a couple, a stark-looking old man and his small plump wife, a good deal younger, who were sitting on a sofa a few yards away from me, with a space between them. They might have quarrelled, or have been expecting a third party.

They looked vaguely familiar but not more than that; I did not know their voices. The man seemed to address himself angrily to a bowl of rhododendrons, as if their mauve Edwardian silkiness, their opulent, upholstered domestication, somehow annoyed him.

I

'. . . I'd let them die before I turned out for them.'

She must have said, 'Let who?' Her gaze touched the flowers, twitched away from them. He said, 'Wanting everything for nothing, pills for the slightest finger-ache; thank God I'm free of it.' 'Oh,' she said. She leaned forward so that she could see, through the doorway into the reception hall, the girls, the porters, the desk, the switchboard, the lift. 'What *is* she doing? Shall I go up?'

'Leave her alone, she's all right.' He picked up the evening paper, thrust it under her nose. 'Look at that, there's what I mean. Some poor damned doctor hauled over the coals again.'

'Do you want any coffee?' She fumbled on the wall behind her, trying to find the bell.

'Oh, leave it alone,' he said, 'leave it alone. It always keeps you awake.'

A woman who had been sitting next to me took off her glasses, folded her *petit point* with a decisive air, yawned, smiled a little above my head and went off towards the lift. She had left her own paper behind, and I was grateful. In it I found the story of a doctor upbraided by the coroner for refusing to come out at night to a farm labourer, who had then astonished and embarrassed him by dying.

When I had finished reading this and every other item (with the deep, illuminated pleasure I took to any kind of reading-matter if it were the only kind available) I saw that my angry doctor and his wife had gone, that I was the only person left in the room, and that a porter was going the rounds, discouragingly turning out every standard lamp but mine, and keeping a dulled, rapacious eye on that. I thought I would go upstairs and write to Gerard, which would be like talking to him.

It was still raining next morning, but there was a faint bloom of light upon the horizon, and over the West Pier a strip of cobalt blue just big enough, as I used to say when I was a child, to make a man's shirt. I sat in the lounge for half an hour, waiting for the sun to come out and finishing my letter. My couple were there, still with the space between them; this space, as in Giorgione's *Storm*, now seemed to me to be pregnant with action. I should not have been surprised to see it suddenly filled with Banquo. The woman lifted her arm, raised it to her head, and I knew what she was going to do next: she was going to see that her ear-rings were firmly in place, to give each screw a turn. It was so familiar a gesture that I was filled with irritation. Who were these two, and where had I seen them before? They were not speaking this morning. He sat reading the *Times*, she sat touching her ear-rings, her cheeks, her hair, now and then slightly changing her position, recrossing her legs, redisposing her arm along the chair as if it were some *objet de vertu* that must be precisely displayed.

I went out to post my letter, go to the bank, do one or two pieces of shopping. Then I walked down to the promenade and leaned over the rail to watch the scurrying sea. The light had now spread across the skin of the water, and the olive greyness was giving way to a firm and resonant blue. Sun flickered on the wet pebbles. Along the groin, acid-green with weed, a child teetered like a tightrope-walker, balancing spade and pail. It was still chilly, but there was hope of a fine afternoon, and to the left of the bay the cliffs sparkled through ectoplasmic mist as though to them summer had already come.

Suddenly the sun tore the clouds open and poured through. The pebbles sent up steam. The pink and shiny roadways steamed, and the roofs of cars. Soon there were deck-chairs on the stones, men wearing handkerchiefs knotted at the four corners, girls in bathing-suits spreadeagled on

3

towels as if to be torn by horses. All the edge of the sea glittered with children.

I sat through the morning on a scrap of sand, enjoying the surprise of the heat. It had been a day like this when Gerard and I were married. I felt very happy. I did not feel like returning for lunch to the Moray, where they would have all the grainy, sand-coloured shades pulled down against the light. I ate at a café in the open air, went to the county ground to watch cricket (partly because Gerard had taught me to like it, but even more because he loved it himself) and returned at teatime with scorched arms and neck.

I recognised Celia Baird sitting *farouche* and neat between her parents. As usual, she was expensively dressed; as usual, only her hat became her. Her other clothes looked too restrained, too elderly, always a little too large. I noticed that she was wearing a good deal of jewellery, a pearl necklace and ear-rings, a pearl and diamond brooch, a large, old-fashioned ruby ring. She was looking through a smart magazine with the restless, rather angry air she had when she thought about buying things. I thought how much she had aged. She glanced up and saw me. Her eyes, which were rather small and of a very light, clear blue, met mine for a moment without recognition: then she was transformed, her face brilliant and full of expectancy. She said something to her mother, who asked her to repeat it, then quickly smiled and nodded in my direction. Celia jumped up and came across the room to me, leaving the gap for Banquo or Giorgione to fill.

'How wonderful to see you!' Her voice was light and rather thin, pretty, a young girl's voice. She did not prattle, but in such a voice could have done so. 'What on earth are you doing here?'

I had met Celia just after the end of the war. She ran, or partly ran, a small secretarial agency in Knightsbridge, where

I had gone in my search for a typist for Gerard and me to share. Somehow we had become quite friendly; she had been to our house once or twice. She had a false-innocent brand of wit that amused us, and she seemed solitary. We knew little about her except that she lived for the greater part of the year with her parents. Once we had seen her with them in London, at a restaurant, but we were lunching on business so did no more than wave to her then. During the past year or so we had lost sight of her.

She repeated, as though I had refused to answer her question, though in fact she had not given me time to do so, 'No, but seriously, what *are* you doing here?'

I told her I was on holiday, that Gerard was in America on a business trip, that I was tired after finishing a book and that I did not much like being in our own house without him.

'Oh,' she said, 'I hoped he was with you.' She said this with so frank and thorough an air that I remembered how much I had liked her, and wondered again why we had drifted away from each other. I asked her if she were on holiday too.

She looked surprised. 'I live here. It's far less nuisance for Father and Mummy – no horrible servants glowering and hating you, no business of stoking boilers. Dull as death, of course, but what's that? And I'm usually in London midweek. I've got a room.'

She asked after my son. I told her he was away at school.

'Oh yes, of course! I'm so sorry, I don't remember things. I expect he's still as handsome, like a very beautiful stork.'

She looking out of the window, peering under the blind into the bright street. For a moment she seemed to forget me. The light sparked the stones of her ring. I admired it. She turned back to me, smiling. 'It's Mummy's, she thinks it's hideous. You must come over and meet them, but not now. I enjoy being off the chain.'

I said I was wondering where I had seen them before.

5

'But have you? Oh yes, in the Connaught. You were with Junius Evans.'

'Why, do you know Junius?' I asked her.

She said, 'He's the friend of a friend of ours. I waved to all of you that day, but he didn't respond. He was feeling weighty about something. He believes it gives him great weight if he pretends not to see people. Do you like him? I'm never sure that I do. But I do when he's actually present.'

I said I knew him only slightly; at that time he had been writing an introduction to an architectural book Gerard had commissioned.

'It must have been dreadful,' she said. 'He sounds so grand but writes such bad grammar. No' – she had this trick of beginning a comment with 'no', as if I had said something that needed correction – 'it's his partner we know so well. Eric Aveling – have you ever met him? He was the son of Mummy's greatest friend. We've known him all our lives.'

Looking across at her wide-spaced parents, who seemed to be waiting in some side-pocket of time for the liberation of a stray word or the striking of the clock, I was puzzled that she spoke so collectively.

She added, 'He may be down next week-end. I'm not sure. Will you have coffee with us after dinner? You won't want to dine with us, it would be too trying; if I were you I'd fight shy. But if you'd come out with me tomorrow night, we could find somewhere more cheerful. Shall we? I could book a table' – she mentioned an extremely expensive and mildly raffish new hotel in a neighbouring resort – 'and we could dance with seemly pansies who sing the words in one's ear. Do say you will!'

I remembered then her lavish generosity. She was well-off, had inherited money of her own, and she loved to share. Sharing brightened her, gave her warmth and confidence, though she performed this sharing with an air of almost deceitful diffidence.

I said I should love to go out with her.

'We could dress up,' she said. 'I'll have to ask Mummy, but she won't come.'

2

When she brought me over after dinner to introduce me to the Bairds they reacted as if I were the signal for which they had been waiting since the beginning of their lives. The old man sprang up with a crackling of bones and made a great crockery-breaking gesture of the arm towards the nearest chair. Mrs. Baird half rose, grasped my hand and swung back on it into her seat.

'I think we must call you Christine, too. Celia's told us about you so often that we really feel we know you.' She touched the ear-rings to see they were in place, gave a little anticipatory gasp and sat back with an air of relaxation, as if expecting me to start making jokes. As I did not immediately speak, she began looking about her for the bell. 'You must have some brandy, I always think it settles one. Daddy, will you call Simpson? You're nearer than I am.'

Her husband put his finger to the buzzer and left it there. I could hear it drilling away out in the hall.

When the waiter came she said, 'The *Biscuit Dubouché*, mind. Not that other stuff. How's the cold tonight? You must tell Mrs. Simpson that the old remedies are the best – mustard and water.'

Baird gave me a phosphorescent smile. 'Hear her prescribing? I don't stop her. I'm a cipher. How do you like it here?'

I praised the comfort, the beds, the very old waiter concerned because he thought I did not eat enough.

8

'Finnegan,' said Celia. 'That's why I didn't see you before. You must have a table in the L.'

'You haven't seen your friend,' said Mrs. Baird, 'because you've been shutting yourself up in your room. It's unhealthy. And unsociable!' She addressed me suddenly. 'Do try to make her less unsociable, Christine – we hardly get any of her company.'

Celia said, 'Now don't start picking sides again, Mummy. Christine's in my team, anyway. She wouldn't be able to read properly down here any more than I can.' She turned to me. 'Finnegan's very good at the fatherly business, he gets all the biggest tips. Acually, he's probably a pimp.'

Mrs. Baird pursed her lips in mock disapproval, as if deprecating but admiring a forward child. 'What will your friend think of you! She'll think we haven't brought you up properly. Poor old Finnegan!'

'Carcinoma,' said Baird. '*He* won't be here this time next year.' He said the word so loudly that nervous heads turned. There was a sort of rising flutter, then a subsidence, as after a scuffle of fowls. Silence fell like feathers coming to earth.

He said after a moment or so, in a manner faintly propitiating, 'I expect he left it too late. These people always do. He may not know, of course. *I* know.'

The brandies came. He sniffed at the glass, pressed the bell again.

'Simpson! This isn't the *Biscuit*!'

The waiter said he had poured it himself.

'I don't care who poured it. It's more like *Marc*.'

'Oh, Arthur,' said Mrs. Baird, 'your silly old nose can't be working properly. It's lovely!'

'Celia! You smell it. Taste it. Go on.'

'It's all right.'

'You, Mrs. Hall!' Unlike his wife, he did not intend to use my first name. 'Go on, let's have some sense out of you!'

His tone was so rude that I was embarrassed; I could not think at once of a soothing reply. Mrs. Baird and Celia, however, merely looked bored. They withdrew, as it were, to the stalls, and sat with folded hands.

'I don't think I'd know,' I said. 'I don't know anything about brandy. I don't often drink it.'

The waiter filled in time by replacing ashtrays.

'You! Simpson! Go and drink these yourself and bring us three more. The right stuff this time!'

When the waiter had gone Celia said, 'You do love to pay for your pleasure, Father.'

I did not understand what she meant. Seeing this, she smiled at me and patted Baird's arm. The weariness of her face was replaced by a look of strong, secreted happiness; I felt it had nothing to do with her parents nor with me. She explained, 'It is Simpson's Saturday treat. Father doesn't like to say, "Buy yourself a drink", so he complains about the brandies, orders another round and gives the first lot to Simpson. It is *true*.'

'It isn't true,' said Baird. 'He brought us muck. But as he doesn't know muck, and as I don't want him to get into trouble below stairs, I cover up for him. And don't set up your opinions over mine!' This last exhortation was delivered with so savage an air that I was alarmed; however, he said nothing else for a time, but sat back in his chair as though some necessary routine task had been completed.

He was tall, tremulously thin, the skin pocketed upon his bones. Scraps of indigo hair clung like cobwebs over his narrow skull; they seemed to bother him; now and again he smoothed them down with a wetted finger or pressed them back. He had curious flat brown eyes, the colour of pitch-pine, and false teeth that were too shapely and a little too luminous, slightly bluish. He looked like a ruined chapel.

Mrs. Baird would have looked merely comfortable and null but for her restless movements and for her small shrewd eyes that appeared to be faceted about the pupil. They were a curious blue, very pale, with an overwash of hazel; below them the papery skin was pouched and shiny. An expensive, heavy scent threw its gauze about her; in an empty room one could easily have found her favourite chair. Just as Celia's clothes seemed too loose, hers seemed too tight. The ribs of her corset striped with shadow the light-blue silk of her dress; she might have had a broad, barrel-shaped skeleton.

When the matter of the brandies had been settled she began to talk to me easily, while Celia retired into a kind of smiling, daughterly silence. She told me they had lived at the Moray since 1946, when her husband had retired from medicine as a protest against the National Health Act. (It struck me that he was getting too old to practise, in any case; he must have been seventy or more.)

'So I did,' Baird put in. He seemed pleased to hear himself discussed, but a little on the alert; like a writer content to hear his work criticised, but ready to correct the critic on any minor textual slip.

'I'm afraid he hates the working-class,' his wife added surprisingly, lowering her voice slightly as if to reveal a naughty but lovable foible. 'He doesn't march much with the times. Of course, you don't have to, here.'

'The Moray is Father's stronghold,' Celia said. 'If they insist on chanting the *Internationale* in the streets he has only to ring for Simpson and have them moved on.'

'I suppose you think that's funny,' said Baird.

'Or "Men of England wherefore plough". The *Internationale* may be a little strong for the times.'

'Don't tease Daddy,' said Mrs. Baird. 'He knows more about things than you do.' She turned to me again, told me she had read one of my books and expressed astonished admiration to hear that I wrote in longhand and did not type them. 'You must get tired out. I don't know how you do it.'

Celia went out to the reception desk to buy more cigarettes for herself and for me. When she had gone her mother said quickly, 'I do hope you're staying here for a while. It can't be amusing for Celia to see only old people.'

I fancied it was not amusing for Mrs. Baird either.

'Do take her out of herself. Of course, I don't know what she does when she's in London.'

Now the appeal of this was unmistakable: Mrs. Baird passionately wanted to know, and hoped to use me as a spy.

'She doesn't have to work,' Baird said. 'There's no need for it. It's all tomfoolery. She does it to be independent.'

'Of course I do,' said Celia, coming back. 'Why not? It makes me more interesting, if I have a topic of conversation.'

She insisted on paying for my cigarettes. I tried to protest but she stopped me impatiently. 'Oh, don't be silly. You shall buy the next lot.' She pushed away the money I had offered her as if it really were dirty, as if it were in itself offensive. Yet in the next breath she reminded her mother that she owed her seven and six.

'What for? The coat-hangers?'

'I got you three. I can't have you throwing your clothes all over the floor. It's revolting.'

'You see how my little girl treats me?' Mrs. Baird looked delighted. 'That's what we all come to, in time. You've got a boy, haven't you, Christine? You wait till he's old enough to boss you. Celia is very bossy; aren't you, darling?'

'I expect so.' Celia's answer was so distrait that I looked at her, and saw that she was filled with a kind of impatient joy. She said to me, 'Could you bear to walk along the front? It's quite fine out.'

I fetched my coat and we left the hotel. It was a calm evening, smelling strongly of the sea. The white electric moons, strung for miles along the coast in their diminishing rings, were blurred in a slight sea-mist.

Celia said, 'I want to talk to you.'

3

She did not, however, speak until we had gone a hundred yards or so, but hurried me on with a buoyant stride that was almost a skip. It was as if she still feared to be within earshot of the Moray.

Then she said, 'I've got someone coming down.'

She smiled to herself, not looking at me. I thought she would continue, but instead she suddenly stopped. We were at the end of a square, in which there was a garden mound, walled and balustraded, thick with shrubs that had been fixed in a stoop of forty-five degrees by the prevailing wind. Their salty incrustations sparkled in the gilding of the street lamps; they might have been polyps in some dense and rambling forest of the sea.

'*Salicaceae*,' she said, in a new, light voice, 'that's what used to fascinate me when I was at school. They took us to some cliffs by motor-coach once, so we could see for ourselves. There were some bright-green pulpy plants – you squashed them and the sea came out. And there were sea-pinks.'

She walked on. Her fur cape slipped from her shoulders, and she hitched it back impatiently.

After a while she spoke of Gerard again, tenderly, as if she had known him very well. She envied me, she said, but in a nice way; a happy marriage was happy for other people. 'I often wish I'd married; but then again, I don't know.'

I thought I might ask her why she had not, knowing that she did indeed want to confide in me but was uncertain how to begin. She turned to me, then, with an air of eagerness, as if I had released words from her; but I guessed that she was substituting them for others more important.

She told me of a youthful love affair that had lasted some years. The man had been talented, poor and idle; he was always going to make good, to make enough money to marry on. 'I hadn't any of my own at that time, and certainly Father wouldn't have helped. It was quite right of him not to help. That would have been *entirely* the wrong way to go about things.' So the affair had drifted on. They had not slept together, since it had been drummed into Celia by her mother that once a man had had you he didn't want you; he would always 'throw it up in your face'.

She laughed; she was mocking and radiant. 'The things we believe! But he had much the same ideas. I'll show you his photograph, if you remind me.' She stopped under a lamp. With Celia, to propose a thing was very often to perform it at once. She opened her bag, displaying a chaos of papers, cosmetics, combs, pens, pencils; she was so neat in her person that such untidiness seemed a wild incongruity. Raking among the tousle, she pulled out a passport photograph, cracked and dogeared. 'Like Dorian Gray, I think, but you mustn't be misled. It was not that at all. He was very ruttish. It was just that it could never be *me*, because he respected me.' She paused. 'How I used to cry at nights when he'd been making one of his dismal confessions! He was always confessing.'

The affair had finally petered out. Mrs. Baird had never approved of him; Celia had come to believe she was right. He had disappeared for over a year and had turned up again, married, and, she said, 'full of effrontery, he made me a sort of godmother to his wife. She was all right; I didn't care. But I was twenty-seven, then, and it was a bit late.'

Though she had told me this story in order to delay or to conceal another, she had been swept by it into the past. Under

15

her happiness of the moment was the darkening of past defeat; like sand beneath the shallows, it discoloured the water while leaving the surface bright.

Shortly after the end of the affair she had inherited money from an aunt – enough, invested, to bring in five hundred a year. I gathered that Dr. Baird had been much displeased. Though he himself had ample private means and needed no more money, he felt he had been by-passed and insulted. For Celia this had meant a liberty it had never previously occurred to her to desire. She and a friend had bought up a modest secretarial agency and had made it pay. They did not take much out of the business, only enough to pay the rent of a two-room flat on the north side of Hyde Park. 'It works very well; we have a room each, and usually stay in it. We like each other, but not to talk a lot, if you understand me. We have our own lives, and I assure you I have very little idea what she does with hers.'

It puzzled me that Celia, who was more than usually eloquent, should find such a relationship possible. I said so.

'Am I eloquent?' She was flattered. 'No, but, you see, my life with the parents is one thing – I like to please them. In London I like to please myself.'

We were passing a large hotel on the sea front, turreted, pinnacled and blazing with light. The plants on the floodlit balconies showed spinach-green. Music thumped out and the shadows of dancers weaved across the blinds. 'Isn't it appalling?' Celia said. 'Let's go in.'

It was often possible, I thought, to guess the financial position of women by the way they entered public places. Celia pushed open the doors of this sea palace as if they were in the way, as if everyone were in her way. She hitched her furs, put a proprietary hand on my arm, and drew me into the largest and brightest of the several lounges. A waiter led us to a table. She objected to it, made him find us another. With a clink of

16

bracelets, she ordered brandy. I noted that her finger-nails were remarkably small, that the pink varnish contrasted oddly with the utilitarian brown of her hands, which she used oddly. When she drew out a note from her purse she crooked her little finger like someone over-genteel lifting a teacup. The crooked finger, I felt, was a kind of secret sign for the benefit of waiters; she was treated with great deference.

She sat for some time listening with pleasure to the music. The band was playing some nostalgic tune of the early 'thirties. I thought of Ned, to whom I had once been married, and remembered that we had danced to it.

'Tunes of our era,' Celia said. 'I feel about them as Mummy feels about *The Belle of New York*. I think of people like us, you and me, as veterans of the Spanish War. I used to carry banners, I and my young man. The parents were incensed. Did you care?'

I said I had cared, that they had been horrible years, but at least we had been alive. We had gained more than we knew from having a Cause.

'Oh, but do we want Causes?' Celia asked, looking suddenly prim and rather shocked.

I said that now we could see the effect of everyone being without them.

'That's what Father can't understand. For him, the revolution howls up the front night and day. He doesn't realise that to all intents and purposes it's been consolidated. At any rate for the time being. Eric says he intends to be the last grandee.'

It was as if a light had flashed up. I knew beyond doubt that this was the name she had wanted to speak.

'Eric Aveling,' she said. 'Junius is the junior partner. Aveling, Hart and Evans.'

She spoke the name of this firm as if it were a line of poetry, beautiful and gnomic.

'He's coming down next week-end. Will you be here?'

She did not wait for a reply. She was released, she could now speak.

'He's someone I want.'

This wanting gave her a look of fulfilment. She lay back in the deep chair, relaxed with love. 'Oh, you don't know,' she said, 'how wonderful it is to talk!'

She told me how, after years of friendship, they had fallen in love, had become lovers. She still felt strange with him; whenever they met she felt an initial shyness. Her parents, of course, knew nothing; this was an affair of secrecy, snatched moments, snatched nights – there had once been a snatched week. 'It's so extraordinary,' she said, 'that it should have been me. When you think that he's been looking at me for years. I can't get over it. But the trouble is Lois.'

The look of rapture left her, though the graveness of love remained. Before speaking again, she put out her cigarette and lit another; offered the case to me and dropped her matches, which, as the box was badly fitted, spilled all over the carpet. The waiter ran to pick them up. She waited till he had done so, gave him a smile like an extra tip, and watched him as he walked away to stand, like a limp sentry, against a pot of palms on the far side of the room.

'He's married,' she said. 'Lois is in hospital.'

Lois Aveling had Barbellion's disease and was now dying, very slowly, and with a kind of ironic cheerfulness. The process of paralysis had begun five years ago; for the last two she had been in hospital.

It was not until she went away that Aveling had made love to Celia, and then suddenly, somehow practically, as if it had been settled between them a long time ago.

'But it's terrible in a way. You see, I like her very much, I always have, and she likes me. I have to visit her. I feel abominable. But then I tell myself that she will never know.' She paused. 'All the same, I don't go alone if I can help it. Junius comes, if he's down here. He's got a house at Black Rock, you know – very chichi; he lets it sometimes when he doesn't want it for week-ends. It's too absurd, it really is: you should see it. Eric calls it the Zenana. Of course, Junius is *right* among his friends here.' Her eyes glinted with a kind of affectionate malice. 'He amuses Lois. He's awful, but he gives life.'

She fumbled about in her bag. I expected her to show me a photograph of Aveling, but instead she showed me a snapshot of herself and of a very thin, bright-eyed woman sitting in a wheel-chair under a hedge of roses. 'That was before she was really bad. She had the chair, but she didn't need it to get about the house.'

I said, 'She's elderly!'

She told me Aveling was forty-five, and his wife perhaps eight or nine years older. She had done a great deal for him when they were first married, had helped him to set up in business. 'But he didn't marry her for that,' she added. 'She used to be quite beautiful in a thin sort of way, and rather hard-smart, like the Duchess of Windsor. Not that she *was* hard; she was very kind.'

Quite suddenly she changed the subject. 'No, but we really must dance tomorrow. Do let's.' Under her breath she hummed the tune the band was playing. 'You shall dance with dear little Mr. Webster, and he'll tell you all about his budgerigars. Oh, it is nice to have you here! You can't think!'

4

Celia came downstairs in a dress of maroon brocade that looked as though it belonged to her mother and in fact did.

'Mummy insisted on lending me her garnets, as we were going gay, and they wouldn't go with anything of mine.'

She admired my own dress, characteristically insisted on going upstairs again to fetch a necklace, which she made me wear. 'It's hideous on me, and perfect on you. Do take it, because if you don't it will only lie in a drawer gathering fluff. It's of absolutely no value, and I should only give it to a sale of work.'

There was something of Haroun al-Raschid about Celia, which was also entirely inoffensive.

She asked if I drove a car and, hearing that I did, suggested that we should take her father's. 'I can't drive, I've never been able to learn. I've always been afraid of killing a child, or a dog, even.'

Dr. Baird looked me sharply up and down. I fancied he might at one time have been a coroner. What was the make of my own car? It was the same as his. 'Well, that's one comfort. Are you safe?' I said we could just as easily take taxis, that indeed I had no wish to bother him in this way. He repeated, 'I said, are you safe?'

His wife, who had been sitting forlornly beside him, looking now and then at the clock as if calculating how many dull hours lay ahead of her, touched his sleeve. 'Now, Arthur, you're not to be silly.'

'Be quiet, my bunny.' This incongruous endearment was snapped out in the same sharp tone he had been using to me. Indeed, I thought for a second that he was addressing me. 'I'm talking to Mrs. Hall.'

I said I had had a clean licence for ten years, but would still prefer not to worry him. I felt annoyed with Celia for putting me in Baird's witness-box, but as I glanced at her saw she was regarding him with a comfortable and tender smile.

'Good for you,' he said, and gave me his sunless grin. 'Why this girl of mine can't do a simple, practical thing like propelling a motor-vehicle I can't presume to imagine.' Mrs. Baird laughed relievedly. I realised that this ponderousness of expression was his only idea of making a joke. 'But you take it and welcome. Have a good time.'

'Always this fuss,' Celia said, as we went down the steps. 'It makes him feel so big, poor dear. Everyone uses his car, of course; he never does nowadays, but he can't bear to sell it. It's like people having pianos they can't play.'

The dancing partners she had arranged for us were two small men called Raby and Webster. Raby was as she had suggested, but I found that Mr. Webster had a wife of whom he was very fond. He talked about her most of the time we were dancing, and only now and then sang with the music.

At the end of each dance they left us, returning when the music started again. I gathered no money was likely to pass; Celia knew how to arrange these things in advance. It was all as mysterious to me as the proceedings of Eleusis.

She, I saw, was a good dancer – far better than I. She danced easily and with delight; I knew Mr. Webster was envying Raby, and said so.

He said, 'Miss Baird is very good; with a bit of training she could have gone a long way. Mr. Raby says he always enjoys dancing with Miss Baird.' He paused, then returned to the topic nearest to him. 'My wife's a good dancer, exhibition class. The trouble is, she's got so much else. The little boy, and then the house to look after.'

He was a decent little man, very gentle, rather distrait. I thought how strange it was that he should have been endowed with the bizarre skill that had led him to spend his evenings, away from Mrs. Webster, on hire to Celia and myself.

He had a small, gentle, chinless face, and his eyes were empty. He plodded on round the floor, patient with me, his mind far away. I asked him what Mrs. Webster was like. He said, 'Oh, nothing all that much. But *thoughtful*! I thought she wouldn't remember my birthday, but she did. A new Lilac she gave me – a real beauty. I came down, and there it was in the cage. I had one who was a talker, so this one may be. One never knows with budgies.'

After each dance Celia returned exhilarated to our table. She was full of such joy that it did not frighten her to inflate it. This was not, as it was for me, an evening of purely artificial pleasure. She was enjoying herself wholly. Webster and Raby were more than substitutes for delight: they were its symbols. She did not notice that the dancers were few and elderly, nor that they thinned away as the evening wore on until there were only three couples, ourselves included, on the floor. It was very late. The tired waiters lolled against the wall.

I went upstairs to the cloakroom and, lifting up the blind, looked out upon the shore. The full moon had risen, the tide was low. There were few people on the front, and the illuminations bore a derelict look, as if they had once shone over a city, and that city had sunk beneath the sea. A clock struck twelve, tossing melodious notes like soap bubbles upon a city almost asleep.

When I came back the third couple had gone. Webster and Raby were at our table; Celia had bought them drinks. Raby, alert, was chattering away in a smooth sub-Cockney that had an air of caricature, but Webster's eyes had glazed, his collar was limp and his smile had gone to sleep as it lay stretched upon his face. I was sorry for him, and thought it was high time Celia and I went home. I nudged her, but she took no notice. In that high, bright, empty room, where the band played above an empty floor, she sat on remorseless.

It was one o'clock before she rose. As we drove off I said, 'I'm afraid we kept them late.'

'Oh no.' There was something inflexible in her voice, inflexible and heated. 'They are extremely well paid. They know me, they know I like my money's worth. No one pays them better than I do, and they must give value.'

Then she asked me to drive on for a while, up into the higher part of the town, which, by that time, was deserted. 'Turn up to the right here, will you?'

We were in a street of small houses, once slum houses, now reclaimed and smartened. There were lights in only one of them; a chandelier held its rainbows steady behind the window veils.

'Junius is down,' said Celia. 'I thought he might be.' She made me stop for a moment while she gazed, smiling, at the house.

She said, 'It's very absurd, but even to look at a place where a friend of his lives makes me happy.'

5

Celia spent the next day with her parents, listening to her mother's talk of friends, relations, clothes, cinemas, and to her father's ground-bass of general denunciation. He seemed to take ease and comfort in disapproval; he drew attention to any item in the paper likely to stimulate moral indignation, and if he could not rouse this in his daughter did not fail to imply that this was because she approved of fraud, murder, cruelty to children or whatever fault lay under discussion. I should have found this extremely irritating; Celia did not appear to mind, but regarded him with an amused and filial tenderness. I observed how easy it was for her, under her father's half-facetious bullying, to relapse into a comfortable semblance of childishness; there were moments when she seemed to be giving an amateur's imitation of childhood – embarrassing because it had overtones of truth. But there was something worse: Baird's compulsion was hypnotic. If I had not taken myself in hand I should have sat side by side with Celia, acceptant of his authority, grateful to have the problems of adult life by-passed for me. As it was, I had begun to be drawn in further than I wished.

Once, when Celia was out of the room for a moment, Mrs. Baird put her hand on mine. 'It's so nice for her to have you here, Christine. She needs somebody sensible, like you. Arthur and I are really grateful.'

At tea-time I found a letter from Mark in my pigeon-hole. There would be a holiday on Thursday; I could come and

24

take him out if I liked, but he expected it was too short notice. I was sure to be busy, and it didn't matter anyway, but he thought he might as well let me know.

I went back into the lounge and asked Dr. Baird if he would allow me to use his car. I explained the circumstances, said that, of course, I should pay for the petrol.

'Well, I should think you would, wouldn't you?' He told me not to crash it into a wall; he knew women drivers.

'He doesn't mean to sound ungracious,' Mrs. Baird murmured, 'do you, dear? He just doesn't care how he sounds.'

He smiled faintly in enjoyment of this character-analysis.

Celia asked if I should be away all day, and looked disappointed when I said yes. Later she said, 'No, I'll tell you what – that is, unless you hate not having him all to yourself, which I should in your place. Why don't we drive over and bring him back here for the day?'

I said it was a long way. She protested at once that it was not more than forty miles, that we could make an early start. She was filled with a kind of strained eagerness.

I hesitated. I did like Mark to myself, though I was not sure he felt the same about me.

'Father isn't bad with boys,' she said hopefully. She paused. 'We could go on the pier, if Mark isn't too old for it.'

'All you'll get on that pier is vermin,' said Baird, with finality.

'Daddy says,' Mrs. Baird quietly augmented, 'that you will never teach people to be clean.'

'That's what I do say.' He turned his savage stare upon an elderly woman knitting harmlessly in her corner.

'Oh you, how absurd you are!' Celia flared up: her colour heightened. 'You don't mean half you say, so why *do* you have to say it? Christine and I are going to get a drink.'

We went into the bar.

25

'Do let us bring Mark here. I haven't seen him for ages. Besides—' She hesitated.

I asked her what was the matter. She looked as if she were going to cry.

'I can stand the old people if there's nothing else beyond them. But to be left with them *this* week—'

She stopped, jingled her bracelets, and reminded the girl behind the bar in a high, cold, pleasant voice that we had not yet been served. I understood her need for me. Her excitement, her joy, was so intense that she could not bear either to be alone with it or in the company of anyone from whom she had to conceal its existence.

'I want to give him a good time,' she said. 'He needn't see Father, of course. We could do all sorts of things.'

When I had at last agreed to her plan her edginess disappeared. She began to talk about her father with a curious, self-deceiving romanticism. He was brusque, of course; his ways might seem odd to people who did not know him; but at heart he was a good man, sentimental and responsive to affection. 'Mummy's so taken up with herself and him,' she went on, without any appearance of resentment, 'that she doesn't really care about me – at any rate, not on any deep level. He's different. I have to indulge him.'

It seemed to me, remembering Celia's outburst, that he must indeed be fond of her, for I could imagine him taking nothing of the kind from anyone else. I could not, however, believe that he was either good or sentimental. Behind the pretence of savagery was something of savagery itself; it was like an ugly mask upon an ugly face.

She added, 'But believe me, if Mark could bear to talk to him, only for five minutes, he'd love it. I mean, of course, Mark wouldn't: no one could; I mean, the love would be on Father's side.'

26

Mark's memories of Celia, though vague, were agreeable, and he seemed glad to see her. What did disquiet him was the prospect of two long rides in one day.

'I get a bit car-sick, as a matter of fact,' he said airily, looking around the sky.

'But you won't today,' Celia assured him, 'because it will be quite different. Utterly and entirely different.'

Her masterful air may have had some hypnotic effect upon him, since he did not complain at all, but arrived at the Moray announcing that he was very hungry.

After we had eaten, I took him into the lounge to introduce him to the Bairds. He was growing very fast, and I saw that he had begun to stoop slightly, as if his height worried him. Baird saw this too. 'Well, stand up, stand up! What you'll get, young man, is a dowager's hump.'

It was not a good start. Mark flushed. He gave an uncertain smile, half-angry, half-placatory.

Mrs. Baird began to talk rapidly. Did he like his school? Did he get enough to eat? A friend she knew had a boy who was always hungry at Eton, but it seemed to be traditional. Through this solacing murmur the doctor's voice ran on.

'You get in the habit once, you never get out of it. Copy your mother, that's what you ought to do; she's straight enough. Millie, give him some coffee.'

Mark said in a stilted, almost genteel voice that he didn't like it; Baird instantly put him through an interrogation. Why not? Didn't he like the taste? Was he faddy? Didn't he know French boys drank coffee?

'You know perfectly well, dear,' Celia said very gently, 'that you think it's bad for people.'

'What's that got to do with it? I'm not making the boy drink it. I simply want to know *why* he won't drink it.'

Mark, goaded, spoke with unpremeditated loudness. 'Because it's foul.'

The doctor was silent. His flat eyes went blank. 'Well,' he said at last, 'so that's that. One can't say fairer than that.'

He stared at Mark, seeming to itemise his features. Suddenly he asked him if he knew a certain name.

'He's my housemaster.'

'I knew him when he was a boy.' Baird began to ask questions and to wait for the answers; he spoke easily to Mark, as to a man of his own age. The tension had passed.

But Celia, as we left the Moray and set out along the front, was tight and unsmiling. She said, 'I must apologise for my absurd father, Mark. If I were you I should want to hit him.'

He said surprisingly, 'Oh, that's all right. I liked him.'

We had a pleasant day; Celia was good with Mark. When we got to the pier she asked him what he would like to do. 'Whatever you want,' he answered, with polite unhelpfulness.

'I'm afraid you wouldn't like what we want. Christine and I are going to sit in the sun and talk, which would be dreary for you.' She gave him ten shillings. 'If I were you I'd simply disappear till tea-time.' This was said with so thoughtful an air, as if her whole mind were bent upon the problem of pleasing him, that he took not the slightest offence.

'I say, thanks! Thanks awfully.'

He disappeared rapidly into the amusement hall. Celia looked after him. 'How lucky you are! He's very nice, isn't he? And he seems to like you.'

We saw him only once during the afternoon. He had managed to hire a bathing suit and was picking his way down over the sliding stones, holding himself together in a stiff, scurrying fashion, like a woman ashamed of her clothes. He climbed on to a groin, stretched his arms and dived cleanly into the sparkling, cineraria sea. His fair head flashed up above the water, bobbed steadily outwards.

'I envy you,' she repeated, 'though I expect he's been a worry. Children must be. People conceal it.'

The Bairds were expecting us for an early dinner. It was a lavish one, imaginatively chosen to please a boy. There were potted shrimps, duck and green peas, a sweet made of strawberries and tangerine water-ice. Baird ordered a bottle of hock. 'Does he drink?'

I said I thought Mark would rather have lemonade.

'Bosh. I won't buy it him. If he gets used to a drop of wine now he won't rush into the public houses and make a clown of himself the moment he's eighteen.'

Mark did not care for his drop of wine, but was flattered to have it imposed upon him. Throughout the meal Baird kept up a kind of brutal badinage with which Mark appeared to be at ease – which, indeed, he seemed to enjoy. Though his face kept a delicate ice-cream flush, he answered the old man gracefully, and even with humour. I was proud of him.

Celia put in such words as were possible edgeways, but made no great effort to join in the conversation. She looked from her father to Mark with the appeased air of a producer who has obtained, perhaps fortuitously, the effect he wanted. She had relaxed her domination, sat smiling like a daughter in her father's house.

Mrs. Baird whispered to me, 'Daddy's bark is worse than his bite.'

When we were ready to set off on the return journey Dr. Baird called Mark before him and ceremoniously folded two pound notes into his hand. Mark made a polite protest.

'You want it, don't you? You can do with it? Don't buy muck with it, mind.'

He and his wife came to the door to watch us drive away.

Mark said he thought he would sit in the back, as he was less likely to feel sick.

'Do as you like,' said Celia, adding, like a domineering sibyl, 'But you are never going to be sick again. Absolutely never.'

She and I talked, Mark looked out of the window. He was not a conversational boy and was content to be left alone. By the time we had crossed the Sussex border dusk had fallen and yellow lights shone among the hills. The breeze went with us, rattling the hedges. At the top of the sky was an arena of the last, the purest, blue.

Mark spoke as we were coming into Godalming. 'I say, Celia, your father gave me an awful lot. Is it all right?'

She said, 'My dear boy, he's not mental. Of course it is. And, anyway, you've earned it.'

We came to the school gates. Mark, who was now fretting in case he should be late, forgot his manners, jumped out of the car and walked away. Then he came back, wrenched open the door and pushed his head in, nodding it like a mandarin. 'I say, thanks awfully. It was very nice. Thank you for taking me out.'

He walked away, stately for a few yards, then broke into a run.

'It must be painful to see them go,' Celia said, 'because you really don't know to what. They never tell you. He might be walking off the planet, mightn't he?' She added, 'It is so disconcerting to know nothing of a person's life, not even the ordinary things, to know them only when they're with you.'

We were not back at the Moray till past midnight, since she made me stop at two hotels for drinks, at a third for coffee. It was as though she could not bear to sleep, to waste hours in which she might have been aware of bliss.

6

On the following evening Celia took her parents to the theatre, and I was in bed before they came in. I was not sorry to be alone. Though I liked her, was attracted by her, she sapped energy. To be with her was absorbing, even exhilarating; but whenever I left her I felt virtue had gone out of me. I wrote a letter to Gerard, to whom life was a long, complex, image-clustered novel, and told him about her. In theory he always welcomed the appearance of new characters, but in fact liked to delay the moment of meeting them. It interested him to match his own conjectures with the reality.

Next day she did not appear at breakfast. It was usual for Dr. and Mrs. Baird to have a tray in their rooms, but Celia, as a rule, was downstairs by half-past eight. At ten o'clock there was still no sign of her. I was just going out for a walk when Mrs. Baird came up to me, looking distressed. 'Christine, I wish you'd do me a favour and see what's the matter with my girl.' She told me that Celia had left them after the theatre, saying she wanted some air, and had not come back to the hotel until half-past four. 'I kept waking up. I never can sleep properly till I know she's all right. When I did hear her come in I looked at my watch.' She had not gone to question Celia then, probably remembering that she was no longer a young girl; but at nine o'clock she had knocked. 'I know she's there because I can hear her moving about, but she won't open the door and she won't answer.'

Though I was disturbed myself, I did not think Celia, whatever her motives for hiding from her mother, would relish my intervention, and I said so.

'Oh, do go! She'll listen to you. It's all we hear these days, it's all Christine.' She was worried enough to be quite unable to conceal a touch of resentment. 'Please! I'll take you up.'

The Bairds had three rooms at the end of a corridor on the fourth floor. These were set in a wing of the building, almost shut off from the rest of it.

'Come into my room for a minute first,' Mrs. Baird said. I followed her, and was astonished by what I saw. It was the room of a woman who did not mean to settle down. She had been living for three years at the Moray, yet she seemed scarcely to have unpacked. Trunks and suit-cases, open, contents rumpled, were pushed against the walls. The door of the wardrobe, ajar, showed only a few clothes upon the hangers. The dressing-table was splashed with powder. In the gloomy and shaded air hung a strong flower scent mingled with a curious ammoniac smell which I could not at first define. Then I saw, in the corner by the bed, a cat basket and a box full of sand, the latter scrabbled and damp. 'It's my Tiny,' Mrs. Baird said. 'They don't allow animals to be kept here, really, but no one says anything about him if I keep him quiet.' A long-haired white cat jumped on to the unmade bed and gave a little, emasculate mew.

A key rattled in the door and a chambermaid looked in. 'Not now, Nora,' Mrs. Baird said, 'you can't do the room now. You'll have to do it later.'

She gave me a cigarette. 'Do sit down, if you can find anywhere to sit.' She pushed some underclothes off a chair. 'I expect you think I'm silly, worrying like this, but she is so moody. I'm sure you aren't. I'm sure you're quite different. I don't believe you ever gave your mother any trouble.'

32

I asked her why, if Celia were obviously up and about, she should worry so much.

She said obstinately, with a trace of ill-humour, 'I don't know why, but I do.' She rummaged in a suit-case and handed me a silver-framed photograph. Even this had not been unpacked. I saw a pointed face, rather small, wide-spread eyes, a meek, slightly ironic smile; long dark hair tied with a limp ribbon, falling in tubular curls; a party dress with frills.

'That was Celia as a little girl. She was so affectionate then; it was Mummy all the time.'

She was not far from tears.

I said I would do what I could.

'Oh, finish your cigarette first. After all, there's no reason why we should run after her.' She picked up the cat and fondled it; it jumped down, leaving small cirrus clouds of fur upon her skirt. 'No reason at all, really. Her life's her own. One day you'll have to lose your boy.'

She sat smoking in silence for a while. I felt that the whole morning would go by, and we should just sit there. At last she got up and pressed my hand. 'See if you can get some sense out of her. I'll go down.' As she opened the door for me the cat tried to run out; she nudged it back again with her foot. 'I have to pay Nora extra for cleaning Tiny, of course. But she's very good.'

She left me, walking swiftly away down the corridor towards the lift.

When she had gone I tried Celia's door. 'It's Christine.'

She answered me at once. Her voice sounded strange. 'Oh, is it? Wait a minute. I'll let you in.'

She was still in her dressing-gown. When she had admitted me she went straight back to the bed and lay down.

'I've got to get right,' she said. 'For God's sake help me to get right.'

33

The curtains were drawn back, but the blinds were almost down, leaving the room in submarine translucence. But it was not dark; the greenish light was clear and steady.

I had never before seen her without make-up. She looked younger, though her skin was dry and flaky. At this moment there were pouches under her eyes, which were squeezed and bloodshot. She had her hair pinned in a net.

'I can't stand Mummy fussing; it would drive me mad.'

I asked her at once what the matter was, and when she told me I was so relieved that I laughed.

It appeared that after parting from her parents at the theatre she had walked along the front, and by chance had met Junius. 'He was bright and very full of himself, and I was in a sort of dream, and he said we ought to have some fun. He wasn't too sober; he'd gone for a walk to shake it off. He took me into a couple of clubs – places he goes to—' She managed a faint smile that instantly dissolved into tears. 'Not very *nice*. Not within Father's range of experience. We met all sorts of people.'

She was talking more easily now, and her tears did not appear to bother her; they seemed more like some painless affliction of the ducts than an expression of emotion.

'And of course I started drinking too much, which I hardly ever do, and I knew I was doing it; but life seemed so marvellous, and Junius was so insidious, and wouldn't let me go.'

At last he had driven her back to the Moray, where she had somehow aroused the night porter, had somehow found her way to her room. 'I did pin my hair up,' she said, with a touch of pride.

Then she had fallen into a black sleep, and had awakened about eight o'clock to sickness, a tearing headache and a giddiness so violent that she had only been able to cross the room by clinging to the walls and furniture.

'I have been sick,' she said, 'which helps. But my head is awful, and I look hideous. I have to be well before he comes!' I was sitting on the edge of the bed. She heaved herself up and fell weakly across my lap, letting her arms trail. It was horrible, somehow, to feel her so exposed before me; I believed she would dislike me for it when she was herself again.

'So you see,' she said, her voice muffled, 'that there is nothing funny about it at all.'

I thought it was strange that between her pleasure in the prospect of seeing her lover and its realisation she had put this curious barrier. It was almost as though she had preferred to anticipate rather than to meet the reality. She was fastidious, she cared for her looks: she had flung fastidiousness and looks away.

I asked her what time he would arrive. 'About half-past two. But I'll never be right by that time.'

Would he care, I asked her then, if she simply told him what had happened?

'I don't know. He'd laugh and say he didn't. But he isn't like that himself. He'd be amused, but I shouldn't be the idea he has of me, if you understand.'

Then she was quiet. She lay for so long in her helpless, humped position that I told her she needed sleep, that after all she had had nothing of a night.

She said, 'But you'll wake me if I do? Promise?' She yielded almost hungrily to a desire for the dark.

I promised, made her lie down again, gave her some aspirin and went away.

In the hall downstairs, of course, were her parents. They were waiting outside the lift for me, so that I should not escape.

I did the best I could. I told them Celia had met friends, had gone dancing, had stayed up too late and woken with a bad headache.

'I'd better look at her,' said Baird, starting forward with an air of angry purpose.

I said she was sleeping, that she would be better when she awoke. It was all I could do not to bar his path.

'Are you sure that's all that was wrong?' Mrs. Baird asked me. She felt for her ear-rings. 'Truly?'

I reassured her.

Baird said, 'Millie, go and get your coat. We've wasted enough of the morning. I don't want to stuff indoors if you do.' When she had gone he said to me, 'What was it, too much to drink?'

I lied, saying I did not think so.

He shook his head. 'The trouble with that girl,' he said unexpectedly, 'is pride. If she will go out with fools and make a damned fool of herself, she has only to admit it *to* herself. It's pretending not to be drunk that makes people drunk half the time; there's not much more to it.'

He pushed his way, with his long, scissor-man's stride, through the swing-doors out into the street; I saw him jerking down towards the sea. He did not wait for his wife, and nor did I.

At half-past one I took Celia milk and biscuits on a tray. I had taken her key with me, so that I could let myself in. She was still sleeping, and now she looked so serene, so peaceful, that I hated to arouse her. However, she awoke at once and smiled at me. 'Bless you.'

I asked her how her head felt.

'I don't know. I shan't until I move. Prop me up, will you?'

She shuddered at the milk, but drank it. She ate the biscuits by breaking them into very small pieces and swallowing them like pills.

I noticed now the sour smell of the room; it smelled of the night's misery. I pulled up the blind, and the sun poured in like sea through a breached dam. Celia stumbled out of bed, staggered, and stood up straight. Then she smiled. 'That's better.'

'Not hurting?'

'Hurting just round the corner, but not actually. I'd better have my bath.'

She made me wait till she had drawn the water and had put in some thickly-scented bath salts. The smell of roses was overpowering in the small room.

'Good,' she said, 'good.' She walked gingerly, not to jolt herself, several times up and down. 'Good.' She thanked me for helping her – 'I think I can manage, bless you' – and sent me away.

7

It was her day now. I stayed away from it. When I came in at dinner-time I looked at the visitors' book and saw that Aveling had arrived. His signature was very graceful and firm, he used a bright blue ink in his fountain-pen.

I could not see the Bairds from my corner, but at the end of the meal Celia came to me. The night's adventure had given her a look of frailty that was not unbecoming, and she had been sensible enough not to put much colour on her face. She was very neat, very smart; she wore some jewellery I had not seen before.

'I'm still trembly,' she said, '*but all right*. Join us later on, will you?'

She carried with her an aura of happiness so palpable that I felt myself drawing back, as from someone who had just undergone a mystical experience.

When I did join the Bairds in the lounge Eric Aveling said, 'We have met before.'

It was true. He had been casually introduced to me some years ago at a party.

'I think it's inconceivable of you not to have told me,' Celia smiled.

'She wouldn't know, she wouldn't know,' he said, 'there was too much noise going on. I don't, I confess, remember the precise occasion; I do remember the noise. It was exceptional.' He made a direct, assured comment on a book I had written and he had liked, and we sat down.

I had thought Celia would be unable to hide love, but I was wrong. She presided over us with a spinsterish, *Cranford* air – pleasant, cool, astringent. If there were a betrayal at all, it was Aveling's. He loved to tease her, and when he did so his gaze lingered on her face, her quick, confident, jewelled hands. He was as tall as Baird, and narrow-chested, his head carried a little to one side, as if he were listening carefully to everything that was said to him. Though he was elegantly made, his body had a disjointed air that I associated vaguely with grandeur; Velasquez often disjointed a king at the elbow or the knee. His fair, fine hair was turning grey, growing high on a tall, lined forehead that plunged sharply downwards to make a sort of shed-roof over bright and sunken eyes. His nose was handsome and birdlike. He had a gentle, broad, good-humoured mouth, the lips folded and recessed at the corners. He had an air of physical and mental ease, disposing his body in a chair as if the mere act of movement gave him delight, and immediately switching his full attention to anybody who addressed him.

He was to stay at the Moray for a week or ten days. He had needed a rest for some time, he told Mrs. Baird, but it had not been possible to leave his work before.

'Not possible?' said Baird. 'Of course it's possible.' As usual, he sounded furious. 'If a man needs rest badly enough he can always take it. Anyone would think you were a Wren.'

'Ah,' said Aveling, nodding with grave attention towards the doctor, 'Wrenn. I think there is a Slavonic expert of that name. With two N's.'

Celia turned her head away, and I saw a smile.

'Not that Wren!' Baird exploded. 'The Saint Paul's Wren, man.'

Aveling looked illuminated. He raised his hand in a

pontifical gesture, dropped it to his knee. 'That one! I see. Now, that would explain what you said.'

'Arthur dear,' said Mrs. Baird, 'you never know when Eric's making fun of you. You are an old silly.'

Baird looked depressed. 'Making fun, is he?'

'I saw Junius last night,' Celia said lightly. 'He took me to a club, and we stayed far too late.'

'Junius must go home on Monday. We can't be away at the same time. Yes, he'll have to go home. It would be sad if we were required to design a new comprehensive school in the absence of both of us.'

'Talking of comprehensive schools—' Baird began, bright with fresh disapprobation.

'As you say, admirable. We'd have been better men if we'd had the luck of these lads.'

'I say the whole ideal's damnable!'

Aveling nodded. 'You may well be right.' He smiled. 'Between ourselves, Doctor, I know you're right. May I say how good it is to see you both?'

Mrs. Baird said it was always good to see him, that they knew his nonsense of old, that he was a tonic.

He said, 'And you are looking well and extremely nice, putting Celia quite in the shade.'

I noticed, as they all talked together, that his tone towards Mrs. Baird was so gentle as to be almost compassionate. He tried his best to please her, treating her like a much younger woman, and a pretty one. She did not believe his flattery, he did not expect her to; but it warmed her and made her more at ease. Baird, too, plainly liked him, but was worried by him. Aveling was not a man to hector, and it put the doctor at a loss to be deprived of his normal conversational approach.

I wondered if Aveling had been alone with Celia that afternoon, how he would next contrive to be alone with her; under her hostessly calm, I felt her impatience. But it was easy enough for him. When we had talked a little longer he asked Mrs. Baird if she would mind him taking us away for a while; it was a beautiful night and he wished to breathe in a great amount of what his grandmother used to call 'the ozone', 'which is always better, in fact, from the end of a pier: which is the reason for piers'. He asked her then if she would care to come, but she refused. I did also; to my surprise Celia pressed me.

'Please, darling.' The unusual endearment was significant; it was rare for her to use the ordinary words of affection, except to her father.

I said good-night to Mrs. Baird, but as I spoke saw she was staring past me at Celia, her face loosened with anxiety.

Celia and I went upstairs for our coats, while Aveling waited for us in the hall.

When we were alone I asked her why she had insisted on my coming.

She said evasively, 'Because I like you. Because it will be nice.'

'It doesn't seem sensible to me.'

'Well, then.' She stopped halfway along the corridor and seemed to think. 'Well, then – when I am tremendously happy I like to share. Some people are like that.'

'If I were you I shouldn't want anyone else.'

'Perhaps I am using you a little.' She put her arm through mine. 'But I tell you, quite seriously, it isn't only that.'

I asked her what she was using me for.

'It will look harmless to the parents if the three of us go out together.'

I remembered the expression on Mrs. Baird's face. I told Celia it was too late. Baird might not know, but her mother did.

41

She answered me at once. 'You're wrong. Mummy's as transparent as glass. I assure you, you're quite wrong.'

I knew by the quickness of her response that she had suspected her mother's knowledge and had refused to accept the idea. Her love for Aveling was of the specifically private kind which can only be displayed, paraded, gloried in, to a stranger, and never, at its beginnings, revealed in the ever-reserved intimacies of the family. To Celia, whose words of endearment were few, who had a nervous avoidance of physical contact except in sexual love, the thought that her mother's mind should as much as touch her own where Aveling was concerned was something raw, almost repulsive.

She repeated lightly, 'You're quite wrong.'

'I don't think I am.'

'Listen: she couldn't keep it to herself, do you see? She would have to drop hints. She would have to look cunning. Do you think I don't know her?'

She began to laugh – the musical, fluid, never quite genuine laughter of an actress off the stage. When we came downstairs together she was still laughing, and as we walked with Aveling out of sight of the Moray she threw her arm around his waist and for a moment leaned her head on his shoulder; it was the reckless, hot candour of a woman in the first uprush of love.

I was worried, and Aveling saw this. He said to Celia, 'You must learn to walk like a young lady or your father will send you to a comprehensive school.'

Yet as I listened, I knew he wanted to be as reckless as she was.

He gently removed her arm, replacing it more decorously above his own.

'I told you Christine knew.'

'Yes, my dear, but we have to behave. Bishops have been known to stay in this town.'

42

I walked on with them for a while, then said I should go back, as I was rather tired. As I turned away he put his hand on her shoulder, and she raised her face to him. I knew they would be together that night.

8

It was true that in happiness she loved to share, for though I deliberately stayed in my room next morning, so that she should not feel obliged to include me in any of her plans, she came up to fetch me. She was radiant, she had a look of beauty. She threw herself into a chair and lit a cigarette. 'How nice your room is! Half-neat, like mine. Isn't Mummy's revolting? Father has managed to make his like a very orderly cellar – so clever of him, since he gets all the sun.'

She smiled at the flecks of sunlight fluttering like moths about the ceiling.

'Junius is coming for the afternoon. Could we all go out together, or are you doing something nicer? I'm afraid he isn't to everyone's taste, but he can be fun. Do say you'll put up with him.'

She asked me if I liked Aveling, listened delightedly to my praise.

'Of course,' she said, 'it is very squalid. I do feel that creeping about hotel corridors at my age is not at all the thing, but obviously he can't come to me.' With sudden, unsmiling energy she asked me a question.

I said, 'I am sure he loves you.'

'Yes – so am I, really. But Lois is there, you know, and it hurts him. We're both happiest when we turn off thinking, like a tap. He's going to see her tomorrow, and I'd better go next day. I would like it if you came.' She got up; her tone

44

changed. 'Only it wouldn't be fair. You mustn't let me impose on you. I do, on people, when I like them.'

She did not speak as though this were a courteous hypocrisy, but as if it were the simple truth. I said I would visit Mrs. Aveling with her if she wished.

'It's not a strain,' she said eagerly, 'because she's so lively. She holds court. You don't feel you have to entertain her – she entertains you. I'm fond of her, but I hate going there. All the same, I never watch the clock and wonder when I can decently go away. She makes time race when one's with her.'

We went downstairs.

There was some excitement going on. Lily, the pinched and stately girl who served in the bar, had fainted that morning and had been put to bed. Dr. Baird was explaining to Boldini, the manager, in a circumlocutory but nevertheless comprehensible fashion, what was the matter with her and how he had known it for weeks. Luckily only the manager, the Bairds and Eric Aveling were in the lounge; even so, Boldini looked hot with embarrassment and fright.

'Don't try to bamboozle me,' said Baird. 'I always know. I can usually tell by their necks. Mind you, I can't say so – it's slander for a doctor to mention the obvious, when the patient won't talk.'

'But, sir,' Boldini said unhappily, 'Lily is a very good girl.'

'So she may be! My God, the narrow-mindedness of people-there's no law against good girls going wrong! Boldini – you make her talk. Then we can give her a helping hand.'

Boldini protested that Lily was subject to liver-attacks, almost anything would upset her.

'Liver be damned,' said Baird. 'I tell you, I can tell by her neck.' He looked sulky. 'Well, just wait and see for yourself. Don't say I didn't warn you.'

'The neck?' Aveling enquired, when the manager had gone away and Baird had retired to his room in a huff. 'I must say that sounds like a piece of folklore.'

Celia said her father was bound to be right. 'He is so absurd, one forgets that he was a very good doctor. The trouble was, he really did detest people outside his own small circle. Lily, you see, *is* in his circle; he's passionately interested in everyone here – the Moray's his life. Boldini thinks he simply wants to interfere, which isn't so. Father is honestly upset about Lily.'

By lunch-time Lily was back in the bar, looking stern and rather white, but performing her duties briskly.

'Wait and see,' said Baird, 'wait and see.'

After lunch we went to look for Junius, who had asked us to meet him at the swimming-pool. The afternoon was hot, the turquoise water already crowded. We sat down beside it and waited. As usual, people were screaming with excitement at the simple fact of being in the water; the air resounded with cries like the cries of wheeling birds. The flag on the dressing-pavilion fluttered only a little against the mast. Young men standing motionless on the diving-boards seemed to darken with sunburn as they stood there.

'I have always wanted to know,' said Aveling, stretching his legs, 'whether people enjoy diving. My view is that they do not. If they did, they would be eager to do it. But the vast majority stand up and hug themselves and look at the water, and only fall into it as a response to public pressure.' He was wearing a suit of dark flannel that looked incongruous in this holiday scene yet gave him distinction. He looked cooler than the half-clothed bathers about him. 'Look at that girl there; she can never make up her mind to dive until a large, impatient queue forms behind her; yet she climbs up again and again. I have her on a ceiling at home, pretending to be a centaur; it is really a most remarkable discovery.'

He told us that he had stripped off some plaster from his flat and discovered an Adam ceiling – in poor shape, but still retaining a leisurely, classic grace. 'Urns and centaurs and beautiful oxen with horns made of icing-sugar.'

Celia said she would love to see it.

'I'm having it restored,' he said, 'and you shall see it when it's finished. It's costing me far more than I can afford. But when the roof crashes over my head it will be the best roof.'

Out of the water by our feet came a great smile and, behind it, Junius. Like some marine animal, stomach silky as a seal's, he wallowed and plunged and rose; clinging to the rail, he greeted us. He said it was nice to see me again, that he thought I must have grown, or perhaps it was the illusion of looking at me from shoe level. To Celia he said, 'I hope you've recovered from our strange little excursion. You look wonderful. And the dress! It is almost too much.'

He was a small man, still in his thirties, but his stoutness made him seem older. Curly black hair, Assyrian hair, lay plastered back by the water from a ballooning, babyish forehead, in which every lump charted by phrenologists seemed to be present. His nose was small, too small for his face, fine, sharp as a pencil, a critical nose. He swept it round from person to person as he talked, as if it were a compass needle; it had that kind of quivering precision. His blue eyes were large and shallow, the whites very clear, the pupils restless and sliding; they were amused and secretive eyes, the eyes of a fat man. They sparkled with life, yet were disturbing. One wanted to share the joke, but could not be sure that it was not directed against oneself. As he climbed out and sat beside us on the hot concrete, I thought that in two sentences he had managed to suggest something to disquiet. He had added an absurd comical-sinister touch to the 'excursion', and he had made Celia seem overdressed.

47

Aveling said, 'We should like you to get your clothes on. This is a pretty scene, but there's a constant smell of dubious frying fat around this part of the beach.'

Junius jumped up, his body drying patchily in the hot sun. 'I'll be with you almost at once, and we'll drive out to some nice genteel place inland.' He paused to ask me about Gerard. 'Educational publishing,' he said, 'that's the thing. Generations of little children always clamouring for more. I wish he would ask me to write more prefaces.'

'I hope your husband will not,' said Aveling, as Junius went off towards the pavilion, 'because I have to write them, while Junius gets paid. He is quite clever, entirely clever, but he has a disorderly mind.'

'He is not clever,' Celia said, 'he really is not. He just sparkles.'

'Well, I do not. So he supplies a deficiency.'

'If you weren't there the business would fall to pieces.' She was angry with Junius and could not conceal it.

He looked at her gravely for a moment, then reached over and took her hand. 'My darling, I know your trip with Junius was perfectly respectable. He implies that it was not, of course, in order to needle me.' She coloured. 'You, however, should have the sense to know that I know Junius. It is an extraordinary metaphor,' he added, ' "to needle"; and, I must say, a baffling one. Do people stick needles into others as a recognisable activity?'

'Perhaps hypodermics,' said Celia, recovering her good humour.

'Oh no, no, no! They would stimulate or put to sleep.'

Junius came back, wearing a suit of fawn seersucker and an orange tie. 'American,' he explained, pirouetting before us. I thought he looked like a debased Pickwick; I was not yet prepared to like him.

He took us to a garden on the far side of the downs, where we were able to have tea under the trees. It was too expensive

48

and too remote a place to be crowded, even on so fine a day. He was obviously well known to the proprietress, who greeted him with something between respect and complicity; he responded to her in an odd, monarchical fashion borrowed, I thought, from Aveling and insisted that she should find us wild strawberries. 'Don't pretend now, don't pretend, you know you keep some tucked away for me.'

All through tea he clowned for us, made a fuss of Celia, made amiable fun of Aveling. He seemed to enjoy his role as a jester, while hinting that he was a jester of a peculiarly powerful kind, a grey eminence in motley, in whose good graces it was as well to stand. If he made jokes at Aveling's expense he was nevertheless in awe of him. He admired him, was jealous of him, would have liked to own him; yet was too shrewd a man to betray himself by deference. I gathered that they were dimly related, had known each other as boys and had followed each other, though with an interval between them of eight years, through school and university. Aveling, being the elder, had felt a responsibility for him; he had felt obliged to guide him. It was he who suggested that Junius should study architecture and had later taken him into the firm. Now, I thought, Junius had become the kind of amusing incubus it is no longer possible to throw off; whom, in fact, one hardly desires to throw off, being adjusted by years to its weight.

After tea, Aveling and Celia went off for a walk together. I watched them as they dwindled through strata of sun and shadow. He was much taller than she; he had to lean over a little to hear what she was saying.

Junius spoke to me. His manner had changed, and was energetic. 'What a pity it is for them!'

I said they were happy.

'Of course. And one's glad. But it's hard on them. It must be hard to refuse to hope.' When Junius talked seriously his

49

face was wrong for it; it was essentially a comedian's face. Nevertheless, it became appealing. 'After all, how can they?'

I asked him, did he mean the hope of Lois's death?

He nodded. 'It must be a most difficult position. It would be perfectly natural for them to hope to marry, but they're stopped from doing anything so natural. Other people can, they can't.'

I asked him if he, too, were fond of Lois.

He did not reply at once. He took out a cigarette from a case absurdly enamelled with the colours of his school and fitted it into a filter-holder. 'Beastly things and spoil the taste, but I believe they do reduce the risk of cancer. One owes it to oneself to take reasonable care.' He smoked with his head thrust upwards. The round green shadows of elm leaves fell upon his face, floating upon it like the lights of the sea. At last he said, 'Lois is just about old enough to be my mother. And, ridiculous as it may seem, I was in love with her. Not for long – just long enough to last.' His eyes slid round; he wanted to see what I was thinking.

'Let us walk too,' he said.

He rose, pulling me up with him. He was easy in the gestures of immediate friendship. We walked over the lawn and in the shadow of a yew hedge.

'You know, Christine, I don't *pretend* to people much. It's boring. And the kind of people I like aren't prigs. I've never been very different from what I am now, and I shan't change. But Lois was the only woman who ever made me think I might be able to care for women. As I say, she was much older than I was; and that was ten years ago. I am telling you the truth,' he said.

I was touched for him, liking him now, but wondering why he should confide in me like this.

'Celia's a wonderful woman,' he went on. 'So odd, she doesn't know how odd she is. I quite adore her.' His mincing

50

manner, half-natural, half-protective, had returned. 'Locked in with that ferocious dad, that sinister mum, escaping to that absurd little business so she can go on her absurd little benders. I am *passionately* for her. But Lois has to come first.'

The dangerous aspect of Junius's conversation was easy enough to see: he would destroy anyone's trust in a friend by surrounding that friend with little question-marks, little, nebulous suspicions. I thought, however, that the people who knew him best must by this time be mithridated against him; I doubted whether he really did much harm, and was sorry for the kind of loneliness, the kind of outsiderhood, that must have driven him to it.

'You must come and see my house.' He changed the subject decisively. 'It was a hovel when I bought it, no less – six hundred I paid for it, and now I could sell it for five times as much. What I've put into it you wouldn't believe. Eric's rude about it, but then he really likes places to look as much like the Athenaeum as humanly possible.'

He glanced across the lawn. The breadth of sun, lime-gold, was narrowing, and the shadows of the tree-trunks strode almost to the edges of the grass. Celia and Aveling were coming back.

'But he shouldn't have these stately tastes,' said Junius, 'because, really, the business is hardly up to them. And they did not ask us to design London Airport. Ah, here you are!' he shouted, in the comradely voice of someone who wishes to conceal the fact that he has been making confidences.

They came up to us, their faces softened, appeased by love, by the words they had spoken to each other, by the incandescent beauty of the summer evening.

9

The hospital where Aveling's wife lay dying was on the downs no more than five miles away, a cleanly bare building of sand-coloured brick with the clouds behind it. It was windy up there, the salty grasses whistling on either side of us as we walked along the concrete path to the bright-blue door.

'I hate hospitals,' Celia said, 'I'm always afraid they'll get me inside and never let me go. And when the visit's over, and I have to leave her, I feel ashamed all down my backbone, I want to run as fast as I can, because I know she's looking after me, and *she* can never go.' She stopped for a minute on the step, lit a cigarette, puffed at it a few times and threw it away. 'It's just this moment I hate. When I see her I'm all right.'

Lois Aveling was not in a room by herself; she did not wish to be. She liked company, and had been moved from a private room at her own wish. She was in the far corner of the ward, and when she saw us come in began to wave eagerly. My first impression was one of shock that she should look so young; she might have been a dark and skinny girl. But as we drew near and spoke to her, I saw that her face was dry and withered beneath the sun-tan she had acquired from lying for two years by a window; and saw also – it was a second shock – that she had once been extremely handsome.

She greeted Celia lovingly, told me how much she had been looking forward to this visit, like a hostess saw that we were comfortably seated and told the nurse we should all want some tea. 'I'm having a round of excitement these days,' she said, without the least appearance of irony, 'Eric, Junius, one of Junius's friends and yourselves, all within a week!'

'You've had your hair done,' said Celia. 'How do you manage these things? You always look twice as smart as I do, and I am *not* exaggerating.'

'Well, I've only half of myself to work on – everything you see above the sheet – and infinite time to do it in. Bed can make one extremely vain.'

There was a good deal of truth in what Celia had said; Mrs. Aveling still had a kind of smartness. Instead of a bed-jacket she wore a short coat of tailored linen, a little lighter than her hands and face. Her dark hair was neatly arranged; one of the nurses, she said, had set it for her.

I told her we had bought her some books.

'Books!' She opened the parcel at once, cutting the string with her nail-scissors, rolling it up neatly into the drawer of her locker. She was full of praise for our choice – we might have been psychic. 'But you,' she said to me, 'of course you'd know. You'd know what one ought to read, which is surprisingly often what one enjoys, don't you think so, or is that a haughty kind of reflection?'

Celia asked her if she were finding it easy to read a lot.

'Perfectly, thank God. I've had none of that trouble again.' She turned to me. 'Last year I thought my eyes were going to give out completely, but they put themselves right again. In fact,' she added cheerfully, 'I'm righter in every possible way at the moment.' She lowered her voice. 'They don't seem half so pleased with me here as they ought to be. I've almost expected a medal. Of course, they may be afraid I'll be fit enough to decamp, and that would be a loss to them.'

This was the recognisable euphoria of her disease: merciful to herself, to others something bizarre, almost sinister. She seemed really to believe what she said: that she would one day escape.

'Poor Eric, he pays and pays. He will do it; I'm perfectly willing to become a free patient – why on earth not? But there you are. Sister!'

Her voice, gay, a little strident, carried across the ward.

'Sister, what do I get for my money here that I wouldn't on the N.H.S.?'

'More visitors and pink china,' the nurse answered promptly.

'Well,' said Celia, 'I shouldn't find the second a consideration, but the other does seem so, or would to me.'

When tea was brought, Lois asked me if I would pour it. I saw then that although she had made an energetic effort to greet us, to unwrap her parcel briskly, to show how neatly she could dispose of paper and string, the effort had exhausted her. She could not sit up unaided. As a nurse raised her on to the pillows she wore, for a moment, the painful, hilarious smile of the ventriloquist's dummy. She ate a little, but hardly touched her tea; it was all she could do to hold a cup steady.

Yet she was, as Celia had said, good company. The ward was her world; she enriched it, expanded it, with description. She had a lively imagination, a ready tongue. She could be very funny. She was also slightly malicious, but her malice seemed trustworthy. I did not believe that she used it for more than a momentary effect, nor that it did more than add a touch of tartness to ready and easy affections.

She began suddenly to talk of her husband. He was, she said, wonderful; because, look at it as you liked, it must be a bore to him, having an absentee wife. 'It is really half a life for him – less. I know that. But you'd never think it, never in this world.' She touched the locker and nodded to it. 'And I have his letters. That's one thing I'd never have if we were together again; his letters. Celia, they are—' She sighed, gave a broad, helpless smile. 'Oh, you don't know!'

54

Celia's eyes flickered. This was hard for her to bear. But she put out her hand and touched Lois's. 'I expect he loves writing them just as much as you love getting them.'

'You are a dear,' Lois said. 'You always say things I want to hear. Darling, keep a weather eye on him, will you? Don't let him work too hard or get run down, and above all let him enjoy his miserable little holiday, such as it is, and don't let him feel he has to come racing up here every day.'

Celia said quickly, 'I don't often see him.' It was unnecessary; to me it sounded false. But Lois was looking across the ward to a bed where a woman lay on her side, unmoving, humped in the sheets. She pointed her out to us. 'Poor dear, she can't move at all now, only her eyes. And she has a frightful husband. He comes up three times a week, and just sits and grumbles quietly the whole time. God knows what he says; she never answers. But one knows he hates her.'

The long white blinds billowed out in a stiffer breeze, giving the high room the air of a dream or of an hallucination. In the pure, the watered light, the light of a Yermeer, Celia sat with her hands in her lap, her head down. Beside Lois she looked very young, young not with the youth of the hair or the skin but with the youth of helplessness. For she was helpless, all love and guilt, concealing both under a housewifely primness that she had long ago discovered to be part of her own personality, had painstakingly eradicated, and now and again reassumed as a disguise or a protective coloration. I knew that her heart was beating too hard, that it would be an effort to her to speak again. She could not, for the moment, raise her eyes because they were not serene, as Lois's were. For a moment I was frightened that she would be asked a question and be quite unable to answer; that in her silence she would be compelled to reveal her sudden and awful nakedness.

'That's why I'm so lucky,' said Lois. 'When Eric comes, he likes it. And Junius does too. I get fonder all the time of Junius.'

'He's not all that nice,' Celia said. She looked up and smiled. 'In fact, I never see how one can be precisely fond. But he seems part of one's life, in a funny way, whether one wants him or not.'

'Have you met—?' Lois mentioned a name. 'Junius brought him up to see me. He's quite his most pleasing acquisition to date.'

Celia had not met this man, but I had. I said nothing. He was a young actor of extremely shady reputation, who had at one time turned his hand to journalism and probably to blackmail. I felt angry that Junius should have imposed him upon Lois.

However, she began to tell us stories of his visit. She was not a fool. If she had little idea of what he was like, she certainly had no doubts about Junius. She was very amusing; yet I found myself feeling faintly uncomfortable that the very sick should not also be unworldly. It was a prig's feeling and I was not proud of it; but when the visit was at an end, and we were walking away, in a kind of shame and relief, from the many-windowed building now flashing its semaphores in the light of the falling sun, Celia said angrily: 'I wish Junius would keep his horrible friends to himself! It's swindling Lois, in a way; she thinks she knows everything, but she really doesn't. One can't help feeling he is having a sort of nasty joke at her expense.'

We drove along by the sea. The tide was far out; the sands caught a plum-coloured glow from the deepening sky. A few children were still playing on the rocks, small in the immense freedom of the shore. Each rib of sand cupped a narrow shadow of violet. The breeze had fallen; the sea, unbroken by a ripple, reached onward and out to the immaculate union.

'Whenever I leave that place,' Celia said, 'I feel I want to go back and tear it down and take her out of it, and let her look at the sea. Sometimes it seems almost a practical idea.'

She stopped. We shared the same thought; the thought of the reality of her disease, the professional, paraplegic, sickroom realities.

'What do you think of her?'

I was surprised that, for a moment, I found it hard to reply.

IO

We were to visit Junius after dinner that evening. When we started out I thought Celia looked tired and in low spirits. She had not bothered to change her dress, though she had made up her face again, and made it up too heavily. As we went towards the garage where Aveling had left his car, I saw that he was regarding her with a tender, worried look; but he asked her nothing about our visit to Lois, nor made any direct attempt to comfort her.

The garage was in a mews behind the hotel. Opposite was a small, brightly-painted public house, with sunblinds and geraniums, tucked in between a storehouse and a men's lavatory.

'Let's have a drink first,' Celia suggested. 'To go to Junius stone-cold is too much for me.'

Aveling looked at her. 'We'll be late.'

'He won't care. Come on, I'll show you my private place. I don't reveal this to everyone.'

She took us into a shaded, cheaply-smart little bar. There were several people perched on the stools; two brassy-looking women, three or four men who looked as though they had something to do with racing.

The barmaid greeted Celia familiarly. 'Well, well, who's a stranger? I began to wonder what we'd done.' Celia gave her a charming, distant smile and a jingle. She ordered for us, led us into a dark corner, all oak-panelling and mock-Tudor benches.

'You would never suppose it,' Aveling murmured, 'but the bressummer there, over the fireplace, is genuine. Very strange. I wonder where on earth they got it?'

He leaned back, folding his hands behind his head. The seat was so narrow that he could do little more than balance on it, keeping himself in place by stretching his legs out and wedging his heels against the floor.

The little crowd at the bar were discussing, with every appearance of special knowledge, the possibility of a royal marriage. One of the men made an off-colour joke; a woman nudged him, nodded her head slightly in the direction of our corner.

'Upon my soul, darling,' Aveling said to Celia, 'do you own this place? You are obviously a person to be reckoned with.'

'I've spent money here,' she replied. Her tone was curiously stand-offish, as if she did not care whether or not she pleased him.

He was noncommittal. 'Extremely nice. I see you get your money's worth in respect. She has an authoritative air, Christine, and others notice it besides ourselves.'

For a moment she said nothing, not responding to his teasing. His gaze rested anxiously upon her.

I asked him some question about telling genuine wood from faked, and he began to answer me with the clear and measured courtesy of one who loves to teach, but is afraid to assume too little knowledge in the pupil. 'Well, you know, of course—' he said; and, 'You'll have noticed that—' He was interesting. I was enjoying myself, listening to him, when Celia broke in.

'Lois was in very good form this afternoon.'

He turned to her, giving her his entire attention as he had given it to me. 'I'm glad. I must say I found her very lively yesterday.'

Celia said, in her lightest voice, falsely warm, 'Your letters mean an enormous amount to her. She was telling us.'

He replied, 'They're all I can give her. I do my best to write in the way that pleases her.'

As she turned away from him I saw that her eyes were full of tears. 'Anyway, they work wonders.'

He laid his hand on her bare arm, pressed it gently.

'Well,' she said, 'what are we hanging about for? Do you want another drink or shall we go?'

When Junius opened his door for us I had the impression of a fashionable stage-setting. There was a blur of golden gauze, golden light, golden ropes climbing a narrow sky-blue stairway.

He said nothing for a moment, his eyes on me, waiting for me to enjoy his triumph.

'This is beyond words,' I said.

'Chichi,' Junius murmured, 'ineluctably chichi. I am not so stupid as to be unaware of it. But, you see, I adore chichi. I actually like it. Most people do, but daren't confess.'

He took us upstairs into his drawing-room. Two small rooms had been knocked into one narrow one of reasonable size, running from the front to the back of the house. Venetian looking-glasses hung on pale-blue walls; sofas were striped with regency silk, plum-coloured and gold. From a gilt basket high on the wall, trails of ivy were spread into a two-dimensional pavilion.

'Eric and Celia can make themselves comfortable while I show Christine the glories. You know where the drinks are.'

He took me up a further flight of stairs into his bedroom. This, also, consisted of two rooms knocked into one. The ceiling was covered with a dark-blue paper spotted with silver stars; nearly a third of the total space was taken up by an enormous four-poster bed hung with crimson tapestry and crowned with Prince of Wales feathers of gilded wood. 'It makes me feel like the Grand Turk. It was hideously expensive, but worth every joint.'

He took me to look out of the back window. Outside was a small courtyard, originally designed to keep coals, now painted white. Cages of flowers hung on the walls. In the middle, between two elaborate garden seats of wrought iron, was an indifferent Victorian statue of a woman, an Alma Tadema beauty with an amphora upon her shoulder. And this was floodlit; it glared in the light.

'Now that,' said Junius, 'is the purest extravagance. But I only switch it on for my best friends, never for the *canaille*. You must come and sit out there some time. It's hideously uncomfortable but ghastly gay.'

He was caricaturing himself so wildly that I was suspicious of him. Junius had, I felt, something up his sleeve.

He had. He said abruptly, 'All go off well today? Was she wonderful?' He sounded like an ordinary man, a troubled and angry one.

I made some reply.

'It's amazing how she manages to upset Celia, though I saw it the moment she came in.'

I said, 'I think the circumstances are upsetting, not Lois herself.'

'No, no, no, Lois does it. Angel as she is, she does. Sometimes one would think she knew, only God knows how she would. Celia is impeccable – besides, she rather loves her; and nobody would be such a cad as to drop hints.'

'I never felt that anyone had,' I said.

Junius gave his odd smile that was almost a smirk. 'It would be awful if it were true, because nobody could ever convince Lois that it simply didn't matter. It's purely a physical thing. He's never going to care for anyone as he did for her – age difference notwithstanding. She was the entire world, and she still is.'

I said I did not believe him. Between Celia and Aveling was love; it would be much less sad if there were not.

Junius's smile faded. 'You may be right. I'm prejudiced. I told you why.' The critical nose pointed, whitening at the tip.

In this over-decorated bedroom, under the paper stars, the golden feathers, it sounded absurd. Yet I believed the confidence he had made me, though I could not understand it.

He said, 'Lois is a natural empress. There are so few left. Let's go down.'

As we entered the drawing-room Celia and Aveling drew apart, she with a kind of rough jolt, he with the slow dignity of a man who does not care to embarrass others, while having no great concern for their opinion.

'Christine has admired everything,' Junius said, 'and will now make herself comfortable.'

It seemed for a while as though the evening would go better than I had expected. Junius and Aveling talked for a while about matters concerning the business; there was the prospect of a good contract. Celia asked questions intelligently. She had heard a good deal about their work, was familiar with various architectural trends, knew the names of possible rivals. Aveling consulted her again, cocking his head to her reply, explaining why he accepted or could not accept her opinion, and at the same time teaching her. Once when he had applauded her, saying, 'That's an idea, that is not at all bad', she made a movement of nervous withdrawal. 'I'm only repeating your own words back to you,' she said, 'only you don't realise it. I actually know nothing whatsoever.'

'You're always worth listening to.'

'No, I'm not. You're just kind to me.'

We talked about books; the taste of Junius was fashionable and narrow, Aveling's surprisingly robust. Both listened to what I had to say, but Junius smiled while listening. He knew. He needed no telling. He felt himself a connoisseur rather than a critic, one to whom absolute truth is revealed in a flash. He knew, also, about the theatre, and here he seemed to me entirely without discrimination; but Aveling and Celia conceded to him the rôle of expert.

We were all, except Aveling, who was putting soda-water into white wine and sipping it as a social formality, drinking too much. Junius became more talkative and more amusing; but Celia very quiet. She spoke less, seemed to draw herself farther apart from us. When Aveling touched her she did not respond.

Junius was talking about an elderly actress who, hideously dyed and bedizened, hung about with beads and bracelets, had now become a clown even in her private life.

'I think she is absolutely adorable,' he cried. 'I think she is the most wonderful creature, still entirely glorious. One's absolutely at her feet.'

Celia said, 'Oh, shut up, Junius!'

There was a silence. His mouth opened, but he found nothing to say. Aveling stirred. He smiled, raising his eyebrows, leaned over to squirt more soda-water into his glass.

Celia was white; her face had tightened, as though some-one had turned a screwdriver.

'Strong,' said Junius at last, 'very strong.'

'I don't care. I detest hearing you praise bloody women like that! You don't mean it. Do you know why you do it?'

'No, but I shall be interested to learn.'

'It's a trick you and your friends go in for; I've heard it again and again.'

'Look, my dear,' said Aveling, 'these are surely not party manners.'

'You do it because they degrade themselves in old age, because they make women into figures of fun. When you say they're "glorious", "adorable", you're laughing yourselves sick. You know they're reducing all of us to the state you'd *like*

63

to see us in, so you could really despise us, you'd genuinely have grounds for hate.'

Aveling stroked her arm. 'You must not be unkind to Junius. He is our host, and we're both fond of him.'

Junius, without thinking, detached every leaf from the trail of ivy hanging nearest to his fingers. He was beside himself with rage.

'How pleasant for Christine,' he said. 'She must think she's in a mad-house.'

'Tell Junius you're sorry, my dear,' Aveling said gently, 'and then he won't be sorry he asked us. I really think you must.'

'Does he deny what he is?' she cried. 'No! He's far too brave; he's open about it; he thinks they all ought to be. So why shouldn't I be open as well?'

'Be as open as you please,' Junius said slowly, 'in your own establishment, but not in mine.'

We all stood up. Aveling put his arms round Celia; she leaned against him, averting her face. There was nothing anyone could say to restore the situation. I could not even make an ordinary social remark, thanking him for the evening; it would have sounded ridiculous.

Aveling put Celia aside, and on his arm. He said to Junius, 'I'll be up to see you before you go tomorrow, and we can get our business sorted out then. I've got one or two new ideas.'

'I'm taking the two twenty-five,' Junius said. His mouth seemed to hurt him.

I managed, then, to say some words of thanks, and went downstairs, Celia close behind me. In a moment Aveling joined us and opened the door. Junius stood at the head of the stairs.

Then Celia turned and ran up to him. 'Junius, darling, I'm so sorry! I've been beastly to you and spoiled everyone's evening.'

64

He did not answer. We saw her lean over and kiss his cheek. For a second he did not stir. She stood facing him on the landing, her hands knotted tightly behind her back.

At last he said lightly, 'Get along with you. We all know what you're like, we've had experience. Forget about it, and we'll go for another excursion one of these fine days.'

As we walked across the road to the car, I saw that Celia was weeping. Aveling put his arm round her and pulled her against his side. 'Poor dear, never mind. You have a lot to bear. We both have too much to bear.'

II

Next day I saw little of them. They went out together in Aveling's car soon after breakfast and did not, so far as I knew, come back either for lunch or dinner. I had some work to do, so to avoid Dr. and Mrs. Baird, who seemed to be sitting all day with the invisible Third between them, I spent the afternoon in my room. On the following morning I had to go to London. It was late by the Moray's standards when I returned, past eleven o'clock; but a single lamp was burning in the lounge and under it sat Mrs. Baird. I caught sight of her on my way to the lift and called out good night, but she had been waiting for me. She jumped up and came across the hall. Could I spare a moment, she asked, if I were not too tired? Perhaps I would have a drink with her.

It was not an ordinary invitation: there was urgency behind it. Besides, the mere action of ordering a drink at this hotel at such an hour would be an event in itself.

She went back to her corner, leading me there with an air of resolution, and rammed her finger hard on the bell. She tried to smile, as if this were an ordinary social occasion; her lips were unsteady.

She asked me if I had had a pleasant day, whether it had rained in London. She was wearing a dress I had not seen before, pale blue, too tight, a little too short in the skirt. She pulled at the hem with one hand, with the other felt for her ear-rings.

The night porter came up and asked us, with a rather ghastly alacrity, what we should like. When she told him he said, 'Certainly, madam!' trying to cover, by a jocular, up-spouting voice, the fact that he thought it was high time we were both in bed.

'Arthur's gone up,' said Mrs. Baird, 'he's had a long day.'

I wondered why the day had been longer for him than any other; I had never seen him do anything whatsoever but read the paper, walk down to the shelter on the front, and on one occasion visit the theatre.

'He isn't strong; he gets tired easily. I tell him it's all mental, if only he wouldn't worry so much he'd be all right.'

I asked her what he worried about.

She looked surprised. 'Well, about what most men do, I suppose. World affairs, and all that. I'm afraid they're a bit beyond me.'

The porter returned with whisky, soda-water and ice. He rattled the ice so vigorously that I felt he would awaken the whole hotel. Tinkling echoed in the vast empty room.

'It is nice to have company,' said Mrs. Baird. Her look was timid, cunning, pitiful. 'And nice of you to keep me company. One doesn't always want to go upstairs with all those old women.' She paused. 'Of course, Arthur's older than I am; he never feels he needs more than he has. I expect you get tired, though, with all the work you do. I'm sure I can't imagine how you do it.'

The windows were open. The wind was blowing strongly from the south. We could hear the inexhaustible sea breathing time away.

I did not want to sit there, late at night, waiting for Mrs. Baird to involve me still further into her life and Celia's. I had in my bag a long letter from Gerard that I wanted to read again. He had a tiny, almost illegible handwriting that often seemed to me something of a blessing, since it made his letters last longer. There was a sentence I had even now failed to elucidate, a tantalising sentence that began 'I want you to know always that I ...' 'Have'? 'Love'? 'Have my' – 'love you'? The words lay there under my hand, meticulous, gnomic. I longed to look at them; I longed to see him again.

'I expect your husband is very proud of you,' said Mrs. Baird, 'and your parents must be.'

I had no parents: they had died long ago.

She went on, 'I often wish Celia had got married. There was someone once, but he wasn't at all the right sort. There would only have been unhappiness.' She put the glass to her lips but did not drink.

The night porter wandered about the room, adjusting a curtain, tweaking a cushion here and there. He looked remote and solitary, with the long and featureless hours before him. He gave us a hopeful glance to see if we had finished our drinks, and went out again. Only half the lights in the hall were on; the space of the polished floor held a subdued and brownish light. The clock, inaudible by day, ticked loudly now, like a garrulous guest who has at last managed to hold the floor because the other talkers have fallen into exhausted silence.

'I know you are wise and kind,' she said. 'Celia is so attached to you. I know you mean a lot to her.'

I replied that I had known her well only for a very short time, but that I was indeed fond of her.

'I am so much older than you, old enough to be your mother, but we both have children, you have that nice boy. It gives us something in common.'

Her distress was beginning to break through. Though she had scarcely stirred except in her nervous movements of smoothing and tidying, she looked somehow dishevelled.

Taking out a purse of gold mesh, she counted out some money and put it on to the tray, as if it gave her something to do.

She burst out, 'Tell me, is there something between her and Eric?'

I did not know what to say.

'They've known each other for years, they were like brother and sister.'

I said something meaningless.

'Don't put me off, Christine.' Leaning forward, she put her hand on mine; it was moist and trembling. 'If anything happened to poor Lois, would he want to marry her?'

I said, 'Mrs. Baird, I'd help you if I could, but I'm only a very casual acquaintance of Celia's. I haven't any real knowledge of her, or any right to talk about her.'

'Any mother has dreams for her girl. I used to imagine her all in white on her wedding-day – she can look so pretty when she pleases.'

I thought Celia could look ugly or nearly beautiful, nothing between. I waited for her to go on.

'But she wasn't really interested. If she had been she'd have married David, no matter what her father and I thought about it. She's not really interested in men, she's happy in her little business, she likes being with us. She knows I love her as no one else ever could. She may fancy she's fond of Eric in that way, but it's wrong. She will grow out of it. It wouldn't last.'

'But Lois may live for a long while,' I said. It was cowardly, it sounded callous: all I wanted to do was to be free of the Bairds – at that moment free of them all, even of Celia.

Mrs. Baird kept her hand over mine. It was like a children's game of piling hands; if I drew mine out I should only have to put it on hers, then she would put hers on mine, and so on.

'I'm not a selfish mother. If there had ever been a real chance of her marrying I'd wish her joy. But it's so late now, and when Arthur goes I shall be all alone except for Celia.'

'This might be a real chance,' I said. I was past pretending.

'We all like you so,' she said irrelevantly. 'Even Arthur does, and he's not easy to please.'

She went on, 'No, it's not real. It's only because of the circumstances. He feels lonely, any man would. He's only turning to Celia because she's nearest. I don't want it to go any further.'

I repeated, weakly, that he was not free.

Now she wore a look of terror and aversion; her fashionable, too-tight clothes were suddenly like some bizarre fancy-dress. She looked round her, as if to be sure there was no one listening. 'I don't mean that. I'm afraid they might do something rash.' She knew this 'rashness' had already occurred; she could not bear to admit it.

'I know I'm not modern. I try to keep up with Celie' – the infantile name came out without her realising it – 'but I do have standards. I couldn't bear to think of my girl doing anything that wasn't right; and it would kill Arthur.'

I suggested that Celia was not a young girl: that life might have been lonely for her.

'I wish I knew what she did in town, I wish I knew. She's far too old for me to keep an eye on her, she has to have her freedom; but I hate it, Christine, I hate it. You'll know what it is one day. You never break the cord that ties you to them.'

I saw, horribly, the cord like vermicelli, run through with a ribbon of pulsing, captured life, a sort of moss-rose pink.

'It would be adultery,' she said.

I was too far now from the ancient Christian acceptances to hear, at once, the leaden weight of the word, the *peine forte et dure*, as it sounded to our grandfathers; in our own time it has become a police-court word, a mere mischief, has lost its blue-black coloration, its association with the scaffold, the stone and the tarry gate. Yet Mrs. Baird saw it printed with the letter of Hester Prynne, and saw it on her daughter's

70

breast. I knew now why Celia had so wild a look beneath her daughterliness; it was because she was forced to hide continually behind the image her mother had made of her, an image classically draped, with marble hand to breast and to pudendum. It was an image all the more frightening because it had been made in *hubris*. Mrs. Baird herself did not believe in it; in the African bush of her uncharted mind the true image stood, the juju, sly and passionate and sad; but it was not this one that she worshipped.

'I love her,' she said, 'and she loves me, though she doesn't show it. Celia never wears her heart upon her sleeve. She wouldn't do anything to hurt me, I know.'

The night porter was on the prowl again. I did not know why he should be so eager to see us up to bed, unless he had a book he wanted to read and felt he would never be able to settle to it until he had cleared away our drinks and had turned out the last light.

'I'm sure,' I said, 'that she would never want to hurt you.'

It was true. There was no cruelty in Celia, who longed only to please; she was kinder than I, in a way less ruthless. Her real longing, which is so often the tragedy of those who are wild in temperament, lay in her longing for smiles and softness about her, for everyone to love and to give, and for no one to be unhappy at all. She was one of those rare people who, at certain moments, feel a yearning for the traditional heaven, the crown, the harp, the glossy, waveless sea; to her it would not seem ineffably boring.

'You must try to warn her,' said Mrs. Baird. 'She would listen to you. I know there's nothing wrong now, but there so easily might be. Of course there *is* temptation. I'm not narrow, I can see that. And poor Eric has a tragic life.'

I said then that I could not warn Celia, that I could not speak to her of these things. She was no younger than I; we were not even intimate friends.

'But you could drop a word. You are so clever. You would know how to drop a word without her noticing. Oh, Christine, I feel so alone! *He* is nothing. There's nothing to be gained from *him*.'

As she spoke, I realised that she hated her husband, had hated him for years. In this bare, unreal moment, in this dim room where a whisper ran round the walls like a rat, this room filled to the brim with the quiet yawning of the sea, she had betrayed herself. The tidiness of tone, the tight solicitude, had gone; she spoke in a strong voice, with scorn, and perhaps with sorrow for a better past she knew had existed, but which she could no longer recall.

'Nothing at all to be gained from *him*.'

She rose stiffly, telling me I had been very kind, that I had been a comfort to her. As we went together to the lift the night porter darted into the lounge, eager to remove all trace of us. The last light clicked off.

As I was about to get out at my own floor, she leaned forward and touched her dry lips to my cheek. 'You are a good friend, I know you are a good friend.'

She went upstairs to her restless room, to the smell of cats, to the trinkets and powder scattered about the dressing-table, to the silence, to the length of the night.

12

Sometimes a change in the weather, even for the worse, produces a lightening of the spirits. The rain poured down, it was chilly again. Cardigans appeared in the lounge. It was my last day at the Moray.

After breakfast I found Aveling and the Bairds together, all looking lively, even the doctor. Celia made me join them. She had a jaunty air, her skin was fresh. Baird was conducting one of his cross-examinations; Aveling, the subject of it, was lying back in his chair gazing at the ceiling, apparently engaged in serious consideration of all that was said to him.

'Now if you're going to tell me we've all got to admire a woman with one eye and six feet, I tell you you're out of luck. Some of us aren't afraid to speak out; we're not afraid to be thought shell-backs. Eh? What do you say to that?'

'I am not sure,' Aveling replied in his measured and courteous way, 'exactly what picture you mean. Now I do know one of a woman with three eyes, but, if my memory serves me – and you'll realise I see so much – no feet. Could that be it?'

He flashed a look of pure fun at Celia, who turned her head away.

'Now look here,' said Baird, 'you've enough sense to know that I'm speaking generally. It's the kind of picture I mean, not one damned particular one.'

'Yet you must,' Aveling continued thoughtfully, 'have something positive in mind. Obviously you would not have

73

had six feet impressed on your mind if in fact there were none at all. If you could be a little more specific I could try—'

'I am trying to get into your head,' said Baird loudly, 'a *type* of muck that I detest, not one special piece of muck!'

'Arthur,' Mrs. Baird murmured, 'I think Eric is pulling your silly old leg again.'

The doctor gave a brief moonstone smile in acknowledgment that a joke might have been made, then turned back to attack Aveling. 'All right, try to get out of it by foolery. What I want to get at is, why do you admire this trash?'

'If you knew Eric better, dear,' Celia said, 'you would know that it is no *use* hectoring him on this subject, because his tastes are extremely conservative. He is behind the times himself.'

'That's what he pretends! And then he puts up houses that look like tube stations. I wouldn't let him build me a pig-sty.'

Even for Baird this was rude; yet he himself was unaware of it, and in cheerful spirits.

'Now you've raised an interesting point there,' Aveling said, leaning forward with an eager look. 'So much has been done in agricultural design – I have seen some splendid barns – but pigs have been curiously neglected. If I were to turn my mind to the matter I could suggest something altogether revolutionary—'

'I think we will play cards,' said Celia.

'But you have to consider the animal itself. The pig can be curiously "choosy" ' – he separated the word as if it had a new and piquant flavour on his tongue – 'it is not realised nearly sufficiently how counter-suggestible such an animal can be, if the intelligence is there.'

'Oh, bosh,' said Baird.

'Bosh?' Aveling enquired, as though willing to be instructed.

'Bosh. They don't even feel as we do – Millie had a cat who broke its jaw. Had to set it under anaesthetic, stitch it up.

When it came to, it tried to eat its dinner. Catch a human being with a broken jaw doing that – as I say, they don't *feel* as we do. Bosh to say they're concerned with art.'

'Ah! But you shouldn't generalise, doctor. Animals differ. In the matter we were discussing it would depend on the particular pig.'

'If no one's going to be more sensible than this,' Baird exploded, 'I'm going upstairs.'

'You're not, Father,' said Celia, 'because we're going to play gin rummy.'

I excused myself.

Baird turned on me. 'Why? Why not?'

I explained that I seldom played cards, and found it difficult to remember how.

'It must hamper your social life if you're like that,' he said. 'Everyone ought to be able to take a hand, makes the wheels go round. People can't chatter all the time.'

I said I was afraid most of the people I knew managed to do so.

'Can't understand what they find to talk about,' he said.

In the afternoon Aveling went to visit his wife. Celia, resisting her mother's suggestion that we should go to a cinema, asked me to come and help her with some shopping. Mrs. Baird was disappointed at first, then eager to send us off alone; I think she thought I might find an opportunity for 'dropping a word'.

The rain had stopped but it was grey and bleak, and the town was crowded with aimlessly wandering men, women and children, who would normally have been on the beach. Now and then a weakly sun flashed on mackintoshes, making a sudden shine of water as though the sea had flown into the streets; children looked hopefully at the sky and tugged at their mothers' hands, but longer queues formed outside the cinemas and buses went by full up.

We went into a shop. Celia stopped at the perfumery counter and bought several things: two lipsticks, some face cream, soap, a small bottle of expensive scent. As we moved off she gave the scent to me. 'I think it will suit you. Do have it. It's wrong for me, but I love it on other people.' I protested. 'No, no, no,' she said almost irritably, 'I bought it for you.'

It was obvious from the attention she received that she was a frequent customer. One of the saleswomen addressed her by name. 'We've got those stockings in, Miss Baird – the ones you were asking about.' Celia moved in this atmosphere, to her familiar and consoling, like a queen; as though she were expecting a lady-in-waiting to appear and pay for her purchases. She did not, however, keep an account there. 'It would make me extravagant. I'd feel I got everything for nothing. As it is, I spend much less.'

I wondered how she could spend much more.

Afterwards we went into three or four bookshops; and in each she made sure that my own books were in stock. I felt embarrassed, afraid the assistants would recognise me. 'Oh no they won't,' she said, with her occasional air of contempt. 'They're all far too stupid. They never look above one's elbows.'

I said I would take her to tea, asked her where we should go. I had imagined she might show me somewhere a little hidden, a little dubious, a little odd, as her public house had been: but instead she took me into a small, stylish, glossy shop that might have been decorated by Junius. I said so.

She laughed, then said, 'I hadn't a chance to talk about it before, but I want to tell you how sorry I am about that hideous silly scene the other night. It was so unfair of me, with you there.'

I said I had been sorrier for her than for Junius.

'Of course you wouldn't have known it,' Celia said, 'but it wasn't unique. We've had scenes like that before. It means nothing to him.'

I thought of Junius, compact with rage at the head of the stairs, and wondered whether she could really believe what she said.

She settled herself in a corner, put her fur cape on the seat and piled her small parcels upon it.

'I shall be miserable when you go.'

I asked her why.

'Oh, I know Eric will be here. But you make me feel safer. As if I shan't do so many wrong things.'

She looked at me earnestly, her eyes strained and bright. 'Whenever I see him I think it will all be so wonderful, and then I do things to spoil it. Like being drunk the night before he came. Quarrelling with Junius.'

She asked me if we might see each other often in London; it would be better, away from her parents. We would have a good time. She did not want to lose me again.

I told her, with the selfishness of love, that Gerard would be home in two weeks and that I might not be so free after that. I could not control the happiness in my voice.

'Yes, of course,' she said, with a disappointed smile. 'He'll want you all the time, after being away so long. Besides, you must be fed up with me and my affairs.'

'It's not that.'

'Then do see me when you can. Will you?'

I made some sort of promise.

'Christine, isn't it horrible that he has to write those letters? That he has to write her beautiful love-letters when he can't mean it?'

The sky had darkened again; beyond the windows a loop of black rain-cloud dipped behind the roofs. The yellow-shaded lamps on the tables sparkled up.

'It must hurt him to do it. Can't you think of that?'

She said obstinately, 'Not as much as it hurts me to know that he does it.'

77

She was pitiless in her jealousy; for the moment it had taken her beyond compassion for Lois.

'What would you think of him if he denied her something so small as that?' I said.

'At least I'd know I came first.'

The squall broke. Rain rushed across the panes, spurted up like cats' heads, ears erect, from the roadway. Umbrellas went up, further darkening the street.

I said, 'You do come first. One has only to look at him.'

'Has one?' Warmth and brightness returned to her face. 'Are you sure? I want it to be true! I know I'm behaving badly, I'm ashamed. But I couldn't stop thinking of those letters – if they really sound to her as though he loves her, then he must love her a little, don't you think so? Or he couldn't write them.' The brightness had gone again.

She went on detachedly, as if examining some academic proposition, 'But if he doesn't love her, and can still write them, he must be something of a hypocrite. He could write to *me* in love and not mean it, isn't that so?'

I told her that in this one thing she seemed to me bitterly unfair.

'I know, I know, I know,' she said rapidly. She pushed a plate to me. 'Do eat some of these things – I can't. Yes, everything you say is true. I'll try not to be like that, I'll try my hardest. You must help me to try.'

I had been debating for a while my relative obligations of loyalty towards Celia and towards her mother, and had decided in Celia's favour. I did not tell her much of what Mrs. Baird had said to me, only that she knew of the love-affair and was pretending to herself that it had no physical basis.

Celia looked thoughtful. 'You mean she likes to think it is simply romantic?' She smiled without humour. 'Really, how very little she knows of me. She can be very nice, but she is really quite obtuse.'

I noticed how she had accepted instantly what she had refused to accept before – the fact of her mother's knowledge. Her love for Aveling had become so obsessive an emotion that anything relating directly neither to him nor to herself seemed trivial in the light of it. Before his visit she had been desperately anxious to keep all knowledge of the affair from her mother: now she did not care what Mrs. Baird knew, providing the pretence of ignorance was maintained.

'Well,' she said, 'I shall be in London again next week, and I shan't know what anyone's brooding about, thank God. But I'll be careful. I will do that.' She took out her purse to pay the bill, forgetting she was my guest.

'Oh, I'm sorry.' She put the purse back. 'Thank you for telling me about Mummy. I am truly grateful.'

She and Aveling came to the station to see me off. She kissed me fondly but ceremoniously on both cheeks. She was wearing some sweet, hot scent a little too heavy for her. 'Bless you,' she said. 'We shall see you again very soon.'

They waited until the train moved out. I saw them turning back along the platform. She was leaning towards him, her head against his shoulder. He moved his arm about her waist. The train swung outwards, cutting them away as the safety curtain of a dream cuts away another dream, at once obliterating it. I felt an instant lightening of relief at being free of them all, their anxieties no longer mine as, indeed, they need never have been. They were nothing to do with me. I told myself I would not be drawn in again. Yet within ten minutes they were crowding back into my mind, jammed there like passengers in a tube lift.

I began to wonder what it was that sucked me so easily into the affairs of others; it was not some professional vulgarity like the obtaining of 'copy' – a myth believed in by people who do not write; deliberate observation is almost valueless to a writer. No; I thought it was something more than prying;

79

it was a kind of vainglory, and an easy one. For if, as the impartial observer, we meddle with lives, it is perfectly easy, when we survey the wreckage we have caused, to step tidily out of it and expect a thank-you before we go. (Moreover, we shall almost certainly be thanked; even the dying – perhaps especially the dying – tend to be polite.) The thought depressed me and made me sick with myself, so I began to look for something more; perhaps something better. But one of the hardest things God requires us to do is to praise ourselves upon those rare occasions when praise is due: we simply cannot do it without remembering the sin of Pride, and then we praise ourselves falsely because we have had the decency to remember it.

I thought of something Gerard had once said in a letter to me, after we had discussed this subject between us, and was comforted.

'Everyone on earth exists for the interest, if not the enjoyment, of everyone else. It's when people cease to be interested that the real harm's done. For every person who wants you to mind your own business there are ten in prison-cells wishing you wouldn't. So I shouldn't worry too much, if I were you.'

13

At the end of the week Celia telephoned me, asking if I would like to come and see her rooms. I wanted to refuse; I had enjoyed a week of my own affairs, even though the house was lonely and I had had no visitors. I seldom asked people when Gerard was away, for I felt that our cook-housekeeper would be more complaisant after a good rest. She was not very good either at cooking or housekeeping, and her ill-tempers too often infected the house like a fog; but she seemed to us precious and delicate as Waterford glass. We were afraid, in fact, to break her; she had been hard enough to find, she might be impossible to replace. At the moment, her relative idleness notwithstanding, she was in a black mood. I knew by experience that it was unlikely to have been caused by anything I had done.; nevertheless it was upon me she wreaked it, answering in monosyllables, going from room to room with that ominous, elephant-like sway of the buttocks which was always her warning of mental disturbance. So I accepted the invitation – firstly, to be out of Mrs. Reilly's way; secondly, so she would have the evening entirely free, and thirdly, because I wanted to see Celia again. I had seen a part of her life; I was curious enough to want to see the rest.

I dined at a restaurant, and afterwards walked across the park to Bayswater Road.

Celia lived with her partner in. a flat consisting of two bed-sitting-rooms, a kitchen, a bathroom, and a very large cupboard converted into what immediately turned out to be a photographic dark-room; for I was no sooner inside the flat than this cupboard door flew open and a stout woman appeared against a red and lambent background suggestive of flames.

She excused herself, and shut herself in again.

Celia knocked. 'Don't disappear just like that, Hilda. I want you to meet Mrs. Hall.'

'In a minute. I'm just finishing something up.'

Celia took me into her own room, which was expensively if too heavily furnished. 'It's the bits and pieces Mummy didn't sell up,' she explained. 'I'd sell them myself, if I had my way, and have nice bare modern stuff, but Eric likes them.' That night she sounded airy and cheerful, like a woman for whom life runs easily and without much incident. 'You'll have to be nice to Hilda for ten minutes, but she won't stay. We live side by side, but not really together.' She told me that Mrs. Haymer was a war-widow, that her husband, an elderly staff officer, had been killed in a raid upon his head-quarters. She had not, Celia said, appeared to mind very much. She was a comfortable woman, self-sufficient, able to take care of herself, given to hobbies.

Mrs. Haymer came in to be introduced. She was in her early fifties. Her face was amiable, full, a little too broad. She asked if I would like to see her room, also – 'It's a contrast to Celia's, I can tell you. I expect you'll laugh.'

It was indeed. It was almost as bare as a monk's cell, except for two armchairs of excitable contemporary design; but the walls were almost covered with photographs she had taken. It was not her room she had wished me to see; it was these photographs. She stood with her hands behind her back, anticipating an inspection. Celia winked at me.

I imagine that technically Mrs. Haymer was an excellent

photographer; but her choice of subjects was so dull as to be prodigious, and so was the captioning, neatly pencilled on the mounts. Pride of place was held by a hugely enlarged photograph of a featureless suburban road, the whole of the centre space filled with macadam. This was called, 'Evening Quiet'.

'I try to get the atmosphere,' she explained.

It was flanked on either side by two exceedingly ordinary studies of trees reflected in a river, one called 'Still Waters', the other, 'Nature's Mirror'.

'Those were tricky,' Mrs. Haymer said professionally. 'I used an Ensign Selfix 820 Special for that one, but a reflex for the other. The light wasn't quite right – still, I'm not altogether disappointed. Now if you come over here I'll show you something I did with an 1860 box camera I picked up in a sale – that was my lucky day; four and six I paid for it, though it cost me over five pounds to get it working again.'

'Oh, Hilda, Hilda,' Celia said, 'what a happy woman you are!'

Mrs. Haymer looked at her brightly. 'Keep busy, that's all there is to it.'

'You mean, I let you run the business while I fritter my time away.'

'I meant nothing of the kind, and you know it. Look, Mrs. Hall, this is the one I wanted you to see.'

When we had left her Celia said, 'She never wants to know what I'm doing because she doesn't mind. And I *do* know what she's doing, so I keep away.' She opened a drawer. 'But she did do this. It was the purest accident, I'm convinced.' She showed me a photograph of Aveling, so barely stated that it might have been taken for a passport; yet it was excellent. 'Pure luck,' said Celia. 'He will never have a better.'

83

I asked whether Mrs. Haymer knew about it.

'About Eric and me? I couldn't tell you. She sees him sometimes, when he comes here, and of course we are circumspect. If she did know she would think it none of her business. I have never been her business, thank God, and we've been working together now for five years. This place is all I know of Heaven.'

'And Mrs. Haymer has all she needs of hell,' I said. 'The dark-room,' I explained, 'that's what it looks like.'

'Sometimes I am so slow about jokes,' said Celia, 'and when I'm happy I'm even slower than usual.'

She suggested that we should go out. 'I'll take you to my haunts,' she said. 'I rather want to. Eric wouldn't approve of them at all; he can be very stuffy. Wait for me a minute, will you?' When she came back from the bathroom she had made up her face again, had put green shadow on her eyelids and blackened her lashes. She was wearing one of her dowdy-smart dresses and too much jewellery.

We went out into the street. Dusk had fallen, and the last of the sun lay in a lime-coloured ribbon behind the trees of the park. 'Watch,' Celia said, 'watch the traffic-lights. I love to see a mile of them changing at once. They're red now. When they all go green everything will have altered, the whole world will look quite different.'

She was full of a curious imaginative excitement. She gripped my arm hard to draw my attention to a prostitute mincing slowly by, her white shoulder-bag swinging as she walked, banging against her hip. 'Isn't she beautiful? Did you see? Now she is *truly* beautiful, but so odd that she won't have much luck.'

The prostitute spoke to a man in a bowler-hat. He swerved a little out and away from her and walked quickly on.

'You see, I told you,' Celia said. Stopping a taxi, she told the driver to drop us at Soho Square.

'You don't mind walking? It's in a mews; he'd never find his way. Hardly any of them know their London at all – they can just about find Big Ben without their maps.'

She was full of such absurdities, such overstatements; they seemed to cast upon the world a contempt that sprang, not from hatred or disappointment but from a pure happiness of heart: why could not everyone be as happy as she, as filled with certainties? She despised all who could not join her on her mysterious heights. Though she still spoke to me with a kind of exaggerated solicitude, almost a deference, which had the effect of slightly annoying me because it forced upon me the feeling that I was an older, more settled, duller woman than she, it now seemed more of a mannerism maintained for courtesy's sake; really, her mind was not upon me. She was glad I was there, glad of my physical presence, but her thoughts were far away. When we left the taxi she took my arm and hurried me along; she walked with a light, jolting step as if soon she would be dancing.

'Here we are,' she said.

We were in an alleyway lighted only by the glare from a coffee-stall, a Soho backwater, rancid-smelling under a surface odour of coffee and garlic. On one side was the jagged shape of a bombed building, on the other an anonymous wall, stuck with wooden doors and barred or blinded windows, that might have been the back of a derelict hotel or a hospital. One of these doors was slightly ajar. Round the edge of it a string of golden light rippled and sparked. Somebody beneath our feet was playing an accordion in a squeezed, spasmodic, rasping fashion, as though the musician, having the misfortune to be buried alive, and finding speech had deserted him, were attempting to attract our attention by the only means available. Celia pointed out to me that we were standing on a grating above the club.

'It's not a very grand club, but it amuses me. Come on.'

She pushed the door open. Beyond it was a curtain of dingy beads, beyond that a flight of cellar steps lit by a naked bulb. 'I shan't give your writing-name,' she said, 'because if by any bizarre chance they have happened to have heard of it they would get terribly excited and bring out the most hideous drinks in your honour.'

We went down the steps and along a dingy passage to another door. Outside this was a wizened negro, defending a visitors' book. Seeing us, he rose and bowed to Celia. He said, in a surprisingly dry and cultured voice, 'We thought you had deserted us, Miss Baird. Mr. Cargill was extremely upset.'

'Well, Tom, I haven't, and I've brought a guest. So, as you see, neither you nor Mr. Cargill should be so mistrustful.' She signed my name and her own. 'Busy tonight?'

'Only so-so, Miss Baird.' He paused. 'Mr. Tomlinis back.'

She raised her eyebrows. 'Already?'

He shrugged and grinned.

We went into an ugly little underground room, bleak, ordinary, garishly lit. There were ten or twelve tables, covered with scruffy check cloths, a small bar with another room behind it; there was a little dais, on which a very dirty young man, who nevertheless looked genteel, was playing an accordion badly. There were only three or four couples there, drab, anonymous, hard to place by class or even by race. On most tables there was beer; one couple seemed to be drinking Pernod. A very small stout man with enormous and silken brown eyes that would have been beautiful had they been set on the same level, darted out of the inner room, came round the bar, and seizing Celia's hand, kissed it.

'I would never have believed it, never, never! I said to Ilse, depend on it, we shall never see Miss Baird again; she is tired of our little *boite*; she has gone to Claridges, where she truly

86

belongs and sits among the great. That is what I said, and you may ask Use if you do not believe me!'

He did not release her hand; she seemed to have no wish to withdraw it. She smiled upon him, a happy, sarcastic smile that was not without tenderness. 'Jimmy, you're being absurd. Aren't I loyal to my friends?' She introduced him to me. 'You must meet Jimmy Cargill; his name is Ali, but he hates it. So he is Jimmy to everyone.'

I thought it also unlikely that his name was Cargill.

'Jimmy, this is my very great friend Mrs. Hall, and you must be as nice to her as you are to me.'

Mr. Cargill promised that he would; he seemed about to cry. He said we must drink with him, that this was a great occasion, but Celia refused. 'You do this every time, Jimmy, till I'm afraid to come in. If ever I do disappear for good, you can tell yourself you've only yourself to blame for embarrassing me with generosity.'

She ordered whisky for us both and took me to a table in the corner.

'But there will be no bill!' Mr. Cargill shouted defiantly after her.

'I don't need bills, Jimmy, I can count.'

He left us, 'to tell Ilse', he said.

The boy with the accordion stopped playing and came to Celia. 'Hullo. Doing all right? I got a hunch we'd see you soon.'

The genteel air was misleading; he spoke a harsh Cockney, with the glottal stop.

She asked him about somebody he knew and bought him the drink he was now silently awaiting. She requested him to play a popular French tune for us. He nodded, drained his glass, and went back to the dais.

Mr. Cargill brought Ilse, his wife, to talk to us, but she spoke English hardly at all and could only stand flittering her

87

head about like a canary, beaming, flashing very tiny teeth and occasionally pushing her cheek affectionately against her husband's. More people began to come in; the Cargills retired behind the bar.

A pasty young man in a stiff new pin-striped suit came up to Celia and swept her a bow. 'Joe!' She greeted him with an air of delight. 'I was hoping you'd be in. This is Joe Tomlin,' she said to me, but did not give him my name. He ignored me completely. He sat down opposite to Celia and gazed silently at her, letting his gaze linger on her jewellery. 'You'll be done for that one of these days. You don't know enough to come out of the rain, you don't.'

'It's Woolworth's, Joe. I never can imagine how you can be so stupid.'

'Get along,' he said. His eyes strayed to the bar.

'Go and get a drink,' she said, regarding him with her peculiar, happy, contemptuous look, 'and tell Jimmy I'll pay.'

'Thanks. Ta a lot.'

While he was away she said to me, 'He's just out of prison.' She seemed proud of this.

'What for?'

She smiled. 'Not burglary, as you're thinking. No, it is very sad. Poor Joe is a psychopath. He steals perambulators and then just leaves them in the street. This is his thirteenth conviction. He has had all sorts of treatment, but it's no good.'

She looked for his return, but he was leaning against the bar, talking to a girl.

'I know you thought he was too interested in my jewellery. Well, he wasn't. He's simply anxious about it. He always is. He worries about people dreadfully.'

Nobody came near us. The psychopath stayed at the bar; the accordionist went to drink with another couple. The Cargills were busy. I thought it was all very dull, and began to wonder if this sordid and uninteresting club were a screen for something. I was not to be told. Conversation with Celia became difficult, as her attention was wandering; she continually smiled about her, acknowledged a greeting here and there, seemed to be waiting.

At last she said, 'Oh, let's go on somewhere else.'

Seeing us move, Mr. Cargill returned, all smiles, to take her money. 'Now don't leave us for months next time! I say to Ilse, "When Miss Baird comes in, the sun comes up!" You ask her if I lie!' Joe and the accordionist came to say goodbye to us then, and she bought them another round of drinks, not ordering for herself.

I said, when we were in the street again, 'Is there anything behind that club?'

'Behind it?' She looked blank. 'Not so far as I know. There may be. But it's no affair of mine. I think people just come to drink.'

We went to two more cellars, as dull in themselves and in their clientele. At each Celia was greeted with radiant enthusiasm; at each she spent money; at each we found ourselves, if not alone, carrying on desultory conversations with people who seemed to have something else on their minds. I became bored and uneasy for Celia; she had been so happy, she had desired such an evening of adventure!

Then I realised that she was having it. The glow was still upon her face, the radiant, queenly, joyful contempt. This was her romantic life, her secret freedom, her delicious squalor, her imagined contact with the raffish, the rotten, the sinister, the Eleusinian. What I myself had seen was at least the greater part of the truth: the dullness and the cadging. There might have been 'something' behind these dreary squander-holes of night, but Celia knew no more than I what it was, nor needed to know. She had woven about them her own arabian nights fantasy, could play Haroun al Raschid to her heart's content, feel fortified against the final submission of her will to Aveling's by knowing that there was, in her life, something he would not approve, something his fastidiousness would reject. Here she was where her parents could never touch her; but here her lover could not touch her either, and here, if only for a little while, she could feel safe from him also. She needed, if she should ever be made desolate, to have something of her own.

14

A letter from Gerard came by the afternoon post. I was in the hall when it dropped through the box and I opened it there, at first seeing only his writing.

'Don't let my address alarm you, as there is nothing seriously the matter. If there had been I'd have cabled, but there was no need to terrify you.'

I saw the heading then: he was in a hospital in New York.

I turned sick; I could hardly go on. Mingled with this terror was a feeling of rage against him that even now he could not write distinctly. I managed to decipher some more.

'I picked up this wretched germ somehow – it's a virus pneumonia, if that means anything to you, and it made me so very uncomfortable that I got hold of a doctor, who said I'd be better off in here. Apparently it doesn't yield to penicillin, but passes off of its own accord. Anyway, I'm having the best of attention, so even if I'm not fit enough to catch the boat on Monday you'll know there's nothing whatsoever to worry about.'

It was Mrs. Reilly's day out; I could not even turn to her. There was only the quiet house, and myself, and the sun rosy in the fanlight, and this unreal letter. I said aloud, 'You mustn't make a fool of yourself. If he says there's no need to worry, there isn't'; but the words might have been spoken by one stranger to another. I thought of distance; New York was three thousand miles away. This letter had taken three days to arrive, and certainly, when he wrote it, his hand had been as cramped, as steady as usual. But in that time what had happened? My mind sprang like a grasshopper forward through the horrible sharp grasses of irrational fear; from the wire that would be telephoned to me, preparing me for bad news, to the wire that would tell me he was dead; to the great hole of utter despair. I could not read on, nor could I move. I stood against the wall, looking down at the carpet, noting and admiring a moth like a pale-brown, silver-dusted shaving from a pencil, as it toppled its way from one scarcely perceptible ridge of pile to another, flickering behind it its hair-like shadow. And then the telephone rang.

'Junius here. I thought you might like to come out for a drink.'

For a moment I could scarcely remember who Junius was. Then I said, 'Gerard's ill, I've just heard.'

There was a pause. He said, 'I'm sorry. How ill? What is it?' as if this were purely a matter of medical interest. I managed to tell him what I knew. I was trying not to cry.

He said in a dry, practical tone that he thought he had better come straight round; in the meantime it would be sensible if I rang my own doctor.

I tried to do so. I misdialled twice, and then got the engaged signal. At last the house replied: he was not in. Was it a matter of urgency? I had not the spirit to say that it was: supposing I had him disturbed in a matter of life or death for the sake of a triviality? Nevertheless, the idea of' pneumonia', of a kind even penicillin could not touch, put me past reasoning. I should have telephoned another doctor, if I had not, even in the middle of my terror, been afraid of looking absurd. (I have often wondered how many tragedies are caused because we are afraid to make fools of ourselves.) So I just stood and waited for Junius, though I did not know where he had telephoned from nor how long he was likely to be. I did not think round and about him at all, as one thinks of individuals, winding them in a cocoon of memory, speculation, opinion; I thought only about his coming. All that mattered was that somebody should come.

The bell rang. I opened the door, and Junius, wearing a pink bow-tie like a cat's adornment, stepped briskly in. Instantly he put his arms around me, as one uniquely expert in dealing with the crises of anxiety. I burst out crying, not caring what a fool I must be making of myself.

'There, there,' he said, in a self-satisfied voice, 'everything is perfectly in order now. We shall sort it all out.'

Though he had not been in the house before, he seemed to know by instinct into which room he should lead me. The ruddy light made him look like some benign monster without background; his fresh round face swam in the spinning shafts of the sun.

He had been talking to me for some little time before I was able to pay any attention to what he was saying. Then his words came clear; they might have been printed on comic-strip balloons emerging from his lips.

'Now it really stands to reason,' Junius said, 'that your husband, being a sensible man – as I certainly remember him from one brief and pleasant luncheon – is telling you the precise truth. It would be extremely shabby of him to write to you that all was well, and then let you receive repulsive cable-grams.' He smacked his lips thoughtfully, gave me a stern look which sat upon his broad nose like a pair of spectacles. 'As an outsider, I must say you seem to me to be making rather a great deal of not very much. Your husband is, I imagine, lying comfortably in bed reading a book. But I can understand that you need hard news, and, indeed, I think you ought to have it. Hard news is what we need, hard news is what we must have.'

He stood up, fingered and tweaked his tie, looked gran-diloquently about him. 'But have you no telephone in a more comfortable place than the hall? One simply has to have a chair, or I do.'

I told him where to find the extension, and he went upstairs.

Presently he returned, beaming. He had, he said, booked a transatlantic call to a friend of his in the School of Architecture at Columbia University, who would certainly go at once to the hospital and see for himself how Gerard was doing. 'It will be 2 p.m. their time, or thereabouts, so everything should work itself out nicely.' He added, 'It will be very expensive for you, but I'm sure it will be worth it.' He looked at the clock. 'Well, there is now no hope of me taking you for a drink, because we shall be waiting for a ring; but I expect you have a drink you could give me.'

We sat waiting. Within twenty minutes his call came through. 'Luck, luck, all along the line,' he said as he came back. 'I've got him, I've told him all about it and he's going off right away. Now what shall we reckon – an hour for the visit, half an hour for him to call back?'

I said, dazed by all this activity, that I hoped his friend could reverse the charge.

'My dear,' said Junius, 'he would have to. He hasn't twopence to rub together.'

The moment I knew that help was on the way I felt better: and foolish. As Junius looked quizzically at me over his glass, at home in my home, the old friend, the uncle, almost, I had, a curious sensation of shame. It seemed somehow discourteous to Junius that I should have been so unstrung by an affection that, to him, must be inconceivable. 'We should have something to eat,' he said, 'only I gather your woman is out and you don't feel like getting anything.'

'But I will,' I said. 'You can't starve.'

He came with me into the kitchen, bustling about it as I cut sandwiches, peering into cupboards, studying the sink,

94

informing me that he had never seen so poor a piece of planning. 'You should not live here,' he said, 'you and Gerard should make yourselves really comfortable. Don't tell me you can't afford it. I don't know why you don't buy an attractive small place in the country.'

I said I did not like the country. I was much revived; the smell of coffee was stimulating. I thought I might even manage to eat something.

Junius hopped up on to the table, and sat swinging his legs. 'I suppose it depends where one's born. I was a country boy, and poor as dirt. My mother was too busy to spend much time on me – there were five of us – so I used to amuse myself alone for hours in the garden.' He added sentimentally, 'I used to play with roses as other children play with toys.' Then he came abruptly to earth; he gave me his quick, self-mocking smirk. 'A pretty picture.'

He carried the tray upstairs. We ate, and waited. As time went on my anxiety began to crowd back again, and with it a feeling of sickness. I no longer listened to what he was saying; I looked at the clock, tried to force the hands round. Junius chattered on. I think he was trying to amuse me by self-caricature, to make me think him something of a fool. He had Gerard's whisky and was drinking that, occasionally picking up the glass and regarding it with a disapproving stare, as if he distrusted either the contents or the quality of the glass itself.

'Have you ever met—?'

I did not catch the name.

'Nancy Sherriff,' he said. 'I wondered if you might have.'

I said no.

'They're one of these enormous, ancient but untitled families, not much money but smart. Handsome girl. I almost thought of her for myself.' His grin was suggestive, malign. 'But I suppose it would never do.'

95

I roused myself sufficiently to ask him why he might have thought I knew her.

'No reason,' said Junius, 'no reason. I think I might take her out: there would be no harm in that.'

It was ten o'clock when the telephone rang. I went into the hall with him. As I stood there, trying to catch what was said, he put his hand out and pressed mine in a fashion kindly and reassuring.

It is one of the most deceiving things in the world to try to guess the purport of a telephone conversation concerning ourselves which is being held by two other people. I had at first been irritated by Gerard's manner on the telephone, but had quickly learned to interpret it. The more hearty, the more jocular he sounded, the less likely he was to be pleased by the caller. He received bad news with a kind of stoical shout of mirth: good news with hubristic monosyllables. Junius, however, barely said more than 'yes . . . yes . . . I see', and once, 'I'll tell her'. His face did not change; it was without expression. When at last he hung up and turned to me, I wanted to faint. I needed to escape whatever he had to say.

'Well,' he said rather crossly, 'that will cost you about ten quid. Ralph's seen your husband, who is perfectly all right and was staggered to hear the lengths we'd been to. He also saw the house surgeon, who seemed quite as flabbergasted. There's nothing to a virus pneumonia but nuisance, so you can sleep in peace.'

It was in this moment of extreme relief that I saw Junius clearly, and knew that he had been utterly and disinterestedly kind. I realised that throughout the dragging evening, beneath my swamping anxiety, I had been wondering what was his motive for this brisk and officer-like behaviour. Why should he have done all this for me, whom he scarcely knew? What did he hope to gain?

Yet it is a common error to believe that people of devious nature, especially if that nature has a strong element of malice, are incapable of any kind of altruistic dealing. In fact it is often by such people that the most startling, most histrionic altruism is displayed. It gives them pleasure, it eases their conscience. For they are seldom unaware of their own crepuscular joy in manipulating the lives of others, and it is a comfort to know that upon occasion they are manipulating a stray event or two, not for their own benefit but for someone else's, for then they can regard themselves as predominantly benign, they can see themselves in the most amiable of lights.

'Well,' said Junius, 'that's that, isn't it? I'd better be going. Come and have a drink with me upon some happier occasion.'

Now I wanted him to stay; I wanted to celebrate; I wanted him to repeat everything he had been saying for the last two hours and a half, so that this time I could really listen. I tried to tell him how kind he had been, but he could not accept gratitude easily; perhaps he had small experience of it. He said, in an affronted way, 'I couldn't have you in that state, I suppose. Our dear Celia would have expected better of me. She is the perfect little Florence Nightingale herself, a helping hand in every pie.'

Statelily he consented to finish the whisky, implying that since I had spoiled the best part of his evening I might perhaps be permitted to make it up to him so far as was possible.

He sat frowning on the sofa.

I said, 'Don't look so cross, Junius: it makes it hard for me to tell you how very thankful I am.'

All at once his face shone. For a second he held this shine downwards, as if ashamed of it, then looked up, his eyes innocent and happy. He said shrilly, in an access of self-mockery, 'But, my dear, you were making such a show of yourself! Honestly, one couldn't bear it.'

'Nevertheless,' I said.

He repeated, 'Nevertheless.' He paused. He said quite soberly, in his ordinary, pleasant, man's voice, 'I like you very much, you know. You mustn't always think too badly of me.'

It was a moment of extraordinary and incongruous intimacy. There was almost nothing that Junius and I had in common; yet I felt him touching my life as he had touched Aveling's and Celia's – whether the touch were agreeable or not was immaterial. It was deep, it was positive, it had made its ineradicable print. Within his cold and shut-away being there was a single point of heat, the heat both of hate and of loving-kindness: he had let me see the glow of it.

He broke the moment, and did it brutally. 'Our Celia – I feel much towards her as Swift did to his. What a bloody thing the other night – really, what a *bloody* thing!'

'You know it was nothing to do with you,' I said. I could be repelled by Junius now, or like him, or feel sorry for him; it would never alter the relation between us, whatever that relation might be. The print was there, inked and smudged, bitten into its whorls and crosses.

'It doesn't matter. Oh, what sharp little teeth! I'll adore her again, of course. I've done it before. But I assure you, if I had not' – he gave a false, simpering smile – 'if I had not been a gentleman I should have pushed her down those damned stairs.'

He got up, straightened his coat, his tie, smoothed his hair.

'It was all right you and Eric hearing, of course. But imagine if it had been anyone else!'

He would rather anyone else in the world had heard. I knew that, and did not wish him to see that I knew.

'I'm afraid,' I said, 'that I took it only as a kind of family wrangle.'

He said, 'Well, of course, you're sensible. That's all it was.' He hesitated, looked at me. 'You're dog-tired. Go to bed. Have some nice cheerful dreams.'

I watched him from the door. He skipped down the three steps, waving his hand airily. In the pale lemon light of the deserted street he looked younger than he was; he might have been a stout undergraduate afraid to find the college gates locked. He set off at a trot.

15

Gerard's sailing was delayed for a fortnight, but at last he was home again; and I was filled with an ease and lightheartedness I seldom knew (though I felt it was selfish of me not to know) when he was not with me. As soon as we had grown accustomed to being together again he wanted, as he always did, to hear of all I had been doing, to have described to him, as minutely as possible, all the people I had met.

He said, 'I must write to R. J. Evans, mustn't I? He really has been very good.' I did not at first recognise Junius by this name. Gerard sent a formal letter of thanks for his kindness to me and asked him to dine with us, but Junius was spending a week or so at his seaside house, and said he hoped we would postpone the invitation until he came back.

At Celia's invitation we lunched with her at the Connaught, and for the first time Gerard met Aveling.

Afterwards I said, 'He wasn't so amusing tonight. I think he needs a rude companion like Baird to bring out the best in him.' I was on the defensive; that day Aveling had seemed to me graceful, pleasant but a little dull, Celia almost vapid. I had wanted them, almost as a matter of professional pride, to match the account I had given of them both and was afraid he would be disappointed.

However, he looked surprised. 'I thought he was amusing. I don't think you exaggerated at all. He's an attractive chap, though not a particularly happy one. From what you say, we could hardly expect him to be.'

I asked him what he thought of Celia nowadays. He said he found her odd, but could imagine some men thinking her irresistible. He could not understand why she had not married. 'The early engagement? That was years ago. What's stopped her in the meantime? Aveling? Perhaps. But I doubt if it was altogether that.'

'Then what do you think it is?'

Gerard looked thoughtful. 'Well, for instance: a woman attractive to men usually puts out horns like a snail, to test the feeling of any man towards herself, no matter if he is the husband of her nearest friend. Celia doesn't.'

I charged him with conceit. He waved his hand a little irritably. 'You don't understand; women never can. It isn't harmful, in ninety-nine cases out of a hundred; it's not meant to be. It isn't followed up. But it is usually *done*, just for self-assurance. She loves Aveling, certainly. To everyone else she's stone-dead.'

It is hard to get beyond the first obsessive jealousies of love. Even though I believed I had done so, I had a fleeting wish that I, too, might seem to be stone-dead, since Gerard plainly found this so interesting.

I said, 'What do you make of it, then?'

'I think I'd guess a low sexual impulse, and a little sexual panic. Also, I think she would have uncovered a little more of interest in those ridiculous night-clubs of hers if it had been otherwise.'

We did not see much of Celia or Aveling for the rest of the summer, since Mark came home for the holidays and we took him to Italy for the last month of them. Celia wrote to me, but she was a poor correspondent, her letters brief, schoolgirlish, oddly lacking in character. Mummy had had an abscess in a tooth; Hilda Haymer had won a prize in a magazine for a photograph of swans. Joe Tomlin was out on bail – she had stood surety for him herself; this was his fourteenth perambulator. She had tried to talk to him, had even offered to buy him a perambulator of his own, if that would help, but he had flung off in a rage as though she had insulted him.

'As of course she had, poor girl,' Gerard commented, 'of course he would feel it was an insult, though I can't for the life of me imagine why. I do wish she would tell us the really fascinating things, though: for example, what title Mrs. Haymer gave to her photograph.'

We were spending our last day at Stresa when a postcard from Celia arrived.

'If Gerard can bear it, do come to the Moray, or both of you, when you get back, if only for a week-end. Lois seems rather bad, it is all very miserable here. Fondest love.'

Gerard thought about it. 'You could go. You could go down after seeing Mark off, and stay over until the Tuesday. I shall be in Oxford, anyhow.'

I was surprised; he had sometimes inclined to the opinion that Celia would, as she said herself, impose upon me. 'Ought I to?'

He said that, for Celia, the postcard was almost eloquent. 'If only she wrote as well as she talked, I would go into general publishing. But this sounds rather serious; I think you should go, certainly.'

As soon as we returned to England, and before I went down to see Celia, however, we received another invitation, this time from Junius.

We had entertained him once since Gerard's return from America, and the evening had not been much of a success. He had seemed to be attempting to play two parts – a sober, scholarly, lordly one for Gerard's benefit, a curiously *louche* and knowing one for mine. Time and again during that evening he had slid his gaze in my direction, had instantly looked away again, grinning with one side of his face. It was as if he meant us to be in some secret against Gerard, some conspiracy that could not be put into words. Gerard said, when he had gone, 'Poor Evans seems very peculiar these days. I don't think I shall ask him for any more prefaces.'

In this new invitation of his Junius asked us if we would dine with him and a young woman – 'She is quite charming and extraordinarily simple.'

'He can't mean that she is mentally defective,' Gerard said, 'so what can he mean?'

'If it is somebody called Nancy Sherriff,' I answered, 'it means that he's impressed by her social standing.'

'Wyndham Sherriff's daughter? The Norfolk family? Not going out with Junius. If so, she really must be simple.'

If I had not been looking out for Junius, I think I should have passed him without recognition. No one would have thought, to see him advancing across the restaurant foyer, that he was other than an ordinary, plump, soberly-dressed young man out with a girl. He might never have possessed a pink bow-tie, or owned a house like the one by the sea. He spoke to us in what was more or less his normal voice, adding to it, perhaps, as a touch of extra grandness, the merest hint of upper-class cockney. For a second his eyes met mine in complicity; then his thick dark lashes swept down, disguising him.

He drew forward a tall girl of wholesome appearance, who gave us a warm, direct, youthful smile.

'May I present Miss Sherriff?' He was stately. He kept his hand upon her arm.

'I know about you both,' she said, 'this is very nice.' She beamed down at Junius, who was shorter than she, and seemed pleased with him.

As we came from the muted light of the foyer into the brightness of the restaurant, I saw that she was extremely good looking, in a rounded, fawn-coloured, bright-eyed, gently aquiline fashion. She looked like a young Roman matron who would be popular with the slaves and trusted by her women friends. Unlike Celia, she did not appear to have given much thought to her clothes; yet she had a gentle elegance, a modest stylishness removed a little from what was precisely fashionable.

Junius sat smiling at her, not like a man who is in love but like one preparing to fall in love at any moment. When he had ordered dinner and we had exchanged a few social preliminaries, he announced that he envied Gerard and me. 'You always look so agreeable together,' he said, 'and without the least touch of smug. There are times when you make me realise how lonely I am.'

'I don't see why you should be,' said Miss Sherriff, looking genuinely puzzled. She had too much good taste to remark upon his bachelorhood; so Junius, who had counted on her doing so, was forced to make it himself.

'The life of a single man,' he said portentously, 'has its selfish pleasures, but sometimes it seems astonishingly empty. I often think I should marry.'

'Well,' she said, 'then in that case perhaps you should.'

Junius pounced. He stared at her with an admiring intense look, which was also a little bulbous. 'I may be waiting for the not-impossible She. Would that be absurd, I wonder?'

Gerard moved restlessly, feeling that Junius was up to something and fretted by not knowing what it could be. I felt I had been thrust out on to a stage without knowing my lines.

Miss Sherriff, however, seemed to know hers. 'Well, no,' she said, 'because everyone might seem impossible, mightn't they? It's entirely a matter for you.'

'Is it?' Junius whispered fatuously. 'Is that really what you think?'

But she only smiled and turned politely to talk to me. She seemed a pleasant young woman, with a sly, elusive sense of fun. She had been born far out of my world; she was at least ten years younger than I; yet she found friendliness easy. All the same, she had the irresistible urge of the impoverished-smart to make her difference clear. It was not snobbery, it was not even deliberate; it was an automatic defence against a world that had roughened since her childhood and would never quite fit her again. She was prematurely forced to live a good deal in the past; it would be harder for her than for many people to come to terms with the idea of so many years lying like a perspective of question-marks ahead.

Junius, catching a reference to some uncle or cousin, was delighted. His chest seemed actually to expand. Was that Lord So-and-so? he asked, as though for him lords grew on blackberry bushes – he could pluck a couple of handfuls for breakfast any day of the week.

'Yes,' said Miss Sherriff. 'He's the dotty one who builds model aeroplanes.'

'Not the one who gave all that money to Peterhouse?'

'Oh no, no, that's Hedley. Victor's terribly mean. He used to give me half a crown once a year when I was a child, and now he takes care never to see me at all, in case I want to keep up the old custom.'

Junius stared into her face again, lovingly. 'I will give you half a crown once a year,' he said.

She suggested he should make a covenant. 'But seriously,' she added, 'he is most repulsive, and not at all nice.'

Gerard laughed at this odd effect of speech.

'You're making fun of me,' she said, with a deep childlike smile that made her seem rosy.

'She is rather nice, I think,' said Junius indulgently, 'I do think she is rather nice. I think Eric would like her, don't you, Christine? I really think they ought to meet.'

16

I returned to the Moray on a wet, wild September day, the wind shaking in the streets like the property-man's tin thunder. I had driven myself down, and had arrived half an hour earlier than I had expected, since there was little traffic on the roads. Boldini greeted me with his bright and swallowing smile. He had put me, he said, in a very nice room on the fourth floor, not far from Miss Baird; he thought I would like that. A guest had vacated the room unexpectedly that morning, so he had been able to give it me; it would be a pleasant surprise for Miss Baird, he thought; he was sure she would be delighted.

I was not so sure. I felt that the fourth floor represented for them all, even for Celia, a kind of lair.

At the moment she and her mother were out. The porter took my cases upstairs, showing me into a bedroom a few doors from the Bairds' alcove, and I unpacked. From the window I looked out at the sea, now a sullen khaki-colour, tumbling about upon itself in a kind of fretful disorder as if trying to shift the weight of the slaty sky. It was chilly in the room, although Boldini had started up the central heating. I put on one bar of the electric stove and began to change my dress. I had left the door ajar so that I could call out to Celia if she went by; but in fact had no chance, since the moment the lift doors opened I heard her and her mother quarrelling, as audibly as if they had the entire hotel to themselves.

'I don't expect to live long,' Mrs. Baird was saying in a tearful, revengeful voice, 'you'll understand better when I'm dead.'

Celia's reply was clipped and swift; hers was a driven voice, only just held within control. 'Really, Mother, you're doing your best to make the contingency seem more bearable.'

I stepped across to the door and closed it quietly. When they had gone by I went downstairs and settled myself in the lounge to wait for them. Dr. Baird was there, of course, sitting by the fire. He made a faint movement symbolic of rising to his feet and told me I had brought some damned beastly weather with me.

I apologised for doing so.

'Filthy climate, filthy country. I don't know why we don't all go to South Africa. The others ought to be back,' he said, as if eager to slough off the responsibility for entertaining me. 'They can't go paddling about in all this wet. How's the boy?'

I told him Mark was well, and had sent his regards.

The doctor burst into a roar of surprising laughter. 'Said the coffee was foul! "Foul", that's the word he used. All too true, did he but know it. Why an Italian like Boldini tolerates such muck is beyond the imagination of humankind. "Foul!" You need have no fears for that young man,' he confidently assured me.

Though I felt I should prefer some other touchstone for Mark's future, I could not help feeling pleased; we are always perversely flattered by the praise of the angry, the contemptuous, the unlovable.

He went on chuckling to himself, in high good humour. '"Foul", he said it was "foul"!'

Mrs. Baird and Celia came smiling in, and both of them kissed me. 'Bless you for coming,' Celia said, 'Mummy and I feel born anew.'

There was no sign that there had been any stress between them. They vied with each other to tell me of recent purchases they had made, assuring me that I should buy some new face-cream which would make all the difference; it was a wonderful discovery, they would not be without it. Both of them looked exactly the same to me, but I had to admire the effect.

'Celia will have told you about poor Lois,' Mrs. Baird said. 'She is not at all well.'

'That's a silly sort of understatement,' said Celia. 'She's looking dreadful, in fact, as you'll see, Christine – that is, if you go there with me. She's been wanting me to bring you again.'

'Now you mustn't be so short with me,' Mrs. Baird muttered. 'Christine would never be short with her mother. Would never have been short,' she amended, having probably learned my condition.

'Oh, nonsense!' The doctor entered the conversation abruptly. 'For God's sake call a spade a spade, Millie. It's cleaner.' He turned to me. 'Lois Aveling seems to be on her last legs, and that's all there is to it.'

'And *you* overstate!' Celia rounded on him. 'Eric wanted to leave Junius in charge and stay here so he could see her every day. The doctor said it wasn't so bad as all that. As it is, he comes from London twice a week.'

'Look here, I know.'

'How do you know? You don't go to see her.'

'Lois and I never got on,' Baird said to me quite mildly. 'She could never take a joke. I went up once or twice at first, but it was too sticky.' He turned to Celia with a face like a fiend's. 'And what do you mean, saying I don't know? I *always* know. Look at Lily!'

Celia began to laugh. He glared at her, then made a contortion of his mouth as if her amusement were half-permissible.

He went back to his crossword puzzle. 'Two months have made Lily very obvious,' Celia said to me. 'She still serves behind the bar, looking very proud and stiff. Boldini is going to see her through her shame and take her on again.' She looked at the clock. 'Half-past five. We can go.'

'Go?' Mrs. Baird was off-guard.

'Go *out*,' Celia said with an appearance of amiability. 'Christine and I are going out.' She murmured to me, as we left the hotel, 'It is too dreadful; she wants to be with me or to know where I am every moment of the day, and I can't bear it. I'm too strained to bear it, I assure you.'

We went into the public house in the mews, where the barmaid greeted us. 'First come, first served. It's all yours, Miss Baird.'

Celia said, 'Put the wireless on, will you, Doreen? Dance-music, if there is any.'

She took me into the dark corner where we had sat with Aveling. 'If the wireless is on she can't hear.' Now that we were free of her parents she let the strain break through. Her face peaked and sharpened; she looked ill. She had not stopped smoking since I met her that day. The cigarettes had rubbed the lipstick from the inner flesh of her lips, leaving only a crumbling, outer line. 'Listen: you will come? I can't see her alone any more, not since she's been like this. I feel guilt all over me like grease.' She shivered, and drained her glass. 'You don't know. You can't imagine. I sometimes think I may go quite mad, and fall on my knees and tell her.' She paused; then with a hard and piercing look, added that Aveling did not seem to feel guilty at all, that sometimes she could almost dislike him because he did not.

'He is only realistic, I think.' I watched my own words carefully, trying to speak in a way that would not wound Lois if she, too, could hear me; knowing that it was impossible. I went on, 'He is in love with you, and he wants you entirely, I suppose. However much he loved Lois, that's over and past praying for. You're asking him deliberately to wish for more unhappiness for you, for himself and for her.'

'If you say anything about a happy release – no, you'd never say it, but if you even *mean* it, and I feel you mean it, I shall be sick. She loves living, she loves that horrible life of hers; his letters keep her alive. Do you know what he told me the other day? That they were becoming more and more of an agony to write. It ought to please me, oughtn't it? Well, I wish he were writing them with all his heart, and loving every word. I can't bear her to be deceived. You may not believe me; but I have *never* been able to bear it!'

Her voice was rising even above the noise of the wireless; the barmaid was looking with interest in our direction, and a horse-racing pair I had seen there before were modulating their own conversation in the hope of catching something of ours.

'Come along,' I said. 'I think we should go and walk in the rain.'

She did not resist. Following me out into the street, she waited for me to choose which way we should go. The rain had ceased now, and the wet pavements glared in a lurid burst of sun. A boy was batting a tennis ball against the wall of the men's lavatory. He missed a stroke and the ball, dirty and wet, rebounded on to Celia's chest. She dived down, picked it up and hurled it away as if it were a hand-grenade. 'Damn you, damn you!'

He shouted, 'It wasn't me!' and gave a yell of outrage as it rolled down the sloping roadway, gathering speed. He began to run after it, stopped, turned and swore at Celia.

'All right, all right, all right!' She groped in her bag, her purse; flung a coin at him. 'Buy yourself another bloody ball!'

He said, 'Ta, thanks!' and grinned at her. He looked foolish, deprived of his wrath.

'Oh, come *on*.' She dragged at my arm. We went through an alleyway into a street of boarding-houses odorous with meals to come, through another mews and down on to the front, where the wind battered the blinding sea.

'I am not a little lady tonight,' Celia babbled mindlessly, 'I am no credit to Mummy, who taught me never to use bad words. Eric would be shocked if he heard me, he would instantly throw me over, which would really be all for the best.' The tears were shining on her face. 'Oh, I wish it were over, I wish she was dead! There you are! That's honest! What else can I wish, what the devil can I? All I want is for it not to go on, and on, and on.'

Quite suddenly she calmed down. She dried her face, powdered it, and made me open my coat so that she could light a cigarette in its shelter.

'It's very cold,' she said. 'We'll go and have another drink, but in a nice respectable place where I can't behave squalidly, and then we will go and have an ordinary, snacking dinner with the parents. You are my guest, you see, so this time you are compelled to share our mealtimes. How sorry I am for you!'

Nevertheless, it seemed to me that in her father's company she was as happy as, at that time, she could be. She could take comfort from his boorishness, derive some faint amusement from it; now that she knew me better, she was no longer embarrassed on my account. Her mother's solicitous anxiety, pushed upon her like food pushed by an officious hostess upon an unwilling guest, grated on her badly. I thought she was easier in contact with a love so little expressed that it might, to the eye of an outsider, not have existed at all. Baird, when he spoke to her, sounded no more intimate than when he spoke to me. He used no endearments, was unresponsive when she teased him. That night her manner was daughterly and cheerful; sometimes she displayed a kind of childlike cheekiness. I knew she was longing for bedtime, to lie in the dark with at least the hope of sleep.

17

Mrs. Baird was waiting for me after breakfast. 'Would you go and see Celia? She's got a dreadful migraine and nothing seems to touch it.'

I went upstairs. The door was left open for me.

'I know,' Celia said, 'that this agony is my excuse for getting out of visiting Lois, but if you'll pull up the blind a bit you'll see that it is none the less genuine.' She spoke in a faint, slurred manner, as if any sound hurt her, even the sound of her own voice. Cautiously I let a little sunlight in. She was a pitiful sight; the left side of her face swollen and satiny, the left eye half-closed by puffiness, and watering down her face. She made me touch her temples, the glands of her neck, to see if I could feel the throbbing. 'I haven't had one of these for five years. I woke at four with this; I've taken everything short of poison. Hemicrania: the Greeks had a word for it.' She winced. 'Pull the blind down again, will you?'

I asked her if her father could not help. 'I won't have him up here, he knows that. It would kill me if he shouted, and he always does shout when I'm ill. Oh no, this is a sort of involuntary malingering. I shall feel better when you've got to the hospital.' She added, in a sick voice, 'I told you I should impose.'

I rejoined the Bairds; I was distressed and said so. 'Nothing to do but forget it,' the doctor said briskly. 'It's a commonplace misery and quite incurable. I tried injecting her with Femergen, but it did no good. It's the penalty nervy people have to pay.' He sounded as though he were glad for them to pay it. He did not believe he was neurotic, thought himself the most level and stoical of men; if anyone had asked him to describe his temper, I fancied he would have replied, 'Even.'

Mrs. Baird said she thought she might go up and sit with her, it was terrible to be alone when you were in pain.

'Only if you're frightened,' Baird snapped, 'and there's nothing frightening about a migraine. Leave the girl alone, for pity's sake.'

So I drove by myself to the hospital, now sparkling in the salty light of the afternoon. The ward sister told me that Lois had been moved to a room of her own – 'She doesn't want people so much now. Not that she isn't still perky – it's wonderful, really.'

She took me along a corridor and opened a door. 'Mrs. Hall to see you, dear.'

The sun was in my eyes. At first I could make out only the white expanse of bed, and on the pillow something rough and brown, like a coconut or the trophy of a Borneo head-hunter. Then eyes flashed, a mouth smiled.

I was so shocked I could scarcely speak. I could not believe that I was looking at Lois Aveling, who, no more than two months ago, had been sitting up smartly in her fawn jacket, hair neat, nails manicured, her whole spirit intent upon escape.

Her voice sounded as easy, as amiable as before. 'Now this *is* nice! I was longing for company, especially yours.'

I explained about Celia.

'Oh, poor darling! Nothing can be more frightful than migraine. I've had it myself, and I can't imagine anything worse.'

Only the muscles of her face moved. Then the sheets stirred painfully, humped themselves below her shoulder.

Out wriggled her hand and arm. I held the hand and shook it gently.

She said, 'As you can see, I've had a bit of a set-back. It won't last, of course, but it's a nuisance at the moment. Do please sit down and be comfortable. *I* don't look particularly comfortable, I know, but as a matter of fact I am.'

When I had last seen her I had realised that she was a tall woman who had once been graceful. I had noticed her unusually small skull, the bones shapely but tiny. Now all I could think about was this little, tobacco-coloured head, severed at the neck by a fold of the sheeting, this head talking cheerfully away to me.

A nurse came in with a vase of gigantic chrysanthemums, white, Chinese yellow, sugar-pink. 'From Mr. R. J. Evans, dear, here's the card. Wired from London, I expect – aren't they gorgeous? Now, aren't you lucky! I never knew anyone like it.'

'Too merry,' Lois said to me, when she had gone out, 'far too merry.' She fondled my wrist. 'You see, all these people here think I'm going to die, just because I've been a bit down lately. I'm not; I've had set-backs before; but they think I am. So they try to be excessively jolly just to deceive me. Now I really hate that.' She looked at me, her eyes unsmiling. 'I do hate that, Christine, people deceiving me, even for the best of reasons. It makes one look such a fool. I hate to look a fool.'

'If they do believe you're getting worse,' I said, 'there is nothing they can do except pretend not to. But I think you're wrong. I saw the sister, and she didn't seem anxious.'

Lois said she hoped I was not lying, too, and her gaze picked about my face, from eyes to brow to lips, back to my eyes again.

Then she said, 'No, you're not', and I felt an uprush of relief that I had done successfully the thing she most hated, had managed to deceive her.

'You can smoke in here, if you like. I do, sometimes, but only when a nurse is in the room. They're afraid I'll set fire to the bedclothes, I think.'

I lit cigarettes for us both and put one between her lips, but in a few minutes it made her cough, and she asked me to stub it out again. 'Can't do anything lying down, except look at you and Junius's ridiculous flowers. He spends much too much. I only hope he doesn't take it out of the business.'

She told me that Aveling was worried. Hart, the sleeping partner, had died recently. Though he had never had a great deal of money in the firm, he had been influential. He had once been an architect of reputation himself, but had become tubercular, and had been unable to work for the past fifteen years. 'Eric gets a good deal of work passed on to him for Hart's sake; now there won't be so much. Even if there were, I don't know how he'd cope with it. I love Junius, but he is an appalling drag on the business. He is *no* good! I have told Eric time and time again. But men are such appalling sentimentalists.'

Her eyes closed, but she went on smiling.

'I am sorry for Celia; give her my love.'

If it had not been for the smile I should have thought she was asleep. She lay quite still, her hand on mine. A bee flew in through the open window and settled on the chrysanthemums, trundling its little brown cask of shadow from flower to flower. The nurse looked in. 'Tea, Mrs. Aveling? Oh! Is she—?' She raised an eyebrow.

'I'm awake, and Mrs. Hall is thirsty,' Lois said. To me she added, 'You will try to enjoy yours, even if I have mine later? I am using a sort of moustache-cup at the moment, but I'm too proud to display it in company.'

She did not speak again until the tray was brought. Then her eyes snapped open. 'I say, nurse. I've been telling Mrs. Hall you all think I am going downhill, but that I mean to surprise you.'

116

The nurse was not taken off-guard; she seemed to be used to Lois. 'Then you're telling her wrong,' she said stolidly.

'Telling her what wrong? That you've written me off, or that I'm going to buck up again?'

'Now you're getting me puzzled, and there are other people wanting tea. I'll have to sort all that out later.' She went away. Lois laughed. 'Isn't she good at it? Her name is Piggott. She is most surprising. I like her best of the lot.'

I thought there was a way in which I could comfort Celia: by telling her what I had just discovered, that we need not pity too greatly people who do not pity themselves. The persistent and indomitable euphoria of Lois's disease made self-compassion impossible. I believed she was also sustained by an immense pride in behaving so well, in making those who visited her feel not merely a sense of duty but a positive pleasure, and in being deceived by nobody. She had said, 'I hate to look a fool', and for that second had seemed to me capable of anger. If she were pathetic, it was despite herself; she could not help the visible brown shrivelling-away of her life, nor the feebleness of her hand upon mine. She would have nothing to do *with what she was*; only with what she meant to be.

The bee buzzed furiously up and down the panes, seeking an exit.

'Look at him, the idiot,' said Lois idly. 'Entomologists try to tell us that he's clever enough to do a sort of dance in Morse code to tell his friends where the honey is, and how many miles away. He can't even find his way out of a window. What a damned silly little bee! Not even as clever as Celia.'

I asked her what she meant.

'Oh, I don't know. She's a dear, isn't she, and amusing? But not really clever.'

Her eyes had closed again.

I was still puzzled.

'Well,' Lois said, 'such funny things, like a child. I expect she told you about the poor lad and the perambulator. It is so like Celia to want to buy him one.'

The door opened. Nurse Piggott put her head in and said, 'Your husband, Mrs. Aveling!'

He came in, smiled to acknowledge me, went straight to the bed.

'Oh, but how lovely!' Lois said. 'And such a surprise this time.'

He took her hand, gently pulled back the sheet and released the other. He kissed both, and her face. 'My dear lamb.'

She looked at him, shining.

I said good-bye to her quickly, not wanting to be in their way. Aveling detained me.

'Will you drive me to the station? I won't be more than twenty minutes.' It was only by chance, he told Lois, that he was here at all. He had been called in to inspect a building site not far away, and had asked his client to drop him at the hospital. I said I would wait for him in the hall.

'Come again soon,' Lois said. 'There's so much to say. Mind you come again. We'll see each other soon, shan't we?'

18

It was a mild evening, so instead of waiting inside in the smells of ether, floor-polish and disinfectant, I walked about the gardens – tidy, shipshape gardens, with ordered geranium beds mitred at the corners, hospital fashion. The paths were bordered with square, chalky stones. Beyond the low boundary wall the rough downs pitched towards the sea in their freedom of grass and gorse. The cooks were busy in the kitchen. I could hear the rattling of crockery, a woman singing *When Irish Eyes are Smiling* in long, sentimental, self-adoring scoops of a reedy soprano voice.

Aveling came out, and rested a hand on my shoulder. It was not an intimate gesture; not the most self-regarding woman could have thought it so. It was an expression of an inner heaviness demanding support, no matter from whom. He was not thinking of me.

His long shadow fell across the glaring geraniums. He stood looking down at them like an absorbed horticulturist brought in for consultation.

At last he said, 'Thank you for waiting.' We went to the car. 'How much time have I?'

I said he had half an hour to spare before his train left – ten minutes more than he needed. I thought he might want to call on Celia, if only for a moment; but he said, 'Don't start for a second or two.' He lit a cigarette for himself, then remembered me. 'I'm sorry. Perhaps you don't like people smoking in your car. I am being very remiss.'

'Of course I don't mind,' I said.

'We might perhaps just go outside the gates and stop there.'

I drove out between stone pillars, each crowned with a bowl of cement filled with more geraniums; against the yellow walls of the hospital they looked hideous. I drew up beyond the wall.

'She is dying now,' he said. 'Even in three days there's been a change.'

I made the formal, unnecessary remark of false comfort.

He shook his head. 'Christine, be very kind to Celia. When it does happen, she'll want you, and I may not be able to see her.' He looked at me with sunken, candid eyes. 'I am very grateful for you. It has always been possible to talk to you, and really I must.'

But having said this, he seemed unable to go on. I did not know how to help him.

I told him how ill Celia had been that morning.

He said, 'I dare say. I don't know if it's worse for her than for me, but it's as bad.'

He jerked his head back towards the hospital and smiled. 'It is so very repellent, isn't it? There was some terrible stuff put up just about that time. I often feel I could bear it more easily if she were in some splendid and handsome place, if she were dying in dignity. Which is, of course, absurd. But it is dreadful that anyone so beautiful should lie in that abominable yellow packing-case.'

I thought of the shrunken head, bronzed by sickness and the sun.

He said again, 'I may not be able to see Celia when it happens, not just at once.'

I told him I thought I understood.

'She's lucky that you're fond of her, that so many people are. Her mother is fond in the wrong way, but her father, oddly enough, in the right one. Or so I think.'

Sitting beside me, his thin long body cramped in a seat too small for him, his gaze steady on the featureless road, he had a judge-like air. I could imagine him on the bench, considering, slowly, painfully, conscientiously, the matter of a life or a death. He would be a judge who made jokes; but not fatuously or capriciously or to leave a legend. He would make them with solemn care in matters not too grave to bring all chance of honour to an end, designing them to lift from the man in the dock just a little of guiltiness, to let him feel he should not be broken for ever by moral indignation, that when the price had been paid he, too, could return to make jokes with ordinary men. For a second I felt for him myself an affection that was almost a stirring of sensual desire; he was warm enough in his nature to evoke that impulse of grateful love which needs to express itself by physical contact, no matter how slight: the touch of a hand upon a coat-sleeve. Yet I thought he, like Celia, did not care to be touched, except in a sexual relationship. I had seen him, while walking with Junius along the street, keep swerving slightly away from him as if the least, the most casual, contact of the body were displeasing.

'It is so extraordinarily hard,' he said, 'to love where one should not. Generation after generation makes its own rules; we get freer and freer, my God, how free we get! And underneath it all is the undertow of the Ten Commandments. They make dreadful fools of us. They're like our grandmother's sideboard, which we don't use any more, but can't bring ourselves to sell. There it is, all the time, weighing us down from the attic or biding its time in the cellar.' He added, 'This is a hellish time. Shall we drive on now? I thought I could say more, but I can't. I don't even know what it was I wanted to say – only: look after Celia. Don't tell her I saw you today – or rather, yes, you must: because certainly Lois will. Why shouldn't she?'

As we drove along by the shore, this 'why shouldn't she?' seemed to rest upon the air like smoke below the ceiling of an airless room. There was no reason; and yet I felt that somewhere the formation of one, of a foetus reason, stirred. There could be no need for Lois not to be frank now in all things, not to make only the plain statement of perfect confidence in men and in events. Her death-cell was too bare to hold secrets; she could not frame her lips to an unspoken word, pass the scribbled slip of paper, without the warders seeing all. She should be lying there as open to the world as a child in the cradle, all her thoughts, her desires, her speculations plain. What had she, any longer, to conceal? I remembered Celia asking me, 'What do you think of her?' Even now I could not have replied. I did not know.

When we came to the station he thanked me and, leaning forward, kissed my cheek. He did not do so very naturally, but as if the gesture had been planned and carried out by a spurt of will. 'Remember me to Gerard, please, and tell him I shall hope to see you both in London before long.'

I watched him as he walked under the sooty, sun-thatched roof towards the booking-office, his head down, his hands in his pockets.

Celia was still in her room when I returned to the Moray, barricaded, she said, against her parents. The headache had gone, but her face was still swollen and she looked exhausted. When I told her I had seen Aveling she said,'Then thank God I wasn't there. Do you know, I have only been together with them once since she went to hospital?'

She asked me how Lois was, and when I told her, closed her eyes.

'I don't think it can be long,' I said, 'and for your sake and Eric's I can't hope that it will be. But she wants to live, whatever life is like.'

'Of course.' Celia got up from the chair in which she had been lying and went into the bathroom. She called to me through the open door,' It makes me so mad when people who want to keep capital punishment tell us it's so much kinder to the victim. If only one could offer them the choice!'

In a few minutes she came out again, and sat before the dressing-table to make up her face. Her hands were trembling. She smudged her lipstick and had to take it off again with cold cream. She threw the soiled cleansing-tissue at the wastepaper basket and missed it. 'Ah, filthy, filthy, I can't do anything right.'

Mrs. Baird knocked at the door. Celia said I had better let her in, and when she saw her, tried to smile.

'Are you better, Celie? You know, I'm quite sure you wouldn't be so nervy if you didn't smoke so much. Do try to stop her, Christine; it would be doing her such a service.'

'Christine is not my nannie,' Celia said.

Mrs. Baird asked her if she were coming down to dinner. 'I do think you ought. It would make you feel brighter. And it's very dull for Daddy and me, all by ourselves.'

'I'm going to have a bath. I'll come down if I feel like it.'

'But you've just done your face!'

'And now I am going to have a bath.'

Celia went back into the bathroom and turned the key in the lock.

'It's dreadful,' Mrs. Baird whispered to me. 'I wish she'd never met that man. Do try to make her more sensible. I know you could.'

We heard Celia whistling above the rush of the running taps. I could find nothing to say.

'Oh, by the way, I was looking through a drawer this afternoon and I came across this.' She jerked out of her bag a little Victorian locket of blue enamel and gold. 'I thought: Now, that's Christine's type, that makes me think of Christine at once, I thought, Now it would be nice if she'd accept it; I don't want it, Arthur doesn't like me to wear period jewels, and Celia hates that kind of blue.'

She twirled it before me, like a hypnotist twirling a watch. It was so pitiful an attempt at bribery that even she could not doubt her own motives. She flushed red. The locket hung between us. I did not wish to hurt her feelings nor be put under some ridiculous obligation. At last I said that Gerard, also, did not care for Victorian jewellery and did not like me to wear it; I could not accept anything so pretty, simply to lock it away in a drawer of my own.

'You could give it to someone,' she persisted.

I thanked her again, but would not take it.

She made the best of matters. 'Well, all right, if you will be proud!' Her smile was forced. 'Make that girl come down, won't you? She must eat something, or she'll be really ill.'

The next few days went by surprisingly normally, with the usual round of shops, tea-rooms, cocktail-bars. Celia went alone to see Lois, and came back looking calmer. 'She really seems to have brightened up a little; she is entirely amazing.'

She was amused to receive a picture-postcard from Junius. 'I hear the Seigneur was down for a flying visit. I wish I could get away, but he keeps my nose to the grindstone.'

'How funny he is,' she said, 'he thinks it just possible that Eric might not have let me know, and that with any luck he might make me feel suspicious and upset. Poor Junius, it must be hard to make trouble so assiduously and with so little result. Everyone's far too used to him to take any notice.'

On my last night we even went out dancing with Raby and Webster; she and Raby giggled together like children, and Mr. Webster told me about his domestic life. Celia said to me suddenly, with an air of discovery, 'I believe I feel better because *she* seems better! That must mean I'm not altogether bad, mustn't it? Do you think so?'

I think she was realistic enough to know that part of her relief came from a lifting of guilt: she passionately wanted Lois to feel happy; she longed, for her own sake, to believe she was doing her no harm. All the same, I did believe there was something in Celia which was purely good, even if it were only the desire to be so. Her nature, like Aveling's, was warm; and, despite the counter-evidence of her quick, humorous and even spiteful tongue, she was not cynical. Celia hoped for joy; she could be charmed and appeased by joy in others.

When I returned to London I half-forgot her, since she seemed no longer in need of my special anxiety. She wrote to me once or twice: all appeared to be well; even at the hospital they thought Lois might be on the mend. I heard nothing from Aveling or from Junius.

Then, at breakfast one morning about a month later, Gerard said, 'I'm afraid it's happened.'

He passed me the newspaper.

'AVELING – on October 10, 1949, Lois Muriel, dear wife of Eric Aveling, after a long illness.'

19

I wrote the usual letters. Aveling answered at once, Celia not at all. I asked Gerard if he thought I should telephone her. 'Time enough,' he said. 'You don't think you've lost her, do you? If I were you I'd wait.'

I took his advice, but reluctantly. Aveling had asked me to help her when Lois died, had warned me that he might want to stay away from her for a while. I wondered whether he was doing so, or whether this had been one of those plans of anticipation that we make to protect ourselves, and then do not put into action. I remembered how, as a girl of twenty-one, I had promised myself that if I ever found myself free from a marriage which had failed I would at once go away somewhere by myself and enjoy liberty like sunshine, needing nothing but to feel it on my face. In fact, I shut myself into my room and wept for my own failure, for the past that was now discoloured and tainted, and for my own sins. I had never felt more a prisoner, shut in by the blanched and unscalable walls of the future.

At last, a fortnight later, Celia telephoned. She was in London; she wished I would come and see her. Her voice sounded unusually light, pitched by will to a high and casual level.

'I'm not going back to the Moray for a while, the parents are so trying. And they would only ask questions and *not* understand anything at all.' She stopped.

I asked her what was the matter.

'Well, nothing really, not more than you'd expect. Eric's feeling awful; he writes to me, but we're not actually meeting just yet. He says he has to hide, and of course I understand. I think he's very wise, don't you? I don't think I really want to see anyone but you, if it comes to that.'

I thought how extraordinary it was that so kind a man could be so cruel. I knew he could not bear to share his pain, nor rub it still more raw by seeing Celia: but I believed he should have forced himself to share it, whatever the cost. He had become utterly self-absorbed, his imagination had failed him; he was desensitized by grief.

'You will come? Gerard can spare you, can't he? We won't go out, we'll just talk.' In the light voice there was an unmistakable note of panic. I knew she needed me now, at once.

I took a cab across the park. It was one of those strange London nights, wet but sultry, that seem to promise excitement if one is happy; and if one is not, to express a world without end of desolation. I rang Celia's bell. I heard steps along the hall, someone singing cheerfully, almost nautically, and very loud. The door opened.

'I can't shake hands,' said Mrs. Haymer, breathless from her song. 'You must take the will for the deed.' She was holding two strings of damp negatives, trailing down from massive paper-clips like kite-tails. 'You'll find Celia in her fastness, I know she's expecting you.' The dark-room swallowed her; singing broke out again.

I went to Celia's room. She lifted a hand to greet me, smiled painfully as if the skin on her bones were scalded and might tear. 'Bless you.'

She had been crying, but had pulled herself together. There were drinks on the table, chocolates, cigarettes in a silver box; it all had an incongruous, partyfied air.

She went across to the door, which I had left ajar, and pulled it very quietly to. 'I must shut off Hilda's noise. Of

127

course, she does it to shut *me* out; she hates me to be upset. She wouldn't notice it for the world. When we pass each other in the hall she very slightly squints, I'm sure she does, so that she won't quite be able to see me.'

I laughed.

'All the same,' she said, 'I feel rather better now.'

She poured whisky for me, only soda-water for herself. When I commented on this she told me she was not touching alcohol; it hauled her up so high that she was frightened of it. She did not mean to be tempted into such comfort for fear of wanting it all the time. I told her I did not think she was ever likely to become an alcoholic, that she was the wrong physical type.

'Well, I'm taking no risks.' She shut her mouth tightly and for a moment looked like her mother; they would look more and more alike as they grew older. I had expected to find her in a state of weakness, yet she had drawn strength from somewhere – enough to carry her through from day to day. She told me about Lois's funeral, which, of course, she and her parents had had to attend. 'I didn't feel I could cope with flowers, but Mummy did; she sent chrysanthemums from herself, and carnations from me. I didn't know till I saw the thing on the grave, a beautiful, Judas-coloured wreath, not as flashy as Junius's, thank God, but bad enough.' Aveling, she said, had been very odd, less like a bereaved husband than a family solicitor. 'You've no idea how much I seemed to notice. Everything was extremely clear, and I found myself making the cleverest analogies. *I* could hardly feel a thing – that is, not emotionally, but I ached. Every bone ached, from the back of my neck down to my shins. I kept thinking I was going to be ill. First it was 'flu, then it was rheumatic fever, and then I had a beastly thought.' She stopped abruptly.

'Yes, I know,' I said. 'I can guess. But it was only a thought.'

'Such retribution it would have been, wouldn't it?'

'On whose part? Hers?' I wanted to drag this ugly little nightmare out of her.

'Oh no, I suppose not. One can't imagine her wanting it. God's, perhaps. Only it would be spiteful. I don't think God is ever that. As you say, it was only a thought.'

Mrs. Haymer knocked, then put her head round the door. 'I've got to run out for an hour. Listen, dear, if someone called Parkinson should phone, will you tell him the title will be "The Knell of Parting Day", *not* "The Curfew Tolls"? "Knell of Parting Day" – can you remember it?'

She withdrew. 'Now where can she be running out at this time of night,' Celia said, 'in the pouring rain? I often think *she's* a mystery.'

I suggested that Mrs. Haymer, now, might be mildly alcoholic.

'But not very. She'll never be "very" anything at all.' Celia leaned forward. She said, in an uncontrolled, despairing voice, 'It will be all right, won't it? He will need me soon?'

The telephone rang.

'Oh, God, that will be her damned Parkinson.' She sprang up and went to the door muttering, '*Not* "The Curfew Tolls". It's "The Knell of Parting Day".'

She banged the door behind her and was away for a long time. When she came back her eyes were shining, she was flushed, she seemed dazed. 'Oh, Chris, oh, Chris, it's going to be all right after all! It was Eric. We're going to see each other on Monday; not quite alone yet – he says he thinks we ought to go to "some place of public entertainment".' She mimicked him, not too badly. 'He must want me. I didn't expect to hear from him so soon.'

Pulling the window curtains open, she looked down upon the rushing glitter of the street, the traffic lights switching the stripes of the rain from green, to yellow, to red, all along the sweep from Marble Arch to Notting Hill. 'I understand perfectly that it won't be easy at first. I think he's absolutely right. I don't think I could bear it myself, to be alone with him yet.'

Relief had unnerved her. She put her arm round my waist, not so much in affection as for physical support. She said she was glad I had been with her this evening. One could endure to be miserable, no matter how miserable, alone; but one felt a fool rejoicing all by oneself. 'His voice sounded *like* him again. If things go well for me now, I shall begin to believe I've been taken in hand.'

I asked her what she meant.

She replied in a rambling fashion that she wanted to be better, not to do harm, not to hurt anyone in the world, but that she did not think she could help herself in any way. If it were *meant* for her to improve, then something would change her, something outside of herself. It was the sort of general-ised idea that springs of a sudden from the mind, rootless, unprepared, not thought out, in a moment of intense relief; and to Celia this curious, confused monergism did, for the moment, seem to represent an eternal verity.

Then her face clouded as the edges of the idea began to blur, to lose shape. 'I expect I'm talking nonsense.'

The telephone rang again.

She said energetically, 'Now that *will* be Parkinson, and you shall answer it. That is one thing I simply cannot and will not do.'

20

I was walking home from a business luncheon through the grid of streets behind Shaftesbury Avenue when Junius sprang up in my path. He had just darted out from a coffee-shop, where he was with friends, and had seen me through the window.

'I knew that haughty gait, it registered at once, so I flew forth. Come and join us; we have good news.'

He took me into an alcove, where three young men were sitting, one of them the dubious actor whom he had taken to see Lois. They greeted me without enthusiasm; they had the proud and furtive air of a camarilla. 'I remember you,' the actor said, as if what he had remembered were discreditable. I had plainly spoiled the party for everyone but Junius. He seemed tired of them, seemed to wish they would go away; which, after a few desultory exchanges, they did.

'Now, then, we can talk. My dear, luck is with us; Eric has landed a really excellent contract, to restore a crumbly old house – a messuage, in fact, other dwelling houses attached and plenty of grounds – for one of Nancy's uncles. She did it with her little hatchet; she is really the most remarkable girl. Not a penny to fly with, but knows every-body.' He stuck his thumbs into the armholes of his yellow waistcoat and gave me a smirk. It was a Dickensian gesture, not at all his usual style; so I risked a guess and said, 'About 1840.'

'What?'

'The house.'

'Only ten years out. What made you say so?'

I preferred to keep the mystery to myself. In fact I had often noticed how Junius would act out his thoughts, and do it with extreme transparency. He had a dramatic imagination, he saw himself in a dozen different rôles a day. He was, in many ways, an exceedingly happy man. The capacity for histrionic escape, which is normally the gift of the adolescent or the elderly, is found as a rule in people of high and tearing spirits. The gnaw and rub of continuous anxiety, the anxiety that persists in some fantasticated form even through dreams, and which presents itself in normal guise, all ready for action, immediately upon waking, is a condition unknown to the congenital actor: for if he does not like what he is, he can always become someone else.

'If you won't tell me, you won't; though I assure you, you make my flesh creep. Have some more coffee, now that the lads have gone.'

I made a comment, unflattering, upon the actor.

'Oh, I know,' Junius said, 'I agree entirely. That's why I was lurking in here, because I wanted to hide him. Eric loathes them all, he gets extremely stuffy, he actually takes me to task. He doesn't like me to be seen with people, if he thinks it will harm the business. So long as I don't mix business with pleasure it's all right; but if he thinks that's just what I am doing, he comes the governess.' He was trying to shock me, watching to see what I thought. I said Aveling didn't seem to me unreasonable.

'No, but one can't drop old friends, however horrible, *just* like that. Of course, I may have to when the time comes.'

I asked him what time.

He assumed a dreamy, Byronic air. 'I often think,' he said, 'that I shall change my way of life. There is an inducement.'

I asked if Aveling had met Nancy Sherriff.

'Yes, once. I took them out to lunch. I had her well primed, though she didn't know it; I wanted her to think she was doing it all by herself.'

'Doing what?'

'Dear Christine, you snap. Well, I knew that this ridiculous uncle, who has so much money it is sickly, wanted a job done. I'd got it out of her. I thought it might occur to her that we would be the ideal people to do it; and, bless her, the inspiration occurred bang in the middle of the savoury. One could see her darling brains working.'

Junius leaned his elbows on the table and regarded me steadily. He asked me if I thought he ought to get married. I said no.

'I find that extremely censorious.'

I replied that I had not meant to be (though, in fact, I had, for there was something about Junius which invited censure, something in his nature which delighted in it); I had given a straight answer to a straight question. 'Anyway,' I said, 'you won't.'

'Why not? Would you condemn me to be an object of disapproval to people like yourself for ever?' He put out his hand into the brilliant, dusty limelight of the October sun, looked at it as if it were a work of art. It was an astonishingly small and slender hand, with beautiful square-cut nails. He was a little sulky now, and disappointed. If he were not immediately accepted in a part he had chosen to assume, he felt like a first-night failure. 'It happened once, with Lois. For a while, she changed everything. I told you that.'

Suddenly I knew he was lying, that this had been just one more of his romantic inventions. I knew it because his voice had not changed; it was the same voice he had used in speaking obliquely of Nancy Sherriff, and this was the same sort of

133

fantasy. As if he realised his error, he shook himself and sat up straight. He said naturally (but it was too late), 'Even I get fed up with myself.'

Then there was nothing to say for a while. I drank my coffee, Junius looked out of the window.

At last I asked about Celia.

'Oh, they're going around together as usual. I believe she'll be getting in touch with you; they've got a sort of celebration planned.' He paused. 'By the way, there was something I wanted to ask you. Ronnie – that's the oldest of the lads you met just now – wants to go into publishing; he doesn't mind how humble it is. I suppose Gerard couldn't find him a little niche, reading, or something? He's desperately intelligent.'

This was said selflessly; Junius genuinely wanted to help a friend. I told him I would ask Gerard, but was very doubtful of the result.

'He's full of ideals, he wants to make something of himself. As a matter of fact he's got a girl in Birmingham. He did think about the prison service, they're always wanting people; only the trouble is he once slipped up himself. Not that it ought to matter,' Junius added with curious naïvety, 'it ought to be an advantage. I mean, having real insight from the other chap's point of view.'

Still we heard nothing from Celia.

On a dark and rainy morning at the beginning of November, however, Mrs. Baird telephoned. She and her husband were in London; they would like to meet Gerard, they would like us to dine with them.

Gerard was not pleased at the idea. Boorish eccentrics, he said, sounded all right by report, but were depressing to meet. One hoped for so much from them, a constant outflowing of their most preposterous qualities; but the flow always turned out to be a thin, sporadic spattering, and between the spatterings was tedium. 'Can you imagine what Mr. F's aunt was like in her off-moments – which must, after all, have been in the majority?'

Still, we could not get out of it.

We found them in a dull, old-fashioned hotel that lived on its past and charged for it. Mrs. Baird wore brown lace, and we drank Brown Windsor soup. They had taken tickets for the theatre; it was a play we did not want to see. It looked as though Gerard had been right in his anticipation, for Baird seemed disinclined to perform, sitting back like a spectator, occasionally turning upon us his bluish and isodontic smile. His wife was ill at ease, too conscious of her position as hostess, too concerned that we should enjoy ourselves to show any pleasure at all of her own. Baird was frankly bored by the play. 'Takes a long while to get nowhere, doesn't it?' he said loudly, during the first interval. 'I remember when plays had you out of your seat. There was always something happening. All they do now is talk, nothing but talky-talky; one longs for somebody to fall downstairs.'

'Do you remember—' Mrs. Baird said timidly.

He flapped her to silence. 'Yes, of course, the chap who used to fall down that flight every night on his head. Knew how to fall soft, certainly, but God knows how he didn't break every bone in his body. I must have seen him do it six times, and every time I wondered whether they wouldn't start shouting for a doctor in the house.' He added, 'Not that I'd have gone – I'd have sat tight and said nothing. When I go out for the evening I'm off duty.'

Seeing Gerard repress a smile, I felt that he might not think his time altogether wasted.

At the second interval Mrs. Baird said she did not think she wanted a drink; she would rather stay where she was. In politeness, and with a sinking heart, I stayed with her, while

Gerard and Baird went out to the bar. She seized upon me at once.

'Christine, do tell me what that silly girl's doing! Hardly a word, hardly a postcard. Is everything all right? Oh, I know she's not a child, but she's been so sheltered in some ways. I hate her living here on her own.'

I said I had not seen much of her.

'But will you make a point of seeing her? She depends on you, she'd never resent anything you said. Do tell her Arthur and I don't like to be treated as strangers.'

I tried to comfort her, tried to impress on her as tactfully as possible, and with much circumlocution, that Celia had her own life to live, and was indeed old enough to make her own mistakes.

In error I used that word.

'What mistakes?' Mrs. Baird's eyes widened. She grasped at my arm. 'How is she making mistakes?'

'It was a figure of speech,' I said.

'Is she seeing much of *him*?'

'I don't know.'

She paused for a minute. 'Naturally you'd be loyal. You're a good friend, so you would be.'

I said, 'Why should it matter so much if they did get married?'

'It's too late for her. Far too late.' She added, with sudden pinched brutality, 'She's too old. And, besides, she'd never stand being second-best.'

I was utterly taken aback. To find anyone so little disposed as Mrs. Baird to gloss her own motives was extraordinary. The excesses of human beings in their selfishness are endless; selfishness brings with it a surprising power of invention, it tends to create its own ontology. Even the dullest in spirit can be spurred to a kind of poetry when attempting to explain why they desire to lock up a husband, a wife, a daughter, a

136

son, for their own benefit; their reasons may even attain the appearance of profound and beautiful self-sacrifice. But Mrs. Baird was singular in her rejection of disguise: for a moment I even wondered if she were a little mad.

The two men came back, Baird stumbling all the way along the row and muttering, 'Feet, feet, nothing but feet, like a lot of bloody centipedes.'

He was taking time to seat himself, aggressively assuming possession of both arms of his stall. As the lights went down Mrs. Baird whispered rapidly to me, 'Arthur had a nasty turn the other day. It scared me. If anything happened to him I couldn't bear to be left all alone—'

Then the act began and she had to be quiet.

When the play was over they would not hear of us leaving them. We must come back just for half an hour, for one more drink. Gerard said he had to be up early in the morning.

'Early?' Baird demanded. 'What do you call early? When I was in general practice I was up at six-thirty, rain or shine, and up half the night as well.'

'Then I won't tell you what I call early,' Gerard said gently, in a manner so reminiscent of Aveling's that I felt Baird could never fail to get the same response from everyone, 'since it might not match your standards. Let's say, early for me.'

'Nonsense. You're still a young man. Not elderly yet, anyhow,' Baird added, somewhat spoiling the effect.

So we went back to the hotel, which, like the Moray, had an appearance of being open after ten-thirty at night only on sufferance, and Mrs. Baird took me at once to the cloakroom, where I did not wish to go.

The attendant had gone home, having turned out nearly all the lights. There was still a heavy smell of powder in the air. I thought I was fated to hold private conversations with Mrs. Baird in the drowsy, half-lit rooms of the world, rooms which, like old age, were always waiting for the last light to go out, for the last squeak of the closing door.

'I don't want you to think I'm selfish. I'd do anything for Celia's sake. But I don't want her running off and leaving me and then being unhappy.'

I said I thought she might not be.

'She's been unhappy ever since this started with him. If it's like that now, in the first flush, what will it be later? Arthur's twelve years older than I am. What am I going to do with twelve years on my own? Tell me that.'

'I can't say anything,' I answered, 'nothing you'd agree with. I wish I could.'

She remarked in a matter-of-fact tone, as though it were not specially interesting or important:

'Lois knew about them, you know. She knew it all.'

With that she walked straight out of the room, without another look at me; I had to hurry my step to catch up with her. 'Why do you think so?' I asked, but she did not reply.

When we got back to the dim, brown lounge, Baird upbraided us.

'You women, I can't think what you do in there. Except, if you'll excuse me, the obvious.'

Gerard's smile became a little fixed; he was, in some ways, prudish.

'I believe you sit there plastering your faces and telling each other all about your grandmothers. And your faces don't look any the different for it – eh, Hall, do they?'

'I think,' Gerard said, 'that their faces look very nice, but that if Christine will finish her drink rather quickly we should go.'

'Oh, don't,' said Baird, suddenly disconsolate. 'Don't go rushing off. Life's full of people rushing off. I like to talk to a man like yourself, not women all the time.'

I thought I saw, behind his eyes, the disappointment not of a moment but of a lifetime. He had never been able to resist the momentary pleasure of cutting off his nose to spite his own face, and it had left him defenceless with a wife who bored him and who steadily and coldly disliked him.

I made my drink last as long as I could without too greatly irritating Gerard; meanwhile, Baird talked about war. 'Do you know what I'm afraid of, Hall? The stray maniac. The majority of men aren't fools, they know where their bomb-dropping will lead. But let loose, say, one mad admiral, for the sake of argument, just one crazy admiral. Whang it goes! And back comes its *vis-à-vis* – not on the admiral; most likely on us.'

'Oh, don't,' said Mrs. Baird, 'it's too horrible to think about. I shut it all out of my mind.'

'I'm not really afraid at all,' Gerard said. 'I think we may find our way through, and no harm done. I believe there's more control on the madmen, in any country, than we realise.'

'I shut it out, I shut it out,' Mrs. Baird repeated.

'She'll stand there on the day of Judgment with her fingers in her ears, so she can't hear the Last Trump,' said the doctor. 'That will be a fine sight. Mind you,' he added, 'I don't worry myself. I don't suppose I'll be there to see it, whatever happens.'

Very reluctantly he bade us goodbye. 'Oh, don't thank me, the pleasure's all mine. I've heard some sense for once.'

Gerard and I walked away towards the park. 'He wasn't bad value, after all. Poor old thing, he doesn't get much out of life.'

I told him what Mrs. Baird had said about Lois, but he was not inclined to believe it. 'She's rather a dangerous woman,' he said, 'because she never for a moment doubts her own impressions. However wild they may be, they instantly become eternal truths. Never give Mrs. Baird an impression, my darling, never, not of any kind.'

When we got home Mrs. Reilly had left a message on the table in the hall to the effect that Miss Baird would be telephoning me at ten o'clock next day.

21

She explained the reason for the celebration. 'It's terribly short notice, but the only time we could get people together. Just Eric and I, and Junius, and some hapless deluded girl Junius is running around with, and her uncle, who gave Eric the contract. You must come, *whatever* you're doing, you must put it off. And black tie for Gerard: we're all going to dress up. The Connaught, eight sharp.'

She sounded happy and excited. I asked her if all were well. She did not hesitate. 'Oh yes, going along as it should. Everything's splendid, really. I'm dying to see you!'

When we met I saw, somewhat to my dismay, that she was wearing a brown dress not unlike her mother's; but she had added a necklace, brooch and bracelet of yellow zircons, costly and, I thought, new. She seemed pleased to be acting as Aveling's hostess, yet did it gracefully, and with no proprietorial air. Junius, at his most sober and most stately, congratulated her on her appearance, and in acknowledgement she caught for a moment at his hand.

Hedley Sherriff was an elderly man, thin, jerky, a little deaf. His evening clothes were old and rather shabby, but, mysteriously, he looked rich. He had the nervous, self-deprecating air of a man with enough money to have a bad conscience about it. His throat was weak, and he spoke in a kind of forced whisper. 'I've every confidence in you, Mr. Aveling. Really, I feel pleased about the whole thing, extremely pleased.'

'I hope you will be when it's done,' Aveling replied.

'Hope I will be when what—? Oh, when it's done. Yes. I'm sure of it.'

Nancy, more youthful, more Roman than ever in a dress of dark red velvet, shouted in his ear. 'He doesn't like the conservatory, Uncle!'

'Doesn't like the conservatory! Doesn't he?' He turned to Aveling, who looked disconcerted.

'It does spoil the place from the south aspect, you know.'

Sherriff looked puzzled. 'They admired that sort of thing in its day. It was my grandfather's especial pride.'

'So were the griffins, dear,' Nancy shouted again. She explained, 'There were horrible red marble griffins in the hall.'

'Mr. Aveling must do away with the conservatory if he thinks fit. After all, it is his taste and judgment that I am acquiring.'

Nancy said to Aveling in her normal voice, 'There, you see, that's one trouble over. I always take bulls by the horns.'

We went in to dinner, where Celia briskly seated us. On Aveling's right was Nancy, with Gerard next to her. I sat on his left, next to Junius. Celia put Hedley Sherriff at her own right hand.

Junius murmured to me, under cover of the conversation, 'The girls are superb, don't you think? And you also. Celia looks like Madame Verdurin in her most successful days. There is really just a touch of the arty there, tonight, all those yellow gauds, or am I being unkind?'

I said I thought he was.

'You never believe I love Celia, do you? I'll show you one of these days.'

Sherriff was saying, 'Isn't it true to say that age always has its own elegance, if we except the past hundred years?'

'I have seen some repellent Jacobean architecture,' Aveling replied, 'as bad as anything I know. But it's hard to disassociate historical romanticism from natural taste.'

'It's a relief to me,' said Nancy, 'to know it's sometimes all right to dislike things. I hate half-timbering, really hate it. One wing of my school was half-timbered, the rest was beetroot, like Rugby. Everyone hated the beetroot except me, but I used to tear up and down at lacrosse thinking how much I'd adore to set fire to the old part.'

'Which is most perverse of you, if I may say so.' Aveling leaned forward over the flowery table. He looked composed and princely above a knoll of tight, red-streaked tea-roses, paid for, I imagined, by Celia. 'Perverse even by my standards, though I have to admit I'm rather in sympathy with your original view. The zebra walls of Tudor houses make me feel a little seasick. To tell you the truth,' – he spoke as though this were a supreme confidence, bestowed to give an extra lustre, an extra depth to the occasion – 'I don't much care for anything before the eighteenth century.'

'You'd like to have lived then, wouldn't you, Eric?' Celia asked him. They must have discussed this before; yet she gave no sign of intimacy, not even of ideas previously shared.

'As a rich man, mind: a rich man. Whenever we fancy ourselves in the past, we always place ourselves comfortably in the upper or upper-middle classes.'

'That's the understood thing,' said Junius, 'it's perfectly natural.'

Aveling said, 'Who ever knew an Elizabethan-fancier who imagined himself as a groundling? Of course, he sat on the stage.'

'What about the French Revolution?' Gerard asked.

'Especially the French Revolution! How splendidly we die, how dignified we look in the tumbril!'

143

'I should have been Mob,' Nancy said decisively. 'I'd have knitted away like mad, two purl, two plain, while the heads fell, especially some of my relations'. Of course, not Uncle Hedley's.'

'But you, my girl,' Junius said affably, eyeing Nancy with a bold and quizzical assurance, as if to stamp her as his own in our eyes, 'would in fact have been the only one making a good end. The rest of us – your uncle, naturally, excepted – would have been howling around the place, dancing the Carmagnole.'

'Oh, come, I don't think I should.' Aveling had the air of one who feels precise self-assessment is only fair to other people. 'I should have been a provincial lawyer, or something of that order – not the political type like Robespierre, need-less to say. I should have dealt exclusively in harmless trivia such as land tenure.'

Gerard remarked that this might not have been such harmless trivia at the time.

'No, no, of course not; you may well be right; in fact, land must have been a peculiarly touchy subject. But I should have kept myself respectable and safe, and carried on quietly into the Directory and the First Empire.'

Sherriff said to his niece, 'One of your forebears was believed to have got as far as the Conciergerie; don't you remember?'

I fancied she did; I fancied she knew her own family history in the most minute detail. But she said, 'I'm not sure. Which one? Was that Mademoiselle de Champ-something?'

Sherriff identified the name carefully, adding a warn-ing that the whole Conciergerie story was doubtless apocryphal.

'Oh, I know! She must be that girl like a pekingese, in the black-looking portrait Aunt Cissie has. She is holding a rose-bud and glaring.'

'How very splendid it all sounds,' Junius murmured to me. 'Poor Celia is looking so envious. She would have adored to be an *aristo*.'

I looked across at her. She was in fact eyeing Nancy with a kind of wonderment, but I did not think it was envy.

'So would you,' I said to Junius.

'My dear, I don't need to. I have the touch naturally. It's something Celia will never acquire.'

'Of what has Junius a natural touch?' Aveling asked pedantically.

'My dear fellow! It wouldn't become me to tell you. Of simple greatness, perhaps.' He shed his fat smile over the table, the flowers, the glass, the napery stiff as eggwhite; he loved a celebration.

'Junius *is* a natural touch,' Nancy whispered, leaning across him to me. 'He grossly overtips. How he can expect decent treatment I can't imagine.' She smiled at him with a familiarity that was soft and charming. 'He will probably ruin the business.'

'You're grand enough to give threepence when you only have threepence,' he retorted, 'which is far grander than deciding to give threepence when you have a spare half-crown. You can afford to be mean even when meanness is a crude necessity. But do you never get sworn at?'

'I can swear back,' she said mildly.

Junius was deeply impressed by her; she knew it, but thought none the less of him. She was young, she was as yet unformed; one day she might become a clever woman, distinguished in her own right: but at present she felt her birth was her sole claim to distinction, and she appreciated its practical advantages as coolly as she might have appreciated having a good figure or a clear skin. Aveling, better born than Junius, or Celia, or Gerard and myself, his forebears for at least a century professional men sufficiently well-off to send their sons to public schools and universities, did not share this adventitious interest; he had met many people like Nancy before. But he seemed amused by her. After dinner, when we had withdrawn for coffee and brandy to another room, he observed to me, 'She is a very nice young thing.'

Celia came up to us. He said, 'Thank you, my dear, it was all excellent', and touched her arm briefly. They looked at each other in a flash of intimacy, tender, yet also strained; I knew that all was not yet well.

I told Gerard so when the party broke up; and, getting into our taxi, we saw Aveling pull Celia hard against his side.

'Why do you think so?' Gerard said.

I told him I thought something was wrong, but could not put my finger on it. Under the easy flow there had been something uneasy, something obscure.

'You don't mean Junius and his young woman? That's all eyewash.'

It was not this that worried me, for I thought I had detected in Nancy a strain of healthy irony; she gave herself easily in friendship, even in apparent confidence, while holding part of herself in reserve. She was young, she was inexperienced, and she was nobody's fool. What fretted me was the strangeness that surrounded Aveling and Celia. They gave every appearance of happiness, of a problem solved, but I felt sure that another problem lay behind it.

I said they hadn't a married look.

'Would you expect them to have, so early?'

'They haven't, all the same.'

He knew what I meant. 'But I don't believe the trouble's with Celia. It's Aveling who bothers me. He is so very sorry for her, you know. And when that happens there is always something wrong.'

I thought it was true. There is nothing which strikes such cold to the heart as a lover's look of compassion, the look that goes straight through the body into the ground, like lightning striking. In love we like to be pitied a little, but only in fun. In fact we may be pitied (in fun) because of our own qualities or disqualifications: but never, without ruin to the spirit, *because of what is about to happen to us.* Aveling had looked at Celia in the tender way we look at a sick person, the nature of whose disease we know, while, out of mercy, we join the general conspiracy to conceal it from them.

22

Gerard happened to remark to Aveling, who had recently become a member of his club, that I did not welcome Christmas. It had been agreeable enough when Mark was a little boy, when it was his day, worth the planning; but he was nearly fifteen now and passing through a phase of aggressive religious orthodoxy. He remarked grandly to me that Christmas had entirely lost its original significance: it was simply an occasion for pigging, spending too much money and wearing silly hats. 'Of course,' he added with his usual redeeming realism, 'I wouldn't want not to have presents.'

It was partly to please Mark that we accepted Aveling's suggestion. Why didn't we, he had asked Gerard, spend Christmas at the Moray? It would save me work: it would be pleasant for Celia and very pleasant for himself.

Gerard and Aveling had recently become very friendly, though not as yet intimate. I felt faintly jealous, as a woman is apt to be when a friend or acquaintance of whom she is fond transfers his confidence to her husband, through the sheer proximity of London club-life. Aveling had been a friend of mine: now he was Gerard's. Yet I need have felt nothing of the kind. Though he gave no appearance of reticence, Aveling appeared to speak very little of his private affairs. He seemed, Gerard told me, to be in one of the becalmed phases of life, never particularly cheerful, never obviously downcast.

It was much the same, I felt, with Celia, whom I saw fairly often. She spoke of Aveling with a deep and tender joy, as if everything were now decided; but also as if the decisions taken would not become operative until some time in the fardistant future, and that there was no need, meanwhile, either to discuss them or to think beyond one day and the next. She was delighted that we were to join her for Christmas, more frank than Aveling about the reason.

'The parents are shocking at that time, all sentiment and bad temper. Father openly detests it, but goes through the forms; Mummy doesn't think she should do other than revel in the turkey and the pudding and the caps, so she gets excessively strained with the effort of trying to enjoy herself, and trying not to wish it were all over and the shops were open again. The deprivation of shopping is very serious to Mummy.'

She added, 'Also, I am afraid she has rather taken against Eric.' She paused. 'Which won't add much to the general aura of junketing.'

She told me that Aveling hoped, on Boxing Day, to drive us over to Hedley Sherriff's estate. His plans for it had been more or less complete when Sherriff accepted an offer from the Ministry of Works to stand part of the cost if certain buildings were leased for government use. 'They've got a small research station almost next door, and can do with more houses for their people. Of course it means that Eric will get a far larger fee, and can expand his ideas a bit.'

We all knew by now that Hedley Sherriff had remained a rich man; I happened to have gathered that his brother Wyndham, Nancy's father, was behaving like an impoverished one.

'I should have thought,' I said, 'that some of his money might go to helping less fortunate Sherriffs. Gerard says—' I stopped; I had no right to repeat what Gerard had said, which was that time and again Wyndham Sherriff only just managed to escape being posted for failure to pay his subscription to the club. 'Gerard says Nancy doesn't look too prosperous,' I put in, though this was absurd, since he had seen her only once, at the dinner of celebration, and on that occasion she had looked extremely well. But Celia did not notice my slip. I suggested that perhaps the Wyndham Sherriffs were too proud to take money from their relations.

'Oh no! Nancy would take money from anyone. She's in debt as it is.' She added, a little anxiously, 'Do you suppose people like that do pay their debts, or do they think the humbler part of the world owes them a living?'

I questioned her. It appeared that she had lunched recently with Nancy, who had borrowed twenty pounds. Now Celia, as I had noticed before, loved to give, hated to lend. She would give absurdly, in a wave of pleasure at the mere action of doing so; had she lived in the Middle Ages she would have scattered largesse, not simply by casting it down but by first tossing it up into the air so that the shower of gold tinkled on the blue sky, as the dying leaves of the elm tree glitter and tinkle on a windy autumn day. But to be imposed on made her feel a fool. She could imagine her debtors nudging and giggling–'Oh, Celia Baird. You don't have to worry about her, she's rolling in money.'

When we arrived at the Moray on Christmas Eve the first thing she told me after we were alone together was that Nancy had repaid her. 'I am so glad! Because I like her very much. Do you know, I simply cannot bear even the smallest financial dishonesty. I think I'd really rather have a black-mailer. Just to get a bus ride without paying a fare seems to me to indicate something *deeply* rotten. Yes, I am quite sure I should prefer a blackmailer.'

She was in very high spirits; I had never seen her looking so young or so smart. She took me into her mother's room, where Mrs. Baird was anxiously combing out a new, too-stiff permanent wave and Tiny, now a large, hunted-looking cat, was squatting in his tray.

'Darling, how smelly it is in here! Really, I think you should give him to someone who can let him have the run of a garden.'

Mrs. Baird greeted me affectionately, kissing me on both cheeks. 'Don't you let her take my puss, Christine; he wouldn't be happy with anyone but me.' She told me I looked pretty, commented wistfully that I was lucky to have long legs. 'Mine are so short, clothes look nothing on me. Celia's escaped the family failing, thank goodness. *I* think she's more like her father's side though I know most people don't.'

When she was ready we went downstairs into the lounge, which had been decorated by Boldini with an entire lack of reserve. There was holly on almost every flat surface; above the elderly heads hung a great ball of mistletoe tied with red ribbon, and over the chinmeypiece was an enormous arrangement of crêpe paper, streamers, chains and fans, pegged with drawing-pins to the wall.

'Lily did that yesterday,' said Celia, 'on a stepladder. Everybody was terrified, but no one could stop her. It was her last action before going off to her sister, who will see her over the event.'

Gerard and Aveling had ordered tea for us, but Dr. Baird and Mark were missing. 'They've gone down to the games-room,' Aveling said.

Mrs. Baird looked at him as though it were his fault. 'But they must have known it was tea-time!'

'I don't think Mark did,' I said, impelled to exculpate him. 'He wouldn't know what time you did have tea here.'

'Well, Arthur knows. I think I'll go and fetch them.'

'Oh, Millie, I shouldn't!' I had not known that Aveling called her by her first name; I thought I had never heard him use any form of address to her before. 'They were both very wrought up about Russian billiards. It was nice to see such enthusiasm.'

She said tightly, 'But Arthur must not play ping-pong. I do think I'd better go and see that he doesn't. A boy like Mark might egg him on.'

Celia said, 'Please, Mother', in an exasperated voice, and looked at me quickly.

I said, 'I think I ought to go and see, in that case.'

'Well, then, I wish you'd tell them that tea is on the table.'

'Tea can be taken off again,' Celia said brightly. 'It is very easy to do so. We will let our little victims play.' She murmured to me, 'Don't disturb them on any account. This will be Father's only Christmas treat.'

I found my way to the games-room, which was far away in the basement beyond a gloomy square of store-cupboards. It was not marked in any way, but I was led to it by Baird's upraised voice.

'Damn it, don't scoop the ball back at me! Has no one taught you any manners? Get down and pick it up like a decent human being.'

Feeling apprehensive, I opened the door gently. Neither of them heard me.

They were using the full-sized table at the far end. A single light glared down on it: the rest of the room was in shadow. Baird, in his shirt-sleeves, crouching and glaring, dancing on his toes in imitation of the table-tennis professional, slammed Mark's serve into the net.

'Bad luck, sir,' Mark cried, in a jovial, conventional manner he never employed while playing the game with me.

Baird leaned forward, poked at the ball, tried to prod it over the net: he was doing exactly what he condemned in Mark.

'Oh, I'll do it, sir; don't you fag.'

Mark raced round, retrieved the ball, and served again. This time it flew back hard, struck the extreme edge of the table and spun off at a sharp angle. Mark jumped for it like a cat after a piece of string, and flicked it back right into Baird's chest.

'Here, here, what do you think you're doing? Do you want to break my glasses?'

'Sorry, sir. Fourteen-six; your serve.'

'That was my point!'

'It was on the table.'

'It was on me!'

'Well, I think it *would* have been on the table,' Mark said politely.

'Then you think wrong. Do you realise I was playing this game before you were born?'

They caught sight of me.

'Hullo, Mother,' said Mark. He turned back to the doctor. 'All right, then, we'll call it thirteen-seven.'

'How do you do?' Baird snapped at me. He glowered. 'We won't *call* it thirteen-seven, young man, it *is* thirteen-seven!'

'Right, sir, it is thirteen-seven.'

'Yes, but are you satisfied? I won't be humoured, mind. When I play this game I like to play it straight.'

I said I was very sorry to interrupt, but that Mrs. Baird thought ping-pong might exhaust him: and that it was tea-time.

'Now listen,' he said, 'I'll come up when I'm ready, Mrs. Hall, and not before: and you can tell my wife I'll play what games I please. You, there, Mark, don't stand with your mouth open, you'll catch a fly. Seven-thirteen; my serve.'

Though I thought he looked uncommonly flushed and remembered what Mrs. Baird had told me about his 'turns', I could see nothing for it but to leave them. .

When I returned to the lounge she seemed to have forgotten her husband's absence. She was asking Aveling about his work, and doing so with the over-courteous, peering attention of dislike. 'But won't you be afraid to destroy the whole character of the place, Eric?'

'It has some bad character which I very much hope to destroy.'

'I know I'm old-fashioned,' Mrs. Baird said, 'but it does seem hard to want to pull down things the original owner was so pleased with!'

Aveling appeared not to resent her. 'Millie, dear,' he said gently, 'whatever I do now must change his ideas a good deal. And, believe me, I shouldn't have agreed to do the work if Mr. Sherriff hadn't approved my own plans.'

'Well, I expect he feels you're the expert, so he wouldn't like to complain.'

'I hope he'll have no cause to.'

She looked nonplussed by this, and for some time said nothing else.

Indeed, for some time no one spoke at all. She had the gift these days, I noticed, for bringing conversations to a halt, and it was hard to push them on again. Aveling lay back in his chair. He seemed neither eager nor uneager to talk, his silence social. If a question were asked him, he would have no distance to travel back to it, his answer would be ready at once. Then Celia leaned across him to stub out her cigarette, and her arm brushed his knee. She did not notice the contact. For the moment she had not been thinking of him.

But at once a change came over his face, and in a naked instant I saw that he was utterly sad. His eyes, shining out from beneath their curious porticoes, were strained with anxiety. He sighed, not audibly but visibly, moved a little, and with an effort recaptured his air of social peace.

At last Gerard asked if we were likely to see Junius over the holiday.

'Well,' Aveling replied, 'he's spending it in his house and I think he's got friends down, but he may look in on Boxing night.'

'Oh, might he?' Celia said, as if this would please her.

She turned to me. 'It will be a great favour if he does. When Junius has friends he is usually incommunicado.'

'If they're nice he might bring them for a drink,' said Mrs. Baird. She looked at the clock. 'Eric, I do wish you'd make Arthur come and have his tea.'

Gerard said tactfully that he would like to see the games-room himself: might we all go there?

'I won't,' said Mrs. Baird, 'but you four can if you like.'

It was strange, this giving of permission; she would not have allowed herself such an expression six months ago. She was now so full of her own worries that the ordinary formalities of adult intercourse were slipping away from her, and we might all have been children.

Aveling said, 'You don't want to stay here all alone. Come with us, or I'll stay with you.'

'No, no, you go. I'm alone here often enough.'

Celia rose with a sharp movement and walked towards the door. After a second's hesitation we followed her.

'I should rather like to play ping-pong myself,' Gerard said, 'if there's a table free. I used to be rather good.'

We found Mark and the doctor quarrelling over Russian billiards. By this time their curious amity had begun to wear a little thin. Mark, accused of surreptitiously setting up a skittle after it had fallen down, was red in the face; had he been a few years younger he would have found it hard not to cry. He was saying, with a kind of turkey-cock emphasis only partially masked by an attempt to be patient, 'The ball wasn't within miles of it, sir. It fell down by itself and I set it up for you.'

Gerard said, 'I must side with Mark. I saw it happen.' It was untrue, but the situation had to be saved.

Baird did not doubt him. 'Oh well, if that's so, all right. Well, young Mark, you're let off this time.'

'But look here, there's nothing to *let* me off! I mean, it would be foul to do a thing like that—'

It was the witch-word: Baird burst into his braying laughter. 'Very well, very well. I'm not accusing you. You go and amuse yourself somewhere else now, and let these others have a go. I want my tea.'

He drew on his coat. He looked ferociously hot. He was sweating. Celia told him he should take his pleasures more easily, and he snarled at her.

Mark thanked him politely for the game, and said he thought he would stay with us for a while.

'Oh yes,' said Baird as a parting shot. 'I'm all right when I'm playing games with you, but otherwise you're bored stiff.'

'Now Mark, dear,' said Celia firmly, when he had gone, 'I know my father is dreadful, but there is nothing personal about it. I'm sure you're old enough to realise that.'

'He isn't half bad at table-tennis,' Mark said, 'for his age.' He was quite serene again.

23

We had all made a general agreement, when the plans for this holiday were mooted, to give one another the most modest of gifts: so it was something of an embarrassment when Dr. Baird, at breakfast on Christmas Day, walked across the dining-room to Mark and put before him a ten-pound note. Mark flushed red and then went white. He looked at it and swallowed. 'I say—' he began, but Baird had returned to his own table.

It was the most awkward thing he could have done. Mark, who was as fond of money as the next boy, saw in a flash what marvels this would buy; but he also knew instinctively that it was too much, and that he could not accept it without protest. Yet he could scarcely have gone to Baird's table, where Mrs. Baird, Celia and Aveling were sitting, and offer such a protest with his thanks. For all he knew, the others had no idea of Baird's munificence. He was hopelessly lost.

Gerard tried to help him. Catching Baird's eye, he mimed astonishment, gratitude, decent rejection: Baird simply stared back at him as if he were an importunate busker in a theatre queue.

'You'll have to catch him in the hall,' Gerard said to Mark, 'and do the best you can.'

But it seemed that the Bairds would never rise. We, also, sat on; and Mark fingered the note with a kind of fearful reverence. 'I say, I've never seen one of these things before.'

At last the Bairds got up. Mrs. Baird and Celia went towards the lift, Aveling and the doctor towards the lounge.

Mark darted after them, almost cannoning into a waiter. Gerard and I followed quickly, feeling that he might need our assistance.

He gripped the doctor's sleeve. Aveling, who did not know what was happening, stopped and waited.

'Look here, sir,' Mark said, 'this is super, but I can't take it. It's ever so much too much.'

Stepping back, Baird twitched his arm away. He looked down from his stiffened height. 'Now look here, that's not the way to do things. What do you know about it? How do you know what's "too much" to me? What standards have you?'

Mark stood his ground. I was proud of him. 'It's far too much by any standards I've ever known, sir. Please— I say, you honestly must make it less.'

'When I was a boy,' Baird said, as if beginning his autobiography, 'I would have given my ears for a surprise like that. I had never even *seen* a tenner. Had you?'

'No.'

Gerard fidgeted.

'Exactly. Well, I go to considerable trouble to give you something you've never seen and never dreamed of, and you throw it back in my face. Do you know these aren't even issued nowadays? You've got the one I was keeping for myself.'

Mark looked miserable. 'It's not that, honestly. It's—'

Aveling had moved out of earshot.

'Well? What is it? Can't you even talk now?'

Gerard said, 'It's extraordinarily kind of you, and Mark was delighted. But Christine and I would both have thought less of him if he'd just put out a hand and grabbed.'

Baird said rudely, 'It doesn't matter what you think. What does *he* think?'

There are certain moments at which a child is beyond help. We cannot speak for him without denying him his coming maturity; and it is at such moments that we realise the maturity which is almost upon him. I did not know how Mark would deal with a situation that seemed so hopelessly beyond his scope; he had been forced into the position of prime participant in a quarrel waged above his head, a quarrel which, in its deeper sense, did not concern him. For a moment he teetered back and forth from his heels to his toes. Then he looked up, smiled, and said quite easily, 'It's very kind of you. Thank you very much. I shall put it towards a new camera.'

Baird began, 'Put it *towards*? Towards? What do you boys pay for cameras, for God's sake?' – but the moment of awkwardness was past, and he smiled to himself as he walked away.

'Extremely well handled,' Gerard said to Mark.

'Oh, was it? Good. I didn't see what else there was to do. And – well, anyway, it *is* a beauty, isn't it?'

He went upstairs, with an air of rectitude, to prepare himself for church.

Christmas dinner was a curious meal. It was not the custom at the Moray for guests, whether resident or not, to pay much attention to one another. The Bairds knew all the residents by now, but they hardly ever exchanged more than a good-morning or a remark about the weather. I myself had commented upon two old ladies who, having lived there for more than ten years, occupied seats on opposite sides of the chimneypiece and had never spoken together in anything resembling friendship. 'But they aren't relations,' Mrs. Baird had said, puzzled, 'though they do look a bit alike. They don't even know each other.' At dinner on this particular day (it was served at the usual time, which was half-past seven) a feeble attempt was made at general comradeship. All through a well-cooked but poorly served meal (Boldini cooked it himself, but his regular staff, with the exception of old Finnegan, insisted on spending Christmas at home, with the result that their places were filled by an army of mercenaries, having not the slightest idea where anything was kept) well-known solitaries braced themselves to look around, nod and smile blindly at random; elderly married couples, who wanted nothing but to be alone, bobbed quickly at other married couples, while hoping the gesture would not form a precedent; and one or two more determined diners even leaned across with their crackers to adjacent tables. Mark began by annoying Dr. Baird; he chose the beef in preference to the turkey (we were seated, for that occasion, at the Bairds' table). 'What do you mean, no turkey? All boys like turkey. Seems silly to go without, just to try to be different.' Mrs. Baird was nervously and determinedly festive; her crackers contained riddles, and she made us all guess them. Celia and I, slipping our paper hats under our plates, were rebuked by Aveling, who was wearing a green mitre covered with gold stars. 'But you must wear your caps, it is important.' Gerard agreed, and put on a puce one; only the doctor and Mark obdurately remained as they were. 'Well, thank God,' Baird said, 'this tomfoolery will be over in another thirty-six hours.'

'I must admit,' said Aveling, 'I rather enjoy it. What other chance do I get to wear headgear straight out of the Beauvais tapestry?' Mark giggled. 'I can appreciate your point of view,' Aveling added, 'at your age you haven't the dignity to support it. But Gerard and I are filled with inner satisfaction.'

'Mummery,' said Baird.

His wife surreptitiously removed her pale-mauve crown.

'Now you are spoiled, Millie,' Aveling said, 'and you were looking so queenly. Come on, pull this last one with me, and let us see if we can't find you something as charming.'

Mrs. Baird put a finger in one ear, hunched her shoulder against the other. With her free hand she pulled nervously, leaving the inner casing of the cracker in Aveling's hand. He took out the explosive strip and gave it to Mark. 'You bang it.'

Mark made dramatic preparations for the snap, and everyone watched him except Celia, who was watching Aveling, and myself, who was watching Celia.

In that moment she was off her guard as I had never seen her. She had a look of such longing, such sad and patient hunger, that I felt my heart turn over for fear that she might not recover herself before the others saw what I had seen. Her head was strained forward, and between her eyebrows were two small converging lines that dragged her forehead up. Her lips were a little open; she might have been holding her breath. The strip parted with a loud bang, a little flash and a curl of smoke; Celia jumped and suddenly laughed out loud. She was herself again, or perhaps she had mercifully ceased to be herself.

It was as though the noise had brought the formalities of Christmas to an end. People rose and began to drift back to the lounge where, as on every other evening, they read or knitted or wrote letters. We rose also, leaving behind us the bright scattered rubbish of the festivity, the screwed-up caps, the litter of mottoes and riddles, the little whistles and squeakers and rings of ruby and emerald glass. 'I think,' Gerard whispered to Mark, 'that after a decent interval you and I might play ping-pong again.'

Celia was waiting for the lift, the doctor had gone along to the lavatory. Aveling and Mrs. Baird were walking a little ahead of me, and I heard her say, 'It seems dreadful, caps and all that, with everything still so near to us.'

For a second he looked angry; I saw him catch his breath. Then he said, 'I can't believe, knowing her, that she would have wanted it otherwise.'

I had a sudden impulse to go to Celia. I stepped after her just before the lift-doors closed and she said, 'Come and have a cigarette in my room. I have had all the family I can bear for one day – not meaning yours, of course. I've got some brandy up there; we shall drink it.'

I remembered the June night on the front, when she had wanted to talk to me but found it hard to begin. She had just the same determined and excited air; she swept me into her room as into a palace, cleared a chair for me, and saw that I had all I needed.

'They'll all be all right for half an hour. The parents are tired of being festive, and Eric will want Gerard to play billiards. I expect Mark will occupy himself all right.'

She kicked off her shoes and fell into a sort of luxurious sprawl. 'How nice it is to be quiet!'

In the room her scent was heavy as an anaesthetic. On the dressing-table was a clutter of lotions, creams, the most recently advertised cosmetics. Hung carelessly across a corner of the looking-glass was her pearl necklace; spilling from a half-open drawer was a new chiffon scarf and a belt like a dog-collar, with gilded studs.

'Restful, oh, so restful, isn't this restful? Really, I'm in a state when nobody can annoy me. I have never felt so calm. And I don't even have to tiptoe along corridors in the night these days.'

This was what she had wanted to tell me. I said, 'Why not?'

'Neither of us wants to, for a while. Anyway, Eric doesn't. I can perfectly well understand.'

I could think of nothing to say.

'It is easy to understand, isn't it?' she pressed me.

I said I thought so.

She clasped her hands behind her head and gazed at the ceiling. 'It is odd,' she said, in a tone inappropriately light, 'but when it happened it was far more of a shock to him than either of us thought it would be. Of course, we are all right really, but he doesn't want us to, yet—' She was silent. Swinging her hands down like a hoop, she banged them on to her knees, stopped lounging, sat up and looked at me very straight, as if I were under rebuke. 'It is only decent,' she said energetically, and she sounded, without meaning to in the least, as if she were mimicking her mother. 'It would be impossible to do anything else.'

Remembering what Gerard had once said about her, I believed she was suffering less from sexual deprivation (which is sometimes, in women of Celia's kind, little more than hypochondria, since the physical side of love may be nothing for them beyond the treasured symbol of being desired) than from suspense and fear. She was longing for him to come to her. She said stiffly, 'I think the more of him because of it. Wouldn't you, if you were me?'

I knew she wanted easy comfort, and of course I gave it, not wishing her to detect the edge of my own fear. And my fear was the worse because, this time, I did not believe that Aveling was being cruel. I believed he *could not* touch her.

'We are perfectly happy and settled together,' she said, reaching out for the bottle and glasses, 'except for that.' Her voice was soft. 'And, after all, that's always the least of it, when everything else is all right.'

When at last we went downstairs together, Dr. and Mrs. Baird were nowhere to be seen; Gerard, Mark and Aveling were still in the games-room. The lounge was deserted except for a bridge four and for the two old ladies, for years acquainted, strangers by old custom, by old custom unspeaking. One of them wore, upon her piled white hair, the paper cap she had perched upon it at dinner and had forgotten to remove; it nodded with the rhythm of her knitting. Near the fire the holly berries had begun to shrivel in the heat, wrinkled and scarlet as gypsies imagined by Sir Walter Scott.

'I don't think,' Celia muttered to me, 'that this will do at all. I must see if I can't make an improvement.' She had a fox-pointed, demoniac look that was none the less free from malice; it was as if she were driven by some angry, yet half-hilarious, pity. She stepped on to the hearthrug and squatted on her heels. She said to the old lady in the cap, 'Have you had a nice day, Miss Ratcliff?'

Miss Ratcliff looked startled. She said warily, carefully, like someone unaccustomed to speaking English or perhaps, like Caspar Hauser, unaccustomed to speaking at all, 'Thank you, Miss Baird, a very nice day. I hope you have all enjoyed it too.'

'And Mrs. Davenport?' Celia swung round to the other woman, 'Has it been fun for you, too?'

Mrs. Davenport was a little younger than her companion-stranger, a little less cosy, a little more brisk. Her hair was a harsh iron-grey, polished and abundant. 'How very kind of you to enquire! Well, it has been peaceful. Perhaps one could not say fun.'

'But you don't want it to be over yet, do you?' Celia cried.

They looked at each other, in defence against her. It might have been the first time a co-operative impulse had passed between them.

'Well,' Miss Ratcliff said, 'I think it's time I went up the stairs to Bedfordshire. It is nearly half-past ten – good gracious, so it is! – and Mr. Boldini will be glad to see the last of us all today.'

'No, no, no! This is a special day, and I'm sure he wants it to be. It probably makes him feel sad, everyone going upstairs too early; he feels his efforts have failed.'

'Boldini cannot be out of pocket through his efforts,' Mrs. Davenport said, with a little edge to her voice. 'Indeed, I don't think he can possibly be dissatisfied even from that point of view. But I must be off myself, or I shall lose my beauty-sleep.'

'No,' said Celia. 'Mrs. Hall and I want you to have a drink with us first, to celebrate.' Her eyes were full of tears.

She had drunk a good deal upstairs, but she was not drunk; she was simply restless, in a mood to give, to make people happy, since she could not be happy herself.

They looked at each other again. 'It's so kind,' said Miss Ratcliff, 'but I don't think we should, or, rather, that I should.'

'But you must feel it's still Christmas, don't you? You are still wearing your beautiful crown, it looks so pretty on you; you must have been feeling Christmassy or you'd have taken it off.'

Miss Ratcliff put a hand to her head. She said wonderingly, 'Oh dear, I must have looked silly!'

Mrs. Davenport said, 'Nonsense. I have been thinking how much it became you.' It was unexpected, this direct approach; she herself jumped a little at the sound of her own voice.

I said, 'It's such a lovely blue, much nicer than any of the others I've seen.'

Celia shot upwards and pressed the bell. 'So you will join us? What would you both care for?'

Still in their timid alliance, the old ladies eyed each other.

'They have got some port,' Celia said, 'some really beautiful port. Boldini hides it, but we'll make him disgorge it. Isn't that just right for the day?'

Both agreed, though looking increasingly ill at ease, that it was.

'But I can't let you—' Mrs. Davenport began.

Celia turned to her. 'Please let me, please, please! Mrs. Hall and I don't want to go to bed yet, we want to have company. You will be doing us a great favour.'

By this time heads were turning from the bridge table. Finnegan came in, with his aged, stilted stride, his tortoise-like out-thrusting of the head.

'We want four glasses of that *wonderful* port, the '27, not Old Tawny or anything dubious like that. You know what we mean.'

'I'm not sure, madam—' Finnegan began.

'Oh, but you will find it, you're so clever. Besides, I want you to pour yourself a glass, too.'

Finnegan found it. Raising her glass, Celia touched it to the glasses of Mrs. Davenport, Miss Ratcliff and myself. The three crystalline bell-notes were piercing in the hot, quiet room.

Miss Ratcliff sipped. She said gingerly, 'This is a real treat. This is most kind, Miss Baird.'

'It is princely, I think,' said Mrs. Davenport. Her colour had risen, her eyes sparkled. She looked quite handsome.' Really, we shall have something to remember, shan't we?'

The old ladies finished their port and thanked us again. They rose in unison, said good-night and went together towards the lift.

'That is the very first time I have seen them side by side,' Celia said, 'they're always in single file. Isn't it wonderful?'

Filled with affection for her, I could not help telling her how much I liked her.

'Oh, do you? Bless you.' She passed a finger-tip delicately under her lower lids. 'But we do make feeble propitiations to the gods, don't we? I want them to be good to me, so I try to please a couple of old ladies. The gods must laugh themselves bloody well silly.'

Dr. Baird and his wife came in. Deserted, they had expressed their resentment by going for a dark and disagreeable walk, which neither had enjoyed.

'Oh, you've both turned up, have you?' said the doctor, in his most atrabilious fashion. 'Just about time. Jolly sort of day this is for us.'

Celia said, without a trace of feeling, that she was sorry. 'We've been revelling with Miss Ratcliff and Mrs. Davenport.'

'Doing *what*?' Mrs. Baird opened her eyes.

'Drinking port with them. Why, here are our menfolk! It's usually they who sit over the port, isn't it?'

Gerard, Aveling and Mark appeared, looking slightly sheepish. They had not realised how long they had been playing downstairs.

'Well,' said the doctor loudly, 'time we all went to bed.'

'Not yet,' Celia said. 'We are all going to play a game, something idiotic, like Donkey, or Old Maid.'

They agreed grudgingly: but Miss Ratcliff and Mrs. Davenport would have made a better end to the evening.

24

On the afternoon of Boxing Day Aveling drove Celia and me to Crowborough.

An odd little scene had preceded our setting-off and had left a sour flavour. Aveling had, of course, invited us all, but Mark had declined politely, since he had made friends on the promenade that morning with another boy and was going with him on a cycle-ride; and Dr. Baird had declined with his customary rudeness, without feeling the need for explanation. It was two o'clock. The doctor had gone upstairs for a sleep, Gerard was working in our room, Mark had already set out, Aveling had gone round to the garage to get his car.

Mrs. Baird stood in the hall arguing with Celia. She had her fur coat over her arm, but had not yet changed her velvet morning-slippers. 'Do hurry up if you *are* coming,' Celia said impatiently.

'But I'm not sure that I am. Perhaps you younger ones would prefer to be alone.'

'Eric asked us all.'

'Of course, not that he's so young. But I think of him as being the same as you and Christine.'

I tried to edge away, but they had somehow penned me into a corner.

'Eric is forty-five.'

'I know Eric is forty-five. I have known him since he was a boy.'

This seemed to bring the conversation to a full stop. I could see Aveling through the revolving doors, chatting to the head porter.

Celia said at last, 'Well, Mummy, please do make up your mind!'

'I should only be a drag on you.'

'Mummy, this is not some great *issue*, you know.'

'You see enough of me. It would be more amusing for you just to go with Eric and Christine.' Meanwhile, Mrs. Baird had pulled on one sleeve of her coat.

I began to say, 'Of course it will be nice if you come—' but Celia broke in, in a quiet, almost childish, enraged little voice.

'If you do feel like that, Mummy, then we'd better be off.'

Mrs. Baird flushed. She put up a hand and touched her ear-rings. 'I only meant it might be more pleasant for you to have an outing with friends of your own generation. I know I must often be a bore to you, that you must long to see the back of me—'

'If you are going to make scenes and try to upset me, it would be far more pleasant for me to go without you. I admit that.'

The reception clerk had moved so far along his pen that he seemed to be trying to press himself through the wall.

'How can you be so beastly!' Mrs. Baird whispered. She seized at her diamond brooch and gave it a wrench.

'I am not beastly. You are beastly. You are trying to make me cry, which you know you always can, but *don't* you imagine it means a thing! It's purely a nervous reaction. It doesn't mean that I'm in the least sorry.'

And, indeed, Celia seemed on the verge of tears; she was trembling.

'Go with your friends. And don't *you* imagine I shall ever come out with them again, so it's no use asking me.' Mrs.

Baird started towards the lift. Celia shot out her small, claw-like hand and caught her sleeve.

'Don't, don't, don't,' she whispered violently, 'I beg you, I implore you, not to spoil everything for me!'

Mrs. Baird twitched herself free.

'You began this. You're the one who spoils things.'

Celia said, her lips almost closed, her teeth touching, ' "I beseech you in the bowels of Christ, think that you may be mistaken!" '

'What?' her mother said sharply. We were alone now; the receptionist had disappeared into a room at the back of his office, the second porter had removed himself to the farthest end of the hall and was pretending to polish doorknobs.

Celia said in a heart-breaking voice, 'Oh, let it go. You'd never understand.' She went to join Aveling, giving the doors such a great swing that they made nearly a double revolution.

I spoke to Mrs. Baird, telling her that Celia was in a highly nervous state and was extremely upset. I begged her (though it was none of my business) to forget what had happened and not to continue the quarrel when we came back.

'Aren't I in a highly nervous state? Oh, I don't know how she can speak to me like that, and before you! To do it before you!'

I had not wished, I said, to be present. I asked her if I might tell Celia that it was all right. That she would bear no rancour.

Mrs. Baird said, 'Tell her what you like, I don't care', and finding that pressing the button failed to bring the lift down, made for the stairs at a tripping run. She ran like a young girl on her small and stubby feet.

I went out to join Celia and Aveling.

So the first part of our drive was an unhappy one, Celia nervously bright, Aveling silent. But after a time he asked her what had happened. 'I think we'd all feel better if we talked about it.'

'You tell him,' Celia said to me.

I did so as fairly as I could. When I came to her Cromwellian outburst Aveling smiled: he could not help it.

'It's nothing to laugh about!' she cried.

'My dear girl, I know. But it is still funny.'

She said, 'I love my mother. I always have. But I can't bear her to want me to *say* it. Surely she must know I care for her? Can't she understand? *Why* has she turned against me? Why does she want to make me wretched?'

Aveling said, 'You've got to remember this. She doesn't take her miseries to heart as you do.' He was trying to comfort her, yet speaking with suppressed irritation, as though angry with her because she had still more to bear. In the same practical, irritated tone he went on: 'I must say, I wish she would take it out on your father. He's tougher than you are.'

'You think she's not in an awful state?' Celia asked eagerly. She had a wild look, as though for two pins she would jump out of the car and run back to the Moray.

'I know her. Believe me about her, at any rate,' he said.

We reached Hedley Sherriff's estate and passed between red brick pillars adorned with pineapples of a smooth yellowish stone into a long driveway tunnelled by overbearing trees.

'Now this is likely to be a great pity,' Aveling said. His manner became brisk; he was relieved to be talking about his own business. He explained that he thought most of these trees might have to come down, he fancied they were dangerous, he was having a forestry expert down to look at them. 'This avenue existed well before the old man's time. I rather suspect he bought the land on account of it.'

Emerging from the trees, we came into a stretch of parkland leading up to the house. It was not, I thought, an attractive house. It was solid and heavy, with horizontal skyline and pillared portico, at a glance not unhandsome; but jutting out behind it to the south, with the cunning and pathetic air of a stout person desirous of concealment who imagines that if his head is hidden his rump is invisible, was the conservatory, now catching the last of the light in its disagreeable panes; and to the north was a meaningless balustrade ending in an equally meaningless string of composite columns. The windows flanking the door had been adorned with some stingy plastering, now chipped and weather-stained. Ivy like wet green mackintosh had seized upon a part of the walls; other parts had been stripped.

'It's a pocket version of Tyringham, very much coarsened,' Aveling said as we drove up to it, 'but then, that is better than a version of something less admirable. The old gentleman's afterthoughts are the chief trouble. We shall have to be tactful about them, very tactful.'

We got out. 'Nobody will be here, of course. Hedley's spending Christmas at Monte Carlo. But he says his man will be there to show us around.'

He rang the doorbell, and we waited. It was not a cold day, though the skies were scumbled and sunless. I considered how many servants had been necessary to keep such a house clean and warm, to draw water, haul coal, cook and serve meals. Hedley Sherriff, Aveling had told me, made do with five: a butler, housekeeper, cook and two women who came in by the day. I wondered how many such establishments were left in the world. I wondered what the manservant would be like, and hoped he would match the house. As we waited we all speculated about him, making bad jokes to pretend we were lighter-hearted than we were.

The door flew open and there, with napkin over his arm, a salver in his hand, plump face screwed into an expression of charged and bursting gravity, was Junius. It was so unexpected, so preposterous, that we burst out laughing; for a moment we became genuinely light-hearted. Dropping his theatrical properties he embraced both Celia and me with the warmth that sometimes gave the illusion of being not only a part of his nature but the whole of it.

'My dears, I could not resist it. Nancy told me you were coming, and we meant to surprise you, anyway. Then we found Robinson sulking because he wanted to be "off" on Boxing Day, so we dismissed him, and I deputised.'

Nancy came smiling out from a door behind him.

'I wanted to put Nancy in a cap and apron, but then thought it would be too *Petite Hameau*.'

'In any case,' said Nancy, 'there is no cap and apron. Really, you are frightfully behind the times! It's as much as the daily will do to put a tea-towel round herself when she washes up.' She asked Aveling whether he wanted to go all over the house again, or whether he would like to sit in the library while she took the rest of us on a conducted tour.

'I think I shall come,' he replied, 'because I do really doubt, Nancy, whether you will get the details right. It always astonishes me how very blank people can be about the houses they live in.'

'I've never actually lived in this one, only visited. But I know it pretty well.'

'Nevertheless—' said Aveling, leaving the word upon the air.

He did not really doubt Nancy's lively and even scholarly interest in any house belonging to any member of her family, or, indeed, in any detail of her family's history: he wanted to show us the house himself simply because he loved to explain, to teach, to illuminate, and because it was another respite. He should probably, as Gerard had once said, have been a professional connoisseur of his subject, a Fellow of a college, the curator of a museum, rather than an architect in practice.

He took us in a leisurely fashion over that dark and dank-looking house, pointing out the essential handsomeness that he hoped to restore to it.

'Your uncle should let me decorate for him,' Junius said to Nancy. 'I could make it look absolutely delectable, if a fraction odd.' For a moment he seemed to have forgotten himself; she looked at him sharply and smiled.

'Yet it could be elegant,' Aveling said. 'It could have style, it could even have lightness. The proportions are splendid. It ought to be all right.'

Afterwards we went out into the dull white afternoon, visiting the farm and the small, but handsome, houses set up in a kind of leper colony just within the wall of the western boundary. It was obvious that the original Sherriff had not welcomed the close proximity of his relations. Aveling showed us the mausoleum, a squat building like a swollen thumb, that stood in the clearing of a copse. 'I love it,' Nancy said, 'it takes death seriously.'

Celia shivered; she looked chilly, tired, heavy-laden. 'No, but honestly: must we?'

'Oh, I think so,' Nancy replied evenly, but she was not joking. 'After all, there's nothing more serious, is there?'

Luckily, Aveling and Junius had walked ahead of us.

'Anything that happens to us when we're alive is more serious! Death is commonplace. It's no one-person's privilege. I wish we could just be quietly removed when our time comes and brushed off the earth.'

A woman more experienced than Nancy would have seen that Celia's nerves were raw, and would have changed the subject. Nancy, however, was pursuing her idea with the concentration of a studious schoolgirl at her homework. 'But it makes us so unimportant in our lives if we're merely pushed out of the way when we die. I think it is important to remember people for as long as possible.'

The light was failing. The grey thumb gathered what was left of it into itself, and gleamed against the fringe of conifers. 'I should like to lie there myself one day, but it wasn't meant for my side of the family.'

Celia ran on ahead and caught up with Aveling.

Nancy looked at me. 'I haven't upset her, have I?'

I said, 'You couldn't know. It's only that Mrs. Aveling's death is still so much on her mind.'

She called at once, 'Celia!'

Celia turned and came back to us. Nancy went forward and spoke to her anxiously, and they walked on together.

When we had seen all there was to see, Junius said he thought we might go to his house for a while. He would follow in his own car with Nancy.

Now I knew that this invitation was important, because it must mean the end of his pretences. As soon as Nancy saw Junius's house she would know what he was, or at the very least would have her suspicions strongly aroused; however much she might play schoolgirl before the rest of us, she was not stupid. I thought she had never believed in Junius's oblique courtship. Like Aveling, she had seemed to regard him as a jester, to be amused by him, never to speak to him except in a tone that was slightly bantering. She rode life very easily, she was in no hurry for it to take definite shape. One day she would fall in love, would marry; but was not concerned with this as yet. She took all the amusements offered to her; theatre visits with girls from her office (she had a job now), jaunts with people who, like Junius, happened to interest her, occasional smart parties and dances with young men and women of her own set. I had seen photographs of her several times in the glossy papers. Yet she was not of wealthy society, since she had no wealth of her own; not of the society of her office acquaintances, since her background was so far different from theirs; and not of the society of Aveling, Celia and myself, since we were so much older than she. She seemed to hang lightly suspended between several worlds, enjoying the motion of the swing, the fanning of the air, as yet undecided which to choose when the time came for her to alight.

I watched her walking ahead of us at Celia's side, a tall girl, easy in her movements, but with none of Celia's taut gracefulness. I wondered how much she had guessed of Celia's love for Aveling, and fancied that she knew a good deal.

It was now almost dark. As we drove off down the tunnel of trees the headlamps revealed every leaf with a pre-Raphaelite clarity, a packed, botanical niceness. When we emerged we saw the downs sprinkled with lights like a lawn with daisies; the night looked festive; still a part of Christmas.

I had forgotten that Junius was entertaining friends. When he introduced them, the oldest of the young men whom I had already met in the cafe, and a delicate, fretful-looking one with a smooth pink face and pinkish fair hair, I realised that Junius had intended his self-exposure to be as complete as possible. He still retained his ordinary, sober manner; but as he took Nancy upstairs to show her the house his eyes were mischievous. The young men, who had been ordered to find entertainment for the rest of us, silently did so. They did not seem to want to talk.

At last Nancy reappeared, cool as a cucumber, no trace of surprise upon her face. 'I never saw anything so attractive,' she said, 'or so thorough. One feels Junius has even decorated the mouseholes with Regency traps and gilded cheese.'

We did not stay long. Nancy was returning to London by train, and Aveling said he would drive her to the station. She and I went up to Junius's bedroom.

She said, 'Isn't he extraordinary?'

She added, not looking at me, 'Eric is all right, of course.'

'Quite all right,' I said firmly.

176

She looked relieved: a bizarre doubt had been dispelled. 'Will he and Celia get married?'

'I don't know.' I realised that I did not know, that I no longer knew anything.

'I think he is attractive,' she said. She blinked up at Junius's canopied bed. 'Oh, really, really!' She paused. 'I think he ought to get married.'

I was dense enough to think, for a moment, that she meant Junius. She laughed. Junius, she said, had twice asked her to marry him. 'What would he have done if I'd accepted?'

I said I thought he might have gone through with it.

'Oh, how dreadful! The mind boggles. No, I meant Eric. But then he is much too depressed, anyway, at present. Did you know his wife?'

'A little,' I said.

Nancy stood up, brushing down her coat. 'I am sure she wasn't so awful as Junius says, because Eric would never have married anyone who was.'

Nancy's remark had so shocked me that for a second I did not wish to know its meaning; my instinct was to pretend that I had never heard it. Then I longed to ask her, but was deterred by something which presented itself as a sort of pride. I could not appear to be 'pumping' her. She was far younger than I, the merest acquaintance, and she had spoken in innocence. I could not disturb her by a question, not when she stood there looking so serene and happy, waiting for me to follow her back, to the others. I told myself that she had misunderstood Junius; he could not possibly have said anything of the sort to her, or if he had, it had been one of his peculiar and tasteless jokes. All these reasons for silence ran through my mind like a strip of film through a projector. The real reason was that I was afraid to speak. I was fond of my friends, even of Junius, who had been selflessly kind when Gerard was ill, and wanted to know of them nothing more

177

than I knew already. The more we love people the less we desire to know them, the more frightened we are of the creature that stands erect within them, looking out through their eyes. What they have shown us already of themselves, what they have already told us, is all they mean us to know: anything else we find out will be the thing they wish to stay hidden, and they wish this thing to stay hidden because they know that, if recognised, it would sow the first seed of hate.

So I said, 'I very much liked what I saw of her', and we went downstairs together.

25

Early in January Celia rang me up, and among other things told me casually that she meant to give more time to her business. It would not be difficult, she said, to extend it, to take on one or two more girls. The lease of the floor below was now available, and it seemed good sense to take it over – 'for there's no reason why Hilda and I should carry on in such a piddling way when we could build up something worth-while. I've got a little spare money I could use.' After that I neither saw nor heard any more of her for quite a long time.

I had a book to finish, Gerard was planning to set up a branch of his firm in Toronto; our minds were full of our own affairs. He brought me, from his club, a little news of Aveling and of Nancy Sherriff. Nancy had given up her job in England and had gone back to Geneva to work there for a few months; her father, a depressed and hebephrenic man with just enough money to keep up appearances, was angry about this, since he hated to live alone. Aveling was still engaged on Hedley Sherriff's work, but otherwise (he had said) there wasn't much doing. He was spending a good deal of time at the club nowadays, and though he was well-liked, did not often join the members in the bar, but as a rule sat in the small drawing-room off it, or played cards upstairs.

One night Gerard brought back for a drink an acquaintance of his, a tall, jolly, comely old man called Henry Fort, who lived most of the year in France, had independent means, and to amuse himself wrote travel books. He was telling me how much I had missed by being born a little too late: the great years, the years of fun, of dazzling personalities as common as poppies in July. He and his friends might, he admitted, have made asses of themselves in their day; but what a day it had been! A new genius with every sunrise, Paris strident with ideas, movements, causes, splendid poses, belligerent periodicals – '*Transition, Blast, This Quarter, Bifur* – how excited we got about them, and how furious! You don't know what it was like, either of you, you live in the age of comfortable dreariness, and you don't complain because you've never known anything better.' He gesticulated at Gerard. 'Dead from the waist down and the neck up, that's what the young people are nowadays.'

'Don't wag your finger at me, Henry,' Gerard said. 'I am not so young as all that.'

'You wanted to be, say, between twenty-five and thirty, between 1930 and 1932—'

'I was.'

'—in Paris. After that, Hitler reared up, and it was never the same again. Of course, I was among the seniors there myself – Pound and Joyce were of my generation – but I never felt it. No one ever felt old.'

His little honey-coloured eyes, almost sheathed in flesh, sharpened with reminiscence. He locked his hands behind his head, where the short white hairs stood up as if in perpetual fright from a scalp rosy as a baby's. He told us of the bars and the night-clubs, the attic rooms two floors above the limit of the lift; of the smell of narcissus and pernod by day, of charcoal in the braziers by night; of friends long dead or grown respectable; of cantrips in Montparnasse better than Nerval's with his lobster. He spoke with reverence of people who had come to nothing, but who were still, for him, illuminated by the fireworks of their promise. 'I remember sitting outside the Dome one night so hot the ice melted as you rattled it, and people looked as though they were in tears with the sweat rolling off them – sitting there with Mary Butts, Bob McAlmon, one of the Crosbys, Lois Harding – she married Aveling, you know, that chap you were chatting to when I came in the club tonight—'

I broke in with a question.

'Yes, I knew her well. Everyone knew Lois.'

He was delighted to be able to tell us something of personal interest to ourselves; he may have felt, with regret, that old age tends to make one's information all too general. 'She was a junior sub. on the *Herald Tribune* at that time. She hadn't much money, she was clinging on by her eyebrows until her mother died, but somehow she was always turned out as smartly as a Frenchwoman.'

Lois Harding was the child of divorced parents; her father had died shortly after the break-up of the marriage. She had drifted around the world with her mother since leaving school and had settled in Paris about 1927. Mrs. Harding, pretty and spoiled, ran from one man to another; Lois, as soon as she came of age, went off to live and work by herself.

'You saw her everywhere,' Fort said, 'in the most *louche* company. Nothing shocked her, and yet she never really joined in. And she didn't, as I believe they put it nowadays, "sleep around".' He recalled her for us; tall, thin, sharp, handsome and young, sitting with her usual crowd at the Dome or the Select. Nobody had quite known what to make of her, though she had been a good enough listener, had had a brisk enough wit, to make herself popular. There were some who believed she had a lover on the quiet – 'but *I* didn't,' Fort said, 'I was damned sure she hadn't. Perhaps her experience of Mamma made her cautious; anyhow, she looked to me like a young woman who didn't intend to make up her mind about anything in a hurry.'

A good many men were interested in her, often the younger, wilder Americans, rootless, raffish, drifting: her peculiar companionable apartness had made her seem desirable, a still point of refuge. She had been a fairly heavy drinker; it had not seemed to touch her. 'Nothing seemed to. She used to pop up in the same dress, day after day, and look as fresh as a daisy. Picasso did a drawing of her, but I believe she sold it when she got hard up.'

Quite suddenly, at the beginning of 1931, she had disappeared from Paris. She made no farewells, gave not the slightest indication that going was in her mind. 'One night she was out on the terrace as usual drinking Mandarin- Curaçao – that was her tipple – and the next night she wasn't.'

He heard nothing more from her until the following year, when she returned to Paris with a husband. She was then thirty-five, Aveling twenty-eight. Her mother had left her nine or ten thousand pounds, and Lois had used most of it to set up this new husband, a stately-looking, rather serious young man, in business on his own. They had spent a gregarious honeymoon, Lois introducing him to all her old acquaintances and dragging him round to party after party.

'I say "drag",' Fort explained, 'because, though he was most amiable and the pink of courtesy, he always seemed to be leaning slightly backwards. But he was in love with her, mind; wildly in love. Anyone could see that. The talk about "baby-snatching" dried up in a good many throats. Though, mind you' – he shot out his hand in an episcopal gesture – 'no one was ever really spiteful about Lois. One isn't, about cool people like that.'

They had stayed for three weeks, then gone back to settle in England. 'I never saw her again. I believe she created a pretty stuffy circle of useful people about her for Aveling's benefit – at all events, she dropped the old Paris crowd.'

During the war Fort heard, by roundabout means, that she had fallen ill. Then nothing more, until he read of her death in the paper.

Gerard asked him if he had liked her.

'My dear boy, everyone did. But she was a queer customer, all the same.'

He asked for permission to kick our fire, an action that seemed to give him great pleasure; and as the coals dropped apart, exposing a crater of pure orange flame, smiled into it at his past. 'What fun we had! What stuff we wrote! *Bifur* – that was a production for you. Boris Pilniak sent me a copy. A marvellous photograph of Caruso embalmed, smiling like a cat, and a small boy peeping over the edge of the coffin. The *frisson*, that was what we wanted: we were all rather nasty, to be honest. Then there were some translations from the Spanish about the tortures of the Inquisition – not such great stuff, I thought, but I remember Lois being struck with them.'

He quoted, in his meticulous, Comédie Française French, revelling in the sound of his own voice:

'*Qui donc pourrait endurer le supplice?*
Plus il est lent, plus il est dur,
Plus il est long et plus il est rigoureux.

Poor dear, I expect she knew all about that before the end.'

I told him that to me she had seemed cheerful and full of hope. That I had not seen her otherwise.

As he rose to go he asked Gerard if he knew of a typist who could take dictation from him for a fortnight or so. He had a book to finish. 'I find the pen tires me nowadays.'

I said that I would, if he liked, approach a friend of mine who ran a secretarial agency and try to find somebody for him.

'How very kind,' he said, with a reverential boom, 'how really extraordinarily kind! I can't imagine what I have done to deserve this, Gerard, can you? Out into the wind and the rain,' he added regretfully. It was a cold evening in March.

'He hypnotised you into that,' Gerard said when he had gone. 'He won't even ring a bell for himself at the club. He has only to say that it would be nice if somebody rang it for a harassed member to rise up fatalistically and do so.'

I said I did not think I had been hypnotised. Talking of Lois had made me think of Celia again; I wanted an excuse for seeing her.

I was unlucky. When I telephoned Mrs. Haymer next day she cried out, 'Oh, what a pity! She's in Italy with her people. She won't be back for a fortnight.'

I told her what I wanted; I would like to interview one or two girls for Fort's benefit, if she had any free.

'Well, why don't you come and do it here? It would be so nice if you could see all our changes. You wouldn't know us these days.'

Next day, when I called upon her, I was indeed surprised by the changes Celia had made in a business which, I had supposed, interested her only a little; as a sideline, a counter to move against a possible charge of idleness. She had acquired the second floor of the house (the ground floor was a florist's shop), had redecorated it, partitioned the front room into two offices, for herself and Mrs. Haymer, and had moved the accountant and three girls upstairs. I felt that had I not known Celia's connection with the place I should have guessed it the moment I went in. Somehow the smart, overtly austere establishment had an aura of the defensively feminine, a touch of the perfumery counter; I should not have been surprised to see a string of pearls adorning the carriage of a typewriter, or a bottle of nail-varnish where an inkwell should have been. Mrs. Haymer showed me around with pride. 'It has cost an awful lot of money, but Celia says we shall see every penny of it back.'

She had found three girls for me to see, and left me with them in Celia's room. When I had made my choice, she took me back into her own office.

For a moment she sat looking at me, her pale-yellow eyes unwinking. She had the air of a hidden purpose, but when she spoke it was only to ask me if I would like to see some photographs. Now she became excited, almost furtive, as if indulging some pleasant vice. 'It's something to amuse me, you know. I've been pretty lonely here ever since we expanded. Even when Celia wasn't about there was always the account-ant and a girl to talk to; now they stick upstairs, they don't even come down for tea.'

Spreading the photographs over the desk, she chattered fluently, technically, about each; she might have been a lecturer with lantern slides.

'Here's my best sunset. I did it with a red filter to get the atmosphere. I must say I'm rather proud of it. That's the Hyde Park Hotel.'

I expressed admiration.

She added hastily, drawing my attention to some minute fleck of white hardly visible even when I peered at it, 'Mind you, the negative's rather battle-scarred, but better luck next time. We can't always help these things,' she said with a defen-sive look, as if rebutting in advance a criticism of mine. 'Now here – ah, now here's my latest of Celia. I took it just before she went. The definition's not all I could desire, but I do think it's got vitality.'

Perhaps she used the word 'vitality' in some technical sense; I could not know. But in any ordinary sense it was singularly wide of the mark. The photograph showed Celia full-face, staring into the camera as if in a hypnotic trance. The small, finely shaped, raying eyes seemed slightly

185

unfocused, the lips parted as in anxiety or apprehension. I asked Mrs. Haymer if Celia had been well when it was taken. 'She looks as though she's lost weight.'

'Oh, does she?' Sturdy, steatopygous, she leaned across the desk to have a closer look. 'I don't think so. She was perfectly well, so far as I know.' She hesitated, trying to recall something of the sitter; people to her were only pictures. 'She may have been a bit moody – I think she said she didn't want to go with her parents. But I'm afraid I didn't pay much attention. I say if people are like that it's always kinder to leave them to themselves.'

I asked whether Celia had been working too hard over the business.

'Hard? No, I don't think so. Actually, we're running so smoothly now there's really no need for her to be here at all. She's no cause to worry. I could do it all on my head, I tell her.'

Again she looked at me, staring.

'I suppose you could,' I said.

'I wonder she bothers. I wouldn't, if I had her means.'

'She doesn't look well,' I insisted.

'I do know she'd had a lot of late nights, always going out and coming in again at all hours. Mr. Evans used to call for her after ten sometimes, and they'd rush off somewhere together.'

'Mr. Evans?'

She looked put out. She flushed. She obviously did not wish to be thought a gossip. 'I know she does like to enjoy herself a bit when she's in London, she's so bored at the seaside.' It was not her business, she added, what Celia did: only I had asked, hadn't I? And in a flat that size one couldn't be entirely oblivious of one's neighbour.

Not caring now whether she thought me inquisitive, I asked her whether Celia had been seeing much of Aveling.

'I don't know. He may have called once or twice. I really can't be sure.' She stood up. She could, when she liked, look like a headmistress out of patience with her girls. She swept the photographs into a drawer. I had failed her by my lack of interest in them, my time-wasting interest in Celia.

As she showed me to the door she said again, 'I could do all this on my head. I really do wonder she bothers.'

26

Towards the end of May, while Gerard was in Canada, I went to a cocktail party given to launch a magazine. It was a very hot night and the room was crowded. All the windows were open on Park Lane. Tree-dust and petrol fumes blew in, and the noise of the traffic augmented the usual noise of a hundred shouted conversations. The drinks were warm, the butter oiled and beaded in the sandwiches. It was far too large a party to be enjoyable, to be anything more than a rite. People beamed, bellowed, were uncomfortable, had sore feet and aching spines, put up surreptitious hands to dislodge a clinging shirt or dress from the small of a back. I knew most people there and tried to talk to those I liked, but they could only smile and mouth back at me as I mouthed and smiled at them. I was just thinking that I might now go home when I saw Eric Aveling at the far end of the room, momentarily disclosed by some freak parting of the crowd. He was leaning against the fireplace, talking to somebody I did not know, his head cocked and attentive, his hands in his pockets. I should have liked to talk to him, but the idea of fighting my way through the hot, packed bodies seemed as minatory as the idea of hacking a way through some virgin jungle of the Amazon. I decided not to attempt it, said goodbye to my hosts, and went out into the sultry evening.

As it was not yet dark enough for the park to be dangerous, I set out over the grass. It was that most delicious hour of a spring night when the sky behind the black trees is still

the clear mauve of a Michaelmas daisy, when the lamps sparkling up against the sunset are unnecessary, a mere gratui-
tous delight and adornment of the city. The grass was dry
and whitened by dust, but it smelled sweet, as if the heat had
drawn out the scent from its cool and glassy roots. Men in
shirt-sleeves, girls in cotton dresses, mooned along the crossing paths.

I had not gone very far when Aveling caught up with me.
'I saw you in that inferno,' he said, 'but I couldn't get near
you.' Though he had been running a little, he was not out of
breath. He wiped his face with a large and stiffly laundered
handkerchief, returned it to his pocket and stopped to light a
cigarette. 'Do you smoke in the open air? I heard Gerard was
away.'

Not for long, I said, not for more than a fortnight. He
asked if I were free to dine with him – 'but I expect,' he added,
'that you're going home to peaceful company.'

I said I should like to have dinner with him, though it was
too hot to eat much.

'There's a pub in Brook Street, if you would care for sandwiches. Or don't you go into pubs? You can see that I don't
know much about you.'

We turned and went back in the direction of Park Lane.
Meanwhile he talked to me about his work, told me what he
had already done at Crowborough. His manner was, as usual,
easy, courteous, attentive; but, even for him, uncommonly
formal. I might have met him only that night, at that party. I
thought, looking up at him as he talked, that he was a handsome man, but not an obviously handsome one, or I should
have thought of him as such before. It was the oddities of his
face one tended to notice first, the shelving brows, the heavy,
dark-coloured lids, the extreme ectomorphic construction of
nose and cheekbones. Yet when he was younger his good
looks must have been far more apparent. The oddities were

of anxiety, of concentration, of gravity of temperament or, perhaps more precisely, that cultivation of gravity which was part of his *persona*. It was a kind face, gentle, ruminative; I wondered how he had looked in the heedlessness of youth.

We had come to the edge of the park. He pointed towards Marble Arch, to the blaze of sunset and lamplight, to a belt of lime-green sky above the fogged and ruddy glow of Edgware Road. 'How fine it is, how it conceals all the garishness! When I see that, I am filled with schoolboy romance – James Elroy Flecker, girls called Yasmin. No one can appreciate Flecker without contemplating Marble Arch at this time of night, this time of year. The girls should smell of chypre, musk, opopanax, detestable scents which would be perfect here. No doubt they do.' He said, with scarcely a change of tone, 'Do you hear from Celia often?'

He did not at once allow me to reply, but made some comment on a woman in a sari who was waiting to cross the road. Then he was abruptly silent.

I said, 'I had two postcards from Italy, and one letter since she's been back. She said she hoped to see me soon, but that life was hard.' I knew he wanted once more to talk to me, as he had talked in the road outside the hospital: I had to help him to begin.

'It is hideously, monstrously hard. And the whole fault is mine.'

He had not used the two adverbs for effect. For him her sorrow was monstrous, was hideous: and for some reason he had to let her suffer. He was full of pain, he had to talk to somebody. Yet I fancied that to him 'talking' was not just a simple release. It is not often that we make our deepest confidences for so simple a reason. We do so – often to someone who is almost a stranger – because we have a wild idea that they might find some magic solution to our difficulty, that because they are detached from us they might speak the word of manumission. Every confidence is an unuttered cry for help.

We walked through the streets of Mayfair, and for the time being said no more of Celia. He made a casual comment or two, and I answered as casually. We went into the public house, a quiet one at the corner of a mews, and sat down with sandwiches at a table in an alcove. The proprietress had an enormous gentle dog who lolloped up and down the narrow stairs, ran beneath the bar and out again, came to lay his head on our knees. Aveling made a fuss of him, rolled his great head between his hands, protested when he was called away. A radio set was playing just loudly enough for a tune to be distinguishable, not loudly enough to interfere with conversation. 'Barring the grave,' he said, 'this is probably the *most* quiet and private place.' He asked me about my work, asked about Gerard.

Then he said, 'I want to tell you this, not to exculpate myself from any unkindness to Celia – at least, I hope that is not my motive – but because I must tell somebody.' He clasped his hands, fingertips touching, around the glass tankard and regarded them closely, as if admiring their whiteness against the golden-brown of the beer. It was cool in the room; an electric fan fluttered its dusty ribbons. 'The last time I went to see Lois, which was the day before she died, she told me that she knew about Celia and myself.'

It was a shock: I had not believed Mrs. Baird could have been right.

'It was just before I was leaving.' He looked up, letting his gaze wander about the walls, which were adorned with American pennants. At the moment he seemed scarcely interested in what he was saying. 'She was as cheerful as usual, but I thought she had a rather excited look, as if there was news of some sort, or a secret. She suddenly turned to me and said in a – in a lazy way, the way she would often say things that were important – "Have a wonderful time with your Celia. I know you'll both be happy." '

I said, 'How did she know?'

He looked me full in the face, earnestly, his brows drawn together. 'I simply cannot guess. One might think . . .' He paused. 'I suppose one might think there is always an instinct, an atmosphere. That she felt it. That she simply became aware. Christine, I do not think it can have been like that, not with us. Celia and I would have died – I almost think that's literally true – before giving away to Lois what must have hurt her more than anything in the world. I'm sure Celia let nothing escape by so much as a look. And I can vouch for myself.'

Trying to help, knowing how hopeless it was, I asked him whether Lois had not spoken in generosity, whether she had not in fact meant to make him a present of future happiness.

'No,' he said, 'it was not like that. I've seen her smile in that way when she was bitterly hurt. She didn't mean me to be happy. She wanted – I beg you not to think I'm speaking cruelly of her – to get her own back.' He repeated my own words. 'How did she know?'

I went cold. I had thought of Junius, the intimate, the constant visitor, Junius and his friends brought to the hospital for her amusement, little sessions that might not have been unlike those on the café terraces twenty years ago. I did not believe he would have 'told her', in so many words: I believed he had hinted his knowledge into her mind. I said, and it was hard to speak, 'It can only have been her instinct. She must have been jealous, alone for so long with nothing to do but think.'

'She was never jealous in her life before. I gave her no cause to be. How could I? Everything that I am, such as it is, she made me.'

Then I said, 'That, anyway, isn't true. You are as you are.'

'Let's take nothing away from her: she had so little.'

I asked him whether it was not possible to think unsentimentally, even in a circumstance that only sentiment could soften and make decent. He had been without her, as a wife, for years. Wasn't it in the nature of things that he should have found it intolerable to be alone? She was ill, she was dying; for all her courage her mind had been troubled. If she had been a healthy woman, and the case had been not hers nor his, but had concerned two friends of them both, would she not have understood that, after a death, life must go on? And would she not have condemned as selfishness any attempt to spoil that life?

'She was not selfish,' said Aveling. 'But she just could not bear it.'

There was something I wanted to ask him, but could not as yet.

He said, 'I am hurting Celia terribly. But I can't at present, anyhow, take things up where they were. I know how she's suffering.' He dropped his hands to his knees. 'Will you try to understand that I am, too?'

I said, 'I know.'

'Lois is between us all the time, or I feel it so. It's rather like *Thérèse Raquin*; I thought that was preposterous melodrama when I read it as a boy. And of course it still is. But melodrama only excites people because it has an element of the worst kind of truth.'

Then I did ask my question. I asked him if he loved Celia.

He said, 'I don't know. I can only tell you I don't know. I can't bear to be with her, I can't bear the thought of being utterly without her. All I can do is to let things drift and hope I shall wake one morning – as you say, unsentimental: or seeing straight again.'

The dog came round, sat expectantly before us. Aveling fondled him, and gave him a piece of his sandwich.

'Come on, Basra,' the proprietress cried out, 'you're annoying people. I won't have you sucking up.'

He crawled towards her at once, to sink humbly at her feet. She gave him a gherkin.

Aveling said, 'I am so tired, Christine. I can just about manage to work. I find it hard to think. I don't feel I want to take any sort of action, do anything at all.' Somebody had turned the wireless up; dance-music thumped down upon us. 'I know what I ought to do. I ought to go out now and tele-phone Celia.'

I asked him if this were really impossible.

He said it seemed to him as if it were. He dreaded her unhappiness, because it would match his own. He found his only comfort in being with people who seemed to have no griefs, whose lives, so far as he knew, were smooth. He had gone to the party only because he knew that people there would at least behave as though they were happy. 'I seem to be locked in this horrible selfishness, or it has locked itself on me. It's something I can't help.'

We left the place and walked for a while. Even now a sunset greenness lingered in the upper air, and the city smelled of flowers. 'This night of all nights,' he said, 'I ought to be with her.'

We had come to the edge of the park. I said, 'Go and see her. Please try to go!'

He stopped. 'I can't. I would if I could.'

Thanking him for the evening, I held out my hand.

'Thank you,' he said. 'I've said much too much, and none of it helps.'

'I wish I could have said something to help.'

'Nobody could. I didn't expect it. But I wanted you to think a little better of me, perhaps. I am a vain man, I am afraid.'

I had never seen a man look less vain than Aveling at that moment. Misery accentuated his thinness, narrowed his shoulders, gave to his movements something of the paralytic's irresolution.

'Shall you tell Celia anything of all this?' he asked me. His eyes strayed, following the satiny flash of traffic round the Artillery Memorial and up into Piccadilly, which was blue as watered ink between the lamps.

I said I would do precisely as he wished.

'If you can help her, tell her what she'd be comforted to hear. She wouldn't imagine that I am thinking of anyone but her. But if she should, by any chance – at least let her know that I think of her continually.'

He paused. 'You are nearly home, aren't you?'

'A hundred yards,' I said.

'Then I won't come any farther.' He dropped my hand and at once seemed to forget me. I stood and watched him as he walked slowly away, his head down, his hands linked like an old man's behind his back, towards the scintillating darkness of the park.

27

Had Gerard been home I might not have acted so precipitantly; but the moment I was inside the house I rang up Junius at his flat in Cranmer Court. He answered me in his normal voice and with every indication of pleasure. I told him I wanted to talk to him as soon as possible, and at once his tone changed.

'My dear, this sounds ferocious! What have I done?'

I said I did not know.

'But what's it all about? All this mystery is so bad for my blood pressure.'

I insisted that I wanted to see him, asked if he were alone there and then. He replied cautiously that he was alone, that to see me for any reason would be delightful, but that he was always terrified of surprises. 'You can't think, Christine, how I detested my birthday when I was little, one surprise after another, all nice ones; but that is really not the point.'

'May I come over now?' I asked him.

'Yes, of course, but you really might prepare me—'

I said I would be with him in a quarter of an hour, and I rang off. I had no intention of preparing him, of giving him a chance to invent a good lie. I went out and got a taxi, hardly knowing what I was about. It seemed to me so appalling that he might, for the sake of a malicious, half-comprehended impulse, have destroyed Lois's peace of mind and ruined Celia's future, that I had no idea but to tax him with it directly. I knew well enough that Lois had not guessed the state of affairs. She had *known* them, and for some time past. I remembered her saying, with an odd, angry smile, 'I hate people deceiving me, even for the best of reasons. It makes me look such a fool. I hate to look a fool.'

Lonely, dying; and someone had made a fool of her; humiliated, she had hated it. It had not been the hearty, rallying nurses who had hurt her, though she had made them her excuse for an outburst. I remembered her again, as she spoke of Celia – 'She's a dear, isn't she, and amusing? But not really clever' – words with a half-retracted sting, words that had not been kindly.

Junius opened the door to me. He was wearing an elaborate dressing-gown over his pyjamas, and at once he fussed at me, chattering at the top of his voice as he drew me into the sitting-room. 'I assure you this is *not* the uniform of the professional seducer. You need have no fear. Gerard may sleep with a quiet mind. But I was thinking of bed when you rang, and I just couldn't get dressed again. You can't possibly object. Do sit down, and what will you drink?' His face was flushed, he was caricaturing himself wildly. I had never been to the flat before and was too upset to notice his surroundings, except that they were far less elaborate than at his seaside house. This was not, I guessed, Junius's posing-place: yet he was posing now, and for all he was worth.

He poured a drink for me, but I did not touch it. I said, 'I want to know why you told Nancy Sherriff that Lois was awful.'

He was silent. He sat down slowly on the sofa, disposed the dressing-gown neatly about him, and leaned back on the cushions with a Tiberian air. He was trying to gain time. But when he spoke the air of posing left him. He looked so ordinary and so angry a man that for a second I felt the sobering shock that takes us when we realise we may have been quite wrong about somebody.

197

'Now, listen, I don't understand this. What's it all about?'

'I want to know why you ran Lois down to Nancy. I thought you were fond of her.'

He looked at me steadily. 'I was.'

'Then do you deny—' I began.

'No, I don't deny it. I was fond of Lois, and then I changed my mind.'

I cried, 'Is that why you told her about Celia?' Pity and rage made me feel drunk. I could see nothing but his face, like a flesh-coloured balloon bobbing on mist.

'I told her about Celia?' He sounded aghast.

I said, 'You must have told her. Nobody else could have done so. She knew!'

Junius said, 'Quite.' His lips were almost closed.

'And she told Eric, and it's because of it that things are so wretched between him and Celia.'

'I knew she'd told Eric.' He was like a ventriloquist without a dummy.

The shock took me again, and this time held me. I knew that I had been wrong, but could not understand how.

Junius spoke again. 'It is because she told Eric that I stopped being fond of her. She told me she was going to: I said it was a bloody thing to do.'

'But how could she have known,' I began, 'if it wasn't you—'

He picked up a book that had been lying on the sofa and shied it violently across the room so that it smashed against the far wall. He was blazing with rage, his face like raw meat, his mouth trembling. 'Good Christ, do you suppose I'd do a —ing thing like that?'

We both stood up. We were confronting each other in a nightmare of suspicion, anger and bewilderment. 'A —ing thing,' he repeated. 'You come here, you bounce in out of the bloody night, and you dare to accuse me of that? Have you gone mad? Has everybody?'

It was one of those moments which seem final, as if there can be no life after them. A curtain should fall, and that should be the end. But words have to be found somehow; and I could not find them.

It was Junius who recovered first. He turned and walked across the room, picked up the fallen book, dusted it, and with the flat of his hand shot it back into a shelf. He gave a dandiacal flick to his hair, his dressing-gown, took a cigarette from a box and after a second's hesitation tossed one to me. He said, 'We shall have to get this cleared up. If you really believed what you've just said, then I suppose nobody could blame you for coming out with it. Quite the brave little girl, some people might say. But I, of course, can't feel so objective.'

I apologised to him. This seemed to satisfy not only his hurt but his vanity; I caught a glimpse of a smile, secret, deep, and to me almost intolerable, though I knew I had deserved it. Having once injured him, I had to resist a desire to add insult to injury.

'I accept that,' he said. 'I can see you've been seriously upset. Even I can make allowances.' The pose returned, faintly. 'But all this business of ladies-making-scenes is rather more than I can bear, on such a hot night, and it would be better if you'd put your feet up and have a drink and tell *all*.'

So I told him what I had learned that night from Aveling, and he listened without comment. 'I knew,' I said, 'that you didn't want him and Celia to marry—'

'Perfectly correct.'

'Why not?'

'My business.' He paused. Then he went on rapidly, 'But I will tell you this. Lois and I were thick enough: she was a broad-minded girl. She worshipped Eric, but she did find him a trifle stuffy sometimes. She had to be so much on her best behaviour. She knew all about me, it amused her; and I used to tell her all the gossip, just to cheer her up. I was devoted to her in my own *so* peculiar way – but devoted I was. Nevertheless, my first loyalty's to him. It always has been.' He told me, smiling sourly, that he realised he wasn't in the first flight as an architect, that Aveling had always kept his head above water. Junius was speaking of himself with honesty; and when he was honest he looked as if he were carefully acting out some scene from a play. It was often the truth that brought out his histrionic quality; when he looked the most sincere, the most open, he was the most likely to be lying. 'So he comes first.' He added cruelly, 'And when I heard what was in her mind I didn't give a damn if she was dying a thousand times over. She didn't even come second; she went down to rock-bottom. As for my remark to little Nancy Sharp-Ears – you mustn't underestimate that girl, whatever you do – that was pure inadvertence. In the circumstances I heartily regret it.'

I asked him if there were nothing he could do to put matters right: I hardly knew what I expected of him.

'No, and if there were I wouldn't do it. He and Celia would be hell together.'

'Is it just Celia?'

'What do you mean?'

'Is it only Celia you don't want him to marry?'

His smile broadened out. 'You really cannot be so unsophisticated as to suppose that, for the *most* discreditable reasons, I prefer him not to marry at all. My interests do not – my dear Christine, it really sounds like blasphemy!– lie in that direction. The trouble with women is that if they understand anything at all they are quite incapable of understanding ordinary friendship. You like men. I don't insult you by supposing that you want to go to bed with every man you meet.'

I said very firmly that I had meant nothing of the kind he had suggested.

'Then, bless me,' Junius said, with an assumption of his Brothers Cheeryble air, 'I really can't think what you can have meant! What complex creatures we all are, aren't we? Sometimes I quite hate us.' He lay comfortably back on the cushions, gazing at the ceiling, where the standard lamp had cast a Persian rose of light.

I said, 'Who did tell Lois?'

'I could guess.'

'Who?'

'You had better work it out for yourself.' He sat upright and spoke earnestly. 'My dear girl, I like you, and I am not going to quarrel with you. For God's sake leave all this pother alone. Lois has done her worst. Eric may get over it: Celia may still get what she wants, though I doubt it. I do my best for her – I take her out, I let her cry on my shoulder. But she doesn't want *you*, not at present. She doesn't want to be with people who are reasonably happy in their own condition.'

I told him that Aveling's need was the reverse: he could forget himself only in the presence of the serene.

'Precisely. Can't you see, even that alone makes them different? That it's a great, yawning, howling gap between them?'

'Junius,' I said, 'who told Lois? You must know.'

'She didn't tell me.' He yawned. 'But I imagine it was almost certainly loving Mummy, don't you? Who else?'

I was appalled.

'Not a direct piece of information, I'm sure; just a little hint dropped in the porches of an ear, perhaps.'

'Why?'

'I don't know. But it seems probable; doesn't it to you?'

He resolutely changed the subject, and for a long while we chatted about things that did not seem real. He was determined to make this seem an ordinary visit, to dispel the hallucinated quality of the air in which we sat. Before I left him I asked him once more to forgive me for what I had thought about him, and this time did so without constraint, though I knew that somewhere, in the dark of the situation that lay between Aveling and Celia, he had been twisting, planning and manœuvring for his own mysterious ends. Whatever he was doing was probably bad enough: but he was innocent of the particular badness with which I had charged him.

He did not reply for a moment: then he said, in a high, complaining voice, 'I tell you, I like you; you won't believe me. It's as simple as that.'

'You were very kind to me once.'

'You never did tell me what those calls cost you. It must have been shocking. But worth it, to get yourself out of such a tizz.'

He beamed at me from the hall door. He had quite recovered his good humour. His neck, in the cleft of the orange dressing-gown, was plump, refulgent, almost maternal, and it was with a delicate gesture of pudicity that he drew the silk across it. 'Now do go home and have a nice night's sleep, and try not to be so *agitato*, because it is most trying to those who love you and ruinous to your looks.' He gave me a little wave of the hand and was gone.

28

Within two days I had a letter.

'Junius says Gerard is away for a bit, so would you like to come here for the week-end? *Please do*. I am stuck at the Moray because Father isn't well, but it keeps both of them out of the way, so it wouldn't be so bad if you came. It has been so long. I have something to tell you.'

She ended, in her round, schoolgirl's fashion, 'Lovingly, Celia.'

As I had told her I would come by train, she met me at the station. I saw her on the edge of the crowd at the barrier, rising up on her toes to try to catch sight of me. Then she waved vigorously, her bracelets jingling. I came to her and she kissed me. 'I've got a car waiting, I wouldn't risk a cab. Trippers are pouring in.'

She urged me through the sifting crowds, her hand upon my arm. I saw that though she was looking thin and drawn, she seemed serene; and she was dressed with even more than her usual care, in a blue silk dress with hat of the same stuff, pale shoes, and in her best jewellery: pearls, ruby ear-rings, a diamond sunburst. 'You'll be robbed for all that, one of these days,' I said.

'I am robbed for it now. People take one look at me and put ten per cent on the bill. But I will not keep things squalidly in a safe. I might as well not have them.'

We drove along the front. There was a soft, still shine on the sea. The sands had caught a bluish light, as if the grains had been raked through with powdered amethyst and aquamarine.

'I think we shall creep first into our little pub,' she said, 'so as not to be fallen upon by family the moment we get in. Not that Father can fall; he has fallen. He is in bed.'

I asked what the matter was. 'Oh, nothing much. Only his blood pressure's rushed up a bit – with miscellaneous rage, I dare say – and he's having to be rested. Which makes him even more furious, so what *does* he gain?' She added without flippancy that her mother was worried, that any illness terrified her. 'She has been assured that he is likely to go on for years and years, but she won't believe it. They don't get on, I don't believe they ever have, but she dreads being left alone.' The light, irritable tone returned. 'I believe if the doctor promised her that in the event of Father's decease he would instantly be replaced, Mummy wouldn't turn a hair.'

She told the driver to turn into the mews and dismissed him there. She flicked ahead of me into the public house, which was empty of customers as yet, and said imperiously, 'Wireless, Doreen. Lots of noise, please.'

'Oh, Miss Baird, aren't you smart tonight! You make my mouth water.'

'Have a drink with me, then,' Celia retorted, 'and give us two large Martinis apiece, because we don't want to keep getting up and down.'

When we were settled she asked me about Gerard, what he was doing, when he would return. 'Eric's been wildly busy,' she said casually. 'He lost one of his best draughtsmen the other week and has been tearing around trying to replace him. Or not perhaps tearing – just somehow covering a great deal of ground with no appearance of motion.'

I laughed. She looked back at me with a calm exhausted smile. 'It is so nice to see you. I always say that, don't I? But it's true. And I've been missing you for so long. My fault, I know. But not really.'

I said I knew it was not her fault, that I had understood; all the same, I had been worried about her and was worried now.

'You needn't be.' She picked the little glassy onion from her drink, swivelled it between her fingers, and dropped it into the ashtray. 'It's all right now: at any rate, it's settled.' She paused. 'There is something you will have to know first. Lois guessed about us and told Eric so. That's what all this misery has been about.'

I could not, of course, betray his confidence. He had told me that I might say what I pleased, if only I could comfort her: but I realised that he must have seen her himself in these past few days. I said nothing.

'I had to think about it, I had to make a decision. I have been very brave. I've written to him, telling him that we must forget everything that has happened and simply be friends again. It is the only way now; and the only hope that he'll come back to me eventually.'

Her calm smile persisted. It was disquieting: yet she really did look at peace with herself.

'Has he answered?'

'There hasn't been time. I knew what I was going to do, but I only sent the letter last night. He's reading it today.' She shivered. Then she swung round upon Doreen, shouting out, 'There's an awful draught coming from somewhere. Do shut that door properly, I'm sure it isn't latched.'

The barmaid shrugged, grinned, came through the counter and made a parade of closing doors and windows. 'Don't blame me if the others complain that it's stewing when they get in.'

'I don't give a damn for the others,' Celia said rudely. She turned back to me. 'It was the *only* thing I could do. It was wise, wasn't it?' she pleaded.

I did not believe it was wise; I believed she had destroyed the last shred of their hopes. Aveling was not a coward, would always shrink from a deceitful solution; yet he was likely, I thought, to persuade himself that in her suggestion their final hope might lie, that in accepting his 'freedom' he was only accepting a therapeutic appearance and not a reality. But I could only say, 'Perhaps it was.'

'I have felt so much better since I sent it. Last night I slept really properly for the first time in months, and when I woke this morning I felt calm and light, as if I could walk without touching the ground.' She hesitated. 'I can't help feeling Lois is appeased. It's silly, I know. But I can't live with guilt, and I have felt guilty enough to die.'

She had always known really, she said, that Lois had not died in ignorance. When Aveling confirmed it she had felt the awful shock of certainty: yet it had passed, and the guilt had remained the old, steady guilt. 'I do not think, though I know it sounds ridiculous in this day and age, that our sins go unpunished. Perhaps Eric and I are paying quite properly for what we did. What do you think?'

I said I could not believe in so frightful a God.

'Not frightful, only fair. Or so I see it.'

She pushed back her empty glass and took up the full one, twisting and turning it so that the spring sun, filtering in a single line of light through one of the back windows, penetrated the icy yellow of the liquid and struck a star. 'I am only an average religious woman,' she said in her odd 'social' voice, ' "believing", I suppose, but not doing anything about it. Mummy would be astonished if I even admitted so much; she regards me as a heathen. Father, of course, *is* a heathen.' She seemed to lose the thread of what she had been saying.

'You mustn't believe in hell,' I said.

'I don't think I do. Perhaps in Gehenna: it sounds worse. "A place of burning refuse" ,' she added. 'I know that from

206

crossword puzzles. I assure you I have felt very like refuse. But now—'

She paused. I prompted her.

'Now I am accepting punishment and feeling better. And hoping, of course, as one does – one is an awful sneak before God – that I shall accept it with such conspicuous bravery that He will give me a prize for doing so.' Drinking up the Martini, she smiled suddenly, affectionately, openly. 'We will have a nice time this week-end. I always like it with you. Tomorrow we'll go out and buy things we can't possibly want.'

She walked back to the Moray with a jaunty step, smiling, her face clear. Mrs. Baird greeted us, gave me an abstracted word, said to Celia, 'Are the sweet shops closed yet? Your father wants some peppermint lumps. I thought you'd be back sooner.'

'I expect they are closed. Couldn't you have gone?'

'I would have, only I kept thinking you'd be back.'

'You could have sent Fryke.'

'Not for such a trifle!'

'Oh, for God's sake, Mummy, what are hall porters for? And we tip him grossly, you know we do.'

'I shouldn't have cared to ask a thing like that,' Mrs. Baird said, with a shut and stubborn air.

I said I would go up to the main road; I should perhaps be in time.

Celia said furiously, 'You shall not go traipsing off after anything so ridiculous! Father can have them tomorrow.'

'But he wants them *now*. He's been carrying on and on.'

I noticed that they had fallen into the habit of conducting themselves at the Moray as in a private house, not lowering their voices, not caring who heard them. It was lucky that, on this occasion, they were so noisy, for the scene was brought to an end by Fryke himself, who sidled forward whispering that there might be a few sweets in the bar, and that he would go and see if there were any peppermint lumps.

'How very nice of you, and how very enterprising!' Celia cried, showering her appreciation upon him. As he went off she said, 'It is really amazing; one can live in a place like this for years and not know they keep a *cache* of sweets.'

Fryke returned triumphant, and was excessively tipped.

'Father says he would like to see Christine before dinner. He says he feels like visitors.'

So I went up with them to Baird's cell, where he lay rigidly on his back like a stone crusader and greeted me without a smile. 'Not much fun lying here for hours, nothing to do, nothing to read.'

'I brought you two thrillers this morning!' Celia protested.

'And they were both rotten. I looked at the end.'

'Anyway, Daddy, here are your sweets,' Mrs. Baird said, holding them out to him.

'Are they Fullers'? I don't want them if they're not.'

'You're lucky to have any sweets at all at this time of night,' Celia said, exasperated, 'and you must make do with them.'

'They *are* Fullers',' Baird announced, peering into the bag. He stripped two of paper and put them simultaneously into his mouth. His temper sweetened, he said he was glad to see me. 'And mind you, now you're here, get Millie out with you. It does her no good to hang around me, and does me no good either.'

'Now, Arthur,' Mrs. Baird said, in a tone of false raillery, 'if you talk like that Christine will think you're very ungrateful.'

'I don't give gratitude for what I don't want, nobody does. I'd far rather know you were getting a bit of amusement.'

'But I worry about you—'

'And I hate to lie here watching you worrying. That fat quack says there's nothing much wrong with me, and for once he isn't wrong. You women go to a show tomorrow; I'll be all right.'

I saw Celia make a movement of impatience. She had not wanted, any more than I, the constant presence of her mother this week-end. Mrs. Baird, however, was firm. 'I shall go out if I see fit, Arthur, and if I don't I shan't.'

She did come out with us next morning for a shopping expedition, though she left us alone afterwards. On these forays through the richer stores Celia and her mother seemed more at one than at any other time. Their noses were sharpened; they looked alike. They were in a mute conspiracy to have the best they could find, and to pay, if rather too much for it, not too ridiculously much. In the textile department their fingers played like minnows in rivers of silk and satin, paddling expertly, testing for flawlessness, for durability. They made me think of merchants acting for Marco Polo, with the full responsibility for the maximum value and glory upon their shoulders. When they were tired they drank coffee and ate cream cakes, while they unpacked their parcels and studied each purchase afresh.

Before we set out Celia had murmured to me, 'He hasn't written yet. I wish he would, but I'm dreading it.' Yet, all that morning, she held her spirits high, and Mrs. Baird kept stealing at her looks of relief and of content.

That evening we went dancing with Webster and Raby. When the band played *God Save the Queen* Celia said she didn't feel in the least like bed and that she would take us all on somewhere else. Raby brightened and looked complacent; but the offer was hard on Webster, who had seemed very tired for the past half-hour and was obviously longing to get back to his wife. He stood there irresolute, as the musicians packed up their instruments and filed away, as the lights began to go out, as the last waiter impatiently drummed his fingers on the wall. Celia was an excellent customer, and probably tipped him better than anybody else: he did not wish to offend her, nor did he wish to offend the management by refusing her invitation: nevertheless, desire for home and sleep tore at him. I suggested that perhaps he had a long day ahead of him tomorrow. 'It will do him good to have a night out once in a while,' she said tightly, smiling at him like a good-natured empress, whose patience it is, however, unwise to try beyond a certain limit.

'Well, Miss Baird,' he began, cockney breaking through, 'you really are the kindest of the kind, as I'm always telling people, but I'd have to let my wife know, and if I phoned her now I might get her out of bed—'

'And would that be all the world? Just for once?'

He looked unhappy.

'Celia,' I said, 'I have been dancing the most with Mr. Webster this evening, and I've made him very tired because, as you know, I am not much good. If you had been dancing with him he'd be feeling fresher. I think Mr. Raby could bear to escort us both.'

She turned to me, ignoring Webster as if he didn't exist. '*You* want him to go home? Is that what you want?'

I knew that one of her wild moods was coming upon her: I did not want to make her angry. If I had said something polite to Webster, such as 'It is a matter of what Mr. Webster wants', it would have meant more miserable argument for him. So I said, 'Yes, I do.'

'All right,' said Celia, abruptly swinging back to him, 'you can go. It's all right.'

He thanked her and backed away with extraordinary rapidity, in case she might take it into her head to recall him.

'So the honour is all mine,' said Raby. He rubbed his hands. 'Well, ladies, lead on.'

Celia said, 'Don't let Mr. Webster think I am cross tomorrow. He was perfectly right not to come. Sometimes I behave in a very spoiled way, and I ought to be refused things.'

'Oh, Miss Baird,' Raby marvelled, 'no one could ever call *you* spoiled!'

She took us to a night-club to which Junius had introduced her, a smart, small, basket-hung house in one of the more sordid quarters of the town. As in all such places, there was nothing to do but drink or to dance standing still. 'We shan't dance,' Celia said. 'We're all tired of that, and Mr. Raby doesn't want a busman's holiday. We shall have champagne, because I'm starting a new life.'

'What,' said Raby, 'do we have to congratulate you—?'

'Oh, I'm not getting married. No, I am starting a life of not being worried. Isn't that something to celebrate?'

He looked puzzled. 'Oh, I should think so. I should think so indeed.' He looked covertly about him. There were only a few women there; it was a club for well-to-do homosexuals, a nice, bright, shady place, with nothing unseemly going on. I saw a well-known actor with a conspicuously unknown companion; a racing driver, a male photographer's model, a journalist who lived in the same London street as myself.

'Very much something to celebrate,' said Celia.

She kept us there, making Raby drunk. To please him she invited two strangers to our table, two young men who seemed to despise him and were much more taken with Celia. Time went by: my head was beginning to ache. She was in good form, sardonic and little-girlish by turns: she made appointments with the young men for an evening in London.

At last I said, 'I'm rather tired, and it's twenty to four.'

She stared at me as if she had awakened from a dream. 'Oh, so it is! How selfish I am. You should have told me. And poor Mr. Raby is almost asleep.'

'No I'm not,' he protested, his eyes swimming, 'I'm as fresh as a daisy.'

She rose, paid the enormous bill and helped Raby to his feet. She ordered the waiter to find us a taxi or call one of the car services. 'I shall take everyone home who wants to go.'

The new guests declined; they were inexhaustible, they were going on somewhere else. They thanked her casually for her hospitality, threw scornful glances at Raby, and reluctantly helped to haul him into the car when it arrived.

'Well,' she said, as we drove through the dark town and on to the sea-front, where the first greyness of light seemed to be blooming upwards, as from an arc lamp beneath the water, 'it was nice, I think. And all very right. I feel so composed that it is like heaven. I can't hear from him tomorrow, of course, because it's Sunday. So that will be peaceful too.'

We drove Raby to his home ten miles away. He had recovered sufficiently to stand alone and to produce his own door-key. He seemed to have enjoyed himself inordinately. 'It was a real treat, Miss Baird, a real treat.'

By the time we came back to the Moray the whole of the sky was filled with a strange and steamy dawn. Gulls were swinging over the olivine sea. Celia stood for a moment on the pavement after the car had gone. She said, 'Thank you. You are very good to me. And now we shall both sleep.'

29

On Sunday morning Dr. Baird, feeling jovial, demanded that we should all play rummy with him on the counterpane. His wife was not pleased: she disliked cards. I think she felt they were wrong for that hour and that day. But Celia seemed to be enjoying herself. She won hand after hand, shouted him down when he displayed bad sportsmanship. No one would have thought she had slept for three hours at the most. I was so tired I could hardly keep awake; the doctor was rough with me. 'If you can't pay attention to what you're doing, Mrs. Hall, you'd better not play.'

'And if you can't be polite to my friends, Father,' said Celia, with no apparent diminution of good humour, 'I shall take her away and we shall play skee-ball on the pier till lunch-time. We should both prefer it.'

He said that was rubbish: it was a man's game, not a game for two young women with no more sense than to stay up all night. His eyes glinted triumphantly. 'You see, I know. I heard you come in. And presumably you both came in at the same time.'

Celia retorted that though she loved to be called a young woman, she was in fact old enough to keep what hours she chose.

'That's what you think,' said Baird, with schoolboy rudeness, and I thought I had glimpsed the charm that Mark so strangely found in him.

'That is what I think,' said Celia calmly. She laid down her cards. 'And *out!*'

'It's a queer thing that when *you* deal *you* win.'

'And a queerer one that a remark like that, at another time, in another place, and to another person, might have got you shot in a duel.'

He chuckled. 'Or got *you* kicked out of decent society.'

'I will not stand much more,' said Celia, without heat.

'Arthur, she won't,' said his wife.

'Oh, bosh. Your deal, Millie, and don't woolgather.'

I was aware that Mrs. Baird was eager to get me alone, and I did my best to avoid her: but when Celia went upstairs after lunch she held me back.

'Christine, I must know. What is happening?'

I did not pretend not to understand. 'Nothing that changes anything,' I said.

'But she is so much more like my girl! She must be happier. Is she getting over him?'

I said I could not talk to her of these things, that I had no right to.

'She's all I've got.'

'But you don't want her to be happy through Eric?'

'Any way, any way,' she said feverishly, and hurried away from me. She had spoken as if she meant it.

Celia and I sat on the beach in the afternoon and talked of things that were nowhere near the heart. The sun was hot. We sheltered under the bright-green groin, lustrous in its combed and silken weed. Mussels and barnacles encrusted it with jet and agate. Celia tried to pick them off and broke a fingernail. The sand was warm, dark as Demerara sugar. She lay on her back, hands behind her head, looking up at the shot silk of the sky. She had the restfulness of one with all the time in the world before her, time to play with, to sort, to rearrange, to twist into new shapes. 'Poor Father, he thinks he's miserable because he has to lie in bed out of the sun. If he were up, it is unthinkable that he would go near it, except to dash into

214

his horrible shelter and back. It smells of sickrooms, and there are always damp patches under the seats. Also, there are men who come there to sit and mutter. He was aggrieved because there were no glass shelters in Italy. In Venice he sat *inside* Florian's all day.'

I suggested that she and her mother might have sat inside shops.

'Oh yes, and churches. I hated it all. It is not a place to be with one's parents. We always went to bed early. I tried to be asleep before midnight struck.'

She was not speaking unhappily, but in a kind of relief to be home again. I guessed that in Venice the thought of Aveling had been near enough for agony.

'Which reminds me, I bought you a necklace from Berengo-Gardin. Remind me to give it you.'

I thanked her, asked what else she had bought. 'An ashtray for Junius from Murano, but now I think it is hideous. He gave it a terrible look, a look askance. Have you ever seen Junius look askance?'

A little boy ran by; he must have been four or five. Celia put out her hand and caught him by the ankle, smiling at him before he could cry. 'Hullo, darling.'

'I caught a crab.'

'Have you? Show me.'

He emptied his pail into her lap, wet sand, crab and all. She did not seem to mind. 'It is a wonderful crab. Has it got a name?'

He sat down beside her and chatted until he grew suddenly tired, or perhaps apprehensive of a stranger.

'All right, run away. See if you can catch a lobster. But you mustn't expect them to be pink now, you know. That comes later.'

She smiled at me. 'He was a pretty little boy, wasn't he?' I tried to brush the sand from her dress. 'Don't bother, it will dry out.'

She asked me if I would like to hear some music that evening. There was a Sunday concert at the Winter Gardens. They were playing the second and sixth Brandenburgs. I was surprised that she should care for music, for it was something she had never mentioned to me. She told me she did care for it, but sporadically: sometimes as a passion, sometimes not at all. 'I think it's because no one around me has ever cared, and I'm miserable at concerts alone. Father is tone-deaf, Mummy likes Palm Court orchestras.' Aveling, she said, speaking of him easily, loved music, but for her his taste was too esoteric. 'Not J. S. Bach, always C.P.E., or J.C. And Monteverdi. You know – or perhaps you don't. I don't. It's all very Eric, and the part I am never at home with.'

She was speaking of him in the present.

We went to the concert, and she sat there quite unmoving, her hands folded. At the end she said, as we walked home through the warm night, 'It is just like heaven, isn't it? A formal one, with a glassy sea, and nothing wrong at all.'

The letter came at breakfast on Monday morning. She did not open it then, but put it away in her bag and afterwards went up to her room. Later, she telephoned a message to Fryke that she would like me to go to her.

I found her sitting by the open window, the letter in her lap. 'I thought I'd tell you; I've already told you so much. He says he won't accept it, of course, my idea that we should just forget everything, but he doesn't suggest anything better. He wants things to go on as they are going. But of course he will do as I propose in the end. Here.' She selected a page and gave it to me. 'I think I should like you to read this.'

It began in the middle of a sentence. He had a clear formal calligraphy, Italianate, but so individual that one was not likely to have mistaken it for another's. He used a fine pen, and the letters, though I think he wrote rapidly, were made with a draughtsman's precision. It was both masculine and fastidious. I should not have guessed, from the signature I had read in the visitors' book, the beauty of his writing close upon a page.

'. . . it is often better not to try to bring things to any kind of conclusion. If I really believed I should make you happier by doing as you asked, then, my dear, I should do it; but I can only judge you by myself, and I can't conceive in myself such strength as you are trying to force upon us both. My admiration for you has never been greater, nor my wretchedness that it should have fallen to me to make you so unhappy. I can't accept ordinary friendship from you – or, rather, the pretence that there has been nothing else. It would be a kind of miserable charade. On the other hand, I can offer you nothing else *now*. You must know that I think of nobody but you, of little else but you. Let us try to live as we have been living, but not, dear Celia, to *act* at each other: for could it be more than that? Not for me, I don't think. Sometimes we should have to talk, however much it hurt us. We can't take a pledge not to do that. So let us wait a little longer. I can't accept, in its easier aspect, the escape you are offering me, because, after all, that is what it—'

The sheet she had given me came to an end. She took it back, slipping it neatly between the others. 'It is a brave letter, isn't it?'

'I think it is,' I said. He was the rare drowning man who, before seizing the rope, would at least have a flash of doubt whether he had the greatest claim to it. But he would have to clutch it in the end.

She turned to me, and her eyes were full of tears. 'It is very, *very* brave.' The window blind flapped in the light wind from the sea as if some enormous sun-shot bird, like an albatross, had flown in. Borne in on it was the noise of children, singing and shouting for joy as they skipped the incoming waves. It

217

was a halcyon day. 'But I shan't change my mind. I shall set him absolutely free.'

Her voice was steady, and she herself was steady in her movements and in her eyes as she came down to the station to see me off.

I did not want to leave her. For the first time I really loved her and felt near to her. 'You're a very strong woman,' I said, just at the last, 'but don't drive yourself too far.'

'Aren't you a very strong woman too?' She smiled. 'It's a dreadful fate to be one. In the end we get left quite alone, you know, and nobody bothers to find out how we are getting on. They're so sure we're all right. If I could get born again I would pretend to be very weak, I'd never give myself away.'

It occurred to me, as the train drew out beyond the downs, that she was of the company of those who can make and keep resolutions which must change a whole life; a member of that most incomprehensible of companies, in which are the martyrs and the saints. For most of us can conceive the noble idea, suggest it to ourselves, even go so far as to begin to put it into practice: but the secret planner of the mind knots the invisible safeguards, weaves the safety-net beneath us. We are in no danger of falling too far. We do not quite speak the irrevocable word: we only suggest that we are about to speak it. We envy the saints and martyrs, sometimes with passion: we long to match them. At moments we believe that there is, between them and ourselves, only a filament thin as the spider's, and that if we can make the one supreme effort of will we shall send it torn and floating into the air. But it is in the difference between the desire and the performance that the mystery lies, the mystery we shall never solve. The vast majority of us are expert recanters; we can do it with infinite grace and the minimum of blameworthiness when the time is ripe. During the whole period in which we are planning our gesture of complete self-abnegation, of total change, the daemon inside us keeps up its perpetual murmur, 'Stop! You're not quite committed'; when the time comes, we ourselves say, 'Stop!' – in the human voice. It is possible that it is the essence of the non-human which makes the saints what they are, and that we, not being endowed with it, can no more understand them than we can really understand the martyr or the murderer. We do, however, know that saints exist; not only for the service of God or even for the service of humanity but also, sometimes, for the service of one other single beloved human being. I was moved by an admiration for Celia that was near to reverence. I could not have done, for the life of me, what she was doing: for such a love I would have fought in the open or by any trickery – I could never have let go. And I began to think that if there were any justice or, come to that, any admiration in Heaven, she might yet find her happiness given back to her, like an unexpected and munificent bonus.

For I was incapable then, as I am today, as I shall always be, of the pessimism of the martyrs and of the saints. I still hoped for the galloping horse, the shout from the edge of the crowd, the white paper flashing like lightning in the air, the reprieve.

30

Mark said, 'I say, there's Celia and Mr. Aveling.' We were in Bond Street, on the top of a bus. Mark, home for the summer holidays, was full of a bewildered triumph; he had got seven credits in his Ordinary certificate, a feat he appeared unable to understand. We were too busy to take him away for some time to come, but he was wandering about in London with a calm, surprised air, as if finding life even more agreeable than he had imagined it. He was just sixteen.

'Oh, damn. I wish we weren't up here. I'd like to see them. We never seem to see Celia nowadays.'

They were standing looking into a picture-dealer's window and laughing about something. I was glad we were on the bus: I had heard nothing from Celia since the week-end at the Moray, and Junius, who had taken to calling upon Gerard and me occasionally, had not spoken of her affairs. I felt much in the dark: it would have been embarrassing for me to come upon Celia suddenly.

The traffic-lights changed and we stopped. Mark jumped up. 'I'll follow you later on. I just want to talk to her.' Before I could stop him he had bolted down the stairs. I saw him bounce across the pavement and call out to them. They turned, startled, smiled and shook hands with him. The bus went on.

He was not back till past six o'clock. When he did come in I saw that he was looking perturbed. He smiled at me briefly, said, 'Celia sends her love', and went upstairs. I knew that it was no good asking questions. However, half an hour later he came downstairs and asked if he might have half a glass of sherry. He sat down with it, lit a cigarette (which he did not enjoy) and took up the *Times*. I knew by these signs that he was likely to unburden himself. Smoking and the *Times* were, for him, symbols of the state of being grown-up: and he fortified himself with both on the rare occasions upon which he felt impelled to discuss adult matters.

'Celia took me to tea at her place,' he said suddenly, not raising his eyes from the paper. 'Mr. Aveling was just going off, anyway. Celia thought I'd like to see her flat.'

I made a casual remark.

'I say,' he said, 'she's changed a bit. I thought it was queer.'

'How?'

'Oh – sort of all light and bright and nervy, not like herself.'

I asked if she had seemed to be unhappy.

He frowned. He folded the *Times* carefully, to form a firm base for the crossword puzzle, took out one of his several pencils and balanced it over the paper. He wrote in a word. 'No,' he said, 'it wasn't exactly that. She was – you know – jaunty. She was awfully nice. But odd.' He pencilled in another word. The sports jacket, too short in the sleeves, rode up his fore-arms. His hands looked very large, as if they had grown out of proportion, and were grimy. I thought of Celia, of how she would have liked a child.

Then he said, with an angry air, 'I suppose we haven't been seeing her because something's up. Of course, it's no business of mine.'

I told him as much as I could of Aveling and Celia: how they had been in love, how things had gone badly for them since Lois's death, how Celia had made up her mind to let him go.

'Oh,' said Mark, flushing. 'Bad luck on her. They ought to get married, really.' He gave me a relieved and open smile. He added that when one heard about being in love and read books about it there really seemed something to be said for the celibacy of the clergy. (He brought this phrase out in triumph.)

I said it was not so sad for everybody, and urged him to cheer up.

'I think I'll be a bachelor don,' Mark said, laying down the *Times* with an air of relief – 'that is, if I'm good enough.' He rose. 'Well, thanks.' He was thanking me for the confidences I had offered him. 'I'll go and wash; I've been oiling my bike.'

Within ten minutes Celia herself telephoned me. 'I saw your Mark this afternoon, I took him to tea.' She was sorry, she said, that she had kept away for so long, but she had been up to her neck in the business: she had never realised what it was like to deal with an expanding concern – 'however miserable an affair it is,' she said in a high, prattling voice, 'small beer to real businesses like Gerard's.' Her father, she told me, was well again. Her mother was in a state of maddening irritability since she had decided to stop smoking. 'She says she must, because it's making her short-winded; so absurd, anyone would think she was training for Everest.'

She would not let me bring the conversation to an end; yet she was embarrassed, she had really nothing to say. I was less distressed because she was holding me off than because it was plainly painful to her to do so. She would far rather have talked freely, it was in her nature to talk. But, though she sounded nervous, she did not sound unhappy. I believed she was still upon the plain of acceptance to which she had so painfully dragged herself.

There was a moment in which she fell silent and I could think of nothing to say. I could hear her breathing. She said at last, 'Are you there? Oh, good. I thought they'd cut us off. Darling, I think Eric is all right. I mean, that what I did was wise. It has worked well.'

I said I was glad.

'In a way it's like beginning all over again, from the beginning. Or I hope we'll begin, anyhow. I do want to see you, but just now I daren't.'

She reminded me how I had once told her that 'talking' usually did more harm than good; if we met, she believed she could not stop herself talking about the whole thing again. 'Which wouldn't be sense, because I am doing very well. Oh, I know what I'd forgotten! Raby is going to be married – *Raby*, dear, Mr. Raby whom we dance with. It is most strange. I think it is to please his mother.'

Some days later, on the almost identical spot where I had seen Celia and Aveling looking into the dealer's window, I was hailed by Nancy Sherriff, in the company of an elderly man with a handsome violet-veined nose and sightless-looking blue eyes, whom she introduced as her father. She asked me to come back to their flat for a drink: they had, she said, just moved into three rooms only fit for pigs just behind Bruton Street. I was simple enough to take this for melopoeia, found it was not so. They occupied the top floor of a building in a mews, a little dark, damp flat with flaking ceiling and walls upon which the paint had shrivelled and curled, showing pink distemper beneath. The furniture was fine; but dusty and in poor repair.

'Not *Buckingham Palace*,' Wyndham Sherriff said, touching his finger to the black-speckled window sill, 'but a roof over one's head.' He gave me a pale smile. The term of reference was not, I thought, one he would have used himself, but one he would have expected me to use, should I have wished to evoke an image of splendour.

'The Palace is not at all grand in patches, dear,' Nancy said to him soothingly; her eyes sparkled. 'And my impression is that some of our rugs are better. You must learn to take things as they come.'

She was just back from Geneva, she said, and was to work in London again. She had quite a good job as secretary to a charity: it wouldn't last long, but it would be fine while it lasted. In that shabby flat she had, I thought, the radiance which may make a girl seem more than human, ichor in her veins and a G. F. Watts-like nimbus about her head. I felt a cramp of envy because she was so fresh and her leaves were still so green.

She explained that the move had been made only yesterday. 'That is why we're so filthy. It is not at all in my nature to be filthy, but you must take my word for that. I'm going to repaint the whole place, and Junius will help, but he mustn't hang up any little baskets with ivy.'

I asked if I could help in any way.

'You can come and help me chip ice out of the fridge,' she said at once, and took me into the tiny kitchen. She closed the door behind us. 'Father will now lie on the sofa for fifteen minutes and grizzle inwardly because I can't make him quite as comfortable as he would like to be. We will wait till he's over it.'

She went on talking to me as she prepared tray and glasses. Her uncle Hedley was very pleased about the way the work at Crowborough was going; one would hardly know the place, and yet it was the same: which was genius, wasn't it? She hoped to see it herself soon.

She had a calm and easy way of talking, different from Celia's surprising nervous flow; no one could be afraid of her, as it would be possible to be afraid of Celia. She was all friendliness. She said, carefully measuring gin into a cocktail shaker, 'I thought Eric and Celia would get married.'

It was a jolt: I had not expected such directness, such an assault.

I did not answer. She put down the shaker and looked at me. 'Have I said something wrong? I just thought it was so.'

'Everyone thought so,' I answered, 'but it may not happen.'

'I didn't think they *lived* together,' Nancy said naïvely. 'I just thought there was something. Junius said it was all over.'

I advised her not to believe everything Junius said.

She gave a splutter of laughter. 'I don't. I try to sort it all out and give it a plus or minus. Come on, we're thirsty.'

Wyndham Sherriff rose from the sofa, and dust rose with him.

'I know your husband,' he said to me, 'I meet him at the club.' Somehow he managed to convey the condescension of a great actor who admits his acquaintance with the stage-door-keeper when speaking to one to whom the door-keeper is important.

We all sat down. 'We should put down newspapers,' he said. 'One can't keep one's clothes clean.'

'It isn't so bad as all that,' Nancy replied equably, 'or I should have put them down for my own clothes. If you'll only stay at the club till I've cleared up, you won't know us.'

Hearing that I was a writer, he asked me if I knew a certain woman journalist: and on hearing I did not, said, 'Good.' He seemed satisfied.

'She is a sort of cousin,' Nancy told me earnestly, 'but she is common.'

A long-held idea of mine, that 'common' was a word never used by aristocratic persons, was exploded. I was to learn later that it had for Nancy an inexplicable connotation, and that she knew no word of a more pejorative nature. Also, nobody was safe from it, neither by birth nor by worldly reputation.

'She has,' she elaborated, 'common feet.'

Apprehensive, I asked her what this implied.

'Oh' – she was vague – 'the general shape. And, of course, if you have bows on them.' She turned to her father. 'It is true, dear, isn't it? She has?'

'Entirely,' he replied, fixing the invisible offender with a look of scornful sadness, such as Bonner, in one of his milder moments, might have turned upon a Marian martyr. 'All of them have.' He paused, and spoke to her as though I was not there, as though he were returning to a conversation itself faintly tiresome. 'Aveling is a very distant connection of your mother's family, or so I believe. But they did not do well.'

'The Dorset ones?'

'No, the Heatons.'

'Oh, them.'

'But it may,' he added, 'not be true.' A heavy silence hung on him like mourning crêpe. I thought how much I should enjoy hearing him in conversation with Dr. Baird. It struck me that they had one thing in common, which was not caring a damn. Sherriff did not because he was an aristocrat. Baird did not because he was Baird. Both, in their diverse ways, were singularly free men.

Nancy looked at the clock. 'If you are dining at the club you ought to go.'

'I doubt if I shall. And I shall sleep here.'

'No, dear, you won't. Nothing's ready.'

He began, in his sleepy manner, to reproach her. She had been away from him so long: had he no right to enjoy a home of his own, scruffy though it might be? It was surely little enough to ask, that she should get a bed decently made up.

She dealt with him affectionately; but she was entirely adamant. She was used, she implied, to his nonsense; senti-mentality had no effect upon her. She had got him as far as the door when a thought appeared to strike him. 'But why should I dine as early as this? I'm not hungry.'

'Well,' she said, 'I thought you would prefer to be among men.'

'It would be pardonable if you preferred to have your friend to yourself.' He was stiff with affront: his pupils, minuscule in the glacial expanse of iris, seemed to disappear altogether. He was obviously used to quarrelling with his daughter where and when he chose, without the slightest regard for bystanders.

'Yes, dear,' said Nancy, 'I honestly think it would, when you behave like this.'

He glared at her; then quite suddenly left the room, without saying good-night to me. She called to him down the stairs, 'You've forgotten your key.'

I heard him grumbling below.

'All right, then, I'll leave it in the letter-box. But please *don't* come in tonight.'

She returned to me, smiling. 'He is so nice,' she said, 'but a trial.'

When he had gone she lay comfortably back in a chair and said, with great friendliness, 'This is pleasant.'

I agreed.

'You ought to come down to Crowborough soon. Eric would like it.'

I asked if she had seen him recently.

'No, but I rang the old thing up on Uncle Hedley's account. He sounds most regal on the telephone. You know, I believe I could put a lot of work in his way if people like what he's done at Crowborough.' She spoke with an assurance natural to her. She had been born into a circle of people accustomed to 'putting things in the way' of others. I wondered how long it would be before the Sherriffs of the world lost their confidence in their powers of bestowal, even when the illusion had far outworn the reality. Nancy, unselfconscious as she was, had spoken like a lady with benefices to her hand and a large assortment of aspiring clergymen awaiting her decision. Her eyes lit up. 'Junius thinks we might interest no end of big shots who still have a lot of surplus capital. I'm going down to—' (she mentioned one of the great country houses) 'this week-end, and I'll try to fly a few kites. In any case they daren't have more than twenty people together on the first floor in case the ceiling falls through, so it does look as though Eric might come in useful, doesn't it?'

I suggested that her friends might more plausibly employ a builder and contractor.

'Oh, well,' said Nancy, 'I shouldn't really know the distinction. They would have to sort that out for themselves.'

I retailed the gist of this conversation to Junius next time he came to see me; we were easy together these days, as if there had never been the slightest emotional tension between us. He did not wear his more fancy clothes at our house, and I began to believe that perhaps he was settling down. He had not spoken of Celia at all, and nor had I: I fancied he knew all there was to be known. He laughed at Nancy's plan for improving Aveling's lot, but not so much as I had thought he would. 'Well, there might be something in it.' He seemed to ponder. 'People like that do know people. I tell Eric he should cultivate our Nancy – why not? Others do. It would be hard to see her marrying a marquis before she'd done her little best for such *polloi* as ourselves. Eh? Don't you think so?'

I said, 'Would Celia like it?'

'Celia?' He might never have heard the name. 'One has to look out for oneself, one can't allow for all these little *nuances* all the time.' His full lips pursed over the word as though he were tasting syrup. He gave me his most benevolent beam, which conveyed finality and a slap on the shoulder. 'Besides, that's old history, alas. Whatever one may feel about it, it is as dead as the dodo.'

31

During the holidays I was disquieted by Celia's interest in Mark. Me she would not see; but several times she telephoned, suggesting that he might like to go with her to Hampton Court, to Greenwich, to the Zoo. 'And don't let him sneer at the Zoo,' she said to me, 'because it is really not for children at all. Mark is just getting old enough to appreciate it.' He was glad to go with her, was naturally fascinated by the chauffeur-driven cars she hired for these occasions: and I gathered that she gave him enormous meals. Yet on his return he was always quiet, and I could get little out of him. Oh, she was quite ordinary, nothing out of the way: a bit on the talkative side, but very nice. I also gathered that he had managed to refuse several gifts of pocket-money almost on Dr. Baird's scale.

I wrote to thank her for her kindness to him. She wrote in reply, 'It isn't anything at all. He is very polite and good company. I like to do it.'

I felt that beneath this kindness she was working out a fantasy. She had nothing: but on these special days she had Mark, he was hers. I was not in the least afraid that she would say anything which might upset him; she was too strong for that, too controlled. What I did fear was that he might sense in her behaviour something inexplicable, and be troubled by it. I was sure that in fact he was troubled. When at last we went to France for the last fortnight of his holidays, he said, 'Oh well, no more trips with good old Celia—' and I thought that, though he did not understand his own feelings, he was glad of it.

I did not see Celia and Aveling again until the winter, when Hedley Sherriff gave a somewhat parsimonious little party to mark the completion of Aveling's work at Crowborough. We were gathered there on a bitter, bracing day. The park shone beneath a thin sprinkling of snow, which had taken a trace of blueness from the cobalt sky. Junius, fatly boyish, skimmed stones across the brittle surface of the pond. Only a few of us, besides Aveling and Junius, had been invited: Celia, Gerard and myself, Nancy and her father, a tall woman whose name I did not catch, who shuddered in furs and complained to Wyndham Sherriff of the idiotic life of the country, and an etiolated young baronet, before whom Junius found it necessary to seem excessively carefree, unconcerned and sought-for.

Nancy led us on the tour. She had arranged it with an impresario's skill, so that the greatest triumph should come at the end. Aveling seemed content to let her do so, to offer information only when asked for it. He looked at her in smiling silence, pleased to be shown off, but pleased with detachment, as he would have been if a child were parading him. Celia walked on his other side, her hands deep in the pockets of a tweed coat rather too striking in cut, a coat for winter days displayed in a dressmaker's summer show. She was walking with a stride too long for her height, and too jaunty. Yet she seemed cheerful, teasing Nancy's youthfulness with flattery, behaving towards Aveling as if he were an old and treasured friend, but no more than that. He, for his part, treated her with affectionate courtesy, turning to her sometimes to make some old, obscure joke that was their own. He did not look at her with love but, I thought, with a gratitude almost as warm. I believed that he had begun to consider himself a free man.

I was charmed with the transformation he had made in Hedley Sherriff's estate. He had arranged to thin the tunnel of trees along the driveway. They were still heavy; but the light came through them in harlequin flakes, making the gravelled way enticing; one no longer feared that a hound of the Baskervilles might come bounding from the far end. The perimetal houses had been restored very simply, refreshed with new light, and discreetly turned into flats; there would now be accommodation for over fifty people. But the surprise was the big house: and as we approached we were all silent.

Nancy was right: it was different, and yet it was the same. It matched the intention of the original builders before the owner had laid upon it his own ferocious fancies. The conservatory with its jujube glass had gone: so had the colonnade of yellow stone. To the right and left of the door the heavy sash-windows had been replaced; the ugly moulding about the door itself had been stripped away to expose a fine architrave. There was no need to go into this house to know that it would be light; yet it preserved, even now, the effect of solid business-man's grandeur which Sherriff's grandfather had taken so much pride in.

The baronet said, in his simple, half-awake fashion, 'I can't see what has been done, but I do know it's splendid.'

'Oh, come, Stephen,' Aveling said. 'You've been round the place twice before. You're not blind.'

'He was dreadful at those party games about remembering objects on a tray,' Nancy put in. 'He really wouldn't know.'

'Well, there was some nasty stained glass.'

'Bravo,' said Aveling. 'That's a beginning.'

We all went into the house.

In the drawing-room, still thinly barred by the last rays of the sun, a fire was burning. The yellow light from two handsome brass oil-lamps picked out from the velveting of the walls a tracery of ivy leaves and threw their steady shadows upon the moulded ceiling; oil-light and sunlight flowed together, changeable, dark and pale. It was a splendid room.

Hedley Sherriff offered us British sherry and cake.

'Seed-cake,' I heard Aveling mutter to Nancy, 'caraway seeds. This is the final touch of artistry. I bow to your uncle.'

'Come and look at this,' Celia said to me. She drew me to the end of the room, where she stared as if with critical absorption at a late portrait by Lawrence of a thick-set woman in watered silk, whose mouth was grim. She added, without a change of tone, 'I thought that man Stephen was Nancy's friend.'

I replied that he was, so far as I knew.

'But Eric seems to know him quite well.'

I believed I had guessed the thought which had occurred to her. Unless Aveling had known the young man previously, he must have become intimate with him through Nancy: which might mean that Aveling had been seeing Nancy often.

Most of us are brilliant in forming suspicions vicariously for friends whom we love and who are suffering. I could form them so readily on Celia's behalf that I felt a thrill of supernatural fear lest I should somehow transfer them from my mind to her own. And, indeed, I was by no means sure that such transference was impossible. I myself, when in love and afraid, used to avoid a certain friend not through fear of what he might say but of the thoughts that might form behind his eyes: for if he did have a thought likely to torment me I knew I should at once see it written out as plainly on his forehead as if inscribed with pen and ink. It was for some such reason that Celia had hidden herself from me: she was afraid I should see a danger before it occurred to her and, without the least will to do so, flash her the warning.

'What a bloody old woman,' she said of the portrait. 'Such a brute to wear lappets of lace.'

The Sherriffs and the two others went back to London.

Gerard and I drove with Aveling and Celia to the Moray for dinner before going home ourselves.

Baird and his wife were pleased to see us, though Baird expressed his pleasure in characteristic fashion. 'Well, it makes a change to see a fresh face. Better than talking to oneself.' He was looking much better, was even a trifle less thin; his voice was louder even than before. Millie Baird, I thought, was in brighter spirits, and her colour was high. She had just had a permanent wave; her dust-coloured hair seemed to have been lifted very slightly from her scalp, so that one imagined a little space of air between it and a bald expanse. It was stiff and light: it might blow away. She refused a cigarette. 'No, no, don't tempt me. I'm being a brave girl.'

'Tomfoolery,' said Baird. 'May as well enjoy what pleasures one can.'

'It's not, Arthur. It was beginning to affect me. I couldn't run up and downstairs as I did.'

'Who wants to go tearing around the place at your time of life?' He turned to Aveling. 'Well, did they all pat you on the back?'

'I think they liked it.'

'What have you done, turned it into a jam factory?'

'Oh, that wasn't the purpose. Part of it is to house scientific workers. I don't think any mention was made of jam.' Aveling frowned, as if trying to recall one.

'Think you're clever,' said Baird childishly. 'You know what I mean.'

'Come and see it for yourself,' Aveling suggested.

'Not me. I've got something better to do.'

'Now *what*, Father? You know you do nothing at all.'

'What I do is no business of yours, and if you looked after yourself like Mrs. Hall you wouldn't have a safety-pin showing in your waist.'

'Oh dear,' Celia whispered to me, 'he is so gifted at putting one in the wrong. I didn't think it showed.'

233

Triumphant, Baird led us to the dining-room. In the middle of the meal he said to me, 'Notice anything?'

I did not.

'Finnegan's gone, died last week. I told you so. I knew it was cancer.'

Mrs. Baird tried to hush him.

'I won't be shushed like that! I'll say what I please. And if I put the wind up a few damned fools and make them see a doctor before it's too late I'll have performed a public service.'

Turtle-like heads withdrew all over the room, bowing down to their plates.

I passed Mrs. Baird the salt: she pushed it away. 'I don't take it now. I think it's bad for people. And, anyway, they put too much in the cooking.'

'Oh, bosh,' said Baird, 'the cooking's first-rate. Do you think I'd stay in this mausoleum if it weren't?'

She looked obstinate; she pushed the salt a little further from her.

'Well, *do* you think I would?' he demanded heatedly.

Gerard, the only person to whom he was seldom rude, distracted his attention. Under cover of the conversation Mrs. Baird said to me, 'Don't you find Celia far more herself these days?'

'I don't see much of her.'

'Far less nervy. Of course, we don't see a lot of her either, since she went crazy about improving the business. But she's much more like my girl.' She looked across at Aveling. 'And *he* seems more settled down.'

'You want to watch your blood-pressure,' Baird said cheeringly to Gerard. 'You're the type that has trouble. As for you, Eric, you could do with half a stone. Do you eat properly? I don't know why people can't take care of themselves. Want to be spoon-fed all the time.'

'You can't have it both ways,' Celia told him. 'You retired because you said people were tearing off to the doctor to get everything for nothing. Now you're complaining because they don't consult him enough.'

His colour rose. 'Don't you twit me! I don't like it.'

'But Celia has reason,' said Aveling, with a smile. 'She really has, you know. And for my part, I feel it was selfish of you to leave humanity to its own foolish devices. I remember when you were God in your own practice.'

Baird was mollified. He looked almost shyly down at his hands. 'Tommy-rot. People trusted me because I gave it to them straight. If there was nothing wrong with them I told them to go away. Nobody ever got a bottle of coloured water from me, I can tell you. But the younger men, they sit with their eyes bulging, talking psychology. Damned fools. Let a patient know he's *got* a psyche, and your work's cut out. I never did. Start a lot of morons thinking about the minds most of 'em haven't got, and you'll never be free morning, noon or night.'

After dinner he asked us if we had to hurry away; he fancied a hand or two of bridge. 'If you're driving it doesn't matter when you leave, does it? All you people keep late hours, anyway – don't pretend you don't.'

So Celia, Gerard and Aveling sat down with him: Mrs. Baird and I were left alone.

We sat in a corner under a standard lamp, not far from where the two old ladies reconciled for the moment by Celia at Christmas still sat in their obstinate and alien worlds. I thought that nothing would ever change the life of the Moray, while there was any life remaining in it.

'I think she's got over all that foolishness about Eric. I'm so glad. It's lovely to see her looking normal again.'

She was blind: she saw nothing.

'She's leading a normal life,' she said.

235

One of the old ladies rose up to shift a vase of chrysanthemums which was throwing a shadow across her book. By doing so she destroyed the entire balance of Boldini's decorations: the room was suddenly askew.

I said, 'How did Lois know about them?'

Mrs. Baird looked at me blankly. She said, 'How should I know?'

'Shouldn't you?'

If it had been she, she spoke as though she had forgotten. 'Oh, I daresay she heard someone making a joke.'

'But would that be enough?' I cried.

'It seemed to be. I suppose if you're lying in bed for years you think of things.'

I asked Mrs. Baird whether she had hated the thought of Aveling and Celia together just because of Lois's knowledge.

'No. Though it was awful.'

She made the gesture of looking for a cigarette, drew back her hand as if it had been burned. Then she took a sweet from her bag and sucked at it.

I pressed her.

She looked me in the face. She had a childish air, a kind of unformed roundness; there were tears in her eyes. She could not expect me, she said, to understand. She was not modern, as I was. But she had known Aveling's mother, she had known him since he was a boy. She had trusted him. 'He seduced her. I saw her once, creeping about the hotel, going to him. It was low, like a servant. What respect could he ever have for her? I should only want her to marry someone who didn't *know*.'

This was her excuse, satisfying to her own soul. I tried to destroy it. I reminded her that Celia was nearly thirty-eight: not a girl. She could not have borne a sterile life.

'It was like a servant,' she said. She clamped her jaws.

The head porter, moving around to see that all was well, noticed the displaced vase and dealt with it. The old lady gave him a sharp look, waiting for him to go, biding her time.

Mrs. Baird blinked her eyes. 'But I think it will be all right now. And perhaps she will meet the right sort of man. In business there are all kinds of opportunities.'

I looked across at the card-table. Gerard was staring down at his hand as if bewildered; Dr. Baird was giving him a lecture of some kind. Celia and Aveling were laughing across at each other, their faces unclouded.

32

And then, for nearly a year, I lost touch with them all, except for a stray note, a telephone call, random news from Junius, who appeared to be in the middle of some love-affair: for I found I was expecting a child. In the third month I miscarried. After that I wanted to see no one, not to go out, not to answer letters, simply to be alone with Gerard and to assure myself that this failure had not spoiled me for him. I knew his bitter disappointment and shared in it to such extent that I could not believe I myself was worth anything to him at all. At last the nightmare steadied and was suddenly shredded away. I believed in the comfort he gave me. Mark wrote to me from school, a young, awkward letter in his oddly mature handwriting: 'It must be awful for you, I hope you don't mind too much, though. I quite understood about your not coming down. Only you can take me out any weekend when you feel like it, the headmaster says it's all right. Not if you don't, though, mind. It doesn't really matter.'

It was one of the times in my life when I found acquaintances more comforting than friends. I had got into the habit of walking in the park most mornings with old Fort, who took a regular constitutional there, and listening to his reminiscence of the great expatriate days which were for him becoming more and more the only reality.

It was some time after he knew the news himself, not being in the slightest degree interested in it, that he let it slip to me. We were walking under the trees on a tangy autumn day; the leaves were just starting to yellow. Energetic and old, his white hair catching sparks of fire from the sun, his high-coloured face turned almost to tangerine, he was talking of one of the *Transition* writers, who had just died in Italy; and he added, as it were by free association, 'Yes, I saw poor Lois Aveling with him once. I thought he was a bit sweet on her. I suppose you noticed that her husband was marrying again.'

No, I said, I hadn't. I felt a leap of hope. I said something or other, not daring to ask a question.

'Don't you read your engagements in the *Times*?'

I did not: I had got to the stage when my friends were unlikely to appear there any more. Imperceptibly we mark off the stages of our lives by the things we cease to read. I asked him when it had appeared.

'The day before yesterday – or, no: Tuesday, it would be. He's marrying Wyndham Sherriff's daughter.'

The moment I could break away from him I went home and hunted for the paper, which I found among the supply Mrs. Reilly kept in the wood-box for starting the boiler.

'The engagement is announced, and a marriage will shortly take place, between Eric Aveling, son of the late Lieutenant-Colonel and Mrs. G. Aveling, and Nancy Heriot, daughter of Mr. Wyndham Sherriff of Halecroft, New Marden, Suffolk, and of Mrs. Linton Pargiter of Lima, Peru.'

Gerard, who had been reading it with me, exclaimed, 'What an astonishing amount we don't know about our acquaintances! Aveling the son of a soldier – how improbable it seems! – and Nancy with a mother divorced and remarried. Also, of course, the name of the house poor old Wyndham can't keep up.'

I asked him what I was to do.

'Write to them both, of course.'

'What about Celia?'

He hesitated. 'She may have accepted the situation. For all we know, she has found somebody else.'

Neither of us believed it.

'I don't suppose it came as a shock to her,' I said, hoping.

Gerard said, 'From what I know of him I am quite sure he would never have let it be.'

'She's too young for him,' I said. I felt sick with pity for Celia. If I could have forbidden the banns by crying Nancy's age I would have done so.

He shook his head. 'She hasn't suffered, and I rather doubt if she has the temperament ever to suffer much, whatever happens to her. That would mean a great deal to him. It would be a release.'

I cried out, 'How cruel!'

'We can't judge. Nobody can.' But he flung the paper away as if it had hurt him also. 'We'd better write to them, and get it over and done with.'

33

Nancy replied at once with a joyful letter, inviting us to dinner on the following night. 'Don't bother to let me know if you can come, only if you can't.' Gerard was not free, but I accepted for myself.

I was out all the next day. When I came in at six o'clock Mrs. Reilly told me that Miss Baird had telephoned three times.

I tried to ring Celia back, but no one answered.

When I arrived at the mews flat Nancy opened the door to me and kissed me as though we were old friends. She was looking radiantly handsome, still stately in her Roman way, but beneath it all an exuberance of love. When I again congratulated her she cried, 'Oh, isn't it glorious? I don't know whether I'm coming or going. Come on up. Celia's here.'

It was a shock: and yet, I thought, I might have guessed it. I was worried and embarrassed, not knowing how I should treat her. Nancy led me up the narrow stairs at a bustling pace.

There she was, in a pale blue dress of the kind she and her mother would have called 'little', lavishly jewelled, a celeste of golden charms about her wrist. She also kissed me, saying, 'It has been a dreadfully long time.'

Nancy had darted into the kitchen. She called out, 'Celia, give Christine a drink and bring me one, there's a dear.'

Celia whispered, 'I tried to phone you. It is *quite* all right. You must believe that.' She added, 'Later!'

She seemed perfectly at home in the flat, which was now repainted and elegant.

'I hope,' Nancy shouted above a clash of dishes, 'that you're admiring the transformation scene. I distempered every inch of it myself. Father says it looks like a women's hairdresser's, but then he always complains. I've sent him out,' she explained.

'All girls together,' said Celia to me, in her prattling tone. She gave me a tight little smile, touched my wrist. She had changed. She had always had what Mrs. Baird called an 'old look' when she showed me photographs of Celia as a child: but that had been something to do with wisdom, with sedateness, something which seemed like the result of premature experience. She had a different look now: it was touched with the wintriness of age. Her face was thinner, and seemed to have shrivelled towards the chin. Yet she looked pretty: pretty, assured, secret and calm.

'Do you know, Nancy did the whole of this? She sent her father to the club, cleaned down the whole place, repainted it, stained the boards and upholstered the couch. It is a most *remarkable* feat.' She called out, 'Can I help?'

'No,' Nancy called back, 'I've nearly finished. I hope you both like crab.'

She rejoined us, taking off her apron as she did so, and sat on the floor in front of the fire. 'Oh dear, so much to do, so little done!'

'The wedding's in a fortnight,' Celia told me. She smiled at Nancy. They sought each other's eyes. 'And she has no clothes.'

'But you,' Nancy said fervently, 'are going to take me out and see to that. I have only fifty pounds, and you must make me smart and hard-wearing on that.'

She turned to me. She was to be married in a register office; it was all to be very quiet, since there was not enough money for splendour, and, anyway, it would not do. 'You and Gerard will come, won't you? We're only asking about a dozen people. It's quite enough.' She said to Celia, 'Does Eric ever wear cuff-links? I've never noticed – isn't that obtuse? I thought I could give him a pair.'

'He always wears cuff-links, and you are obtuse,' Celia answered. She was easy and teasing.

'Well, his cuffs don't stick out, then.' Nancy got up, seated us at the table and went to bring in food.

'She is a superb cook,' Celia assured me, 'and so far as I can see, no one ever taught her.'

'Oh no.' Nancy disclaimed this. 'When my Mum was on one of her motherly jags she taught me herself for three months. By the way' – this was to Celia – 'she is sending me twenty pounds.'

'No!'

'Munificent,' said Nancy, 'by her standards.' Her tone was good-natured, but beneath it was the hurt that makes the implacable enemy. She hated her mother, she would not forgive her. 'I do think that if she deserts me she should pay compensation. It is,' she added quaintly, 'ordinary business principles.'

As the meal went on I felt the edge of jealousy. I had become an outsider. Between Nancy and Celia an intimacy had arisen, something that was jocular, not quite relaxed, but at the same time sweet. Nancy was like a big young daughter with a mother who is physically smaller, and who is prepared to play the part of the protected. Sometimes she looked at Celia secretly, with an air of rather puzzled fondness. She had known that there was once love between her and Aveling, though perhaps not the extent of it: and it made her nervous. Yet she believed, she must have believed, that it was over and done with. In her good-nature she was trying to do the best she could: to *include* her, to share her own possession of joy

243

in so far as it was possible. And Celia, talking to her naturally of Aveling, with the special affection and knowledge of an old friend but without the least show of jealousy, was content to accept her as a child, content to seem protected, and yet to guide. She had come to know far more of Nancy than I did: several times she referred to matters that were new to me, and which Nancy, with her usual courtesy, at once explained.

They were both behaving beautifully: I felt uncomfortable.

It was true that Nancy was a good cook; in practical matters she was unusually competent. Her faintly puppy-ish air, a trifle clumsy, was misleading. She was quick, acute, ingenious. But she was too immature to know that in the easiest atmosphere pain may still exist, even if it is only the memory of past pain. She talked of Aveling naturally, happily, in the full newness and release of love: I wished she had not done so. Not that Celia seemed in the least perturbed. Indeed, she urged her on to express joy, as if some of its warmth spilled over into her own being; her face brightened, she was excited about the coming wedding. Nevertheless, an older woman than Nancy, who had known grief herself, would have taken no chances that grief was utterly absent.

I asked Celia how her parents were.

She replied, 'Much as usual. Mummy's taken to having palpitations, but I think that's only to draw attention to herself. No,' she added quickly, though we had not spoken, 'I'm not callous. We all need people to pay attention to us. And my father is getting so delighted with his own company that he hardly addresses a word to her from one week's end to another. I'm not blaming her at all.'

'But isn't she well?' I asked.

'I suppose nobody is, if they think they're not. But Daddy says there isn't a thing wrong with her, and I can't imagine he's mistaken. Poor dear: it makes her very trying, though.'

Nancy, despite her feelings towards her own mother, felt that other people should behave with conventional approval towards theirs. She looked a little shocked. But Celia, as she spoke of Mrs. Baird, had spoken with a high-pitched lightness that told me what she was having to endure. For the first time that evening she looked at me as if I, and not Nancy, were her intimate. 'I go down there as much as I can just to pacify her,' she said, 'but when I do go she's always on at me.' It was an odd vulgarism, not characteristic at all of her normal, skilfully selected speech. For a moment memory had made her careless. She was thinking of her mother, was tormented by her, was resentful because she loved her.

'I can never think why you don't tell her not to be silly,' Nancy said, showing that Celia's mother had been discussed between them before. 'I will not stand this nonsense about blood being thicker than water. In any case, it is meaningless. Who *are* we tied to by water?'

'It isn't nonsense.' Celia lit one cigarette from another. We had finished the meal and were sitting over coffee. 'It is disgustingly true.' She jerked her shoulders. I thought of the vermicelli cord of life, running from female to female back into the awful giddiness of time, soft, elastic, supernaturally tough.

'When I have children I shall feel it, I expect,' said Nancy, 'but I don't feel it of my parents. Certainly not of my Mum.'

Celia said, 'Let us close this subject.' She rose and went over to the fire, throwing more coals upon it. A wave of flame washed over the walls. I saw upon a Queen Anne bureau Mrs. Haymer's photograph of Aveling.

Celia followed my gaze. 'I made Hilda give Nancy a print. Nothing he's had taken since has been half so good. He looks like one of Saint Joan's more kindly inquisitors.'

'Brother Ladvenu,' Nancy said quickly, and with a touch of pride. She did not consider herself as clever as Celia and was pleased to recognise a reference. 'He would be simply mad-keen for her to get off.'

The telephone rang in another room, and she jumped up to answer it.

She came back, flushed, excited, a little doubtful. 'Actually' – she used the long, close-vowelled drawl, as if mimicking some mimic of her own class – 'it's Eric. Shall I ask him round? Or don't we want to be disturbed?'

'Of course ask him round,' Celia said at once, 'you know you couldn't bear not to.' She began clearing away the dishes, as if she were as eager as Nancy to give him an orderly welcome.

He was there within fifteen minutes. I heard him coming up the stairs with Nancy, heard her laughter. Then he came in, kissed Celia tenderly, and after a second's hesitation kissed me also.

'I've just written to you this evening,' he said. 'I had no idea I was going to see you. But it is very nice indeed.'

Declining a seat on the couch, he pulled up a high-backed chair. 'Why wasn't I asked to dinner? I would bet anything you like that Nancy gave you her very best.'

'She did,' I said.

'And excluded me.'

'But you won't be excluded for long, will you?' Celia said, teasing.

'No, not so long.' His gaze, as it rested on her, was peaceful and grave. 'How were they last week-end, my dear? Were they trying you hard?'

'Hardish.'

She looked directly back at him, nothing to be read in her eyes but the privileged and powerless intimacy of love that is over.

'I shall come down soon. I owe Millie a visit. They're coming to the event?'

246

'Of course.' She turned to me. 'You must make Eric tell you about his house. He's busy making it magnificent for the bride.'

Quite suddenly, everything she said seemed a little hapless. She recognised it, for at once she changed her tone and said, without the note of banter, 'Nancy's very fortunate.'

Yet even this should not have been said. Though his face did not change, I saw him flatten his hand on his knee. He said to me, 'I've had my ceiling restored, as I told you, and been lucky enough to acquire two rooms below, one with an Adam fireplace and one with some very decent panelling. Celia must not tell you I have a house. I had a flat: now I have what must repellently be called a maisonette.'

'Father thinks he should live with us, as we have enough room,' said Nancy, 'but I say no. After all, I've made it nice enough for him here.'

'Goneril,' Aveling said. He had to touch her for a second as she passed by him; even he could not resist it. When he looked at her his face brightened and was clear; the years left him. 'But I, also, say no.'

'And quite right.' Celia spoke with aunt-like authority. 'It is always a mistake. Though I can't seriously imagine anyone mistaken enough to take *my* parents in. I mean—' But there was no way out of this. She coloured.

'Anyone who was lucky enough to have Celia,' Nancy said, in a heedless, richly affectionate manner rare to her, but nevertheless part of her youth and of her natural warmth, 'ought to put up with six sets of parents.' It was so sincerely spoken that it sounded right. It should have sounded cruelly insensitive, yet it did not: and Aveling gave her a quick, grateful look.

For the rest of the evening we talked of practical matters concerning the wedding, and Celia was full of plans. We all listened to her. I became as caught up as the others were in the curious magic of making arrangements. It did not seem to me, then, as if there were any barriers of love, of sorrow, even of mere length of friendship or depth of intimacy, dividing us one from the other.

When I rose to go Celia said she would come with me. It was eleven o'clock.

34

'Let's walk,' she said, when we were in the street. 'We always did walk together.'

We went into Berkeley Square, and, without aim or consultation, turned into Charles Street. It was a humid autumn night. It had been raining, and the rays of lamplight were spectral in the damp air.

When Celia spoke again, it was with bitterness. 'You would think she'd be satisfied, wouldn't you? Now she's got me. Now I'm out of danger.'

For a moment I was bewildered. Then I realised that she was speaking of her mother.

'You really would think so.' Her tone held the pettishness of nervous suffering. 'But she demands more and more. Do you know what she'd like me to give up now? The business. Oh, she doesn't say so. But she would. She hints – and her hints are so heavy! "I'm just dropping a *seed*," she thinks. Seed! It drops like a sack of coals. There is something so terrible about Mummy's hints, they make me shrivel inside.'

I said I understood.

'I'm sorry you do understand. It means you've flinched at them yourself.'

'Perhaps,' I said, 'but it wouldn't matter. None of that could affect me as it could you.'

She nodded. Pausing under a lamp, she lit two cigarettes and handed one to me. 'We'd better walk on or we may be picked up – how flattering that would be! The other day a young man whistled at me; I don't think he could have seen me properly. But I was pathetically pleased, I don't know when I've felt so pathetic about myself. I wonder if it was the last whistle I shall ever hear? There ought to be some means of knowing.'

She walked some way in silence, graceful, well-turned-out, a little matronly, the smile pinned across her lips. As she raised her hand to the cigarette her bracelet jingled.

'About Nancy.' Her smile went. She spoke gently and firmly, as if she were putting me in my place. 'She is right for him, you know. And I don't care any longer; I have honestly learned not to. It began about six months ago, and when he knew it he told me. He could not have behaved better. He's been absolutely straight with me.'

I did not know what to say. As she did not speak at once I said that, all the same, I was sorry: that I had been hopeful.

I thought I saw in her face a flash of gladness that I was not overjoyed: but she replied to me in the same grave tone as before, explaining matters to me.

'No, no, it *is* a good thing. You see, she makes him peaceful.' The lamps of the park quivered ahead of us in the bottle-greenness of the night. 'Pretty,' she said. She laid her hand on my arm. 'And he will be able to pretend to master her – though really he's far too kind to impose his will on anybody. But with me he wouldn't even have been able to pretend. I am not that kind of woman – I can't be. But how I wish I were, how I'd love to be!'

She spoke with passion, yet it was a passion directed against herself. She had always longed to be rid of her own strength, her own authority, knowing that in the end she was likely to be lonely, trusted by everybody to look after herself. She would have liked to be able to play the loving game of submission, would have liked to possess in her nature just a spark of its reality. But she was not like that at all. Even in her girlhood she had never known the erotic fancy of a dominant lover, to whom she would kneel, to whom she would cry and beseech. She had always been a leader, perhaps a gentle, nudging one, with the guiding qualities of the shepherd; but a leader none the less. If she had dreamed of submitting to a man, she would have been unable to prevent herself (in the dream) pointing out to him how much more ably he could handle her if he tried it in another way.

'Still, one can't be what one isn't. And I do like Nancy, I really do. It comforts Eric that I like her, because he still feels guilty, though there's not the slightest need for it. She likes me, too. I don't feel shut out. I don't think I could bear to feel shut out entirely.'

Suddenly she laughed. The sound of it rang gaily through the quiet street.

'You know, they say marriages are made in heaven, but, believe me, this one was made by Junius. I think he's been working for it from the beginning. Why, do you suppose?'

As I did not reply – 'But what does he get *out* of it? It is really too mysterious for words.'

We came into Park Lane, clotted at the corners with prostitutes. Like figures by Chirico (they might have had punching-balls for heads) they stood in their marbly group-ings at every turn, their faces fashionably pale, flat in the lamplight, their skirts wagging against their weary calves as they shifted from foot to foot. Their coats glittered in jewel-colours, emerald, ruby and sapphire; they made a sort of elegance, a kind of Greek chorus to the million dialogues of the city.

'These girls,' Celia said, 'I suppose they enjoy it, or they'd do something else. But how they must long to sit down!'

There was a coffee-shop nearby, open till midnight. She made me go in. It was bright and noisy there, the Caribbean decorations flashy. Most of the people there were young, but there was an old and gaudy woman sitting up at the bar, talking earnestly to a waitress.

Celia eyed her. 'There, but for the grace of God – well, I expect that's where I shall end, don't you? I shall become one of Junius's gorgeous, adorable, sickening old women.'

I told her I did not think she would ever change, that she would always be Celia as she was now.

She said vaguely, her eyes roaming, 'Oh, you never know, you never know. Bless you.' She put her hand over mine and squeezed it quickly. She was freer with gestures of affection than she had ever been, yet I felt she had begun to lose me out of her life.

She asked me, in her most normal fashion, about Gerard, how his affairs were shaping: and hearing that he was about to go away again for a week or so said at once, 'Then you'll come to the Moray with me. Please do. There's no reason why you shouldn't. Come after the wedding and tell me all about it, especially what everyone wore.'

'You won't go?'

'No, I don't think so. Father and Mummy will. I shall have a strategic cold, a very bad one.' She added, 'Don't think I wouldn't like to go. It wouldn't upset me, not in the least. I want to see them happy. But I have a sense of the fitness of things. And for me to be there, after all that has happened, would not *do*.'

I told Gerard what had happened that evening.

We went to Nancy's wedding at Caxton Hall, and afterwards to a small reception at Claridge's. The first thing Nancy said to me when it was over, and she was able to speak a word in private, was, 'Is it true about Celia? Has she really got a cold, or wouldn't she come?'

I replied, untruthfully, that Mrs. Haymer had insisted upon keeping her in bed.

Mrs. Baird, in grey with a flowered hat, like a bride's mother, was feverishly cheerful. 'How well they do look together! Eric needs a tall wife, a small one would only make him look silly.' I remembered her telling me that he was too old for Celia, and wondered what she thought of the difference between his years and Nancy's. Yet today he looked young, springy, full of open joy: he could not conceal it at all, and he did not try to.

Wyndham Sherriff, wandering disconsolately up behind me, said, 'Well, I hope it will be all right. He seems a pleasant enough fellow. I think he must be a sort of connection of ours.'

Junius detached himself from some smart friends of Nancy's, waited till her father had wandered away again, and spoke in my ear: in profile, in his frock-coat, he looked like the letter D. 'It's extremely suitable, don't you think? We must have a real old gossip at the week-end. Celia says you're coming down. You must both dine at my house.' At the words 'my house' a proud smile spread across his face: he might have been referring to Holkham or Chats-worth. 'I imagine the very last of poor old Wyndham's fortune must have gone on this "do", or is Eric quietly assisting? No one ever tells me anything.'

Dr. Baird was loudly demanding that Aveling should tell him where the honeymoon was to be spent.

'Well, we had thought of a little place near Clacton, but, of course, it will be cold.'

'Clacton? What the devil do you want to go to Clacton for?'

'There is shrimping. We're both keen on that.'

'Now look here,' said Baird, 'if you think I'm going to swallow that, you're wrong. And if you're trying to tell me I should mind my own business, you can do so straight out, and not play the fool.'

'I shall be very distressed if you are angry on my wedding-day.'

'I'm never angry. I simply like to get things straight.'

'It's odd,' said Aveling, with a gleam of fun, 'that you should say that. I was thinking only the other day, "I have never seen Arthur in a state that could really be described as *angry*".'

'I'm glad you realise it,' said the doctor. He turned to Nancy. 'Well, you seem a fine healthy young woman. Good luck to you both.'

Gerard whispered to me later, 'I've been having a dreadful time with Mrs. Baird. She is trying to get me to persuade Celia that the business is upsetting her nervous health and that she ought to give it up. She told me that as a business-man myself I should understand what a strain that sort of thing could be on a young woman. She is also hinting that Celia is irritable and disobliging to her because she is beginning the menopause. I think you should be prepared for some rare old nonsense.'

But Mrs. Baird, having raised these things with Gerard, was content merely to tell me of her own physical discomforts. She was not, she said, at all well; and Arthur was too self-absorbed to notice, or to care if he did notice. 'Oh, I know what you think of me, Christine,' she said, her voice rising on a fume of champagne, 'You think I am very selfish about Celia. I expect that's what she tells you about me. But I only want her happiness.' She looked across at Nancy and smiled sentimentally. 'That girl will do Eric all the good in the world. Say what you like, but Lois was always too old for him.'

We remember an atmosphere, Proust says, because girls were smiling in it. I had other reasons to remember that wedding – but, if I had gone there without any history I should have remembered it because Nancy was smiling; because her bliss was beautiful to see. She was not at all put out by the excitement. She talked with everyone in turn, giving to each her undivided attention, and when she turned to seek Aveling's eyes, it was not a look that shut out others: it was a look so full of gratitude and of bounty that it seemed meant for us all.

Once I heard Aveling say to her something private, for her ear alone.

When they had gone away, when Gerard and I were leaving with the other guests, Mrs. Baird came up to us. She looked suddenly piteous, unbalanced, awry. She put her hand on my sleeve. She whispered, very quickly, 'I do want Celie all I can. I don't think I shall make old bones.'

'What's that?' Dr. Baird bore down upon us.

'Nothing.'

'Better not be,' he said, with meaningless, jocular menace. 'Well, Mrs. Hall, we shall see you soon, I believe. Give my regards to the boy. He's too old to cheat at table-tennis now, eh? I expect so. He must be getting pretty smart these days, he must be a downy bird.'

35

When I arrived at the Moray Celia was in the hall to greet me.

'We are in the thick of a domestic tragedy. The cat. You'd better come and console her.'

We went up in the lift.

Mrs. Baird came out from her room like Electra from portals of brass, and stood weeping with her back to the door. 'Tiny is dead.' She stood aside to let us enter into the ammoniac gloom. The white cat lay in his basket, looking like a soiled tippet at a jumble sale. Already the fleas were leaving their host. Mrs. Baird knelt beside the body and stroked it; mourning gave her gestures a kind of formal nobility.

'He's been ill for several days,' said Celia, 'and Mummy's been dosing him. We didn't know he was as bad as that, though. We came up after lunch, and he was dead.'

'Tiny, Tiny, Tiny,' said Mrs. Baird in a small voice.

The doctor came in. 'Phew, what a fug you've got in here! For God's sake, Millie, open a window. It smells like the lion-house at the Zoo.'

'He cared for me, Tiny really cared.'

'Cats don't care, Millie, they're only out for what they can get.' This, oddly enough, was meant as consolation: he was trying to make her believe that she had not lost a friend.

'You don't know. What do you know about animals?'

'We'll have to get a box for him. Better ask Fryke.'

Celia said to me, 'I am seldom at such a total loss. What does one do with a cat who dies in an hotel? If we had our own garden we could bury him.'

'They'll put him in the incinerator,' Baird said bluffly, 'they'll know what to do.'

'How can you, Arthur?' Mrs. Baird raised her head and the tears spurted out from her eyes.

'I don't know what you mean, "how can I?" No need to try to put me in the wrong just because this poor chap's gone. After all, they're going to cremate me when I go, and what's good enough for me's good enough for a cat.'

'You know, Father, your words of comfort aren't very successful. I think you'd better go downstairs and do your crossword.'

'Well, it's up to you to get your mother out of this state, then. You talk to her, Mrs. Hall; you've got some sense.'

But I did not talk to Mrs. Baird. After consulting in whispers with Celia I went downstairs, recounted the story to Fryke, and made arrangements for a box to be brought. I told him it would help matters if the box were seemly in appearance, and he took my point at once. He knew where he could find one, he said, and he would put some cotton-wool in it. 'Make it like a proper coffin,' he said, with a gleam of creative pleasure, 'you leave it to me.'

He did it very well, so well that even Mrs. Baird was calmed by the thought of death's dignity. Celia tipped Fryke lavishly, and the body was borne away.

'Now come downstairs, Mummy, and have a cup of tea. It will do you good.'

'No, dear, you go. This isn't very lively for Christine. I'll lie down for a bit, and they can send me a pot.'

She lay down, suitably turning her face to the wall.

Celia hesitated for a moment, then said with a touch of

impatience, 'Oh, all right. I'll help Christine to unpack. She hasn't had a minute to herself.'

When we were in the passage she blew out a great explosive breath. 'Thank God, I may at last be able to clean that room up! That is, if she doesn't immediately buy another pet and perpetuate that hideous tray. Let's walk down. I need exercise.'

As we made our way through the sun-slotted silences of the Moray, sliding our hands down the brass rails, our feet noiseless on the crimson pile, she reproached herself because she could not speak with sympathy when she really felt it. 'I am dreadfully sorry for her, she adored that animal. She is at least ninety per cent as miserable as she seems. But it's the last ten per cent's drama that dries up the wells of my decency. I cannot *bear* pretending.'

We went into the lounge, where we found Dr. Baird half-asleep in the window. When he saw us he opened his eyes. 'Plenty of other places to sit,' he said ferociously, 'no need to crowd round here.'

Celia did not seem to be disconcerted. She shrugged, and took me away into the farthest corner. 'He's like that, these days. His own company enchants him.'

The day was fine, the muted sunlight falling redly on Boldini's vases, now filled with leaves. Miss Ratcliff and Mrs. Davenport were knitting and reading respectively by the fire, and the lounge waiter was tiptoeing about emptying ashtrays. The fire from the sun and from the hearth made the air rosy; on such a day the Moray was a pleasant place to be in.

We saw Fryke coming across the room to us, in his wake a dark young man with a nervous face, who walked with the edgy precision of a horse at the Royal Show. Fryke indicated Celia and retired.

'Miss Baird?' The young man cast the name in the air as if he were tearing it up and throwing it away. 'My name's Atwell. Dicky Evans asked me to call in.'

Celia smiled. 'Well, how nice. You must sit down.' She introduced me.

He hesitated. 'In fact I can't stop. Only Dicky said he hoped you could come to dinner tonight. You and Mrs. Hall.'

'Why, we'd love to! And how good of you to be messenger. I wish you would sit down, you look so uncomfortable standing there.'

He sat gingerly. He was extremely handsome in that frail, sharply cut manner which makes the features look a little raw, as if the chisel has been dangerously precise. He was perhaps twenty-three or four. He was carefully dressed and he spoke with care, as if afraid a cockney note might break through. He looked spoiled and beloved.

'We are going to have some coffee,' said Celia, 'and I know you'd like a cup.'

'In fact I honestly can't wait. I'm tearing about doing some shopping.' He fidgeted, as if afraid he had not been sufficiently conclusive. Then he spoke to me about a book of mine which he had read. 'I read it at Dicky's. He said I'd be meeting you.'

It is always hard to believe that those who admire one's achievements can be utterly without virtue. I began to think him rather agreeable.

He told me, lowering his eyes, that he wanted to write himself. He had, in fact, made a small start, a little reviewing, nothing to boast about.

'You are Mervyn Atwell, then,' I said. I had always been quick to associate a Christian name with a surname; and I remembered a modest half-column on some modest travel book, signed by him. He jumped and blinked his eyes: said naïvely, 'I say, how ever did you know?'

When he left us he was walking less like a show-jumper and looked less contemptuous. He would be seeing us at dinner that night.

'He is a herald,' Celia said, looking after him, 'Junius has a herald. He should wear gold back and front. Now why was he sent? Because there was no need for the invitation to be issued in that way. He could have telephoned, as he always does. No: he must have wanted to display him. So he must be special. Junius must be happy.'

I asked her if she wanted him to be.

She replied thoughtfully, 'I'm not at all sure. It depends. There were several things I meant to ask him tonight, and I don't think I shall allow the herald's presence to put me off.'

Junius had branched candlesticks sparkling upon the dinner-table, and sacerdotal lilies. The lamps were out; only the candles shed and spirted their radiance over the whiteness of linen. All was planned for an adoration. He himself, at his most orotund yet most secret, seemed not wholly serious; his eyes flashed sideways as he welcomed us, flashed back again, daring us to laugh. 'Though I can't do you as proudly as our dear Nancy, I can give you a tolerable dinner. I, alas, cannot cook; but Mervyn here has a gift for it.'

Mervyn, rather sulky, rather pleased, brought in cold Vichyssoise. 'Well, I hope it's all right, because it took me nearly all day to prepare, and my feet are aching.'

'He will pretend to be of common earth and talk about his feet,' said Junius. 'As a matter of fact he has been cooking with an air of supreme negligence. Celia, you are looking most regal again, all your glittery-bits on to do me honour. And Christine is delightful. Christine, you should wear more black. The time has not yet come for pastels. You have at least another ten years to go before it does.'

When Mervyn sulked in again with lamb cutlets, Junius poured and tasted the wine as if it were a sacred rite. His lips crinkled on it; he closed his eyes, slowly exhaled. 'It is an unassuming little wine, but it will do. Quite unassuming but quite seductive.'

It was, in fact, an ordinary wine of a poor year; but Junius had no palate.

This was pointed out at once by Mervyn, in a genteel plaint. 'I say, this isn't much good. Why didn't you ask me to buy it? Now that I do know about. My father was a wine-merchant,' he explained to Celia.

'Oh, don't make it sound so grand,' Junius said cattily. 'You needn't exaggerate.' Then his smile broadened and grew tender. 'And don't look so glum. If you will try to expose me in front of my guests, you must expect reprisals.'

'He's crazy,' Mervyn said to me simply, 'he really is, some-times. My father was quite a humble wine-merchant, but that is what in fact he *was*.'

Junius looked at him for a long time, a look that invited the looks of others. He was not so lost in admiration that he could not try to make us admire also. The young man blinked about him. Despite his haughty airs, which arose from defiance of those who might laugh at him for belonging to Junius, he was modest at heart: he did not understand the ceremonial that had been built about him.

'*Ow*, I say!' The cockney vowel popped out like lead from a pencil.

'And what do you say?' Junius breathed over velvet.

'I meant to tell you. I think I can get an introduction to B——.' B—— was literary editor of a weekly of middling importance.

'You won't go near him, Junius said, 'he is no good at all.' He rose to help Mervyn with the plates. We heard them argu-ing in another room. The young man returned with a soufflé: he was flushed. 'Damned thing's sunk a bit,' he said to Celia, 'but it ought to be eatable.'

When we were all seated again Junius, to show his power, returned to the subject of B——. He was thoroughly undesira-ble; he could do nobody any good. He had his pets, no new pets need apply. And, in any case, Mervyn was not to get in touch with him.

I knew and liked B—, and I said so.

'There you are, Dicky!' Mervyn cried.

Junius swung towards me. 'My dear Christine, he can't do *you* any harm. But he can ruin a man like Mervyn here by promising him the earth and then letting him cool his heels until they drop off with frostbite.'

'How picturesque you can be, Junius,' Celia said. Her smile tightened. She was enjoying his jealousy. 'But you can't issue a ukase, surely?'

'I think we will forget about B—. And you forget it, Mervyn.'

'I'll have to see about that.' The young man tossed his head, then turned and stared fixedly at the window. He looked like a lover by Marcus Stone.

'I don't think Celia and Christine will enjoy a family squabble,' Junius said, 'so we shall refer the matter to a later date.'

We went into the drawing-room, candlelit also.

'Well, now,' Junius cried, 'let's gossip about the wedding!'

'Let's gossip about the primal cause,' said Celia, stretching out her legs to a *petit-point* footstool and clasping her hands behind her head. We were alone with him now. Mervyn was clearing the table and making coffee. 'We are all friends together. Why were you so determined he should marry Nancy?'

Junius told her she was talking nonsense. His eyes were wary.

'Oh no, I'm not. Let's agree that it wasn't right for Eric and me to marry.' She sounded perfectly cool, entirely unembarrassed. This might have been a matter far back in her youth, only the fact remembered, the emotion dead. 'But why have you been working so hard for Nancy all the time?'

He seemed to take a decision. 'All right, let's agree that I didn't *interfere* between you and Eric – my dear, those earrings are far too old for you! I bet my bottom dollar they're Mamma's.'

'You admit that you wanted him for Nancy.'

'Only when it was perfectly plain that things weren't as they should be between the two of you. You can't say I wasn't sympathetic.'

'We went the rounds together,' said Celia, 'and I wept. But why Nancy?'

Junius got up and assumed a Victorian pose before the fire, stomach jutting, hands behind his back.

'Eric and I weren't – and are not – doing such good business. Not all that poor: but rocky. That young woman knows everyone on earth. She will be a tower of strength to Eric. She will bring her rich friends to him. Also, she will cheer him up.'

Celia was silent. Then she said, almost with admiration, 'I do honestly believe you are telling the truth. I believe you've been acting out of nice, plain, mercenary considerations.'

'Not mercenary. She hasn't twopence.'

'But you hope she may bring the money in.'

'I hope so, certainly.' Junius looked at me. 'Do you believe me? Christine attributes the most extraordinary things to me sometimes. She turned up at my flat once, at a preposterous hour, and went for me like a pickpocket. Yes, there are things even you didn't know, Celia.'

'Oh dear,' she said, 'whenever I come to your house I step into a certain amount of murk. You are such a mystery-monger, Junius.'

I said, 'Mervyn's coming with the coffee. Can we stop being mysterious now?'

'We shall. We'll play the gramophone.'

Mervyn stepped in and smelled the silence. 'What's up? Not a crisis?'

263

'Of course not a crisis.' Junius took the tray from him. 'We're going to have some music.'

'Oh lor'.'

Junius informed us, like a guide before a museum exhibit, that Mervyn needed to be developed. He could write a little, his literary taste was good. But in everything else he was entirely raw. 'If I let him, he'd buy a record of *In a Monastery Garden* and sing the chanting monks part himself. Sing it flat.'

Mervyn protested, glowering, but he did not seem displeased. 'Oh, well, you won't mind if I read.'

'Read by all means.'

'But let's have the lights on, for pity's sake. This place looks like a funeral parlour.'

Junius stepped across to the switch and the chandelier flashed up. In the sudden brightness his face was angry and hurt. He went to the gramophone, put on a Bach chorale, took a book from the shelf and tossed it to Mervyn, almost hitting him. The young man managed to catch it. He lay down on a sofa, crooked his legs, balanced the book upon them and removed himself from our company.

I had not known of Junius' fondness for music, that he and Celia had this in common. She was instantly appeased by it, and he, after a minute or so, gave himself to listening, only now and then stealing at Mervyn a look of gentle, jealous, humid affection. I felt sorry for him: I believed this attachment would bring him nothing but misery, for I thought I recognised in the young man the signs that he would not always be as he now was. Even now, he was not altogether content. He was vain, he liked to be flattered, but he was also ashamed. When he spoke to Celia and myself, it was not with the ironic, buttering note of the invert who pays court to a woman; there was a touch, however slight, of genuine sexual interest. Junius, I thought, might be barking up the wrong

264

tree in his fear of B——. He would be wiser to watch out for the first strong and personable young woman who was not prepared to regard Mervyn as lost to her.

When we rose to go, Junius took Celia and me up to the bedroom. 'You needn't tell Eric about young You-know-who downstairs. He will only be stuffy and tiresome.' His eyes were bright: he was longing for us to be gone, willing for us to recognise his longing. 'And, moreover, he would think things, which would not in the least be true.'

As I was driving Celia back she said, 'He is strange, isn't he? I don't think he understands the half of his wickedness. Come to that, do we? Do we seriously believe that he plotted, from the moment he met Nancy, to throw her at Eric, just because she might be able to help the firm? Or is it something more? Sometimes he hates me, you know. I really wonder whether he doesn't do so all the time.'

The mists had fallen away and the moon was up. The tide was low, the smell of the seaweed strong. Celia asked me to stop for a moment. Leaving the car, we leaned over the rail of the promenade, looking out upon the romantic sea. 'I wish I were on a luxury liner, going a long way away.' She paused. 'You remember poor Joe Tomlin? He's in jail again. But not a perambulator this time, somebody's bicycle. That's what shakes one in life, people stepping out of their parts. Don't ever step out of yours, promise me.'

I asked her what my part was.

'Oh, just to be here. I don't really know.' She looked drained and peaceful, at the end of pain; I had seen her look like that after the migraine had left her. 'Isn't this nice?' she said. 'Don't let's go indoors, not just yet a while.'

36

'There is one thing about Nancy,' Aveling said, touching his hand to the nape of her neck, nobody could possibly say she was a snob.'

'I am not!' She was caught unawares, she had let her voice rise. 'It is only that I like *facts* to be right. The Hill-houses aren't at all grand; the old gentleman only got his title for pouring money into the Tory Party and sucking up to Disraeli; he was quite a common old man, and my grandfather said that at one time he was little better than a fence.'

'Not at all snobbish,' said Aveling, 'just factual.'

'He is laughing at me,' Nancy told us, 'but he knows nothing at all.'

Gerard and I were sitting with them on the balcony of Aveling's home. It was spring, and the lamps, just lit, threw their yellow transparencies into the freshly budding trees of the square. Even in the falling light I could see the coarse and rugged varnish on the energetic green of the buds.

Nancy looked at her husband sternly, as if to show us that she was a match for him. 'Eric can be very silly when he likes.'

'No, no, no: nobody could call me a silly man. It is not at all the right word. Opaque, perhaps.'

Stuffy, I suggested.

'Yes,' he said, thoughtfully, 'one might say stuffy. It has been said, I believe.' He turned to Nancy. 'Then do I take it you don't want us to go to the Hillhouses because there was a fence in the family?'

Of course she wanted him to go, she replied. They were as rich as Croesus and it would be very good business, but he was quite in error to suggest that there was anything grand about them. 'They are only hideously rich. And after all,' she added naïvely, '*you* are a sort of vague cousin of mine, if Daddy is to be believed.'

Aveling laughed. 'I simply cannot follow all this!'

She said patiently, 'Well, Lady Mary married Julian Hill-house, which gave them all a terrific social lift, and she used *their* money to haul them up with her, but fundamentally, though it doesn't matter in the least, they are oicks.'

'And you're not snobbish at all,' I teased her.

'No. It's snobbish to stick your nose up at people who don't pretend to be better than they are, but there's nothing wrong in getting things clear about people who do.'

'Yes, there is,' said Gerard.

'I agree,' said Aveling promptly, enjoying himself. He was looking at Nancy as if she were a silly and delightful child; he loved her very much. Yet she was not silly, and she was only pursuing her absurd line of conversation to amuse him. Very young, sculptural, now a little plumper, she shook her head slowly.

'I'm sure Christine doesn't.'

'Why,' I said, 'what should I know? I am always afraid I might have common feet.'

'What's that?' said Aveling, grinning.

I said, 'You weren't there.'

'But yours are not,' Nancy said earnestly to me, 'and if you'd in the least understood what I meant, Christine, you couldn't think it.'

'It was better for people like you,' Aveling murmured to her, 'when you could meet your end splendidly, with people screaming with joy as the executioner held up your head. Now you are merely dying out, like the bison.'

267

'I vote Labour to hasten the process,' Nancy retorted. 'It's only sensible. This is a far better country for the vast majority of people than it has ever been before, I can see that. And it is by no means a disagreeable one for me.'

She was beginning to speak like Aveling, to catch his speech-rhythm.

'We shall go our separate ways to the polling booth,' he said, 'and not speak to each other for several days. For my part, I am propping up the last shreds of privilege. After all, mine's still a luxury trade. And there's no need for Nancy to fall over backwards.'

'You are very dense politically. People don't realise it, but you are.'

'That will be enough nonsense from you, my girl,' he said with an assumption of firmness, and she instantly looked meek, smiling up at him under her lashes.

Gerard told them that we were both off to Canada for six weeks at the end of the month. His Toronto branch was well established, I was temporarily at the end of my work, and it would be a holiday for us both.

They looked at each other.

'Well, in that case—' Nancy began.

'—I can see no room for concealment,' Aveling followed.

She said, 'We are terribly happy tonight because we're going to have a child. It's quite certain.'

I rose and kissed her.

'I congratulate you, and I envy you,' Gerard said to Aveling.

'I am pleased,' Aveling said, 'I can't tell you how much. In a way I hardly hoped for it—'

'I can't think why not,' said Nancy.

'Nevertheless, I hardly did. So it is pretty splendid.'

'It will arrive in November,' said Nancy, 'not a nice month, but one can't arrange these things. Would you believe that my father is not pleased? It won't have my name, you see. And will only distract even more attention from himself. I am letting my Mum know by the slowest possible sea-mail, second class.'

A little wind sprang up, tossing the leaves across the lamps, stirring the boughs to a sound like the sea. In the green sky to the west a line of violet clouds, like rocks at low tide, marked out a paler lagoon.

'You mustn't try to sound hard,' Aveling said, 'it will be less becoming to you now.'

'I am hard about my Mum, just as she is hard about me.' She closed her lips.

'But poor Wyndham isn't hard.'

'No,' she conceded, 'I was being silly.' She sought his hand and held it tightly. He drew a line about her with his eyes, from the crown of her head along the slope of her long neck, her shoulder, her rounded arm.

When I went to visit Celia a day or so later I found Mrs. Baird there; she had just had dinner and was making ready to go. If Joe Tomlin had stepped out of his part, she had stepped back into hers. Cheerful, dressy, she was full of talk. They had had such a day's shopping, their feet were in ribbons: but at Marshall & Snelgrove's they had found a new foundation cream to put *under* a foundation cream – it kept one fresh from morning to night. 'You really ought to try it, Christine. It costs fifty-nine and six for a large jar, but a little goes a long way.'

'We've been discussing Eric's great news,' Celia said, smiling, 'I heard it from Nancy this morning.' She was lying on the couch with her shoes off.

'He always wanted it,' Mrs. Baird said, 'but poor Lois never could. Not that he ever said anything, except once, to Arthur.' She drew on her kid gloves, carefully smoothing the leather over each finger in turn. She added, with an

269

effrontery none the less staggering because it was unconscious, 'Well, Celia, that's one thing you never did for me.'

'I was sought, as they say. But never really found. Do sit down, Christine. Mummy is always on her feet for hours before departing, and, anyhow, we're waiting for her taxi.'

There was a sound of hammering.

'Hilda's making some alterations in her dark-room, it seems that the lights are all wrong.'

'When are you coming down to see us again?' Mrs. Baird asked me affectionately. 'You know it makes a nice break for us, even though Celia keeps you to herself. She's a greedy girl.'

I told her I was going to Canada shortly.

'Oh, aren't you lucky! That's what I'd like, a nice long ocean trip.'

'I was saying the same the other night,' said Celia. 'Why on earth don't we take one?'

'I don't really like to leave Arthur. Not that I mightn't almost not be there, for all the notice he takes of me. But he doesn't like to be lonely, all the same.'

'No,' Celia agreed, 'but I suppose he would miss us in a dumb-ox kind of way.'

They were looking very alike that night, and sounding alike.

Mrs. Baird said, making a rare joke, 'Not a dumb ox, exactly, when he's always bellowing.'

'Let's ask him if we can go,' Celia said. Her tone, relaxed, rather sleepy, had not changed; but her eyes were sharp.

'But, darling,' said Mrs. Baird, 'even apart from Arthur, I think it would tire me too much.'

'You're as fit as a fiddle.'

'You say that because your father says so. I do have a lot of pain sometimes.'

'Indigestion,' said Celia. She listened. 'Your cab's come.'

270

Mrs. Baird kissed her good-bye, kissed me fondly. 'Well, well, we have had news! We have had news, haven't we?'

When she had gone Celia sat up, and showed me some of the day's purchases. She must have spent twenty pounds on oddments. 'I shall have to buy little garments for Nancy. She is excited, isn't she? But anyone would be. I expect it will embarrass Eric a bit, to talk about it with me. You've no idea how much I wish he'd stop being self-conscious. Honestly, it seems like a dream to me now. He would have felt far worse if he'd married me.'

She stuffed the purchases back into their bags, and went to put them away. When she came back she sat beside me on the couch, and did not speak. Mrs. Haymer stopped hammering. The flat was quiet. Celia's hands lay in her lap, the hands that were too small, too old for her. She picked at her rings, studied them closely like a jeweller. 'They ought to go and be cleaned soon. There's some nasty sink-like matter in the settings. I don't know how one gets in such a state.'

She turned to me. All at once her face was suffused by a flush so dark and hot that she seemed to be sweating even upon her eyeballs. She tried to speak, but could not. She shot out her hands and gripped my wrists.

'What is it?' I said. 'Tell me.'

Her throat moved. 'It's hard.'

'I know.'

She burst out, 'I can bear it if she doesn't have a son!'

Releasing me, she bore her head down to her knees and up again, several times, as if in pain, her hands clasped over her stomach. Then she did an extraordinary thing. She threw herself forward on to the floor and lay there outstretched, arms at her sides. For a moment or two she pushed and ground with her shoulders, her hip-bones, in a burrowing motion, as if trying to dig herself through to the extremity of earth itself: afterwards she was still, the wailing sobs breaking from her body as if thrown there by a ventriloquist. I dared not speak to her or touch her. I sat at her side while the noise of her crying tore on, in its misery, its rage, it aggression, and its utter disappointment.

Celia had not been able to make that muscling leap of the nerves which turns the human being into the saint. She had tried hard enough. She had deluded herself into a spurious peace by 'accepting punishment'. For all this long time she had battened her suffering down till she had convinced herself of her triumph over it. Perhaps, unconsciously, she had hoped that Aveling might somehow find his way back to her. But it was all over now: the reality of Nancy's pregnancy had broken down in Celia all pretence, all courage and all hope. She was like the rest of us, like myself. And she was weeping as much for her own final failure of will as for her total loss.

Outside, Mrs. Haymer began to sing. She was singing to drown the crying, her voice deliberately bluff and hearty. It was no business of hers what Celia chose to do, how wildly she behaved: out of politeness she would take no notice, would make everyone aware that she was taking no notice. So she sang as she went between the dark-room and the scullery, and made as much din as she could.

After a while Celia came stiffly to her knees. For a second she remained on all fours, like a clothed animal. Then she hoisted herself on to the couch beside me, and put her head in my lap.

I said, 'It helps to let go. One always has to, in the end.'

'Possibly.'

I tried to tell her how much I understood. She wanted me to talk: she steadied herself by the run of my voice, as if it were a hand-rail.

'It is always you who have to endure me like this.'

'I'm glad,' I said. 'I'd rather it was I.'

'Than whom?'

There was a flicker of interest in her voice.

'Than Junius,' I said.

'I don't really talk to him. Though he sometimes makes it easy.'

She lifted her head. As if she were awakening from a nightmare she pushed the damp hair back from her forehead. Now she was very white. 'Have you ever done that? What I did just now?'

'Once,' I said.

She held my hand. 'Light a cigarette for me.'

She drew at it. Then she ran to the door and opened it. 'Hilda! You can stop that singing!'

Mrs. Haymer appeared, startled. 'What's the matter?'

'I'm not making a noise any more, so you can stop yours.'

Mrs. Haymer turned to me and spoke over Celia's head. 'Is she feeling all right?'

'I can answer for myself, Hilda. Yes, I am feeling all right, and *will* you stop singing?'

'Sorry. What's up, got a headache?'

'A damned, bloody headache.'

'Make her lie down,' said Mrs. Haymer to me, 'nothing else is any good.' She tiptoed away into her refuge.

Celia laughed, her voice shaking. 'I have never spoken to Hilda like that before. And I shall never be able to apologise, because she would hate it. It would be too personal.'

She stood against the grate, on tiptoe. 'You really did do that yourself?'

'Once,' I repeated.

'One always thinks one is the first. Poor Chris.' She said passionately, 'I am so sorry you ever had to do it! I am so sorry!'

She said later, 'I shall miss you when you go. I may go away myself – I don't know where. Yes, I think I might. Only,

273

of course, she will want to come. Perhaps I shall take her. She enjoys things with me, you know; and any company is better than none at all.' But she had a rooted, dazed look. I did not believe she would stir, did not believe she would nerve herself for a departure.

37

When I returned to England in the middle of July I learned that Nancy had narrowly escaped a miscarriage and was to spend the rest of her pregnancy lying down. When I went to see her I found her lying on a couch in the drawing-room window. She had all she could need, books, sewing, crossword puzzles, a solitaire-board with marbles of sea-green glass, a sick-room abundance of flowers.

But she was furious. 'It is too awful, Christine! Here I have to lie like a log, when I feel so healthy I could slide down the banisters.' As I laughed she said, 'We had wonderful banisters at Halecroft, steep enough to make you feel daring and broad enough to be perfectly safe. I remember my Mum trying them once, when I was very small – my father was furious; he thought it was so sinister. As, of course, it turned out to be, since she ran away to Peru.'

I asked her whether the thought of saving the baby was not sufficient compensation for inactivity. She cried out that it was, infinitely worth it: but that it was human nature to want your cake and eat it, and that though she would not for the world budge from her sofa, this did not mean that she was enjoying herself. 'If it weren't for Celia, I really should have gone mad. Eric's frightfully busy – I was right about the Hillhouses, they have got something in the wind for him, awful as they are – and I'm alone for hours and hours sometimes. Celia bought me the solitaire and the crosswords. And she comes along and drinks at my side, which is very comforting, even though I don't drink much myself.'

She began to praise Celia with the consistency of a public orator at Degree Day: nothing was too good for her. She was so kind, and so much fun, and almost embarrassingly thoughtful – after a while one hardly dared to *think* a wish, in case Celia turned up with it in tissue paper. She spoke, in fact, with all the enthusiasm of a woman who would genuinely love another woman if she were not a little jealous of her. Nancy, the most natural and open of girls, was nevertheless a normally suspicious one.

She broke off suddenly in the middle of her praise. 'Tell me about Lois. I shouldn't ask you, as Eric talks about her so little: but one is human. You knew her. What was she really like?'

Priggishly, I considered how much older I was than she: only a very young woman would have asked for my confidence in this way, and I had no right to give it. Yet, abandoning priggishness, I did so. I told her what I had learned of Lois' early days in Paris, of her oddity, her shut-inness, her remote and friendly calm: how I had at first liked her, and had always been sorry for her, reverent towards her courage: and then doubtful in a way I did not altogether understand. By the time I knew her, I said, her disease had set her apart; one could not get near her. 'But she was always very cool.'

'Always very cool,' Nancy repeated. Her gaze wandered to a yellow butterfly, flicking about the tubs of flowers on the balcony. 'I'm not. I sometimes get into a state. But I try not to show it, because Eric's not keen about states. I think Lois conditioned him against them.'

Folding her hands behind her head, she stared up at the ceiling. Her breasts were abundant under her cotton dress; she was like a Rubens woman incongruously gifted with the power of reflection. A flap of light-brown hair fell away from a forehead unlined as a child's; and her eyes were childish as she said to me, 'I know about Eric and Celia, of course. But I don't know whether she slept with him. It hasn't been made clear.'

I began, 'Nancy, I can't possibly—'

'I suppose she must have, not being exactly a *girl*. But one doesn't know in so many words. And not knowing upsets me.'

I told her that in love most of us had to be content with not knowing everything. There were worse states than this.

'Not for me.' She looked obstinate. 'I should feel differently towards her, one way or another, if I knew. I don't mean feel *worse* – but differently. I have this nag at the back of my mind that I am being made a fool of.'

She was more like Lois, I thought, than she knew. The clock, gilt and icing-sugar, struck six. 'Tell me,' she said steadily, 'because Eric will be in soon.'

I said I knew no more than she.

She rolled her head from side to side. 'How disappointing you are! You're exactly like everybody else, and I didn't think you were. Oh, how could you be!'

I asked her whether it were not enough for her that Aveling loved her deeply, and would never care for another woman.

'I'm afraid he may care for her again.'

I said I thought the renewal of love was a very rare thing; that nothing was so completely destroyed by time as a love affair of the past. Sometimes, I thought to myself, one fantasticated it, believed that if the once-beloved object were to reappear all would begin over again: but believed wrongly. It did not matter so much that time altered people. What did matter was that it altered our idea of them. They became, in the moment of our love, what they could never be again once the gauze of that love had been withdrawn from them. They were just men and women, flesh and blood, a pimple at a lip,

277

a vein in an eye-ball, a broken finger-nail, a loosened muscle, a smile too short, a stare too long. For we did not love men and women, but only the angels we made of them.

'You won't tell me,' said Nancy, 'what I want to know.'

Aveling came in. When he had greeted me he lifted her half up in his arms, gathered and bundled her, kissed her cheeks and her lips. 'Has it been a long day?'

'Not so very. And I've had Christine.'

He asked me about Gerard, about our journey. It was characteristic of him that he did not give us his good news until I had risen to go. 'My dear, we have won. Hillhouse has stampeded them.'

She cried out, and hugged him.

He said to me, 'Nancy's family of fences have proved extremely useful, no matter what their social shortcomings may be.' It appeared that Lord Hillhouse was a director of a wholesale house in St. Paul's Churchyard, which had held an open competition among architects for a building design. 'And due, I don't doubt, to his shady influence, Junius and I have been successful. Mind you,' he added, 'that doesn't mean that they will necessarily decide to put our building up. I believe the chairman, who appears to be rather like Celia's father, can't stand the sight of it. But we are a thousand or two to the good.'

Nancy gave a smile of pure, confident self-satisfaction. She had always known what she could do for him. She had never expected to fail.

He insisted that I stay for half an hour longer and drink to his good fortune. 'Because this is a genuine chance for us. Crowborough was delightful, but a freak for a luxury trades-man, the greater part of the job, anyway; if this goes on they will permit me to build vast municipal "launderettes" – as I believe they are called – and I shall at last become a useful member of an exceedingly dull and comfortable society.'

He said he would walk with me to the cab rank.

We went out into the summer dust of Bloomsbury.

I told him I was sorry he had been so worried over the baby. 'I have hardly known a worse moment in my life,' he replied. 'It was all the more horrifying since we had been so confident. I had thought of Nancy as a sort of *Gaea Tellus*. Now it seems that her pelvis is very narrow and they will have to assist the birth. They tell me it will be easier for her at the end, though.'

For me, also, Nancy had an aura of unfailing abundance and increase, a cornfield ripeness.

'They see no reason why all should not go well,' said Aveling half-defiantly.

Despite his deep and fundamental happiness, he had aged in the past year. One had thought of him as an old-young man. Now he was a middle-aged one; beneath his pose of sobriety was a real sobriety.

'Celia has been very good to us. She seems as anxious for Nancy as I am. We have got into the habit of caring for her together. Do you think Celia is happy?'

He was profoundly anxious that she should be; to put it crudely, he wanted her settled and out of the way, out of the back room in his mind where she was so securely lodged. Sensitive people are always anxious for the felicity of those they have deserted; they can never be entirely at peace with themselves until they are assured that the flesh has knit over the wound they have made. They are compelled to go on feeling guilty, because they believe that guilt is in itself an atonement. Yet this guilt is not of the slightest use either to the hurter or to the hurt, since the latter cannot imagine it. The injured always envisages the injurer in a condition of bliss and high spirits.

I said, 'I know she wasn't, some time ago. But I think she may have come to terms with her life.'

279

He said, in a strong voice unlike his own, a voice distorted by honesty, that for him Nancy was the present and the future: he meant that Celia would have shut him into a past he could no longer contemplate. 'When I speak of it to you I take care not to think about it. I only use the words.' Then he said, 'You must know that we ceased to be lovers a long while ago.'

'Nancy worries,' I said, 'because she is never quite sure whether you ever were.'

He stopped. His look of astonishment was almost comical. He looked like a lecturer interrupted in a difficult exposition by a whistle from the back.

'But, my dear girl, I told her about us!'

I explained what Nancy's worry was.

'But she must *know*,' Aveling protested. He was silent for a moment. 'Would it make a difference in her attitude to Celia? They seem genuinely fond of each other.'

'In her attitude, perhaps. Not to her fondness, I think.' I explained as delicately as I could that some women (I was not one of them) felt a special nearness to the lover of someone they loved.

'Oh, lord,' said Aveling, with an odd, fastidious jerk, 'you make me feel like Macheath.'

We had found ourselves in the maze of that kind of conversation which, between a man and a woman, has its own allure and its own tastelessness, and gives both a sense of sex-betrayal.

We had come to the cab rank. 'Give my love to Gerard,' he said, 'and tell him I hope to see him at the club soon. I don't go very often, as I like to be with Nancy. By the way, Junius is in a very miserable state. It seems that a young man by whom he apparently set much store has left him. I knew nothing of it till the other day, and then only by chance. I've always found it hard to be tolerant, as the custom is nowadays, towards Junius's way of life. But I am extremely sorry for him. He likes you very much. If you see him, do what you can. He doesn't unburden himself upon these matters to me.'

I saw Junius a week or so later, when Gerard and I were spending a few days at the Moray, and I met him by chance on the front.

My first impression was that he looked dilapidated. His flesh seemed to sag, his hair was greasy, his summer suit should have gone to the cleaner's.

'Come and have coffee,' he said, 'nice to run into you without a pride of Bairds cluttering you up.'

We walked along a little way. The weather was mild, the sky pale, the sea the thin blue of watered milk. Junius turned into a self-service café, the kind of place he would not normally have entered without a sniff, or a joke about the *canaille*. He brought back two cups of coffee, which he had slopped into the saucers. Then he folded his arms and stared at me, trying to reproduce his old malicious, inquisitive beam. 'Very nice, you look extremely nice. My dear, I really do believe you are having your hair touched. Has it come to that?'

I disclaimed this.

'I should be the last to blame you. I think women have a duty to the public to make themselves as pleasing as possible.' He went on, with scarcely a pause, 'Mervyn has packed his bags and departed. His damned interfering old mamma thought I was an unhealthy influence, and suddenly dragged him off to Italy.'

I said I felt it unrealistic of him to expect me to be altogether out of sympathy with Mrs. Atwell.

Instead of retorting, he launched into an extraordinary tirade of sorrow. At this moment he was genuinely broken-hearted, and misery lent him eloquence. He spoke of the young man, not as a lover mourning his loss but as a father whose child had left him to the loneliness of age. Describing him to me as if I had never seen him, he did so with a kind of loving paternal candour; he might have been saying, 'Of course, I know they're all the same, but with one's own boy one feels differently.' The apple of his throat moved up and down like a lift going between floors. His eyes were moist and luminous, pale as the milk-blue sea that glittered far off behind the middle-distance of scarlet umbrellas, the background of the sifting holiday-makers in their sugar colours of hundreds-and-thousands. All was festive, the pale world shone, all things were joyful but Junius, sitting above his cooling coffee, his hands fretting on the glass-topped table where somebody had spilled a milk-shake, Junius alone with his spoiled hopes.

'You understand a bit,' he mumbled, 'I think you do. Oh, my God, I've got to go back to that terrible little house without him! And nobody cares. Not a soul, not one single soul, cares.'

38

We were to go that night, much against Dr. Baird's will, to the theatre. To punish us, perhaps, he said that we must all spend the afternoon with him in the shelter on the front. It had turned warm, and he saw no reason why normal, healthy people should fug indoors. I said that Gerard could not come.

'That's all right, *he's* working. I like a man who works. But the rest of you are just prepared to sit inside and stare at your navels.'

Mrs. Baird tried to cry off. The sudden heat, she said, had made her feet swell (and, indeed, the slender girlish ankles, the equine arches, were badly puffed), she could not walk even so far as the shelter.

'You must expect to swell, Millie, if you will spend all the morning in and out of shops like a dog at a fair. You come on, when you're told to, your feet will soon go down.'

Yet I thought she looked hot and tired, her cheeks also puffy, her face and neck unusually red.

We sat together in a row like birds on a twig, Mrs. Baird, the doctor, Celia and myself. The places on my right were taken by two young men wearing knee-length tweed coats with velvet collars, tight black trousers, ties thin and straggly as a little girl's hair ribbons. One, who was high-shouldered and robustly built, had brassy fair hair with a greenish shine on it like verdigris, elaborately arranged in a sort of pompadour. The other was small, dark, white-faced, and had a boil at the corner of his nose which seemed to worry him since he tried repeatedly to burst it into a spotless white handkerchief. It was Celia who drew upon them the doctor's stupefied attention: perhaps she had hoped to amuse him.

He said, in his most carrying tones, 'What do they think they are, Oscar Wilde? The East Pier is the place for them. Why don't they keep to it?'

The fair one leaned forward. He said, with a hideous simulacrum of courtesy to the old, 'Why, what's up with grandpa? Could the gent be talking to us?'

'I was not talking to you but about you,' the doctor retorted. There was a rustle of interest from the sides of the shelter.

'Be quiet, Father,' Celia whispered. 'We don't want to get into this sort of thing.'

'What you want,' said the young man, still addressing Baird, 'is a push in your bleeding face.'

'And what you want,' cried Baird lustily, 'is a right-about-turn, back to where you came from. Where do you think you're going, a fancy-dress ball?'

'Arthur, Arthur,' Mrs. Baird whispered in terror.

'And where do you think you're going, to a bleeding funeral? If I had a face as long as yours I'd get a bit carved off.'

'Leave him alone, Denis,' the pale one said, in a sick fashion. He might have been going to vomit, not involuntarily but as a deliberate action, designed to make himself more comfortable.

'Any young man in my day who dressed like you,' said Baird, to whom this sartorial phenomenon was plainly a new one, 'would have been thrown on his backside into the nearest rubbish dump.'

'If you don't stop that, we'll do you, see?'

'I cannot believe,' Baird persisted, 'that you can be drunk at three in the afternoon.'

By this time a small crowd had collected.

'Oh, don't, Arthur, don't. You'll only annoy them.'

' "Ew, dewn't, Arthur. You'll ewnly ennoy them!" Better take her advice, – face.'

Celia got up. She said to the young men, 'If you will talk this over with me quietly, where there isn't such a crowd, I think we can smooth things over.'

'She thinks she can smooth things over, do she? She really thinks she can, Charlie.'

'Oh, let's – off. They're all off their bleeding nuts.'

Purposefully, Celia opened her bag: they took no notice.

'You shut your trap, Charlie, and leave this to me.' He turned to Baird with something like a bow. Had he been wearing a hat with feathers, he would have swept it across his stomach.

'So grandpa thinks he's King Muck, do he? So he thinks he owns the bleeding place?'

'You come over here and talk,' said Celia masterfully, moving towards the promenade rail.

'Now I'll tell you something,' Baird stated. 'Instead of loafing around here, looking like an old Bessie, you'd better take your friend to a doctor. See he gets a blood count, and say that I said so.'

The fair man perceptibly recoiled. 'What the – hell are you talking about?'

'I'm a doctor. You do as I tell you.'

'Doctor, my arse. You're all right, in't you, Charlie?'

'Course I'm all right.'

'What's up with you, grandpa? Have you gone off your bleeding chump?'

'Mind your language in front of my wife, if you please.'

'Which one? Got a harem, haven't you?'

'Get that wizened fellow to a doctor. And have a blood count, I say.'

The one called Charlie looked terrified. 'Here, Den, let's make a move. They're all crackers. I don't want to spend my day in the bin.'

The fair one rocked gently from foot to foot. The crowd, making a neat ring, looked on with mild interest.

'Oh, come on, can't you,' Charlie nagged, 'he's a proper cretin.' He pronounced the word as if referring to an Aegean islander.

He got up. He had been transfixed up till now. The two strolled towards the rail and leaned with their backs to the sea, looking at us. The crowd, which had had to part for their progress, re-formed in two arcs. Celia went towards the young men. I followed her.

'Now go along,' she said.

The fair one looked at the ten-shilling note. 'What's this for?'

'For going away. I don't mind an audience, but my father does.'

'She says for going away,' said Charlie, with a weak snigger of bravado.

The other looked us up and down. 'You're not a bad-look-ing pair of dolls. What about the pier tonight? Take you on the Ghost Train, we will.'

'Oh, go away,' said Celia.

He pocketed the note. They strolled off, looking back-wards to jeer and whistle and chi-hike: then they were gone. The crowd moved on.

Celia returned to the shelter. 'How could you, Father! Why can't you leave people alone?'

'People shouldn't listen to what isn't meant for them.'

'It was meant for them, and you know it.'

'I feel awful,' said Mrs. Baird. Over the flushed cheeks was a yellowish swelling, cloudy and coarse in effect, like the plas-tic material used for making teacups. 'You oughtn't to upset me like that, Arthur, everyone staring.'

'No need to be upset. I'm not upset, am I? Got rid of 'em by white man's magic, too. What's the betting they go over to the nearest poor swine sweating his heart out on a panel?'

'What was the matter with Charlie?' Celia asked curiously, her anger subsiding, 'do you know?'

'I'm not one of your doctors in those tomfool films. But it might be pernicious anaemia. And serve him right. This end of the town ought to be kept decent, at least. Let them stay where they belong.'

Mrs. Baird retired, and lay down for the rest of the afternoon.

We dined at six, since the play, a comedy being given a try-out before coming to London, began early. At a quarter to seven, just as we were ready to go, she went along to the cloakroom on the ground floor.

'What an age she is!' Celia said impatiently. 'If she doesn't hurry up we'll get there after the curtain's up and have to madden people by lurching across their feet. I'd better go and tell her.'

'I'll come,' I said.

We went into the neat room, with its looking-glass walls and hangings of cottage chintz. The attendant had gone off duty: by the bowls of powder, the clothes brushes, was a saucer containing a shilling and two sixpences, sprats to catch a mackerel. Mrs. Baird was not there. We went into the inner room, where there was a row of lavatories. One was engaged, but when we called her there was no answer.

'Damn it, I bet she's gone upstairs,' Celia said. 'I'll have to chase after her. You wait for me here or go back to the others.'

I returned to sit with Gerard and Baird. The doctor was arguing to Gerard that there was no sense in educating most people since they were too stupid to profit by it, and as for publishing books for them, any decent teacher could give them the rudiments with a blackboard and a bit of chalk.

Gerard was soberly agreeing with all this, not feeling that Baird was either capable of changing his opinion or was in the least desirous of doing so.

Baird cried, 'Where the devil is Millie? That's the trouble with women, not an ounce of consideration.'

Celia stepped out of the lift. She looked perturbed. 'I can't find her,' she called out, as she came towards us.

'Perhaps she's waiting outside,' I said. Any suggestion was better than none.

Celia went to look. 'She's not.' I joined her. 'Better look in the lavatories again.'

There were five of them in a row, two inches or so of space under the doors, but the partition walls flush with the ceiling.

Celia lay down on her face. I was reminded, despite my anxiety, of the night when she had broken down utterly. She wriggled along, peering under the doors. As she came to the one marked 'Engaged' she gave a heave of relief. 'Nobody there. One always gets worked up.' Then she looked, more for luck than anything else, at the last in the row, where the bolt seemed not to have been driven entirely home, and the sign stood at '-aged Vac-'. Meanwhile I pushed at the 'Engaged' door, and it opened; the handle governing the sign had stuck, and the last occupant had left the door very slightly ajar.

Celia cried out. She scrambled up. She was trembling. 'She's in there. She's been taken ill.'

I looked myself. First I saw the base of Millie Baird's navy-blue bag, the calfskin one with gilt trimmings. Then I saw just the toes of her blue Ferragamo shoes. Her feet seemed to be wedged with the heels to the wall.

'Mummy!' Celia shouted.

'Don't,' I said, 'I'll fetch Fryke.'

The porter came with me at once and went straight to the 'Engaged' door, which, in my agitation, I had slammed shut. 'Not there,' I said. 'There's no one in there.'

For a second he seemed more concerned about the slur upon the Moray implied by ineffectual signs than about Mrs. Baird. 'Silly gadgets, those. I said when they put them on they was no good.'

Celia was leaning against the washbasins. She looked as if she would faint. I showed Fryke the right cubicle. He knelt, looked, sprang up and banged at the door. 'Here! Madam! Are you all right?'

'Of course she's not all right!' Celia cried hysterically.

'Another rotten gadget; look at it, it's shut all right, but it hasn't quite gone home.'

'Damn the gadget! Get the door open! Chris, go and get Father.'

I said I thought we ought to wait for a moment, to see what had really happened.

Fryke contemplated the door. 'Not easy to open them.' This time his voice held a degree of professional pride. 'It's double, you see; the screw bolt and then the catch. Not going to be easy.'

A wind sprang up, sending the chintz curtains billowing in, filling the room incongruously with a phantasmagoria of roses and bees and humming birds.

Fryke stepped back. Then, in a sideways spin, he hurled himself at the door. The noise of the impact was startling, but there was not so much as a cracking of wood.

I went to fetch Baird. When he had heard me he only said, addressing Gerard, 'You stay where you are. I'll send for you if I want you.'

He followed me into the cloakroom, and without a glance at Celia stationed himself before the lavatory door. 'Millie! Millie! Come out!'

This stentorian demand made Celia jump, and recover her nerve a little. 'Don't be a fool, Father! If she could come out she would.'

He looked at Fryke, who responded with a glitter of understanding. They were engaged together on men's work. Together they ran at the door, the doctor adding little to the total force. The result was as before. Frail, jangling, Baird stood back and gripped the cool edge of the basins.

Gerard stepped quietly in: behind him was uproar, for the noise had roused the hotel. He said, looking out into the hall, 'Nobody is to come in just now. Mrs. Baird may have been taken ill.'

Fryke renewed his assault. After three more attempts he gave up. 'No use,' he said. 'We'll have to get a carpenter to saw the lock off.'

'For Christ's sake,' Celia cried, 'we haven't time for a carpenter! We must get to her *now!*'

Gerard put his arm round her. She leaned against him, her eyes closed. Baird, who had his breath back again, was regarding himself in a glass, passing his chin over his hand as if unsure whether he had shaved that morning. 'Listen,' Gerard said to Fryke, 'there must be somebody here who's stronger than we are. Isn't this place run on coke-boilers? If so, who makes them up?'

'Ah,' said Fryke, 'now that's a scheme.' He appeared to have forgotten Mrs. Baird; the technician in him was uppermost. 'If he hasn't gone. But he usually does 'em about now.' He ran to the door. 'Joe! Go and see if Dibber's there, and bring him up.'

He came back to us. There was nothing to do but wait. Boldini had joined us, and was smoothing his damp palms, pressing sweat to the finger-tips.

'Damn silly,' Baird said to him, in a helpless pause, 'to have doors like that which you can't open. Anything might happen, old people, anything. It's criminal carelessness, that's what some would say. Some people might sue you.'

290

'Oh no, oh no,' said Celia, her eyes still closed.' Oh, Father, stop it, please.'

Dibber came in, a small, square man in overalls. He pushed the door tentatively. Then he took a run at it himself, crashing it with his shoulder. There was a faint splitting sound. 'Here,' he said to Fryke, 'two of us ought just about to do the trick.'

Fryke smoothed his wet-looking hair, pinked out a piece of gold braid that had curled itself inwards on his lapel.

'One, two, three—' Dibber began. They swayed and muscled for the spring – 'Go!'

The door smashed open, tearing the lock away with it.

'Crummy!' Dibber exclaimed, in an involuntary burst of delight at the success of physical effort.

We all saw what lay inside, before Celia and her father came forward to block the view.

Millie Baird lay across the plastic seat, knees sagging against the pedestal, heels stuck hard against the wall on one side, head dangling over the other. Her hat had toppled off, and was hanging to her stiffly waved hair by a single pin. Her skirt was pulled up over her thighs, clinging in peaks to the rucked-up corset. Around her calves was a kind of twisted bandage, formed by the pink silk knickers which she had rolled down. I caught a glimpse of her face, pallid and relaxed, the dulled eyes open wide as if in distasteful surprise at this intrusion; for a moment I shut my own.

Celia tried to lift her.

'Leave your mother alone,' said Baird sharply, 'and get out of the way. Far too many people in here.'

He shoved her into my arms.

Now she could see nothing, since his body covered the doorway. As I held her she began to pull and twist at her bag, to wrench at the clasp. 'What is it?' I said.

She was doing what came to her automatically. Raking out a couple of notes, she thrust one at Dibber, one at Fryke. They looked at her in utter bewilderment.

Baird began to talk, as it were to himself.

'She pulled the flush, she was just getting dressed again. She was standing at the side of the pan when she fell. Somebody get Dr. Cust, and do it quick.'

Then he stood up and faced us, his flat eyes staring open, his mouth moist and trembling. 'I didn't know! I should have seen and I didn't see it. I didn't see, I tell you! I – *I* didn't see it! *I* didn't know!'

39

After her mother's funeral Celia went to London and did not return to the Moray for some weeks. Her father did not seem to need her; he was too busy 'kicking himself', she explained, using the phrase with an affectation of lightness which sounded strange. For he, who had prided himself with reason upon his diagnostic powers, had failed to believe in the sickness of his wife. How he had failed he did not know, but his failure had been utter, and in death she had made an ass of him. He had not liked her much for many years past. Now she had made an ass of him, and he could not forgive her.

At the inquest, Celia told me, he had sat with his face in his hands. 'It was extraordinarily unlike him. Fortunately, it passed for grief. In fact, he was eaten up with rage.' Mrs. Baird had made even more of an ass of her husband than he had guessed until he heard Dr. Cust's report: the cause of her death was coronary thrombosis, and she had almost certainly had a previous attack.

'Why did she conceal it?' Celia demanded. She was still deeply shocked. She looked, at this moment, almost as old as her mother and grotesquely like her. 'What earthly reason could she have had? When I think she went through *that*, alone, I could cut my own throat.' She added, more gently, 'She was a pathetic woman, you know – so many aren't. And pathetic people know they are pathetic.'

She had not been so attached to her mother as to her father, though they had had more in common, even if it were only the passion for spending, for delighting in advertised luxuries which seemed so entrancing once they had passed from the printed dream to the touchable reality in the drawer or on the dressing-table. Yet Celia had a filial feeling almost religious in its intensity, and entirely religious in its rawness, its sensitivity. She railed against the tie of the blood because to her it was a profound reality – far more so than it had ever been to me. She had hated her mother to touch her; it was not in her nature to give her the comfortable love she craved: but it tortured her to know that Millie Baird had died undaughtered and alone.

She repeated, 'Why did she conceal it?'

I said, 'She may have been touching wood'; but in fact I simply did not know. It was extraordinary to me that she had not told her husband of what must have been a terrifying attack, that she had not seen her own doctor. It was years since she had consulted Cust. I found myself supposing that her selfish and tenacious love for Celia had risen at last into something of splendour; that she had wanted to spare her a bitter anxiety, or perhaps to leave her free to come and go as she pleased. If Celia had known of her mother's disease she would never have left her side. She would have given up the business, as Mrs. Baird had for so long wanted her to do; she would have rooted herself at the Moray, patient, watchful, outwardly tamed. It is possible that Millie Baird, foreseeing her end, had wished her at last to be, not the daughter she had wanted, but the woman Celia could not help being.

These, however, were the kind of reflections, complex and charitable, that most of us incline to make when we come up against the inexplicable. To the end, Millie Baird had remained mysterious. She had been baffling to me in her frankness, in the very candour of her extreme selfishness; now she was baffling in her final concealment.

'People do touch wood in amazing ways,' I said, and was glad to see Celia shrug, as if too hurt, or perhaps too weary, to press the subject further.

'I suppose I shall have to go home, sooner or later.' It was the first time I had heard her call the Moray by anything but its name. 'I shan't stay, though. I shall give Father the odd week-end, but I'm going on working.'

She was feeling that she had nothing else left.

'Come into my bedroom,' she said.

There she showed me a clutter of pigskin cases, tossed one upon the other. All had been expensive, all carelessly used. 'Mummy's personal effects. I haven't had much time to go through them. But there's some stuff here I can't do with, and if you like to take it and give it to your char you will be doing me a favour.'

It was her way of making me a gift: but it was done far less circuitously than was usual with her.

She opened one of the cases, full of scarves, belts, gloves, odds and ends of what is called costume jewellery. I saw at a glance that this was no random selection: Celia had picked carefully what she thought I might like. The first thing I saw was the enamel locket with which Mrs. Baird had tried to bribe me. 'I'd like this, if I may have it,' I said.

'Oh, do take the rest! I've given Hilda stacks of underwear, all too small for her. But Mummy grossly overbought, and I don't feel I can wear the stuff myself.'

I said, 'I can't take all this. There's pounds' worth here.'

'Oh dear,' she cried, in a kind of exasperation partly put on, partly real, 'do for pity's sake cart it out of the place. *I* don't want it. Surely you've got somebody you can pass it on to?'

I thanked her. She would not have my thanks.

'Mummy left a surprising amount of money,' said Celia. 'I don't know how she did it. Even Father was startled. She left what she had to me.'

I thought, as I watched her parcelling up her gifts for me, that she had changed; and at first I could not understand how. Then I realised that she was not so urgently feminine as she had once been. Though she was still expensively dressed, though she still wore her jewellery, the hyper-femininity of the 'powder-room', the perfumery counter, the novels of Colette, had left her. She was using no scent. She went about what she was doing with a kind of impersonal, Stakhanovite precision. She was well-to-do now; when her father died she would be a relatively rich woman. And by then she would no longer care about the pretty, wasteful oddments money could buy.

'I say, an odd thing happened the other day. I was round at Nancy's – here, put your finger on the knot, will you? – and we were talking about Eric, as we often do' – she wrenched at the string, double-tied it, tossed the parcel into my lap – 'and I made some remark without thinking, you know how one does, which made it obvious Eric and I had had a proper *affaire.*' She laboured the word; she was a little embarrassed. 'She knew we'd once cared about each other, of course, and I assumed she'd know it was the *whole* thing. But she went a bright red, all the way down her neck. I felt shocking; of course nothing was said: but I'd have cut my tongue out rather than tell her something she didn't know, especially just now.'

I told Celia, then, how Nancy had been worrying. 'Has it made a difference?' I asked.

'I think she is very childish,' Celia said, as if blaming her. 'She can't possibly still believe in gooseberry bushes, especially now— No, I don't really think it has. In a way we seem closer. I do rather love Nancy, you know.'

I said I did know.

'I can't talk to her as I can to you. But I feel I want to take care of her. She is such a mug,' Celia added surprisingly, since this was far from her usual idiom, 'in so many ways.'

296

I did not think she was right, but I said nothing.

'I don't want her to lose that baby. In a way, I want it more for her than for him. She would be so baffled if anything went wrong, she wouldn't be able to bear it. Life has always gone so much her way.'

Mrs. Haymer knocked and entered. 'Would you two like to see some colour transparencies? I've never done any before.'

She made us look at Waterloo Bridge, the Abbey, Buckingham Palace, all under mauve skies.

'Not too bad, I think. I really think they might be worse. I'll have to take some of you,' she said to Celia.

'I have no colour, so it would be pointless.'

'Of course you have! What things you say. Oh – talking about colour: you know that temporary with the dyed hair who came to us for work?'

Celia nodded.

'She's a prostitute! I saw her actually on a beat! What things people do!'

'I expect she was trying to go straight. We didn't fix her up, did we?'

'No,' said Mrs. Haymer, looking severe, 'because we didn't like the look of her, and she couldn't do shorthand. Even in our business,' she informed me, 'one sees some strange things.' She went out, stopping once more to peer again at her photographs.

'Poor Hilda,' said Celia. 'Life must seem very unstrange to her on the whole. She is so happy.'

Early in November Gerard telephoned me from his office. 'I thought you'd want to know that they've taken Nancy into hospital. She's three weeks early, and there seems to be some reason for anxiety.' He had met Aveling, he said, on his way to work.

We heard the news ourselves just before midnight, when Celia telephoned us. Nancy had borne a son. Both of them were doing well.

She gave me this information and at once hung up the receiver. Her voice had sounded ghostly, as if she had only enough strength left to repeat a certain number of words. She might have counted them out, as on a telegraph form: she could not have been more brief.

40

A few days after the baby was born I had been visiting Nancy in hospital; when I got home Gerard told me that Junius had rung up, that he was coming to see us after dinner. I had not set eyes on him since that morning on the front, nor had much news of him. I asked whether he appeared to want us for anything in particular.

'I don't think so. He said, only for a chat.'

When he came he was wearing his ordinary business suit, and I thought he looked like an ordinary, tired, rather depressed, rather crumpled business man. He was a little thinner, and his face was pasty; for once the small, sharp nose gave him an air of delicacy, of fastidiousness. 'I just thought I'd like to talk,' he said, 'or even to sit around a bit.'

It was all he seemed to want to do. Junius, at his worst, had been a life-giver: devious, malicious as he was, he had always brought life into a room and illuminated it with the spark of his busy, agitated spirit. Now he sat upon our couch as if he had been dumped there, hardly speaking at all beyond a yes or a no. He, of all people, had become heavy in the hand; even Gerard had to grope for new topics of conversation. Drink seemed to have no effect upon Junius. Steadily he drank all we gave him without it showing the slightest effect.

'Did you see Baird last time you were down?' Gerard asked.

'No. He never had much use for me.'

I said, 'It was a shocking thing.'

'Particularly as it was also slightly ridiculous,' said Junius.

Gerard said it would take Celia a long time to get over her mother's death.

'Oh, Celia. Well, the money will enable her to be miserable in comfort.' For the first time that evening his face showed a gleam of animation. 'Do you know just how much Millie Baird did leave her?'

We shook our heads.

'You don't read your newspapers. Thirty-two thousand pounds. And Baird will leave her a lot more.'

Gerard was interested enough to ask how the money had been made. According to Junius's account, Baird, whose father had been a wool merchant in the West Riding, had started with substantial capital; his wife had multiplied hers by playing the markets. Somehow, though I had never heard Millie Baird speak of money, except in connection with what it would buy, or seen her so much as glance at the financial columns of the papers, I did not feel surprised.

I told Junius that Celia had some plan concerning her own business, which she meant to tell me in time.

'Oh, I can tell you. She told me. I think it's mad.'

I had imagined that Junius had been seeing nobody, hugging his sorrow to himself; but it appeared that he was seeing Celia constantly.

'Oh, she came out with it only the other night, in one of those charnel-house clubs of hers. I'd been wondering what was up. She was a bit oiled' – Junius had forgotten to be urbane – 'and she told me. That ghastly woman she lives with wants to buy that tinpot agency, and Celia thinks she may sell.'

'But what the devil will she do with herself?' Gerard cried. 'I should have thought it was the only thing that kept her going.'

'I know what she means to do.' Junius spoke with a touch of his old gleeful mystery. 'She means to live at that dead-alive hotel permanently and be the light of the old brute's declining years. Better her than me.'

We said nothing. I thought of Celia, her last hopes rotted away, seeking for someone to whom she must come first, even if it were a savage old man who would require her to sit all day at his side among the old in that costly waiting-room where the knitting-needles clicked the last of time away.

'She'll do all right,' said Junius, with a sneer that would have seemed callous had it not been so automatic, so far detached from his own absorbing inner contempt and disappointment, 'she's always got the shops. I think perhaps I should train her taste. She might start collecting Georgian silver, and give choice little oddments to me.'

Gerard and I agreed that Celia was mad to think of selling the business – so far as we knew, it was both profitable and stable; and she had no need to spend more time upon it personally than she wanted to.

'Oh, but you don't know her,' said Junius quickly, obviously taking pride in the thought that he did. 'She is so obsessively whole-hog. She's always wanting to cut entirely loose from things, which I do think is one of life's greatest errors. We all ought to have thousands of little strings tying us down, like Gulliver.'

Somebody called Gerard on the telephone. While he was gone, Junius said to me in a furtive, scuttling voice, 'You remember Mervyn Atwell? His dearly beloved mother is *now*, if you please, taking him to live in the South of France. Fantastic, isn't it? A constant flight with her darling boy from temptation. It makes one despair of human nature.'

Though I felt nothing but admiration for the persistence of Mrs. Atwell, I was sorry for Junius's wretchedness. He, as well as Celia, was forsaken, his life a desert; and if there was more hope for him than for her, he was incapable at the moment of realising it.

301

'I'm sorry,' I said. It was all I could say.

'Perhaps you are, more or less. But you don't really like people of my persuasion. All tolerance outside, all Pilgrim Fathers within. I know. You don't have to tell me.'

I said, stung by the revival of his spirits (however low they might still be), that he was trying to have it both ways. It was unreasonable for 'people of his persuasion' to expect women to admire them, at least until the latter were past the stage of hoping for physical joy. I was thinking, there was no doubt about it: the charm of association between the sexes was basically the charm of physical attraction, the delicate sexual tug-of-war, no matter whether this was acknowledged at all or even seriously considered. I said aloud that, knowing that for him and his friends they had no charm whatsoever, knowing they were considered superfluous, even physically distasteful, women were all too aware of being cheated, especially as custom forced them through the ordinary social symbolism of sexual advance and retreat.

Junius laughed for the first time that night, throwing his head back so that a lock of hair danced on his forehead. 'Christine, my old mother would have described you as a "caution", supposing she had been able, God rest her, to understand a word you've said. But you simplify, you simplify maddeningly. You aren't without charm for me – bless my soul, Gerard would look down his nose at this conversation! – don't you think it.' There was a little colour in his face: his mood was Pickwickian. 'Still, I admit it's different.'

At that moment Gerard came back, and Junius, deprived of a conversation which might have led back to his lost friend or, at least, have developed into an interesting discussion about himself, relapsed into gloom. After a while he got up and left us with the barest of good-byes.

'Why does one like him?' Gerard wondered. 'I don't know. But it's odd; one's always rather pleased to see him. And it's sad to see him submerged.'

I said I thought Junius was likeable because life was so hot in him: and also because he was not a genuine villain. Like a child, he wanted people to realise that he was only pretending.

Gerard said he pretended so successfully that he was often indistinguishable from the real thing. It was hard enough for any of us, much more so for anyone as fluid as Junius, not to become what we pretended to be.

But I was sorry for Junius, touched by his desolation, unable to erase from my mind a picture of him, alone in his strange, bedizened little house, alone under the plumes of gilded wood, the pompous canopy, lying wakeful without hope of footsteps returning along the empty midnight road beyond which the sea lay as empty as his own life and, in these dull and windless days of the late autumn, as spiritless.

4I

Three days later, when I was upstairs working, Mrs. Reilly came to tell me that Celia had called. She had never done this before without writing or telephoning me. I went down at once and found her in the drawing-room, standing with her back to the fire, still dangling her bag and umbrella. She gave me a peculiar nervous smile. 'Hullo.'

She looked as though she had had a shock; but of a kind she feared people might laugh at. 'Hullo,' she repeated. 'I didn't think you'd mind. I've only just got back.' She sat down at my invitation but made no attempt to take off her coat. 'As a matter of fact, I came straight here from Victoria. I had to tell you the joke.'

For some reason, I did not instantly wish to hear this joke. I felt vaguely that in her present state she would tell it in a way which would make me unsure how to receive it. To put her off, I said I was just thinking of having a cup of tea, and she ought to have one too.

'Oh, a cup of tea,' Celia murmured. 'Yes, I expect I'd better. I expect I interrupted your work.'

I told her, though it was not true, that I had finished writing for the day.

She sat huddled inside the sable coat which had belonged to her mother, and had now become a little old-fashioned. She was still wearing her gloves, soiled from the journey, blistered over her rings.

Mrs. Reilly, uninstructed, came in with the tea and an extra cup. Celia drank greedily. 'I missed lunch. I didn't want it. No, don't offer me anything, because I couldn't manage it.'

The tea soothed her a little, for in a few minutes she took off her outdoor clothes, straightened her hat before the glass and sat further back in her chair. Yet she still had the same half-hilarious, shocked look. 'It should be written, really, only I can't write. You'll find it hard to credit – I know I did. I still do.'

Then she told me, fluently, with her own graphic detail, what had happened at the Moray that week-end.

She arrived at three o'clock on Saturday and ran up the steps into the hotel, determined that what she had to do she would do at once. ('I thought if I didn't do it immediately my heart would fail me.')

It was a cold day. The sea-mist hung like a wet army blanket over the promenade and had seeped a little way up the ribbing of streets. In the Moray the fires were high. Mrs. Davenport and Miss Ratcliff were both asleep. In the farthest corner a very old man, a widower who had lived at the Moray for twenty years, had surreptitiously removed his teeth and was trying to adjust them for a better fit. There was, however, no sign of Baird.

('Now I had planned just what I was going to say, I'd learned my part. Somehow, it was a terrible jolt not to find him in: it was like bringing out your big speech on a stage and finding the other actors had all gone home. So, of course, I went upstairs and unpacked and read a book till tea-time.')

When she came down again her father, who had been to see a chiropodist, was in his usual chair, doing his crossword puzzle. He asked her without interest if she had had a good journey, gave her a lack-lustre account of his foot-troubles, looked across at the old ladies and decided to follow their example. He, too, fell asleep.

The life of the Moray, in its somnolent timelessness, went on. Boldini tiptoed in to speak to the lounge-waiter. Fryke brought somebody a timetable. Outside, the street lamps loomed up in their globes of mist.

('I knew I couldn't tell him that day. For one thing, the place seemed at its worst, its most dead. I thought I should feel better tomorrow, if the sun was shining. As it was, of course. You remember how sunny it was all day Sunday.')

Yet when next day came, it did not seem easy to announce to Baird a decision that would change her life. He had always been a taciturn man unless his indignation was aroused; and he seemed, since his wife's death, far less indignant than he had been for years. So they sat in the shelter, in silence, watching the sea emerge spangle by spangle from the early fog, like silver plate through the cleaning powder. Baird had acquired a new trick of sucking his cheek in and pushing it out again with his tongue, an action which seemed to give him satisfaction and comfort. He had brought the newspaper with him but made no attempt to read it. The sea shone. Baird, unblinking, his legs peacefully disposed in a manner likely to trip passers-by, sucked his cheek.

('It began to seem more and more as though I couldn't do it. Yet I thought, Here he is, all alone: and what have I to lose? I might as well be in one place as another.')

It was not until after dinner that she managed to speak to him. ('As a matter of fact, I had taken a Benzedrine. I was glad I had, as it turned out.')

She asked him to go with her, not into the lounge but into the writing-room, which was generally unused in the evenings. He did not want to go. 'Why should we bury ourselves in that hole? It's as cold as the grave, anyway.' 'Because I want to talk to you.'

'Well, talk, talk; go ahead. Nobody here ever listens, and they're too deaf to hear if they did.'

He was ill-disposed to change the least of his habits. She believed that he was feeling lost, hopelessly alone, terrified of the slightest deviation from the chalkline of his life. She felt her courage rising to meet her need.

He began to fidget in his pocket for a pen, to fold his paper firmly for the crossword puzzle. 'All right,' he said, 'what is it? Do you need money? I'll make you an advance on probate, if it's that.'

She told him she was going to give up her business.

'What for? It's doing all right, isn't it? I thought you did well enough out of it, for a tinpot thing like that.'

That was not the point, she explained. She had decided that now her mother was dead there was no point in keeping up two homes.

('And as I said it my heart dropped like a lift. I can't tell you how I felt.')

'Well,' said Baird, half his attention on the puzzle, 'where are you going to live, then?' He pencilled in, CARTHORSE.

She answered, 'I'll come and live here. It will be company for you. And there are only the two of us left.'

It was said now. There was no going back. She could hallucinate herself, forever at his side, growing older, perhaps caring less as the years went by. She fancied she saw her ageing ghost pass into the body of Miss Ratcliff, who had at that moment leaned forward to tip a fallen coal back into the fire.

('It was rather dreadful, and yet it was peace. It was somewhere to be. It was something to do, even if it was just a duty. I always think it's sad when even our duties seem better than nothing.')

Baird pencilled in, COTILLON. She watched his moving fingers. Then he said, 'Damnfool idea, if you ask me. You're always bored stiff down here.'

She told him, trying to speak lightly, that she now felt differently. She needed to run about less than before, peace seemed pleasant to her. 'And you won't feel so alone.'

'You wouldn't stick it,' he said, 'not for ten minutes. You'd be sorry for yourself in no time.'

She was touched to affection for him that he should seek to put her needs before his own; touched perhaps to a deeper affection than she had ever felt for him in her life. She fought to persuade him that she was tired of London, tired of living a casual life with a casual friend, that she was used to the Moray, that she would be happy and content there.

She was successful in her persuasion; he believed her; for he said suddenly in a loud voice, 'Well, look here, it wouldn't suit *me*.'

She was so taken aback that she burst out laughing. She could not credit her ears. This was not the kind of joke Baird usually made, but she was prepared to accept it as a new manifestation of his liverish humour.

He said, 'I'm not joking. It wouldn't do. And it's time you saw my side of it.'

'What is your side?'

'At my time of life I can't be bothered with upsets,' he said. 'I have my own ways and I don't want to change them. I like to see you when you run down. But I couldn't give you any company, do you see?'

'Are you seriously telling me that you don't want me here?'

'There's no need to put it like that,' Baird said aggressively, 'when you know it's not the way I mean it. But I'm used to being alone. I like to sit about, and go for a bit of a walk, and think a bit.'

('I asked him what about,' said Celia, 'which was unwise. He got rather angry.')

'There you go,' he said, 'always being clever. God help me when I think what some of your friends must be like!'

'Never mind about my friends. You're telling me you don't want me to live with you: I want to be quite certain about that.'

He clapped his hand down over her knee; it was an attempt to show affection, it was meant as an emollient of what he was going to say to her. He told her then, in an easy, prosing fashion, that for years he had not been getting on particularly well with her mother. 'You're not a child, you know life isn't always roses round the door. I was fond of her, I suppose, but we hadn't anything to talk about. I couldn't join in all that shopping-chat, and she used to sulk because I didn't talk much. What was there to say?' Her death, he went on, had been a shock to him; but he had come to realise how free he was for the first time in his life. He was set in his ways; he didn't want to be made to talk, made to do this, do that.

'Now you'll tell me that you're fond of me,' said Celia.

'Fondness isn't necessarily wanting to live in someone's pocket. You and I,' he added, with his blueish smile, 'understand each other.'

Celia said she understood him perfectly.

'There you go again, trying to make something damned disagreeable out of my words. No; you stick to your job, and have a good time in town. Then you can always run down here when you get fed up with it. For a day or so,' he added quickly.

He rose, saying that it was time for bed, for his bed, anyway. He liked to read himself to sleep. He got tired easily, he was not so young as he used to be. He pecked her cheek, waved his hand to her and went away, leaving her in the hot, quiet room, to the turning-down of the lamps as the residents, one by one, gathered up their belongings and left.

Celia said to me, 'You can laugh if you like. I want to, really. I'm sure I shall feel better the moment I can. Oh dear!' She pushed her cup across to me. 'Do give me some more tea. It all makes me think of such an excellent new ending to *King Lear*. You remember when he recognises Cordelia again, how pleased he is?' In her revised version, Celia said, Lear would not be pleased. He had partially recovered his wits; and it had to be remembered that his most positive action, when he was last in his senses, was to throw Cordelia out. 'He would take one look at her and say, "Didn't I tell you to go away? Well, I haven't changed my mind, don't you think it." And he would shoo her off the stage like a fowl, muttering "The cheek of her!"'

This fancy did release Celia's laughter; she laughed until the mascara made stencils like birds' claws under her eyes. A rejected Cordelia, shooed out of her last refuge, she still admired her ridiculous Lear for his selfish strength; she respected him for the fool he had made of her. That tie between them, that special closeness, that unspoken affection running deep below the callous appearance, had turned out to be the greatest of her illusions.

Baird was one of those people, relatively rare, who are in no need of human affection or even of human care, who are utterly and defiantly wrapped up in themselves. It was not, I thought, always the contemplative, those with deep inner lives, who became like this. It was quite as often the shallow, the easily content, with thoughts so untroubled that they could be lived with in peace. The inner life, if it is a busy one, often needs a rest from itself; it struck me that nearly all the deep-natured people I had ever known had been, sporadically at least, social beings, needing at times to look outwards and to involve themselves in the affairs of others.

Celia was shocked and hurt, not by her father's insensitivity but because he was so utterly opaque. He was not a deep man, though he had once been a clever one, and now that he was old he had ceased to think about anything but the minor comforts of his uniform and solitary days. He was happy; yet his happiness depended upon the trivial routine with which he had surrounded himself, and the mere idea that Celia or anyone else might disturb it had thrown him into a panic.

She stopped laughing. 'So there you are.'

'What will you do?'

'Well, it's difficult. I shall have to disappoint Hilda, I suppose; I'd promised to sell. Poor thing, she's been trying for ages to edge me out, she can't see there's any use for me. But I'll have to think about it. I must think it over carefully.'

As she rose to make up her face again, to prepare for departure, she kept breaking into abrupt, almost noiseless bursts of laughter. She had a deserted look; yet with it something of the strength that often seems to stiffen deserted people, like a stick through a plant. She was a little shorter than I, but today she had a stringent briskness of movement that made her seem tall.

'I do feel I could dine out on my story, if it weren't in such bad taste. I expect Junius will enjoy it, though. I must give him a ring.'

She would not stay any longer, even for a drink. She was busy, she said, she had so many things to do. I wondered what they could possibly be. Now there seemed nothing left for her at all.

42

After Celia made her announcement at the Avelings, I often thought that we tended to remember, with extreme vividness, the moment before the unexpected event. Events, in themselves, could be blurred, for surprise was a muter of colour and of sound; but the atmosphere preceding them, an atmosphere in which we were calm, unsuspecting, probably happier, it was that which we did not forget.

I remembered precisely how that room had looked and everyone in it, just before Celia spoke.

It was the first week of the new year. I was dining with the Avelings, and Celia was there. We had finished the meal and were taking coffee at the table. There was a bright fire. Outside the windows the rain fell in a steady hushing on to the trees of the square. Aveling was leaning back, regarding his beautiful ceiling. Nancy was stretching out her arm from a ruby-coloured sleeve to the dish of walnuts. Celia, on Aveling's left, had clasped her hands behind her head and was smiling to herself, the cigarette sticking up from her mouth. On a console table at her back there was a handsome arrangement of dried hydrangeas, ranging from sea-green to thunder-cloud-blue. They were a frame for Celia's head, and she looked as if she were waiting for somebody to come and paint her.

'I have some news for you,' she said without preamble, her smile unchanging. 'I was keeping it.'

'We'd love some news!' Nancy cried. She cocked her head. 'Do I hear baby?'

Aveling listened too. We were all very quiet. 'No. It's all right.'

We turned to Celia again. Unlocking her hands, she rested them around the stem of her glass. 'Junius and I think we shall get married.'

For a moment it seemed like a joke. This was not her news: she was teasing us, putting us off from the real revelation.

'My dear—' Nancy murmured uneasily.

'It is perfectly true,' said Celia.

Aveling sat up straight. His face reddened. He said, 'You'll do nothing of the kind!'

Nancy started, and looked at him.

For a moment Celia did not speak. She stubbed out her cigarette carefully, putting out the last spark by folding the butt over on to itself. She looked at her ashy finger and wiped it clean with a handkerchief. Then she said, 'My dear Eric, you really haven't any say in this *at all*.'

He left his chair, as if it were intolerable to be still, and stood against the fire. 'I don't think you can possibly be serious.'

'But I am.' She turned round to stare at him, a sad, insolent stare, with a touch of triumph. For she had jolted him into losing control, and before us all.

'You know what Junius is. You know it would be a ridiculous farce. Your life would be a misery.'

'That really is my own affair,' said Celia.

For the first time in over two years they were concerned only with each other. This was between them, and nobody else.

'You're to do no such thing! How can I help feeling responsible for you—'

'How silly you are.' Her smile broadened. 'Will you tell me what possible right you have to tell me my business?'

'Eric,' said Nancy softly, 'you haven't, you know.'

He ignored her. His colour was still high. He had a curious dishevelled look, and his eyes were miserable.

'Of course I have a right. I've known Junius most of my life—'

'I think we shall get on quite nicely,' said Celia, 'if we are both sensible. Junius is happy about it, and I am rather tired of being alone. You'd be surprised how often I long simply to have somebody to talk to.'

'But there are other men,' Aveling said desperately, 'there's no need to do this.'

'Are there other men? I don't find them like flies around a honey-pot.'

Nancy darted frightened glances from one of them to the other. She, too, believed Celia was mad to think of such a thing: but was shocked and distressed that Aveling should care enough to be thrown off his balance.

'Junius is feathering his nest,' he said.

'Oh, but I think he mildly likes me,' Celia retorted. 'Anyway, we get on very agreeably these days. We've got quite a lot in common.'

He said, 'You aren't serious. No one could be.'

She got up, pushing her chair back so that it gave a grinding squeal on the wood.

I said quickly, 'At least you ought to think about it for quite a long time.'

'Shut up, Chris.' She stared at Aveling, her mouth tightened against trembling. It looked like the mouth of an old woman. She burst out, 'What have you ever done for me? What conceivable claim have you for interfering?'

'Of course I shall interfere! I can't stand by after all these years and watch you commit suicide.'

'It won't be anything like suicide. I will not have you spoiling things for me! I'm old enough to do as I please and marry whom I like. Surely you must see that.'

314

Nancy rose with a determined jerk of her body. Only I was left seated.

'Eric, it is Celia's affair. She ought to be left to think it out by herself.'

Again he did not answer her. He was bewildered by shock, by distaste, and, I thought, by the revival of an old jealousy. It is hard for us to let go entirely even of a discarded lover; between him and Celia, at this moment, there was the anger of sexual tension.

'I've finished with him if he does this to you.'

'I really don't think we shall need you,' Celia said. 'As you generously suggested, we are unlikely to be short of money. Junius may start up on his own.'

'He wouldn't be the slightest good on his own.'

'Well, we shall have a chance to make sure, shan't we?'

I said, 'Celia, come and talk it over with Gerard.' I knew she had once had faith in his judgment.

'I don't need to come and talk it over with anyone. If I want to marry, I shall do so. And I don't suppose any of you imagine I am blind to the circumstances. But we shall find a way of living, and I daresay it will suit us both.'

Aveling's flush had subsided. He put his arm around her shoulders. The gesture was easy and brotherly, but she pulled away from it.

He said, 'You matter very much to all of us, you ought to know that by now.'

She walked across the room and sat down. Both of them suddenly seemed to me *produced*; they might have been obeying chalk marks on a stage. I fancied that Celia was nearly enjoying herself, that she felt a residue of pleasure in being, after so long, at the centre of a scene with him. But when she spoke it was without theatricality. She said in a wavering voice, 'Yes, but not as the most important person. In a sense, even if it's only a legal one, I shall be that to Junius.'

315

'Celia, dear,' said Nancy, 'you're making us all frightfully unhappy.'

'Not at all. You're trying to make me unhappy. And I don't expect you two to come to the wedding. I will not be disapproved of.'

I asked her, in a feeble attempt to lighten the atmosphere, if I were to come.

'Oh, of course, of course. If you haven't tried to talk me out of it between now and then.'

Aveling sat down. 'Do let us see this straight, if we can.'

Celia gave a long, impatient, histrionic sigh.

'I have always been fond of him myself,' Aveling began. 'But you mustn't marry him, Celia. He will make you extremely miserable. This is one game he cannot play.'

'And, as you imply, he will be marrying me for my money. But I *shall* have a background. Don't any of you laugh, you're in no position to!'

I said that nobody was laughing.

'I should like a background,' Celia continued dreamily. 'It will be something for me, at least. And Junius and I really do understand each other better than you would think possible.'

'Now that *is* baby,' said Nancy, intently listening, and she raced out of the room.

The moment she had gone Aveling lost control again. 'I absolutely forbid you to do it!'

She smiled. 'Oh, what nonsense! What utter nonsense! As if you can forbid me anything I choose to do.'

She got up. 'I'm going home.' She looked at me, and I hesitated.

'Go with her,' said Aveling.

'No,' she said, 'I don't want Christine tonight. On second thoughts, she'd better stay behind and chew it all over with you and Nancy. It will be so fascinating for you all.'

Nancy came back. 'Nothing much. You're not leaving us, Celia?'

'Yes, I am. I've quite spoiled your evening.'

Nancy said firmly, 'No. We've spoiled yours and been very silly.'

'I'll get my coat.' Celia left the room. We did not speak until she came back.

'Well,' she said, and paused. 'I shall see you all before long, I imagine. I will send Christine bulletins from time to time, and she can pass them on.'

'I want things to turn out as *you* want them,' said Nancy, with a touch of passion rare in her. 'I really do want that!'

'I expect you do. Good-bye, Eric. Don't worry about me, because it isn't worth it.'

She turned and left the room, running downstairs so quickly that by the time Aveling had moved to see her out the front door had banged behind her.

He came up again. 'I wish you'd talk to her, Christine. Won't you go after her?'

I said no: she did not want me.

'She'll have to be stopped,' he said.

Nancy cried out, 'Why? Perhaps it is what she needs! I think we ought to leave her alone.'

The door bell rang three times, an angry piercing ring.

'She must have forgotten something,' Nancy said.

Aveling started down the stairs. We heard the door open, and Celia's furious voice, 'Now you'll have to get me a taxi!' He murmured something. We heard him say, '. . . wait, I'll help you.'

'Do you think I can't walk?'

She came in on a limping rush. She held out to us one of her shoes, from which the heel had been wrenched. 'I caught it in your grating, damn and blast it! I nearly broke my ankle. Look at this, just look at it!' Her hair was streaked with rain.

'I'll ring for a cab,' Nancy said. 'You sit down and wait.'

Aveling took the telephone from her. 'I'll do it.'

'So bloody dangerous! People might break their legs in a thing like that.' Celia hugged the shoe to her and nursed it. She was fighting back tears of hysteria.

'It isn't our grating, dear,' said Nancy, squatting at her side as if to comfort a fractious child, 'it belongs to next door. I'll lend you some shoes to go home in.'

'I don't want them. They'd be miles too big.'

Celia bowed her head right down over the shoe, and her hair swung forward to hide her face.

'You can have my mules, they fit anyone.'

'I don't want them, I tell you.'

'There's a cab coming right round.' Aveling replaced the receiver. 'I'll take you home.'

'I can take myself home.'

'If you took off both shoes,' I suggested, 'you'd be much more comfortable.'

She kicked off the other and tossed the pair into the hearth. 'You can throw them away for me,' she said to Nancy.

'But they're so pretty. Can't they be mended?'

'Do you suppose I went groping round on half-lit pavements in the pouring rain looking for the heel? Because I didn't.'

Nancy offered her a drink. Celia refused it. She would not speak, but waited with hanging head until the taxi-horn sounded outside.

'Come on,' said Aveling.

'I don't want any help.'

'I shall see you home, as I said I would.' She offered no resistance. Without another word to us she ran out in her stockinged feet and down the stairs. In a moment or so we heard the cab drive off.

Nancy looked at the clock. 'Only ten! It has seemed a long evening, I'm afraid. Do you mind if I bring baby in and feed him here?'

She fetched the child and sat with him at her breast. I made up the fire. She looked calm and beautiful, secretive with maternal pleasure, not at all disturbed by what had passed; yet after a moment she said, 'Perhaps you wouldn't think it, but I hated Eric going with her. You'll think I'm greedy and jealous and ought to be ashamed.' She transferred the child to her other arm. Baring her right breast, she wrinkled it down as if it were satin and wedged the crenellated nipple between the baby's gums. He fastened to it greedily, his lids closing to a faint shine of light.

'I feel out of things.' She added affectedly, in a high, mannered voice, 'I'm so afraid of him going to some lengths to comfort her, which I know is mean of me.' She wanted me to know she was serious, was ashamed enough not to want me to know quite how serious she was.

I said I thought she could spare Celia so little as that, for it would be little enough.

'I know, I know. But I shall be glad when he comes back.' She looked at the velvet shoes. 'Will you be very good and kind and put those into the waste-paper basket? I don't want them lying there.'

People can be in love for no reason: and for a reason. Aveling, though he was undoubtedly in love with Nancy, had a reason for being so: she could give him rest. She, on the other hand, despite her ease and coolness, simply loved him out of a tenacious passion. Other men could have given her quite as much, in the way of reason, as he. He would not suffer through jealousy of her, since hers was not the temperament to provoke it; he loved her because he would not suffer through her. She herself, however, had become capable of jealousy, whether justified or not; marrying Aveling had in a sense made her what he would least have wished her to be. But I thought she was well aware of the dangers of ever letting him know this. She would not allow him to suspect. Her release was to pour out her jealousy to me.

She drew the baby from her, cuddled him, changed his napkins and took him back to bed. When she returned she was looking bland and amused. 'I read somewhere or other,' she said, 'that when an Indian wife committed suttee the concubines would rush up and hurl themselves on to the funeral pyre as well.' She paused. She looked like a simple, thoughtful hockey-girl. 'You know, if I caught anyone trying to get on to my pyre I'd jolly soon push her off again.'

We heard his key in the lock. She stiffened, relaxed again. When he came into the room she was smiling, her hands folded, her face raised to him.

He, however, seemed tired and downcast. He kissed her rather absently. 'It's no good,' he said, 'one can't talk to her. Nobody could.'

Her eyes brightened with relief. She had been worrying for no cause; the past half-hour had been nothing but a bad dream. Now she was seeing them in the cab, sitting apart as they drove through the wet and loveless streets, hardly a word spoken between them. She put her hand into Aveling's, and he held it for a long time.

43

As time went on, as the news of Celia's intentions reached me in the form of hasty telephone calls and stilted letters, it became obvious that the pattern of existence between her and Junius and Aveling and Nancy was to show little outward alteration. Celia and Junius would marry: it was all settled – a date was fixed for early March, the reception would be at the Moray, they would go abroad for the honeymoon. But Junius was not to leave the firm of Aveling, Hart & Evans to set up (with Celia's money) on his own. After all, he and Aveling were used to each other. It occurred to me that a lively anticipation of change was far more common than change itself. A climactic event, like the scene in the Avelings' dining-room, makes people believe that lives must be radically altered as a result. They expect a game of Old Family Coach, complete with realignments and sudden changes of residence, new domiciles across the seas, new habits, new enmities, new friendships.

It had seemed to me that too much had been said, that it would not be possible to preserve any viable relations. I was quite wrong. It is not at all rare, in old and intimate relationships, to say almost too much: it is very rare to say the one thing that is altogether too much, that is enough to blow up the past like a bomb. Celia, Junius, Aveling and Nancy, I realised, would find a way of getting on together.

But this complete healing was for the future. One thing she would not do, Celia told me, was to have Aveling at her wedding. 'I will not have persons with forebodings, I will not have hooded eyes fixing me gloomily at the precise moment of my fate.'

I had not been allowed to discuss the deeper question with her; steadily she had held me off with the light artillery fire of factual information – what she would wear on the day, how many people she would invite, what changes Junius would make in the seaside house, what sort of flat they hoped to find in London. From Junius himself I heard nothing at all.

One Sunday in February I drove to Godalming to take Mark out for the day and discovered that he had had visitors the day before.

'Of course Saturday isn't much good, we hardly get any free time. They just took me to tea, that's all. Junius is rather nice, isn't he?'

Mark had never met him before, and was slightly bewildered. From listening to Gerard and me, he had gained the impression of a personality both bizarre and mysterious. The man who had taken him out had seemed to him pleasant and ordinary. 'Like what I imagine a stockbroker is,' said Mark. 'I should have thought he'd bore old Celia. She always seems a bit wild.'

I asked him cautiously whether she had seemed happy.

'Well, she was in tearing spirits, you know; one gets a bit edgy wondering what she'll do next. I felt that if she ran into old H—' (he named his headmaster) 'she might say pretty well anything. She gave me two quid sort of under the table – I don't know whether Junius is the kind to keep her short. Actually,' he added hastily, 'I didn't really want to take it. I do all right for money. But you know how she is.'

Though Mark was fond of Celia, who had long ago captured his imagination, he was never quite easy with her: it was plain to me that he considered Junius likely to have a sobering influence. 'Can I send her a wedding-present on my own, I mean, not just join in yours and Gerard's? I've got her two quid, or rather, I could spare thirty bob of it. I need the rest for some wire and tinned fruit.' (I was never able to understand Mark's purchases.)

'I think she'd be delighted,' I said.

'She asked me to come, only I'll be at school. Pity. I'd like to see Dr. Baird in a top hat.'

I took this for hyperbole. It seemed, however, that Celia was to have a very formal wedding. I wondered who the guests would be. She had always seemed rather friendless; I had never heard of any relatives except for her parents. I hoped the guests would not consist of Junius's old friends.

A week before the wedding he telephoned to ask me to dinner at Cranmer Court. 'You haven't been in my flat since that curious night,' he said. He sounded like his old self, jaunty, mischievous, posturing. 'I do think, when I look back, that we both behaved well, all things considered. We nothing common did or mean upon that memorable scene.'

I said I wished I could be so sure.

He told me he would have the door on the latch so that I could walk in; he might want to hear a programme on the wireless.

When I arrived, he was listening to the conclusion of the Fourth Brandenburg Concerto. When it was over and the applause had died away he turned to me. His face was glistening. 'You ought to have come earlier! It was sublime, I've never heard it better. That Brandenburg, you know, it's the *whole* thing! First he gives us God the Father, then God the Son – all the tragedy – and then God the Holy Ghost; and then by some celestial trick he whisks them into the Trinity. If I were a religious man, which I'm not, I'd see how it works through that.'

If he were talking for effect it was because he had some-how to release his emotion through words. He was genuinely

323

moved. He looked like an overfed boy dazed by some great new feat of overfeeding; yet he was struggling to express a momentary revelation of the divine. 'I've heard it a hundred times, but never have I heard it played like that. If you weren't here I'd weep. Have a cigarette.'

The table was prepared for me. It was a cold meal; he hoped I wouldn't mind. He had managed some hot soup.

Still dazed, yet with businesslike movements, he went to and from the decanter, back and forth to the kitchen. 'I'm moving next week, half my things are packed up. I don't know where anything is.' He thumped his hand in the air to the music he could still hear in his head. He had put on weight since I saw him last. He had always been dapper; soon he would be too fat for dapperishness, would have little of looks to commend him but his colouring, the pale blue eyes, the black hair, the ruddy cheeks.

'It is splendid to see you again,' he said, with a reminiscence of Aveling and a quick little pounce at my hand. 'Such memories we share!' His eyes sparkled with malice and fun. 'Unstiffen yourself, now; bygones are bygones. I am sure they made you wear a backboard when you were a child.'

I could not help laughing at him.

'That's better. Now come and eat, and I will tell you about everything. And you must tell me all.'

In fact, he kept me to my own news and to Gerard's, his gaze steady upon my face as if there were nothing he cared about more than the welfare of my family. He ate rapidly in a greedy, half-furtive fashion, the fork flicking from his mouth to the plate like the tongue of a lizard. The excitement with which he had greeted me, which had derived from a stimulus great enough to thrust him out of himself, had died down. His mood was changing. As he put his brief questions, made his brief sympathetic answers, he was in the process of planning how he should approach the subject of his marriage.

He did not do so until I had nearly given up hope of it, and was thinking of going home. He had been talking of the new flat, of how he had instructed the decorators, of the furniture he planned to buy, of the right place to get the latest fabrics. So far as the words went, it was his typical patter; but his voice was flat, his tone uninterested. Suddenly he stopped.

'We can't put it off for ever, you know. I've been wondering, of course, what you thought of me.' He had spoken simply. Now he stopped again and, raising his eyes, looked at me. I had known him wear much the same straight, simple look when he was lying: yet this was not altogether the same. He had been easy then, he had not been at a loss.

'We didn't know what to think.'

'No, of course, you wouldn't. I accept that. But I should like you to understand just what Celia and I are doing, because you're fond of her and I dare say you've been worried.'

'It was a surprise,' I said.

Junius passed me his cigarette-case with the enamelled school-colours. 'Even for me, it isn't easy to talk about it. The important point is that I think Celia and I can make a go of things. I'm fond of her, too.' He smiled. 'I am, honestly. Old stuffy Eric thinks I'm after her money, which is most unfair. I can't pretend to be sorry she's got some; it's cosier for both of us, and I shall like to be comfortable. But it's not that.' For a moment he looked heroic; he felt cruelly misjudged, he could not help posing. Then his face changed again. 'She is awfully alone. Eric gone, Papa doesn't want her. She would like to be married. And we get on surprisingly well. She'd feel she had something, just to be married,' he repeated.

'What about you?' I asked.

'I should like to seem more like other people. Call it a "front", if you like: it's a good bit more. I'm sick of being alone, and Celia knows all about me. So far as I can, I shall be

325

a reasonable husband. Anyway—' He hesitated. For a moment he sat in silence, stroking the case, rubbing a circle of the silver to a bright gloss. 'I've told her she need never be afraid people will laugh. I shall give them no chance for that. I can't change much, but I shall never let her down in public.'

He emphasized the two last words by raising his voice on them. This had been the hardest thing to tell me, since it seemed to him the most absurd. It was nevertheless the most important.

'She is always afraid people will laugh,' he said, in a slurred manner. 'I've promised her what I told you. I don't think we'll be unhappy.'

'You know how much I hope you'll both be happy.'

'Do you?' he asked eagerly. His eyes lit up. He looked younger, was touched with his old shifty, affectionate laughter. 'I believe you do. Really, I don't think you're dense at all, I think you have a glimmering. Celia and I really do get on nicely, you know. We've made our rounds together, we like the same things, we like the odds and ends. I quite like all her silly little criminals, she's amused by a lot of my friends. We've had so many *scenes*, too; and say what you like, it does help.'

He was laughing at me openly now, but he was sincere. He, too, was looking forward to this marriage, to the outward respectability that it would bring him, to not being alone any longer. It could not be a true marriage; but it might work. The part of Junius that had always longed for the outward forms of a normal life had expressed itself already in the business suits, the crested cigarette-case, the patchy assumption of that manner which had turned him into Mark's idea of a stockbroker. He had been honest about Celia's money. He would be glad to have it. He was not particularly good at his job, he was unlikely to go any further. His tastes were luxurious; he would enjoy being able to gratify them. But for all the advantages he would receive, he was prepared to pay.

326

He would not allow people to laugh at her. He would not let her down.

'You might say with some justice,' Junius remarked dreamily, 'that I'm not good enough for her. Celia *is* remarkably good, you know. She never did anyone a bad turn in her life, not deliberately. And she has an overactive conscience. I shall find it hard to live up to her.'

I thought how true this was. She would do her best for Junius in gratitude, perhaps, for the sin from which he was inadvertently to save her. Celia believed in sin; it had always been inseparable in her mind from her love for Aveling. If she had married him it would have been a taint behind their lives, recognised by them both. Neither of them had been able to escape from the Puritanism deep in their natures. I remembered what he had said to me, several years ago, in the road beyond the ugly yellow hospital where Lois lay dying.

'Underneath it all is the undertow of the Ten Commandments. They make dreadful fools of us. They're like our grandmother's sideboard, which we don't use any more, but can't bring ourselves to sell. There it is, all the time, weighing us down from the attic or biding its time in the cellar.'

In this strange and empty marriage there would be no sin for Celia. If she suffered through it she would have the consolation (of inestimable worth to one of her temperament) of knowing that this suffering was not a punishment for wrongdoing. Her conscience would be clear. In Junius's bright, warm little room, the curtains drawn against the frosty night, I believed she might not altogether lose her life.

'Of course she is a bit of a crackpot,' Junius said, ruefully. His eyes glimmered, his mouth drooped. 'Say what you like, she is. She insists on being married in church.'

He took a turn round the room as if to flex his legs, stopped in front of me and stabbed out a finger like Lord Kitchener's.

'But *that* part of it's going to be quiet. That won't be an orgy. Most of them are going to be asked to the reception only, which may seem odd, but that's how it's going to be. I do feel a church wedding is a trifle farcical.'

I did not think it would be farcical to Celia. I imagined she would be able to disregard Junius at that point, to be married almost by herself. She intended to start well, no matter what the end might be.

'Look here,' said Junius, still pointing at me, 'it will be all right so far as I can make it, not, of course, expecting the earth.'

Then, ceremoniously, he insisted upon opening a bottle of champagne, and we drank to the wedding as if it were any wedding, gleaming sugary through flowers and the bright green tinselling of smilax.

44

The evening was mild and overcast, the air still steamy from the rain that had fallen steadily from noon till six o'clock. The tide was far out, and the sands were like gun-metal in the sullen light. Over the horizon, two lips of cloud had parted to let out a breath of sun.

Celia said, 'It might be fine tomorrow.'

She wore an old raincoat, a scarf tied round her head and under her chin – everything decent, she had told me, was packed; and, anyway, tonight she could let herself go, she need not keep up appearances. The smell of the sea was harsh and strong.

The promenade was empty for miles except for the cars ripping rain from the wet roads as they tore towards the distant glimmer of the town. In the windows of the great hotels only a few people, most of them elderly, sat staring out at the last of daylight. The sodden flag above the bandstand had glued itself to the staff, and the fairy-lamps were black as lumps of coke against the ghostly cupola, stained with winter's rust.

'Not inspiriting,' said Celia.

I said that any resort looked desolate out of season.

'Sometimes I think this is the last resort.' She smiled sourly. 'I don't think I could have stuck the Moray for so long if it hadn't been for the sea. It gives me a sense of freedom.'

I replied that it gave me a sense of being shut in: I did not like to feel there was one direction in which I could not walk.

'Oh, but I can walk on the waters,' said Celia, 'when people madden me. I can go out and out, right over there, and disappear entirely from view.'

She was in a peculiar mood, half-grim, half-elated. She walked with the stride that was too long for her, as she had done upon the day of inspection at Crowborough, as she always did when confronting any sort of ordeal. We passed the colonnade that shut in the garden of trees, salted and crutched by the prevailing wind. The lights came on. The white and orange moons sprang out in the damp pavements, in the great pink stretch of the doubled carriageway.

We came to the hotel where we used to dance. 'Come on,' Celia said, 'we must find out what's happened to old friends.' She ran up the steps, pushed me before her through the swing doors, raced me into the cocktail lounge, that contrived a transition in emotional temperature between the hall and the restaurant. The head waiter moved hastily to greet her; he cast a swift glance over her mackintosh and a hunted look at nowhere at all.

'Well, Miss Baird, you are a stranger! Can I make a booking for you?'

'Don't be upset,' she said. 'We're not coming to disgrace you, we don't want food. But we want to stand a drink to Mr. Raby and Mr. Webster. Are they about?'

'Mr. Webster's left!' he exclaimed, astonished that we should not know. He would have been no more astonished had we failed to hear of the Queen's accession. 'Months ago,' he added; 'he's opened a restaurant in Eastbourne. But I think Mr. Raby's somewhere here.'

'We should like to see him.' Celia spoke loudly and grandly. 'Please let him know. We shall sit out here, in a very dark corner.' She slipped back her headscarf but did not bother to take off the mackintosh, though it was hot in the room. She was for the moment, perhaps for the last time, off-duty from the routine she had designed for her own life.

Raby came gliding to greet us, hands fanning outwards, a deferential smile on his face which, I noticed for the first time, was rather a powerful one. His manner, now that he was not in our employment, differed from that of the paid dancing-partner. He looked at us with a meaningless air of complicity. His eyes danced.

'Poor Freddy Webster! His wife nagged him into it, but I'm sure he isn't at all the type. So gruelling, and so hard to get started. But she didn't like him dancing. She was always sure he'd meet someone hugely rich who'd rush him away to a life of sin on the Costa Brava.'

'What about you?' Celia asked him.

'Me? Oh, thrilled to death! Do you know I'm expecting to become a father in July? Me! I can think of absolutely nothing else, I trample on people's toes and they make complaints. But honestly, Miss Baird, I am so tremendously pleased – you can't think!'

We congratulated him. Celia said it called for another drink. She was moved by his delight; it had thrown her off her balance. For a moment I thought she would cry.

Raby shook his head. It was kind of her, but he dared not take too much before the evening began. He had a client who was very particular. He had to watch his step with her – 'That's good, isn't it?' – in more senses than one.

'It will have to be a son,' said Celia.

He looked surprised. 'We both want a girl. We're crossing our fingers.'

'Will your wife want *you* doing this job always?' she asked; but she had gone too far, for Raby's face tightened, and he answered, 'I'm sure I don't know. We haven't discussed it.' He looked at the clock. 'If you'll excuse me, Miss Baird, I'll have to brisk myself up a bit.'

When he had gone she said, 'This place is becoming a morgue. Let's go round to the mews.'

The lights of the little public house shone out into the street, pasting upon the roadway a stained-glass pattern of rose and amber. The door stood wide open.

Celia stopped. 'I know what it is – new shades.'

We went in. 'Here's a stranger!' cried Doreen.

'That's what they all say. I see you've done yourself up.'

'Had the painters in. Like it?'

'Smart lampshades,' said Celia, 'and a new carpet. Very nice, very nice indeed.'

Doreen asked her where she had been keeping herself. It must have been six months, quite six months.

'I shan't be keeping myself any longer – I'm getting married tomorrow.'

'You're never!' Doreen's face opened wide like a slit plum. 'This calls for one on the house.' She brought drinks for us. The other drinkers in the bar edged a little aside, while remaining part of the scene. There were celebrant looks all the way round. 'Come on, Miss Baird, tell us who he is, where it's going to be, what you're going to wear.'

'All secret,' said Celia. 'I shall come in and tell you about it when it's all over.' In our turn we bought a drink for Doreen. Then we went into our usual dark corner, and for the moment everyone forgot about us.

'The wedding-garments are costing me a fortune,' Celia said, twisting her rings round and round her thin fingers. 'Jacques Fath. Junius helped me to choose them. But I shan't give you any descriptions: you must wait and see. It was such fun for him, I could see he was pretending he'd have to pay. He kept nodding and frowning over the expense.'

She lay back in her chair, smiling to herself. 'I don't think it was at all complimentary of Doreen to be so surprised. I'm not so old as that.'

332

I asked if Doreen were married.

She replied, out of the side of her mouth, 'Yes, and with five children. But she doesn't let it be known. It takes away the glamour.' She wore the maternal look that always came upon her when she discussed some private life upon the perimeter of her own. She was proud of knowing so much about people, proud that they gave her their confidence. 'She is really Mrs. Digby-Cork,' she added with a grin, 'which sounds splendid but makes her seem like somebody else. I gather he's no good.'

One of the horse-racing women who always seemed to be in the bar waved her finger-tips to Celia, cleared her throat, and sang, 'Here comes the bride.'

Everyone burst out laughing.

'I shall look the part tomorrow,' Celia called across to her, 'when I get out of this mackintosh.'

'White bride?' asked one of the men.

'And fully choral,' Celia retorted gravely.

This seemed even funnier.

'Well, God bless,' the woman shouted, 'and good luck! I hope you'll be as lucky as I've been.' She smiled at the salmon-fleshed, check-coated man at her side; we had never seen her without him, and had never heard an intimate word pass between them.

'That's right,' he said, throwing his arm around his wife's neck and leaning his considerable weight on her, so that she skidded a little, 'you do as well as us and you'll bless the day. Cheers.'

Doreen turned up the wireless.

'She is such a good girl,' Celia said to me, 'she always does what I want.'

Under cover of the din we were able to talk again.

'This is pretty, isn't it?' She looked about the room. The overhead lamps were shielded in rose-coloured silk, fringed with gold; on each of the tables was a small standing lamp in a shade of bright yellow paper, and round the chimneypiece was a string of fairy-lights. 'When you *think* of the time people spend trying to make things nicer to look at, all the effort that goes to shop-windows, all the thought that goes into wallpapers and new kinds of sofas—' She paused. 'How odd it is that the general effect is still so awful!'

She laughed at herself ruefully. She was in a mood to find the world transformed and radiant; at least, to try and find it so: but honesty had broken in.

I knew she was not happy: but she was so doggedly determined to feel as if she were, that genuine happiness was almost within her reach. At all events, her excitement was a consoling substitute. So long as she could keep to the pitch of it, all would be well.

When we left the public house to a renewed chorus of congratulation and snatches of Mendelssohn and Wagner, she tucked her hand through my arm.

We both said simultaneously, 'Let's walk.'

'Philopena!' Celia shouted.

'I forget what happens,' I said.

'Doesn't whoever speaks first have a wish? I don't remember now. Oh, *how* many times have we said that?'

'I said it because I thought you would.'

'Dear Chris,' she said. She fell into her long, jolting stride.

I thought I liked her as deeply as I had liked any woman in my life. I had never found an emotional relationship easy with anyone of my own sex and had tended to shy away from it. With Celia it was different. As an only child it had been hard for me to imagine how I might have felt towards a brother or a sister. Now I believed that I knew, or could conceive, an emotion far enough removed from any sexual context by familiarity, or perhaps by taboo, to flow without constraint, to be at the same time cool and profound.

'*Salicaceae*,' Celia said, as we passed by the garden. Her face was peaked in the flood of the arc-lamps, her eyes glittered like sequins. 'You know when Eric saw me home that night I broke the heel off my shoe?' She dropped my arm. 'He tried to talk me out of things: in the end he kissed me. I'd been having extraordinary fantasies about *that* happening.'

She paused for a moment, looking up into the Japanese shapes of the branches against the drizzle.

'But it was only a sort of consolation prize. I felt nothing at all. Absolutely nothing at all,' she repeated in a harsh, wondering voice. She gripped my elbow again, as if to stop herself from falling.

'You mustn't care,' I said. 'It would have been so much worse otherwise.'

'I suppose so.' She drew a deep breath. 'Let's get your car. I want to make the rounds.'

So we went into one club after another, and wherever she knew anybody there was a celebration; but the season was dead and most of the clubs were empty, the pianists strumming listlessly away until such time as they could decently go home.

'I won't get drunk,' Celia said, 'not this time. Never you fear.'

When we came back to the Moray at last it was past three o'clock, and she was almost asleep. She told me she would sleep, sleep well, that she felt peaceful, that all things seemed very simple and clear to her now.

45

The day was dark and rainy. All the lights in the church were on. Junius, in the front pew, was holding what appeared to be an absorbing conversation with the best man, who was elderly and did not look distinguished. On the left of the nave Mrs. Haymer, Gerard and I sat together. There were no other guests. The organist was playing *Sheep May Safely Graze*; he produced a curiously timid sound from the instrument as though he were only practising and did not wish to disturb anybody. 'Isn't it cold for the time of year?' Mrs. Haymer whispered. She pulled her coat closer at the neck.

The music stopped. The organist began again, playing a voluntary of a lively nature which was unfamiliar to me. The clergyman had appeared, and Junius, more like a letter D than ever, moved out to stand in front of him. Almost before I knew it Celia was upon us, walking a little too quickly for the music as if eager to get the whole thing over and done with. Mark would have been disappointed in Dr. Baird, who, far from wearing a top hat, seemed deliberately to have chosen the most shabby of his old medical uniforms – dusty black coat, striped pants that sagged at the knees.

Celia turned and smiled at me, having as yet paid no attention to Junius. For the first time her smart clothes became her, fitted her perfectly: nothing was wrong. Her hat and suit of stiff pearl-grey silk gathered to themselves what light there was, rediffusing it about her like the bloom upon water. She was triumphant at last in her person, as she had longed to be.

336

Junius had had too short a hair-cut. The back of his neck beamed like a rosy face through the clipped hairs; Janus-like, he might have been smiling in two directions.

But he was confident. He had made up his mind about this wedding, he had no wish to back out. He stood stiff and soldierly, his residual nervousness expressed only by the faint quivering of his coat-tails.

The vicar began, 'Dearly beloved, we are gathered here together in the sight of God', not in the usual dutiful drone but in a voice that fondled each word as if it were new, and Celia glanced at me again. Her face was open and calm, her lips tightly pressed together. I saw her put out her hand to Junius, and for a second he held it. Dr. Baird cleared his throat. Jerking his head back, he stared with savage concentration at the vaulted ceiling, as if he were going to pronounce upon it an unhopeful diagnosis. He coughed once or twice, blew his nose with an uninhibited trumpeting. My attention was so riveted upon him that I failed to follow the service, and was startled to hear Junius exclaim 'I will!' in so robust a tone that it made Mrs. Haymer jump. Celia's responses were as clear, but she made them in her lightest, most prattling tone; they could have come from a child.

As the ring was given and taken, Gerard put his hand over mine, and just for a second it was our day. Mrs. Haymer was formally weeping. Dr. Baird was diagnosing a damp-stain on the wall above the pulpit. Celia and Junius were married now, though there was a good deal more of the service to come.

They knelt at the altar-rail. Junius bumped down on to his knees with business-like celerity; but Celia fell with the grace of a debutante trained to a court curtsey. Her back stiffened, her head drooped. Gerard gave a shift of sympathy with her: we guessed that at this moment she was offering up in loneliness her past and her future. Awkward as she was about the approach to God, no church-goer, a kind of irregular, a fellow-traveller, she was concentrating in prayer with the entire force of her will. Small, touching, immaculate, she knelt as still as stone.

I was distracted by a movement upon my right side. Mrs. Haymer was edging stealthily away from me towards the opening of the pew. She assumed a furtive, humped, sideways attitude: she was taking a photograph. The next moment she was sitting upright again, hands in her lap, face innocent. But she could not forbear to murmur to me,' I don't know whether it'll come out, the light's so rotten.'

Afterwards we all went into the vestry where Celia, tautly smiling, her eyes unreadable, signed the register. She and Junius kissed like lovers, with a bounce and a hug; it was so spontaneous that it might have been rehearsed, or at least prearranged. Junius was looking pleased with himself.

Gerard said to Celia, as he kissed her, 'I know you can have a very good life. Christine and I love you, you know.'

'Like the grave in here,' Baird remarked to me, 'place needs a proper damp-course.'

We went out, to *Jesu, Joy of Man's Desiring*. It was no more than two minutes' walk back to the Moray, by way of a side street, but Celia had two excessively large cars with white ribbons waiting for us, and we made a meaningless detour by way of the front. Boldini was on the steps, watching for us.

It looked like a gesture of supreme welcome. In fact, his aim was to hurry us through the hall into a room reserved for receptions, so that we might disturb the ordinary life of the hotel as little as possible.

At this point the best man, who turned out to be a brother of Hart, the original partner in the firm, had trouble with a shoelace. We all waited till he had re-stied it, and Boldini visibly fretted himself.

In the room, shiny with daffodils and light oak, there were about thirty people, and the noise was mounting. Not a soul, save one correct-looking young man who had not looked so correct when I met him with Junius in the London coffee-shop, was known to me.

'You don't have to talk to them,' Celia whispered, 'they are odd connections of mine and Junius's, and a few old friends of Mummy's. They are astonished to be here at all, which will doubtless make them impart a gaiety to the proceedings.'

Though her eyes were bright, she looked exhausted.

'What a pity you had such an awful day for it!' an aunt-like woman commented, on her way to the buffet.

'I'll be in the sun soon,' Celia called after her, 'we're going to Bermuda.' She said to me, 'I'm longing for that. Do you know, I've never really travelled?'

Junius came up. He looked her up and down proprietori-ally. 'Yes, that really is an excellent suit. Who is that bison-like man with glasses over there talking to Hart?'

'He's my mother's cousin. He's a solicitor.'

'Oh. Will I have to know them all in future?'

'Be comforted, not a one.'

He moved away as another couple came up to greet her by her married name; they did so with an air of inspiration, as if they were the only people to whom the thought had occurred.

'Come up at half-past two and help me change,' Celia said. 'I must do my duty now, make the rounds.'

Soon she and Junius had to cut the cake; Mrs. Haymer took another photograph. Then the best man read out telegrams. Aveling and Nancy had sent their messages separately. Nancy's ran, 'All the luck there is to you both bless you affectionately'; Aveling's, 'My dear love to you.' Celia sat through the reading with a smile as bright, as fixed, as her mother's had sometimes been. Afterwards she leaned idly across to where the pile of papers lay, selected one out of them and put it in her bag.

Dr. Baird tracked us into a corner. He looked hot and cross. There was a cylinder of ash on his lapel, ready to fall. 'I want a word with you, Mrs. Hall. And you too,' he added to Gerard. He took us out of the wedding room, just beyond the door.

'No good beating around the bush. You know about this fellow, I dare say.' He paused.

We said nothing.

'Anyway, Celia wasn't born yesterday. She's old enough to know her own mind, I tell her. I only hope she does.' The ash dropped; he peered at it in a hostile manner and ground it into the carpet. 'I say it's not my business. You can't keep a girl hanging around for ever, once she's grown up.' He was a little ashamed of himself. He wanted us to believe that it had been a sacrifice for him to let her go. 'Millie was a leech in that way; I'm not. It's time Celia led her own life. But will it work?'

'It may,' said Gerard. 'She has to have something.'

Baird's neck went red. 'You can say that,' he retorted in his most hectoring manner, 'but how many women would give their ears for what she's got? She's never had to lift a finger in her life if she didn't want to.'

I remembered the look of quick, naked pleasure that had flashed across Celia's face when she was called, though for the ninth or tenth time that day, by her new name. 'I think she wants as much as I have,' I said.

We turned the conversation somehow, praised the service, the reception, the excellent food we were eating.

'Look here,' said Baird in a desperate fashion, 'it's no good people blaming *me* if it doesn't work out. She's got her eyes open.' He was trembling. We saw the quiver running down his long, striped legs. He was tensing the muscles of his calves. 'It's not my business to interfere.'

'I say,' said Junius from the doorway, 'I was wondering where you'd all got to. Do come back, Doctor, and cope with people.' He looked elated now, full of affairs, a host thoroughly conscious of his responsibility for pleasure. On his face was still the party smile, beneficent and blind. 'We've got to make a move now, Celia's started fidgeting.' He spoke as a husband, fondly, only pretending exasperation.

Baird went back to the party without a word. Junius gave us a flippant wave of his hand and followed.

'It may not turn out so badly,' said Gerard.

I went upstairs in search of Celia. She had already removed and packed the grey clothes. Now she was struggling into a woollen dress, which concealed her head and had twisted itself about her upstretched arms. She said from the folds of it, 'Pull this damned thing down, will you?'

Her face appeared, flushed with champagne and exertion. 'Also Fath,' she said, 'a copy, but dear enough.'

I told her I had never seen her look so well.

'I'm glad of that. There is usually something wrong with me; I don't suppose that you knew I knew. But I have always known.'

I watched her in the glass as she touched up her make-up, combed her hair. She put on her hat and coat.

What further intimacies I had expected I do not know, but it was evident that the time for them had gone. Last night, on our rounds, upon our search for the drugging excitement which would bring her safely to this moment, I felt that I had found her again, that she had returned her friendship to me. Now there seemed nothing more to say. We sat for a few desultory minutes, smoking, chatting of nothing in particular.

'I did tell you Hilda was buying the business?'

'Yes.'

'I thought I did. She'll enjoy herself.'

'You'll write to me?' I asked.

'Floods of picture postcards.' She stubbed out her cigarette. 'I suppose we'd better go down.'

She rose, but instead of turning towards the door went to the window and flung it up. Sideways lay the sea, dove-grey, smooth beneath the feathery rain, the clouds in their pigeon-colours resting low upon it as if sustained by the silk of the water. A stray umbrella here and there pushed along the front. As the cars went by their wheels sent up plumes of water from the roadway. The essence of the sea, the strong green smell of weed and shellfish, the smell of distance and of liberty, stole into the room. Celia breathed deeply in and she out: she might have been doing remedial exercises. Then she closed the window and turned to me.

She put her arm through mine. We did not call the lift but walked slowly down the stairs together, through the Moray's afternoon silences, past its shut-in sleepers, and re-entered into the festivity of strangers.

It was over three weeks before I heard from her, but at last I received by air-mail one of her awkward, childlike letters, affectionate and uninformative.

She was very well, it was wonderful to lie in the sun all day. Junius looked like a Red Indian. They were enjoying themselves, though there really wasn't much to do. When they got back we would all have dinner together.

The whole of the flimsy form was crammed with this kind of thing in her neat examinee's writing. She ended, 'We both wish you both were here. We send our fond love. Affectionately, Celia.'

As an afterthought she had added beneath her name, in parenthesis, as though she were afraid I might have forgotten, but really in a spurt of unquellable pride in having some kind of country she could call her own, 'Evans'.

You've read *The Last Resort*.
Now delve into another delicious tale by Pamela
Hansford Johnson,
An Impossible Marriage

I made up my mind that I would not see Iris Allbright again,
not after so many years. I do not like looking back down the
chasm of the past and seeing, in a moment of vertigo, some
terror that looks like a joy, some joy crouched like a terror.
It is better to keep one's eyes on the rock-face of the present,
for that is real; what is under your nose is actual, but the
past is full of lies, and the only accurate memories are those
we refuse to admit to our consciousness. I did not want to
see Iris; we had grown out of each other twenty years ago
and could have nothing more to say. It might be interesting
to see if she had kept her looks, if she had worn as well as I
had; but not so interesting that I was prepared to endure an
afternoon of reminiscence for the possible satisfaction of a
vanity.

Also, she had had only one brief moment of real importance in my life, which was now shrivelled by memory almost
to silliness. I doubted whether she herself would remember it
at all. I would not see her; I had made up my mind.

But it was not so easy. Iris was determined that I should
visit her, now she had returned to Clapham, and to this end
kept up a campaign of letters and telephone calls. Didn't I
want to talk over old times? If not, why not? She was longing
to tell me all about her life in South America, all about her
marriage, her children, her widowhood – didn't I *want* to
hear? She was longing to hear all about me. ('How you've got
on! Little Christie!') I couldn't be so busy as to be unable to
spare just half an hour. Why not this Wednesday? Or

Wednesday week? Or any day the following week? She was always at home.

I began to feel like the unfortunate solicitor badgered with tea invitations by Armstrong, the poisoner of Hay. Knowing that if he accepted he would be murdered with a meat-paste sandwich, in constant touch with the police who had warned him what his fate was likely to be, he was nevertheless tortured by his social sense into feeling that if Armstrong were not soon arrested he would have to go to tea, to accept the sandwich, and to die. It was a hideous position for a man naturally polite and of good feeling.

My own position was in a sense more difficult, for no one was likely to arrest Iris Allbright, and I felt the time approaching when I must either bitterly offend her or go to Clapham.

In the end I went to Clapham.

In a London precariously balanced between two wars, how is a young woman supposed to make her way in the world? This is the question which Christine faces. Dissatisfied with her life spent working in a bank and living in the shadow of her more beautiful and beguiling best friend, Iris, Christine is quick to fall under the smooth, heady charm of Ned, an older man who seems to hold the key to the future she wants.

But appearances are fickle, and soon, Christine finds herself isolated inside an increasingly sinister marriage. As time begins to tick, Christine must find her way out, at the risk of becoming trapped forever. . .

An Impossible Marriage | 9781473679801 | £8.99 | Hodder

Pamela Hansford Johnson

Pamela Hansford Johnson was born in Clapham in 1912 to an actress and a colonial civil servant, who died when she was 11, leaving the family in debt. Pamela excelled in school, particularly in English and Drama, and became Dylan Thomas' first love after writing to him when they had poems in the same magazine. She went on to write her daring first novel, *This Bed Thy Centre*, aged 23, marking the beginning of a prolific literary career which would span her lifetime.

In 1936 she married journalist Neil Stewart, who left her for another woman; in 1950, she married novelist C.P. Snow, and for thirty years they formed an ambitious and infamous couple.

Johnson remained a productive and acclaimed writer her whole life, and was the recipient of several honorary degrees as well as a CBE in 1975. She was also made a Fellow of the Royal Society of Literature. By her death in 1981, she was one of Britain's best-known and best-selling authors, having written twenty-seven novels, alongside several plays, critical studies of writers such as Thomas Wolfe and Marcel Proust, poetry, translation and a memoir.

Praise for Pamela Hansford Johnson

'Very funny' *Independent*

'Witty, satirical and deftly malicious' Anthony Burgess

'Sharply observed, artfully constructed and always enlivened by the freshness of an imagery that derives from [Johnson's] poetic beginnings' *TLS*

'Miss Johnson is one of the most accomplished of the English women writers' *Kirkus*